In the Shadows

About the Authors

Édouard Philippe, former French Prime Minister, is a lawyer and member of the French Government.

After ten years of varied experience in the French political world, Gilles Boyer became the political adviser to Alain Juppé. He was also a member of the executive committee of a large French media group.

EDOUARD PHILIPPE
GILLES BOYER

In the Shadows

Translated from the French
by Maren Baudet-Lackner

HODDER &
STOUGHTON

First published in the French language as *Dans l'ombre* by
Editions Jean-Claude Lattès in 2011

First published in Great Britain in 2022 by Hodder & Stoughton
An Hachette UK company

1

A CIP catalogue record for this title is available from the British Library

Paperback ISBN 9781529383799

eBook ISBN 9781529383782

Typeset in Plantin by Manipal Technologies Limited

Printed and bound by Clays Ltd, Elcograf S.p.A

Hodder & Stoughton policy is to use papers that are natural, renewable
and recyclable products and made from wood grown in sustainable forests.
The logging and manufacturing processes are expected to conform to the
environmental regulations of the country of origin.

Hodder & Stoughton Ltd
Carmelite House
50 Victoria Embankment
London EC4Y 0DZ

www.hodder.co.uk

For Anatole, Léonard, and Sarah
Edouard Philippe

For Lucie and Manon
Gilles Boyer

"May the best man win."
A traditional French saying originating in Normandy

"Politics is almost as exciting as war, and quite as
dangerous."
Winston Churchill

"Even paranoids have enemies."
Golda Meir

Prologue

I'm an apparatchik.

I always have been. I've never fancied myself a politician. Many have tried to cross the divide. Some of them have even succeeded. But not many, and I don't like the ones who have. People end up in my world for reasons that have little to do with talent: there are women, because there must be; cowards because they're everywhere; and flatterers because they represent nothing—and "nothing" tends to be less harmful than "something" when it comes to politics. I've learned to live with all of them.

What I cannot stand, are apparatchiks who take themselves for politicians. In my world, politicians and apparatchiks feed off each other. Neither can survive without the other. Anyone who doesn't know their place, is a disaster waiting to happen.

Apparatchiks are used to taking blow after blow for their bosses. They are mechanics. Organizers. Advisors. Enablers. They are the heart, the soul, and sometimes the brain of a politician.

Politicians are a different breed altogether. Their empathy can be fierce and their energy unfailing. They know how to touch people when they want to. They convince voters that they are one of a kind.

Politicians want to be seen and heard by an audience. To feel confirmed in their opinions, the fairness of their ideas, to hear that they're the best, the strongest, or the funniest, to be told that they'll make a difference. They don't doubt themselves by definition; let alone envisage that anyone else might do the job better. Better than them simply doesn't exist.

Being elected put aside, I have done it all. I've composed and corrected hundreds of speeches, attended at least as many campaign meetings, and have travelled the world to lunch with established top dogs only to dine with young hotshots vying to replace them. I've fixed things for men I despise and taken out people I hold in high esteem—and vice versa.

I know the intense joy this world can bring. The waves of adrenaline, the rare loyal friendships, the bond that develops between people who want the same thing. I know the gratification of dizzying discussions about making the world a better place. And the fervour that drives those who are foolish enough to believe they've made a difference in drafting an agenda.

In short, I know precisely how exhilarating it can be to live alongside those in power—particularly if you are the one who got them there.

That said, I am also familiar with the less glorious aspects. The everyday betrayals. The messy compromises. The pathetic resignations.

I have spent the last thirty years in a world that is as vile as it is cunning; and I have done so by choice. There is a flipside to every coin, and this is the price I pay to do a job I love.

I got my start in this field because I was passionate about politics. But I stayed because I was infatuated with my boss. *The Boss*. I still am. Twenty-five years of battling side by side in the trenches of world politics have fostered a strong bond between us.

No one else knows him better than I do.

The Boss is a true politician. The real deal. He trusts me because I've never taken advantage of an opportunity to betray him. And God knows, I could have! Some say he couldn't cope without me. That I must know him inside out, given how long I've been holding the fort for him.

There may be some truth in this, but one thing is for sure: it never has, and never will, cross my mind to betray him.

I've spent the last twenty-five years of my life slaving away to make sure he becomes president someday. And now he has a real shot. Two years ago, no one believed it could happen. Only a handful of people—those part of his inner circle.

Today is election day, and I hope against hope that he will succeed. Just two weeks ago I wasn't sure about a damn thing. Not sure about his chances, about him, or even about myself. For just two weeks ago, the beautiful political machine I had helped build collapsed.

It all started on a sunny day in Lille. Or maybe it was on that sunny day in Lille that it all ended.

PART ONE

PART ONE

1

Tuesday 16ᵗʰ February, 10:15 a.m.

It was a lovely day. Exceptional weather for February. The sun was shining all over France, even in the north. Every cloud has a silver lining and for once, climate change was no exception. It's hard to explain that we must make sacrifices to fight global warming when late winter in the North feels like spring in Madrid.

The Boss was on a delicate and important mission visiting the home turf of Marie-France Trémeau, who had been his main adversary in the race for the party's nomination in our American-style primary.

Every MP in the area, including Trémeau—well, all those on our side, and they were a minority in those parts—attended the breakfast. The very fact that they had come, when the previous year they had been at each other's throats and would undoubtedly return to that state of affairs the following year, was a remarkable success in and of itself. The local party officials, who were more enthusiastic and less jaded, were present as well. An intimate, face-to-face meeting with the Boss was a rare opportunity for them. The kind of event that would be relived at party meetings for years to come.

I was with the Boss for once, despite my profound disgust for the groupies who live to follow him around on the campaign trail. They seem to imagine that the fact of sleeping in the same hotel for a night will forge some special bond with the Boss. Repulsive behaviour. I'm far too familiar with the petty in-fighting, the vying for a place in the Boss's car, the privilege of sitting behind him at events, or the collecting of files passed to him while watching him exercise his legendary people skills.

The nice thing about the Boss is that he never asks me to accompany him. If I'm there, that's fine, and if I'm not, that's fine, too. Sometimes when I join him, he seems surprised to see me. Most of the time, when I don't, he seems surprised that I wasn't there. In fact, it's irrelevant to him if a mission is well organized.

That day, the trip was a sensitive one: all major political journalists had come to watch the Boss and Trémeau side by side after the violent clash that had opposed them just six months earlier. The day had to go well to create the appearance of a unified front. Not a single poorly chosen word could be allowed to derail our efforts.

I used to do everything for the Boss. And I used to do it alone, or nearly. But over the years, the team had grown. Now everyone had a role to play. Despite being responsible for everything, I was in charge of nothing, which was both liberating and worrying, as I am a stickler for details.

The lovely Marilyn was managing the press as usual, and doing one hell of a job. The Valkyrie, our head organizer, had handled every detail of this trip, and all the others, and was keeping a watchful eye on the proceedings. Schumacher was ready to pull out at a second's notice to get the Boss to the next location in a flash. As for the Cowboy, he was never more than a few steps away, ready to pounce at the slightest hint of danger.

I was in a corner with Caligny, where we were trying to find a way to make ourselves useful—him because he had yet to prove himself, me because I was supposed to be overseeing people who had clearly learned how to get on without me.

The kid was excited: this was his first time accompanying the Boss. His eyes were bright. First times are always stirring; you never forget them. And it's not every day a twenty-something gets so close to a man who might become president. In his mannerisms and features, the kid looked just like his father, a former minister who had passed away ten years earlier. The same unkempt mass of hair, the same dark eyes, the same smile, and the same way of emphasizing his words with a firm gesture from his right hand. He didn't suffer from the awkward, overdressed elegance of young men who lack self-assurance in their oversized suit jackets, short trousers, and worn shoes. The kid dressed simply, casually, in a velvet jacket, white shirt, and dark-blue jeans. Professional, but relaxed. He had an innate quality, a form of poise and humble confidence I had rarely witnessed in someone his age.

I didn't really know why the Boss had hired him to join the campaign team. Caligny had no experience and nothing to offer. But since joining us, he had shown that he could keep out of the way and even make himself useful. That was already a major improvement over all those candidates with bags of experience and even more ambition.

We stood off to one side to observe the scene. The first step on our tour was General Charles de Gaulle's childhood home and everything was perfect: the line of cars, the party members who had spontaneously turned up to offer their support, and the press area for the journalists, who were following in a bus.

With its flag flying in the bright sunshine, the house on the Rue Princesse would have been quite ordinary, were it not for the illustrious infant who was born inside. But for any candidate wishing to align themselves with Gaullism in any shape or form, it was a mandatory stop on the campaign trail. Smiles, handshakes, waves, pictures with adoring fans, and on he goes. Nothing in his hands, nothing in his pockets, a natural smile; he knows he can never look like he's in a hurry.

I was watching the Boss, as though for the first time. Sixty-three looked good on him: he'd stayed trim (a fact people almost seemed to hold against him since nothing said bonhomie like a few extra pounds) and had never lost his hair, though it had gone quite grey rather quickly over the past few months. We had to help him dress properly. His wife wasn't up for it any more and he couldn't care less, but the French people wanted to vote for someone elegant, so he wore what we chose for him. On that beautiful February day, it was an unobtrusive grey suit, a light-blue shirt, a red tie, and a lightweight black raincoat to ward off any unexpected showers. Far from original, but nothing anyone could criticize either.

I was listening, almost as though it was the first time, too. His pleasant, unique, instantly recognizable voice, which had become his trademark, paired with his kind, benevolent, almost sincere smile. His sentences were short and simple, his questions warm, and his attitude noble but not arrogant. He was good. He was in his element. I watched him, tired but high on the campaign, dutifully carrying out all his obligations, determined not to leave anything to chance.

After a few minutes, I gave Caligny a mission: to ensure Marie-France Trémeau was always by the Boss's side and to never let her stray, no matter how much she might like to. Healing the wounds from the primary had been so difficult that now the press would put every detail under the microscope. The tension was still palpable, and it had to be imperceptible.

It was obvious that she would have preferred to be elsewhere, as is often the case with high-ranking politicians. We all hated her, but had to admit she didn't look her age, which was well past fifty-five. The way she held herself, like a queen, inspired respect. She looked perfect in one of her iconic trouser suits. I imagined she had an on-call personal stylist. Unhappily married and childless, she was tirelessly driven, making her a formidable political adversary: the heart of a man in the body of a woman, the ideal combination for politics, though admittedly not for everyday life.

Since she had no choice but to welcome to her constituency the man who had defeated her, she wore a warm smile, but when she looked at the Boss, there was resentment and hatred in her eyes that maybe only I could see. She kept trying to move away, and I smiled as I watched the kid's desperate efforts to keep her in the right place for the cameras and photographers, while several intruders jockeyed for her abandoned position.

The other MPs were only too happy to tag along. They all longed to be photographed next to the Boss and were eager to proclaim to whoever would listen that they were loyal and doing their utmost to make sure that he won, that they were behind him because if he won, he would defend *our* ideas and take *our* country in a better direction. The fact that the legislative elections would take place just six weeks after the second round of the presidential election wasn't totally unrelated to their sudden enthusiasm, though. By campaigning for the Boss, they were really campaigning for themselves. I couldn't hold that against them. I had decided not to be angry with the MPs during the campaign. Not until the Boss was elected.

This was why the MPs were now not just polite with me, but spoke to me quite naturally and directly. This was only true for the cleverest among them though; the mediocre politicians had just become terribly obsequious.

Jean Texier, Trémeau's right-hand man and an MP in his own right whose constituency was in another region altogether, had even made the trip here, confirming the importance of the event with his presence. He and I provided the same things for our respective bosses: we were the brain power and the men behind the coups and the political banter. But he had decided to run for office to gain independence, an independence which he didn't actually use. Today he had come to watch, feed some sound bites to the press, and accompany his boss, who had undoubtedly felt rather lonely since her defeat.

I have mixed feelings about Texier.

I hate him, for a whole slew of reasons. First, for having so often tried to (politically) take out my boss, my employees, and on a few occasions, me. But above all else, I hate him because I despise what he is: a fake politician and a real apparatchik. I hate Texier, but I respect him. We share the kind of bond that sometimes unites men who do the same job but back different causes. We would smile at each other's blows with a blend of annoyance and admiration. But I also feared Texier: he was unscrupulous, and though people thought as much of me, I knew I would never cross the line he had blithely hopped over.

He's a real bastard, but he has at least one valuable talent: he's a cut above the rest when it comes to crafting caustic but funny remarks that are ambiguous enough to pass for praise. When he'd been a simple apparatchik, we had had a cordial relationship: we helped our bosses take each other out but never attacked one another directly. We talked. We laughed together. It's important to laugh with your political adversaries. If you can't have a good laugh with them, you're either blinkered, anxious, or a pain in the arse. Whatever the explanation, it's a bad sign.

Texier is exceptionally gifted for making people believe he's the exact opposite of what he actually is. His physique fools everyone. People say he's elegant and believe he's young, when he's actually in his sixties. His trim figure, jolly demeanour, and his luck at having lost all his hair in his forties (which means no one ever got to see him go grey) almost make him look like he's just turned fifty. People think he's calm when he's hysterical. They say he's loyal, but I know that he does the most for his friends when they don't actually need his help.

If you listen to him, you might take him for a humanist poet and a rebel. But that image is miles from the truth. Whenever Trémeau had something unpleasant to say, she would send Texier to say it for her. Whenever she was working on a low blow, Texier designed and executed it. If Trémeau had won, he would have become a minister. He had to be furious as he watched the train pull out of the station, realizing he was on the wrong platform.

During the primary, Trémeau and the Boss had put on a good show: a cordial campaign "between friends and may the best candidate win". But behind the façade it was a merciless battle fuelled by an enduring mutual hatred. As for Texier and myself, we were engaged in a never-ending war: we fought to get our hands on new party members' details before the other, to visit swing seats in the best possible conditions, and to leak unflattering information to the press about our adversary.

Now that the primary was behind us, we had swapped roles. Our bosses hated each other, and it was up to us to grease the wheels. Despite the resentment of Texier and his boss, which was all the more acute given the unexpected nature of her defeat and the small margin that had sealed it, we had to talk and get along. Not an easy feat for two men like us, who had always been in the same party but never in the same camp . . .

Texier was there, and I had to handle him, since I knew he would seize any opportunity to claim his boss had been "mistreated".

"It's an honour to have you with us!" I said. I tried to erase any irony from my voice but knew perfectly well that the result would be passable at best.

"I wouldn't have missed it for the world," Texier replied. "Look at them, the best of friends."

"And look at us!" I added with a smile.

"Yes, peace and harmony reign."

He seemed to be in a good mood, which was rarely a good thing.

"You know," I continued, "this is a big day for us. For the party."

"Yes, Marie-France is doing her part to make sure everything goes to plan."

"As are we, I believe."

"Hmm," Texier grumbled sceptically.

"I hope you're not planning to play the martyr!"

Texier smiled. "Have you ever noticed that it's always the victor who asks that question?"

When we were alone, we always pestered one another, but it was rare for things to get out of hand bar a few exceptions. The primary had been one such occasion, and it had left its mark.

"Come on," I offered with a smile and a pat on his shoulder. "Let's go and see the room where the Great Man was born."

Though great de Gaulle may have been, we couldn't afford to spend a whole half-day admiring a typical bourgeois home from the late nineteenth century in French Flanders two months from the first round of a presidential election. In just over half an hour, the Boss had briskly toured the place, signed the visitors' book where all of those who aspired to reincarnate the General had confessed their admiration, shaken quite a few hands, and reminded the press of the importance and modernity of the Gaullist message. Following a nod from the Valkyrie, he had taken his leave and climbed into the car, which sped off towards the medical imaging research laboratory we were scheduled to visit as part of this trip devoted to "Innovation: a solution to the challenges of globalization", if I remember rightly.

The drive would take a little over twenty minutes. In our rush, young Caligny had ended up in the Cowboy's usual spot—the passenger seat in the Boss's car—leaving the bodyguard no choice but to join the Valkyrie and Marilyn in the second car. The Cowboy had to be furious to find himself so far from the man he was supposed to protect. He would have to console himself with Marilyn's presence. I bet he would have jumped at the chance to protect her if only she had expressed any interest. As for the Valkyrie, she was clearly not in need of his services. In hand-to-hand combat against the Cowboy, I would put my money on her.

I was in the back seat with the Boss, who seemed relaxed. Schumacher was driving fast but the ride was smooth.

Trémeau and Texier, who were joining the Boss for the whole day, had got into another car. It would have been better for the Boss to invite Trémeau to ride with him for the short trip, but that was more than either one of them could manage. I was certain a Parisian journalist would notice.

Caligny was listening to his voicemail. The Boss was watching the city as we drove past. His face was impassive; only his eyes moved to take in the scene outside. He was thinking about something. These daydreaming episodes, stolen minutes in the frenzied schedule of the campaign, gave him time to settle for a moment and reflect. I left him to his silence, knowing full well how important it was and how brief it would be. The Boss generally put a stop to his daydreaming by asking his entourage a twisted question. I love his twisted questions. The way they leave most people in a state of confusion is enough to brighten my day.

I think I first realized we'd hit a snag when I locked eyes with Caligny, who had turned around to face us.

There was something strange in his gaze. Not fear, not surprise either, definitely not indifference. Something indescribable, like a blend of incomprehension and foreboding. In any case, he wasn't trying to get the Boss's attention; he wanted mine. Which meant that whatever was bothering him was either trivial or extremely important. And since, despite his young age, the kid wasn't the sort to worry about trivial things, it meant something serious was afoot. I immediately shifted into "protection" mode. Don't stress the Boss, don't weigh him down with things that aren't his responsibility. Wait to know more and have an action plan ready before telling him.

Caligny must have read in my eyes that this wasn't the time to talk about it. He stared straight at me and waited.

That's when the Boss decided to exit his daydream.

"I've always wondered why Napoleon decided to invade Russia when he knew his army wouldn't be able to advance or obtain supplies by the usual methods. There's no victory without supplies."

How's that for a random and difficult question . . .

"Pride, maybe?" suggested the kid, who still didn't understand that the Boss's questions could be rhetorical.

The Boss smiled.

2

"Pinguet knows who rigged the 15th September vote. Pinguet could talk. But Pinguet is dead. A rather interesting coincidence, don't you think?"

Interesting wasn't the right word.

The message was short. I didn't recognize the voice. A man with an unidentifiable accent, speaking slowly. It was a private number and the kid had no idea who it could be.

When we had arrived and the Boss had left the car, Caligny had handed me his mobile and I had listened to the message. I put on the calmest of faces, but I couldn't believe what I was hearing.

The 15th September vote was the vote in which the Boss had been chosen to represent the party in the presidential race. Our primary.

The Boss's victory had caught everyone off-guard; everyone had thought he was finished a few weeks before. But Trémeau, the favourite, had made a few blunders in the home stretch, and the Boss had successfully played the role of peace-maker to unite all the camps opposed to his adversary and her controversial personality. The years the Boss had spent carefully and quietly laying the groundwork seemed to have finally paid off.

This surprise defeat only heightened the hatred Marie-France Trémeau and her entourage felt for the Boss and me, and ever since, we had been spending as much time fending off blows from our friends as from our adversaries. Though Trémeau never said as much, she hoped the Boss would lose, so she could run the next time.

The Boss's victory had been close, less than five hundred votes out of 230,000, but until this mysterious phone call, no one had questioned it.

As for the name Pinguet, I knew only one. A senator from Isère, in the south-east of France. Like most senators, he was old, but I hadn't heard that he had died. And I really didn't see what he had to do with the current situation.

Caligny stared worriedly at me. I was still trying to put on a show, but I could see in his eyes that I was failing.

We're most scared in life when we don't understand.

And I definitely didn't understand what was going on.

In different circumstances, I probably would have listened calmly to the message, feigned indifference, and shrugged. But just two months from the presidential election, I couldn't shrug: nothing was trivial any more.

"Pinguet who? The senator?" he asked.

"You've heard of him? I'm impressed, kid!"

"I've come across his name in articles about my father."

I kept forgetting that Caligny had been born into politics. Knowing that things had happened before he became interested in the field gave him an important advantage: the kid knew his political map and recognized the importance of history. The Boss had brought him into the inner circle for reasons I still didn't quite comprehend, but they must have been well founded. In any case, he was a part of the Boss's entourage, so I might as well treat him accordingly.

"That's the only Pinguet I know. He's been the senator from Isère for nearly twenty years. No one will remember him, for either good reasons or bad. He's a decent man who got into politics rather late, after a successful career in business. He's far from loyal: he's changed parliamentary groups at least twice and backed nearly all of his camp's candidates for president, at least any who had a plausible chance at success. Not particularly clever, but rich, I believe. That said, in politics, money doesn't make much of a difference."

"But what does he have to do with the primary?"

That was the question.

I would have preferred everyone to forget about the primary. Bloody battles within the same family always leave their mark, and everyone knew that it was now in our camp's best interest to focus exclusively on the upcoming election.

"I have no idea, kid, and I'm too old to chase after riddles with imbeciles who have nothing better to do with their time than leave cryptic messages. Unfortunately though, something tells me that the chap who reached out to you isn't finished. I'll have a think. In the meantime, you'll need to stick a sock in it and keep your mouth firmly shut. Not a word. Understood?"

"Yes. But there is one thing that is definitely going to be a problem."

"What's that?"

"You're going to have to stop calling me 'kid'. My name is Louis."

I liked him. He had potential. But everyone on the team had a nickname. He wasn't going to escape that easily.

3

The Boss looked focused and fascinated. He was barely capable of using a computer to check his email but appeared to be completely absorbed in the discussion of medical imaging innovations. He asked questions. He listened to the answers and then knew exactly what to say to each person in the room, as if he was there just for them. These regional trips created opportunities for him to touch people, both physically and emotionally. For a moment, he shared in their lives, their struggles, and their concerns.

Marilyn seemed relaxed. She wasn't. I could tell from the way she nervously ran her thumbs across the joints of her other fingers. A discreet but systematic coping mechanism. I walked over slowly.

Of course, Marilyn wasn't her real name, but it suited her so well. She was a real pro, always in a good mood, at least with the journalists, and she knew her audience and her boss like the back of her hand. When she knew the answer, she was precise. And when she didn't know, she admitted it, which was always the best option. When she wanted to get a message across, she knew how to express it in such a way that the journalists quoted her at length. And when she wanted to muddy the waters, she used her doe eyes and her gift for doublespeak to pull one over on even the most ferocious Parisian reporter. Boop-boop-bee-doo!

Well into her forties with dark, shoulder-length hair, olive skin, and a figure that had filled out gracefully over the years, she still attracted plenty of men in their thirties and already appealed to those in their fifties. I could attest to that. The thing that had always impressed me about her was her ability to charm men without annoying women. When you think about it, it's a rare skill. Take me for example, I charm next to no one and annoy most people. Women who know how to charm people not by their looks but by casting an inescapable spell on whomever they're talking to have my undying admiration. Marilyn is particularly gifted in that department. She's truly interested in others, and the way she spontaneously offers up her talents and intelligence makes it hard for the person she's talking to to believe that such a beautiful woman could also be so accessible. It's not Marilyn's physique that does it; it's what she does with the mind attached to said physique. As a result, she's not one of the many women in politics who, as many are so fond of saying, will lose their influence as they get older. No risk there.

Of course, my impression of Marilyn has become less objective over the years. Nevertheless, I can't help but notice that everyone who has ever underestimated her has regretted it.

"All good?" I asked, unsure whether it was a question or a statement.

"Mm-hm. He's perfect," she replied. "The journalists are happy, they're getting pictures. He was excellent on research policy and solid regarding funding. Besides, political journalists don't know anything about the technical aspects . . . Another twenty minutes and we can head for lunch at the racecourse."

"Okay." I was silent for a moment as I looked around. Then I continued in a tone that I hoped sounded casual.

"Have you had any questions about the primary recently? Or about anything relating to it?"

Marilyn was no fool. She knew I was asking for a reason. A potentially important reason.

"No, why? Is there something I should know?"

"I don't think so, not yet. Let me know if you hear anything like that, though."

I had tried to play it cool, but I realized as I said it that she would never be satisfied with such an evasive reply. Since she didn't want the journalists to see us in an animated discussion, she smiled broadly and gently touched my shoulder as though I'd just said the kindest thing she'd ever heard. From afar, it must have looked like we were the best of friends. Maybe even lovers.

"Are you fucking kidding me?" she said, a big smile still plastered on her face. "You know what will happen if you don't tell me about a potential story, right? Someday soon, one of those journalists you can see over there, the ones with the big camera crews, will ask the Boss a question without any warning. And from there, we have two possibilities: either he knows how to answer, and maybe he comes out with something we would have preferred to keep quiet, at least for the moment; or he doesn't know how to answer or, worse still, he's embarrassed by the question, and we end up with bad footage playing on a loop on every news channel and online, too. So, if there's a problem, you tell me right now what to tell the Boss to answer if someone asks the question, and you tell me what to feed the press."

All this was said in the same calm voice with an unfaltering smile, as if she were asking about old friends we had in common. As if I still had friends . . . That said, she wasn't wrong. Of course, I didn't have anything to tell her. I didn't know then if the message was going to turn into a real problem. Or when. I didn't know if it would be a big deal, or how to frame it. To be safe, I swore her to secrecy and told her about the message Caligny had received. I promised to keep her updated.

She nodded. There was a funny look on her face. I couldn't tell if she was wondering why I had tried to hide something important from her, or if she could already tell back then that this mess was a slippery slope.

It may all be in my head, but I felt right then like I'd disappointed her. Yet again.

4

The Boss had just made a triumphant entrance at the race-course banquet hall in Marcq-en-Baroeul. The atmosphere was festive, the beer was flowing, and the people of northern France were giving us a characteristically warm welcome. Under different circumstances, I might even have enjoyed myself. The Boss had said a few well-chosen words upon arriving. After enjoying his lunch, he got up to visit each of the tables. After thirty years of experience and several terms at the head of various ministries, he still visited every single table at every banquet he attended. Everyone found this habit delightful, but few understood how much energy it took.

The Valkyrie was standing discreetly in a corner, as usual. She was a mysterious woman who had always had our trust, though she had never become a member of the inner circle, a real confidant. When she spoke, it was because there was a problem, and she rarely spoke. A fit bottle blonde with short hair who was always dressed in cargo trousers, a T-shirt, and Converse trainers, she undoubtedly appealed to men (and women) looking for an authority figure. She had worked at an event management agency for ten years before walking out to knock on our door, much to our relief: once she joined us, I no longer had to worry about our trips, which were always perfectly planned to the second, or our rallies, which she also organized. It's amazing how easy organizing major events seems when professionals or Germans are running the show. For her, a banquet with a thousand guests was hardly a challenge, but her real strength lay in the fact that, whatever the event, she handled it with the same energy and devotion to detail.

We smiled at one another, and I gave her a thumbs-up.

With all these people, it was hard for me to begin a thorough investigation into the anonymous phone call. I managed to get away for a minute to call the Major.

"I've got three questions for you when you get back," he said straight off the bat.

The Major excels at what he does. I don't know where he learned to do it, but he always tells you the number of topics he wants to discuss before he starts speaking. That's the only flourish he allows himself in a conversation, particularly on the phone—indeed, he's the overall world champion for the shortest phone conversations in history. In our job, that defies even the most basic laws of physics.

I had decided to let the Major run the Boss's campaign. It came with too much hassle and too many restrictions for me. In all honesty, it was better to be the Boss's real right-hand man without having to manage everything at HQ which could include anything from printing documents and finding campaign funding to planning rallies and meetings with unions and all the other lobbies. I had happily handed all of that over to the Major, knowing full well that people would still come to me with any truly important questions. The Major knew it too but didn't care. That's why I chose him. I had the most enviable position: I was a drudgery-free confidant. I had kept the best for myself and could choose my fights. I went where I wanted and handled what I liked, leaving the obligations to the rest of them. After twenty-five years, I deserved it.

"And I'll be delighted to answer them as soon as I get back," I replied. "In the meantime, I have an emergency. I need you to look into something for me. Quickly. It doesn't look good, but I can't tell you more on the phone. Organize a meeting at HQ with the party's IT manager, you, and me first thing tomorrow morning. It's about the vote in the primary. And I want you to find out whatever you can about Senator Pinguet. Discreetly if possible."

"Is that all?"

Out of the corner of my eye, I spotted Texier watching me. If he could lip-read, I was in trouble.

"No, I'd like to take advantage of this call to discuss the reasons that may have pushed Napoleon to invade Russia in the middle of winter. Any ideas?" I asked jokingly.

"No," the Major replied unfazed. "I'll call when I have something on Pinguet. Meeting tomorrow morning at seven thirty in my office with the IT guy."

The Major was both concise and an early bird. He beat me in both areas. In his defence, I must admit that running a campaign is a shit job. You spend your time juggling important party names, material concerns, strategic decisions, the hesitations of those who are afraid of losing, and the pipe dreams of those who hope to win. In short, you are responsible for a political machine which, despite what most people think, is always on the verge of veering off course.

I liked the Major. He was efficient. Clear. He was sensible and blessed with good intuition—two qualities that don't always go together. I didn't like many people, but I had to admit I liked him. I'm not certain it was reciprocal, but I didn't care.

Noticing I'd hung up, a visibly concerned Texier came over slowly. "Can I ask you something?" he asked. "I've just received a surprising message."

Oh, bloody hell. Our anonymous caller was apparently branching out.

"A message?" I asked as nonchalantly as possible.

"Yes, I'm very angry."

"Oh, hey, let's not get carried away, all right? We don't even know who—"

"Carried away? Carried away? Your HQ just informed me that your boss still doesn't have a date for his visit to my district, and you don't want me to get carried away?"

That was all!

"Don't get upset. I promise I'll talk to him about it again," I said, relieved.

"I don't want you to talk to him about it. I want you to decide he's coming. You *can* decide that sort of thing, can't you?"

"I said I'd talk to him."

Texier walked off grumbling to himself.

I had been so close to giving it all away. It was a bad sign for me to be getting flustered over something so trivial . . . .

5

Tuesday 16ᵗʰ February, 10:28 p.m.

The rest of the day had gone well. We were running a bit behind schedule towards the end, but that was to be expected
and no one was bothered. At the Université Catholique in
Lille, the lecture theatre was packed and the atmosphere was
electric. Events like this one, with students, who were rarely
big fans, were always sure to energize the Boss. He knew how
to talk to students, and more importantly, how to change their
minds. I loved watching him do it. All those young people so
full of certainty when they arrived, convinced they would be
hearing from either a genius or a monster. He made confirming positive impressions while simultaneously overturning
negative ones into an artform.

He had such a good time in the lecture theatre that afterwards he made us all stay for a drink at the university
café, taking up an invitation from a group of students. Great
photo op and excellent interviews with young people saying
how surprised they had been to have the chance to speak so
freely with him. The radio stations picked up a few lines from
an enthusiastic young woman who explained that the Boss
"was really charming and amazing because he talks to young
people like they're adults." The syntax was approximate at
best, but the political message was excellent and the young
woman attractive. It was perfect.

Nevertheless, I was ready for the day to be over. The Boss
had said he wanted a campaign full of relatable images.

The Major had decided that meant that, whenever possible, he should travel by train. And it was easy enough to take the train home from Lille. The trip afforded me an hour during which I could tackle all the important topics I needed to go over with the Boss. In fact, it was almost for that hour alone that I had really decided to come along that day; one whole hour for conversation, decision-making, and planning.

The journalists were at the far end of the train, where Marilyn was commenting on that day's newswire stories. I had made it clear to her that none of them should be allowed to make the trip sitting next to the Boss. Such a coveted opportunity generally helped the lucky journalist to get a scoop, something off the record, or material for a puff piece. The Boss was typically happy to grant them and would undoubtedly have agreed to it then if I hadn't explained to Marilyn that he was tired and that it was best not to put him in a situation where he might slip up. I know the Boss well, and, at the end of the day, when the pressure starts to let up, because he's fatigued or maybe just because things went well, he stops scrutinizing his every word and becomes a little too authentic. These are the moments when he might insult one of his colleagues with a snipe that's as elegant as it is useless coming in the middle of a campaign which is supposed to bring people together.

The Boss, Caligny and I were alone in an empty carriage on the 10:09 p.m. train. The Boss was in a good mood. He was chatting with Caligny. Or rather, he was talking and the kid was listening. I distractedly heard him explain why the people of Lille had suffered more under the first German occupation, during World War One, than they had under the second. Caligny was just about to ask a question when I put down the file I was studying and joined in.

"Sorry to interrupt your discussion of a topic so crucial to the campaign at hand, but I have a few questions we need to discuss before the train reaches Paris. I think it's time for our young friend to go study how Marilyn handles a pack of ravenous journalists without getting bitten."

Caligny got the message right away. I was finally alone with the Boss.

"I like that kid. He learns fast," I offered. "I'm sorry to interrupt, but we have several difficult issues to cover."

"You're still wondering why I asked Louis to join us, aren't you?"

"I do sometimes wonder, yes. He's smart, but that doesn't necessarily make him useful to the campaign . . ."

"A fresh eye is always useful . . . I liked his father, you know. And when a son is interested in learning more about a field in which his father excelled, it pays to encourage him. The end result could be well worth it. Think of Randolph and Winston Churchill . . ."

"I'm sorry?"

"Winston Churchill was the son of Lord Randolph Churchill, a brilliant mind who became an MP at twenty-six, and finance minister at thirty-six. Unfortunately, he died at forty-six. He could have become prime minister, you know. He should have done, really, if he hadn't gone mad. Though madness isn't necessarily prohibitive . . . In his final years, he was still an MP and he delivered delirious tirades when Parliament was in session. His father's madness and especially his fall left their mark on Winston. You can't really understand Winston unless you know that he always believed he would die young. Caligny's death may have left its mark on Louis, too. If we're helping to train a French Churchill, we're not wasting our time, are we?"

I couldn't believe what I was hearing. This had to be the first time a presidential campaign had ever turned into an internship for a potential future head of state. One thing I loved about the Boss was the fact that he could still surprise me after twenty-five years together.

"I see you're sceptical," he continued. "But let's not forget: I'm sixty-three years old, and you're barely ten years younger. Do you really think we can forgo having a more youthful voice on the team? He's an intelligent young man who's eager to get to work. He seems loyal and he understands teenagers."

I had received the message loud and clear: the kid was non-negotiable. But the Boss wasn't about to stop there.

"For example, if I'm ever asked about my favourite contemporary singer, who should I choose?" he asked.

"There's only one option: Bruce Springsteen. The rest isn't even music. If he needs to be French, uh . . . Cabrel?"

"Cabrel? Cabrel? You're even more out of touch than me! I mean, I like Cabrel, but if I cite him as a contemporary singer, the eighteen- to thirty-year-olds will laugh me off the stage. You see, that's why we need Caligny."

"All right. Okay," I conceded, eager to move on to more serious subjects. We couldn't waste the whole hour talking about the kid. "So, Texier is demanding that you visit his district, where you'll tour the naval repair yard and hold a rally. He mentioned it again today and he's starting to make subtle threats . . ."

"Really? Texier? Trémeau's minion who spent the entire primary tarnishing my reputation? And now I should go pay tribute? He does know I beat her, doesn't he? What's he going to do? Use the navy to score political points against me? Is it my fault he doesn't understand that there's no sense in building twenty-five frigates when our soldiers are late to the theatre of operations because we lack transport planes, and we don't have enough heavy artillery ammunition?"

"I know all that," I replied. "And Texier is insufferable. But he's important within the party. He's Trémeau's right-hand man and a symbolic gesture like this could help heal the wound. Plus, he needs your support because his next election is far from a done deal."

"But his district has always been in our pocket!"

"Yes, but it's changed. A lot of new people are moving to the area. Different voter profiles. Polls are showing the opposition in the lead. Since Texier has been spending time on the national stage, he isn't around as much, and the other side has a solid candidate."

"Fine. Yet another reason not to go. Tell him that I'm not coming. Not now anyway. Tell him I said that MPs who want my support for their elections need to back me in mine. Unconditionally and enthusiastically. What's next?"

The Boss was tense now, wound up like a spring. He was right, too. When you win your party's nomination and become a presidential candidate, you have to change tactics to avoid being pulled down to the level of those who used to be your equals. He was right not to give in to Texier's pathetic threats. He would be eating out of our palms when the time came no matter what.

In the meantime, I was going to have to explain that the Boss wasn't coming and make it clear that he needed to start campaigning for him. And all without provoking a fight. The Boss could hold his ground, but I had to be careful not to provide the other camp with any excuse not to comply. That's the problem when your election victory is both a surprise and slim. The losers wanted revenge above all else and we couldn't give them a reason to throw themselves back into the fray. The meeting promised to be anything but simple. I couldn't do it on the phone; I would have to invite him to lunch. When you have unpleasant things to say, it's always better to do it over lunch.

"I'll handle Texier," I said. "One other question though. I have a bad feeling about some rumours circulating regarding the primary. I'm not sure where it's coming from yet, but someone seems to be trying to undermine you. The future French Churchill got a call this morning, which he shared with me."

The Boss, who had just opened a file containing his schedule for the next day, looked up. He said nothing as he tried to understand the implications of this new piece of information.

"What do we know exactly?" he asked calmly.

"For now, next to nothing. But I've already started my investigation. A stranger left a message on the kid's mobile about the supposedly rigged results of the primary and the death of a certain Pinguet."

"The senator?"

"Maybe, but I would be surprised. We would have heard if he had died. I'm on it now. I have an early morning meeting to find out more tomorrow. I'm handling it."

The Boss nodded. There wasn't much else to do. He knew that when I said I was handling something, it was handled. In theory. Both of us just sat there for a moment, staring blankly into the distance. I couldn't help but find the silence a little awkward. Caligny, who had clearly been watching us from the corner of his eye, realized I was done. He came nearer, looking at me to ask if he could sit down with us again.

The Boss called him over before I could answer. "Come here, Louis," he said, "let me tell you about Churchill."

At least something good had come out of this trip: I had finally found a nickname for the kid.

6

Wednesday 17th February, 3:50 a.m.

It doesn't take much to give me a bad case of insomnia. The slightest hitch in the evening—and few evenings were without a hitch of late—was enough. It didn't keep me from falling asleep but always woke me up somewhere between three and five in the morning.

The night after our return from Lille was one of those nights.

Resigned to the fact that I would not be falling back asleep, I stretched. In the dark, in that big, empty bed, I took stock of my impersonal bedroom—a sad sample of my pitiful bachelor pad. I got up, put on a T-shirt and a pair of boxers, and stopped in the bathroom to splash cool water on my face. In the mirror, I saw a man who was older and craggier than I expected. I made my way to the lounge, where I turned on the television to serve as my only source of light for a while, and selected the end of an NBA game.

I made myself a big cup of milky coffee and some toast. I turned on my computer to scan the news sites and read everything that was being written about the campaign. If I wasn't going to sleep, I might as well get an early start on my day.

There didn't seem to be any bad news. The articles on the day in Lille were mostly positive, or at least not negative, which was really the same thing. Over the years, I had learned to settle for neutral.

Another article caught my eye. The deadline for all presidential hopefuls to register was now a month away and the piece was about the list of likely candidates.

The political landscape was fairly traditional: two heavyweights, the Boss and his main rival, Vital, a social democrat. I would gladly have described the Boss as a social democrat, but in this election, he represented the right and the centre, and if we didn't act accordingly, he might not even make it to the second round. Of course, that wouldn't prevent him from pushing the political agenda of his choice once elected . . .

The left had been at the helm for too long. The country's current president, a wily old socialist, wasn't running, and his support for Vital was lukewarm, leaving the field wide open: there was no favourite, and a handful of votes would determine the victor in the second round between Vital and the Boss.

Vital was at a political disadvantage because the French people would most likely opt for change. But he had an administrative advantage because his friends were in power and held the reins of the country's institutions during the election. The Minister of the Interior, the Prefects, the intelligence community, and the police were all unofficially at his service.

Several candidates intended to throw their hats in the ring for the first round to publicize their ideas and try to throw a spanner in the works for the two main contestants. But not all of them would be able to garner the five hundred signatures from elected officials required for an official candidacy.

In the end, Vital would have to contend with the Green Giant, a hardcore environmentalist who stood nearly two metres tall, and the Lefty, a ruthless crypto-communist who had managed to unite the far left behind a candidate for once. I was also helping a new leftist to garner enough signatures to qualify. The journalist called him a troublemaker, who could marginally impact Vital's numbers. Marginally. Everything would be marginal in this election, so I was leaving no detail untended.

In his camp, the Boss would have to manage the Centrist—a centre-right candidate who believed in God and the independence of the centre (as long as both God and the centre continued to lean to the right)—and the Radical, also from the centre-right, but who abhorred the Centrist and Catholicism in general. Vercingetorix was also in the running, but only for the opportunity to condemn the European Union and defend the idea of a Frexit. The Boss and I had also encouraged the candidacy of a right-wing environmentalist to keep all environmentalist votes from going to the left. We hoped she would manage to grab a few points. I was handling her signatures personally. The article reminded readers that her candidacy was, if not encouraged, at least seen in a positive light by the Boss. If the author only knew.

We were aware ahead of time, barring any major blunders, who each of those candidates would endorse for the second round: everyone would stay on their side of the aisle. Their support had a price, but everyone would get what they paid for.

One candidate remained uncategorizable and unpredictable: the Fascist, the far-right candidate who refused the label but did everything to earn it.

In short, under a dozen candidates and two big favourites, one of whom was the Boss. The most recent polls predicted it would be neck and neck.

I closed my computer to watch the television news at six o'clock. I felt my mind drift off and my eyes close. That's when my alarm went off.

7

At this time, the streets of Paris are nearly deserted. I've always found this difference between Paris and the rest of the country rather striking. A hundred miles from the capital, people start work at eight o'clock and eat lunch at noon. In Paris, you have to have a compelling reason to get to work that early, and suggesting a lunch at noon makes you look like a magnificently backward country bumpkin. No one but engineers and campaign managers get up early in Paris. Before, there were factory workers, too, but they've all been pushed outside the city limits now.

I wondered why I had let the Major schedule the meeting. It's not that I don't like to get up early—it's rather nice to enjoy a longer day by waking up in the small hours. And there's something magical about Paris in the morning. The air is purer and the water in the gutters is cleaner. Walking alone through a place that will soon be filled with noise, movement, and faces has always given me an absurd sense of power.

I work best in the morning, too. I'm productive, attentive, and responsive. After two in the afternoon, my body reminds me how little I slept the night before. I've made plenty of mistakes in my life, and I made most of them in the early afternoon. Over the years, I learned not to make decisions during those hours when my mind was dulled.

★ ★ ★

The taxi driver had already glanced at me three times in his oversized rear-view mirror. He was trying to place me. He must have seen me on TV or in the newspaper, but he couldn't put a name to my tired face. It seemed to annoy him. And since I had no desire to speak to him, I conspicuously turned away. With taxi drivers, as with women, it was simple: either I knew right away that we were going to get on, and I asked them lots of questions, imitating the Boss during a campaign event; or they provoked a cool indifference in me that even I found surprising. This one fell squarely into the second category. Maybe it was the way he had called me "sir".

Seven twenty. No one in the streets, but there was that pair of eyes on me. I shouldn't have even had to think about the driver. I should have been going over my to-do list or making calls or shouting at employees, asking them why I still didn't have the daily press round-up, just to see who would dare to tell me that I didn't have it yet because I wasn't at the office. I'd like to find someone who'd answer me like that. I'd promote them on the spot. But none of them would dare. I was too close to the Boss. Many of them thought annoying me meant displeasing him.

The huge rear-view was hypnotizing. I could see my reflection in it. It's always strange to see yourself in a rear-view mirror, especially when you're sitting in the back and off to the side. I didn't look great.

"I think I've seen you on TV," the driver said finally. "On the news."

"That would surprise me. In a late-night adult film, sure, but not on the news. Unless it was a porn news site. Besides, it's been quite a while since I've been on camera. Well, at least not my face. But I'm glad to get a little recognition out in the world, in a taxi, because usually it's not my face that gets people's attention if you catch my drift . . ."

The guy gaped at me. He wasn't sure what to believe. I played it cool, didn't even smile. I pretended to be thinking about something else. We were about to reach HQ anyway. The campaign paid the bill, but before getting out, I gave him a generous 50 cent tip.

"Well, off to work, then. Lots to do . . ."

I was pleased with myself. Seven twenty-five and I was almost smiling. I pulled myself together before going inside, though: I hadn't smiled entering HQ for a while now.

The previous winter, I had started looking for a campaign HQ.

The Boss had asked for the impossible: an easily accessible, secure location with parking places in a neighbourhood that was neither too wealthy nor too depressing. He wanted a big, functional but welcoming space in a street that was busy but not too busy. A place with about a hundred desks and a large meeting room—all available for short-term lease. Oh, and I had to be discreet about my inquiries. Right . . .

Once we gave up on the impossible, I made an imperfect choice: a modern, three-storey building in the 9th arrondissement near Saint-Lazare Station. We had moved in at the beginning of January.

The offices were nice. I had seen what I could do with them right away. The main thing was that everyone would fit. Because everyone was quite a lot of people. Between the publication of campaign documents, the team in charge of organizing trips for the Boss and his supporters, those who worked on rallies, the press relations department, the small legal and finance hub, the team who answered mail and put together leaflets, those who managed relationships with MPs and local officials, and security, there were at least a hundred full-time employees.

We had hung large signs outside to make sure everyone knew what was going on inside, without completely blocking the view into the building, so anyone curious could see we were really working, while also ensuring the privacy and safety of the occupants. Politics: the art of reconciling the irreconcilable.

The lobby was guarded twenty-four seven by thoroughly dissuasive security guards. There was also a reception desk with a combination of pretty young assistants—because seduction is a big part of any campaign—and experienced older women who knew everyone, because we had to sort the useful volunteers from the leeches who came more for what they could get than for what they could give. That's the problem with a presidential campaign: if you win, you're in a position to obtain a lot of things for a lot of people. So, people who need things tend to turn up and offer their help. Even when they don't know how to do anything that could possibly be qualified as "helpful".

That morning, the lobby was empty. The teams often preferred to work late rather than get an early start. At least those who had a life outside of work.

I took a minute to get a coffee. I had decided to put in a free coffee shop for our full-time workers, like in a Silicon Valley start-up. Everyone was delighted, and it had improved productivity. As for the leeches, they still had to pay for their coffee and sandwiches—making it harder for them to spend as much time in the building.

The big skylights up on the top floor gave the place a certain charm. The Major, the Boss and I all had our offices there.

With my large cup of coffee in hand, I climbed the transparent central staircase to join the Major.

He was already there, of course. A force of nature: tall and muscular with short, white hair and solid-looking hands. His handshake was too firm for a politician, who could never go around crushing voters' knuckles, but it gave you a good idea of who you were dealing with. His voice completed the picture of a man who was just over sixty, serious, honest, and ex-military, although the Major was never in the armed forces as far as I know. His name, of course, is not Major either. But he runs the campaign with such a firm hand and with so much verve that I call him the Major. Before, when he was just the head of the party, I called him Sergeant. He wasn't a fan. I'm fairly confident that, of the two, he prefers the Major.

His office was terribly mundane: a large, light wood desk with a hole in the corner for electrical cables. A computer screen. An oversized telephone with a lot of buttons. Files everywhere. A safe. Two armchairs and a coffee table for meetings. Family pictures: Mrs Majorette with a kid in her arms, probably one of their many grandchildren; the Major as *pater familias* in their country house; the Major with the Boss. The decor confirmed the first impression you got upon seeing the Major: honest, solid, loyal, and dull.

The meeting should have taken place in my office. A few years earlier, in a similar situation, I would have paid attention to such a detail because there is a definite advantage to being on your home turf. And, before this campaign, I was reluctant to let anyone have an advantage over me. But I've settled down since then. And my office isn't really suitable for a meeting with several people. I chose a small one on purpose.

Since we'd set up at HQ, any time I needed to hold a meeting with more than three participants, I organized it somewhere else: in an impersonal room, in someone else's office, even the Boss's when he wasn't around and I wanted to impress, in the basement kitchen, at the café, the list goes on.

★ ★ ★

"Nice pictures and a flattering article. Good work."

In other circumstances, I would have been touched. The Major isn't only terse; he rarely congratulates anyone.

"Ah, you'll have to tell Marilyn," I replied. "She's the one who managed everything. He was good, though. He keeps getting better at that sort of thing. By the time he's ninety-eight, he'll be excellent, and we'll really be sure to get somewhere. Hang in there, just another thirty years of hard work!"

"Shall we do this in my office?" the Major asked without a smile.

"Yes, but let's add a fourth chair."

"I thought you wanted just the three of us. You, me, and the crazy IT guy."

"Have you forgotten Winston, Major?"

"Winston?"

"Yes, young Caligny. If he's going to learn anything during this presidential internship, we have to include him. Nothing could teach the future leader of the nation a better lesson than a frank discussion with an IT manager before eight o'clock in the morning. It's a rite of passage."

Though he was used to my nonsense, I could see the Major was struggling to understand. He blinked repeatedly. The Major was probably a good chess player—organized, cautious, sometimes bold. But at poker I imagined he was ripe for the taking.

That said, within his area of expertise, the Major did everything right. As a good apparatchik, he maintained solidly built networks, always returned favours, and when he asked a question, he got an answer.

"So," he said, moving on before the others arrived. "I looked into Pinguet, like you asked. The kind of senator they don't make any more. A few skeletons in the cupboard, but nothing serious. Seventy-four years old. In almost any other position, he would be nearing the end, but in the Senate . . . I checked, he's fine: no health problems or accidents."

"Well, good for him. But that doesn't get us anywhere. Can we tie him to the primary in any way?"

"Not any way I found. He wasn't involved in the oversight committee we put in place to audit the voting, and he didn't campaign for the Boss or Trémeau locally. He didn't even pick a side. In fact, I can't find a single instance where he defended a risky position. Nothing, I found nothing."

The Major's tone was doubtful. Since he knew nothing more, he said nothing more. This was proof of his intelligence, but it was also a fairly radical stance in the world of politics.

Nothing on Pinguet. So now a computer nerd was my only hope. And that was never reassuring . . .

8

Caligny and Paul Froux, the party's head of IT, joined us at the same time.

Luckily for Winston, they looked nothing alike. In fact, Froux didn't look like much at all. His hair was slicked back, but it was impossible to tell if it was hair gel or grease. His yellow polyester short-sleeved shirt might have brightened the nearly grey complexion of a man who clearly felt more at home with computer screens than with other people, but the taupe tie killed any chance of that.

Next to Froux, young Caligny looked like a Greek god.

"What are you doing here, Louis?" the Major asked dryly, despite my earlier warning. It must have been his way of marking his territory.

"Winston's just following orders, Major," I said. "A trait we can all applaud, wouldn't you agree?"

Caligny gave me a dirty look when he heard me using his new nickname. "They say young people are rebellious, that they know nothing of the values of hard work, but here is a young man, just twenty years old, who happily got out of bed this morning for a seven thirty meeting! Take comfort, Major, May 1968 is finally behind us!"

I could tell the Major was annoyed to be in the dark about why Caligny was present—both at the meeting and in general. As for Winston, he didn't seem to care for my sense of humour. Froux trained his usual vacant expression on me. The meeting got underway.

Twenty minutes in, I finally put my finger on what the meeting made me think of. A bullfight. An unusual bullfight. Not the kind of fight that pits a graceful man elegantly dressed in bright colours against a strong, brave bull. No, there was none of the extreme refinement you find in that type of bloody but symbolic battle. This bullfight saw a tired, anxious old cow facing several determined, rather irritated men.

I must say that in his role as the cow, our head of IT was particularly convincing. He had started sweating nervously as soon as the Major asked his second question. His explanations were drowned in a plethora of useless and incomprehensible details.

"Look, Froux. I don't want any of the technical stuff, not for now," I finally said, interrupting him. "All I want is for you to use full sentences—you know, subject, verb, object—to explain clearly how the system worked."

"Well, each party member has a number assigned by us: it's their username for the vote. Then, an algorithm randomly assigns a secret ten-digit code to each member. The username and secret code must be used together to confirm the member's identity and open online voting. The contents of the electronic urn, which is open for the duration of the election, can only be checked once voting has ended, at which point the results are instantly available, with a score for each of the candidates."

We could tell Froux was doing his best to speak slowly. His shirt collar was damp. Sweat dripped from his hairline. And it wasn't even eight o'clock in the morning. In February. I took a mental note to never invite him to an afternoon meeting in the summer.

"Okay. That much I follow, more or less. To vote, a member needs a username and a secret code. Who provides them?" I asked.

"The party assigns the username. We give each new member a number the day they first join the party. Well, when I say 'we' I really mean the computer program, because the number assigned is random."

"And the secret codes?"

"They're assigned by Droid, who use a proprietary algorithm."

Caligny, who had undoubtedly been born with a computer in his hands, like the rest of his generation, nevertheless opened his eyes wide. Realizing he wouldn't look any stupider than we did by asking simple questions, he interrupted Froux. "I'm not sure I understand," he said. "What is Droid? And a proprietary algorithm?"

"Droid is the subcontractor that handles our voting operations because they require software, resources, and expertise that we don't have in-house, because I do what I can, but I don't have the means to handle all that."

"And a proprietary algorithm?"

"Oh, it's just an algorithm they developed. It's the software that assigns secret codes compatible with the voting program. They assign a code to each member and send it directly to them. That way, the party doesn't know the members' secret codes. It limits the possibility for voter fraud. It's very secure, with firewalls everywhere to keep any potential hackers out. Plus there was a compliance officer present at every stage."

His earnest efforts to reassure us were almost touching. The Major was just getting warmed up, though. Why had he looked so worried as Froux spoke? He had brought his hands together in front of his mouth, his fingers just beneath his nose, as if he were about to start praying. In the Major's language, that meant he was seconds from ripping the person across from him to shreds. I didn't mind. The world would be better off with one less IT guy in it in my opinion. But then again, that would mean hiring someone new—which wasn't the best idea just two months from a presidential election. Froux was ugly, slow, and narrow-minded, but at least he'd been around for a while. Handing the IT system over to a stranger was clearly riskier than leaving Froux at the helm. That was the ultimate protection from redundancy for IT managers: whoever decided to sack them had to be willing to take the risk of replacing them with someone even more dangerously incompetent as well as potentially opening up digital security to attacks.

Eager to save the Major's adrenaline, and my own, I decided to rein things in. "Right, it was secure. So, how did the 15th September vote play out?"

"Uh, Trémeau lost?" Froux offered, his voice betraying fear, disbelief, and incomprehension among other emotions.

The guy was killing me.

"Froux," I said, "thank you so very much for clearing that up for us. Perhaps Trémeau's defeat and, by correlation, the Boss's win, somehow escaped Caligny. It's priceless to have an employee like you to provide such deep analyses and remind us of what matters when confusion starts to spread. I can only speak for myself, of course, and perhaps the Major would like to say his piece, but between the two of us, I'm just curious, do you seriously think I'm an idiot?" I wanted to disembowel the man then and there, but I thought that if I continued he might have a heart attack. "All right, Froux, let's get back to business. What I'm asking is how it played out from an IT point of view. Were there any incidents? Hacker attempts? Anything you can't explain? Anything we would have a hard time justifying if asked?"

"Everything was cleared by Droid and the compliance officer! None of the teams filed a complaint. The results are one hundred per cent reliable. There was no fraud."

★ ★ ★

I felt weary all of a sudden. With a nod, I indicated to the others that the cow was theirs to finish off. The Major gave me a resigned look, which was rather unlike him. Caligny, who was less annoyed than us, was still trying to understand the system architecture. He was now asking the questions, and they were good. I even got the impression he understood the answers. With any luck, once he had figured out the system and its subtleties, he would be able to answer the questions that were still popping into my mind.

It was nevertheless embarrassing to admit I needed an interpreter to understand this chap who'd been working for the same political party as me for over ten years . . . If the Boss's enemies found out, they'd have a good laugh. And if, on top of all that, they learned that Caligny was running a meeting the Major and I were both attending, they might even get their hopes up.

"Major, I suggest we let Winston try to get his head around this business while we handle our real jobs. We have a campaign to run and a presidential election to win!" I said.

Caligny would have to get on with it, since the Major and I had to get ready for our morning meeting with the Boss.

9

As we did nearly every morning, the inner circle had gathered around the Boss: the Major, Marilyn, and Régine, the Boss's personal secretary, a formidable woman who would have thrown herself in front of a train for him and who managed his diary, phone calls, and mail like a drill sergeant. And Démosthène. And me.

We were the loyal few who would never betray him and who would be with him until the end. Any of us would cut off our own arm to protect the Boss.

I haven't mentioned Démosthène yet. He's a member of the inner circle though, and as such, he's an indisputable member of the team. He's worked with the Boss for years. He's an intellectual with multiple degrees, who speaks Latin, Greek, German, and English—four languages almost no one masters in French politics. Especially English.

The Boss had recruited him back when everyone had thought he was done for. Démosthène, a dyed-in-the-wool academic with doctorates in classics and geography and a passion for German history, wrote articles, published books, and spoke at conferences. In other words, he wasn't doing anything particularly useful. But since he was clever, he had attracted someone's attention and been hired to write speeches for a former prime minister who hated the Boss. But one day, the two of them met, got to talking, and decided they liked each other. From then on, though he continued to teach courses whose very titles were beyond my comprehension, he became a volunteer member of the Boss's team—a team comprised solely of the secretary and me, because at the time, there were only three of us. Everyone in politics had scorned the foolish intellectual for turning his back on the powerful to help the madmen bail water. But now no one criticized his choice any more.

My relationship with Démosthène has always been a bit awkward, though I can't say exactly why. He's a nice, even-tempered and polite chap, and not at all the type to take all the credit. I've never had a serious fight with him, nothing beyond minor disagreements about wording for the Boss's speeches. In his defence, Démosthène is completely devoid of political wherewithal. He lives in the wonderful world of ideas, where you can think and say anything, a world where the most powerful people are those who know the most.

As for me, I live in the somewhat less wonderful world of electoral marketing, the twenty-four-hour news cycle, political compromises, favours proffered, and blows dodged or landed. In my world, those in power want to stay there, or gain even more. I'm not sure whether my world is more or less authentic than his, but in any case, it's different.

Though he had an intellectual preference for Démosthène's world, the Boss had to live, fight, and win in mine. But even the most abysmal sports commentator would tell you that a good team always includes a variety of complementary abilities. And Démosthène was the best when it came to drafting a foundational speech from an incomplete sentence mumbled by the Boss as he walked down a corridor somewhere.

So there were six of us—if you count Winston—who made up the Boss's team, his entourage, his inner circle. He had chosen us, and we all had a role to play. He counted on us, and we were determined not to let him down. I held a privileged position due to my many years of service by his side, and everyone else knew it, so I didn't have to hold it over them.

We weren't really friends, though we got on well, but we were united behind him, and he brought us together like a shared passion that transcended our differences. It was our responsibility to support him to the end. He would be president, thanks to his talent, drive, charisma, and hard work. And thanks to us.

He would be president soon, but in the meantime, he was in a bad mood. A thousand little details betrayed his feelings that morning. The way he refused to look at us when we came into the office, the way he concentrated on what he was reading as we sat down, the rapid blinking of his eyelids, and his silence once we were all settled.

In such circumstances, it was best to keep quiet and let him run things. His secretary silently read through the Boss's diary. Marilyn typed away on her Blackberry, which was hardly new, since communications managers are constantly striving to show the world they're always communicating. The Major was proofing a report he had drafted for the Boss. Démosthène was trying to make out the titles of the books that sat on the Boss's desk. I was watching everyone else.

I cleared my throat, to remind him that we were there and that we, too, had work to do. No one else in the inner circle would dare to do such a thing. It was one of my privileges after twenty years of loyal service.

"I see you're all here at last?" he finally said. "I guess we can get started then? Because if you have better things to do, I can always wait."

The Boss's hypocrisy could be limitless at times. We had spent nearly ten minutes watching him read, and now he was telling *us* off. But he was the Boss. He was the one in the ring, in the fight of his life. It was hard to be angry with him for a bout of irritability.

He handed me the report he had just finished. "Here," he said. "I don't understand a word. Tell its author there are two possibilities: either I'm an idiot, or he has a hard time clearly expressing simple ideas."

The Major jumped in with the schedule. He always went about it the same way: he made a list of planned trips and addressed any questions they threw up. Only the most delicate issues were tackled during our meetings with the Boss, since the Major, the Valkyrie and I handled the rest. Once he got the answers he needed, the Major moved on to suggestions for future trips, including his opinion regarding the plans drafted by the Valkyrie and her team or by the elected officials behind the requests. I was usually consulted at some point.

Someday, when a journalist looking to make a name for himself by writing a book about the Boss comes to interview me, I'll underscore his exceptional ability to make decisions. The Boss likes making decisions and has never had a hard time with them, even when difficult consequences are involved. But in truth, his decision-making process is incredibly complex. Sometimes he makes decisions quickly, all on his own, making it seem like he is absolutely sure of himself. And other times, he asks everyone's opinion more than once and engages in discussions to weigh the pros and cons. One of the things that most fascinates me, is that, contrary to the impression he gives, when he makes a quick decision, that's when he's least sure of himself.

Of course, making decisions is never easy. People haven't been killing one another for thousands of years just to show future generations how terribly mediocre they were. No, it's because coming to an agreement about how to make decisions is a daunting task. And even once we've agreed on the best way to make them, we must still actually do it.

After the Major, Marilyn usually stepped in, most often to quickly go over any campaign rumours that were making their way through the political milieu, though, thanks to an unwritten pact, they would never reach the papers. The Boss loved these stories. He pretended not to care, but he couldn't keep himself from asking Marilyn or me what was going around. He needed to know what the journalists were saying about the candidates, what they predicted, and what the various entourages were whispering. The Boss would listen with a smile on his face, regularly expressing outrage about the things people claimed he had said, though he didn't always outwardly deny them.

After the rumours, Marilyn dived head first into the more serious business of suggesting a schedule of press meetings—these were planned around the policies the campaign needed to address and the Boss's scheduled trips. The goal was to reconcile two seemingly contradictory obligations: constantly providing new, headline-worthy material, while striving to drive home the same consistent message in order to convince public opinion. All without any blunders.

Démosthène took notes. Every decision the Boss made meant more work for him. For each trip, he would have to supervise the preparation of a file including a detailed schedule from the Valkyrie, background information on the history and geography of the place he was visiting, as well as anything noteworthy or related to the chosen theme. For each press event, he drafted a file summarizing the key points for every news topic to ensure the Boss was never caught out by a question. He also added anecdotes and quotes, of which the Boss could never get enough. The Major added a political memo regarding the state of the party in the chosen district and the ambitions of local officials there, as well as the most sensitive questions or talking points. Last but not least, I added my own contribution before handing the file over to the Boss, who, in true old-school style, read every word we wrote for him. And everything came back to us annotated, crossed out or highlighted. I gave up trying to figure out how he had time to read and absorb everything. That was probably another reason why he was the Boss.

Except for his bad mood, which left a distinct chill in the room, everything was normal. But I could tell that this day, which had already begun badly with that dreadful IT manager, would not be like the others.

"So, what's this story about Pinguet and the primary?" the Boss finally asked.

I was taken aback. I couldn't believe that the Boss was talking about it so openly in front of everyone, even though nothing ever left that room. Once I'd got over my surprise, I summarized what we knew—in other words, not much.

"Caligny got an anonymous call yesterday. A man left a message saying that a certain Pinguet knew that the primary vote had been rigged, but that he had died since. We all immediately thought of the senator, but he seems to be in good health, and, given my past interactions with him, I can attest that he never knows anything about anything. As for the vote, we've started looking into it, to see if there were any murky areas. We'll also keep looking into the mysterious Pinguet and I'll dig through every detail of the primary to see if there were any issues. For the moment I'm told everything went to plan."

The Boss listened attentively.

Démosthène, who was hearing all this for the first time, no doubt intended to lighten the mood when he spoke. The difference between playing the intellectual and playing the court jester is often just a question of perspective. "What could there possibly be to look into? We know who won, though not by much. No one contested the results. Trémeau conceded!"

"It doesn't really matter whether the rumour is true or false," I pointed out. "What matters is whether it spreads and our ability to nip it in the bud. Two months before the election, a rumour about a rigged primary could make a mess of our party and ruin the Boss's reputation as a man of integrity."

The Major, who always preferred to let cooler heads prevail, must have noticed I was getting worked up. "There is no proof that anything unorthodox happened during the primary. Just because some guy mumbles the beginnings of a rumour doesn't mean there's any truth to it. For now, I know three things. First, it's up to us to prove to anyone who wants to spread rumours that the primary was exemplary in all respects. Second, we need to look into Pinguet more seriously. Third, I think we need to keep this quiet until we have more information and, most importantly, we must keep working without getting side-tracked by something we know nothing about for the moment."

Normally, after such a straightforward summary from the Major, the Boss should have wrapped things up, said that he agreed, given two or three orders, and moved on. But the subject seemed to be troubling him.

"Have any journalists questioned you about it?" he asked Marilyn, who already knew everything there was to know. She was surprised the Boss was still on the topic.

"No, nothing for the moment. But I think that if anything got out, it would be bad for us. The primary was a bloody affair and we're still working hard to downplay stories of betrayal and pressure the party may have applied. But that's not what I'm most worried about. I'm most worried about the fact that Vital has been playing the 'a new way of doing politics' card from the beginning, with his participative rallies and open townhall meetings. He'll be riding the 'straight talk' wave, and that will be much easier for him if we look like shady old schemers . . . err, not that you're old."

Oops, that was a bit of a blunder. Even I, who occasionally dared to tease the Boss, was careful about mentioning his age. In any case, today wasn't the day.

Démosthène apparently thought he needed to add his two cents' worth. "If I may, I think we just need to be careful. Vital is doing really well with his 'new way' positioning. He's trying to show people that he's not a part of the machine, that he's not afraid to contest his party on sensitive issues, and that he's really listening to what the voters have to say. People are tired of politics in general and it's rather smart to cast them as stakeholders rather than simple voters. I'm not saying we need to follow suit, of course, but we mustn't underestimate our adversary . . ."

This meeting was headed off the rails. The second one of the day to go pear-shaped. That was two too many. I had to intervene.

"Let's not confuse things. On the one hand, there's the question of the anonymous call, about which the Major has said everything there is to say. And on the other, there's the broader question of how to react to Vital's campaign. And as for that, let's not be ridiculous, you can't 'do politics differently'! Sure, it's a nice slogan, it's catchy, but it means nothing! Differently from what? All elected officials listen. Have you ever heard of someone running a campaign without organizing a ton of meetings with as many people as possible to listen to what they have to say? Do you really think," I said, addressing Démosthène in particular, "that Vital suddenly saw the light and somehow did away with the fundamentals of politics?"

"I didn't say that, I'm just saying—"

"Christ, a politician who says he's going to do politics differently is like the owner of a supermarket chain who says his goal is to increase consumers' buying power. It's bullshit. In retail, the goal is to get more and more people to come into shops again and again so you can take their money. In politics, the goal is to mobilize your electorate, build networks, and develop a message that meets voters' expectations at the time of the election so you can be elected."

"I know that, but—"

"Politics is a profession. Regardless of how you feel, there aren't a hundred different ways to go about it. You've got to get out in the field. All of the men who have been elected president of France travelled to the four corners of the country before deciding it was time to run. And to do that, you need a political party. Anyone who tells you that you can win without a party, without a team, without a network, without compromises, and without money, simply by listening to what people have to say is taking you for a ride."

"All I'm saying is that it's a theme that's impacting public opinion," Démosthène insisted.

"Vital was running surveys for his party while I was still at university. He's an apparatchik through and through. He has a better understanding of his party's members than anyone else, not because he's the best, but because he has more experience than anyone else in his camp. Next to him, I'm as lost as a vegetarian at a steakhouse that his label attracts more buyers. I'll stop there, though, because I'm starting to get worked up."

The Boss had watched me get angry with a smile. I was the only one who was allowed to be irritated in his presence. All eyes were on him. The Boss let silence reign for a moment.

"All right, well, I think we've gone over everything," he concluded. "There's much truth in everything that was said.

Much more than in what gets said on TV. Mind you, the truth often matters less than what is presented as the truth—particularly in this profession. In other words, I run the risk of looking like a museum piece if Vital manages to convince people that he is a modern man while I am an old-fashioned schemer. The press would like nothing more than to tell that story. It wouldn't be true, but it would be a good story."

Realizing that the meeting was over, the Major stood up, followed almost instantaneously by everyone present. Except for me. I dawdled as I got my stuff together. The Boss often had a few minutes for me after meetings. Because even among employees he trusted completely, there were still things he only wanted to say to me.

The Boss had stood up, too. With a friendly hand on my shoulder, he walked with me to the door. I felt obligated to reassure him. "This whole thing is very strange. I'll handle it, but it's the kind of problem we could do without at the moment."

The Boss paused for a second. Then, in a warm voice that contrasted with his hard, cool gaze, he replied in words that keep running through my head to this day.

"Yes," he confirmed, "it's a problem. But your tirade made me think of what President Queuille always used to say about politics. Incredibly insightful. He said that politics isn't the art of solving problems, but of silencing those who create them."

Then he smiled, though his eyes remained fixed on mine, and shut the door to his office.

10

We'd hit the Snag on Tuesday, but I only realized it was going to be trouble two days later.

The Boss's attitude during our meeting had left me perplexed. When you work with someone for so long, you get to know them. I knew him well, maybe not as well as people thought, but much better than anyone else. In general, I could predict how he would react to questions people asked, what he would say, and most often, how he would say it.

This time, I had been caught off guard.

He had brought it up with the team when I had told him I would handle it. He had restarted the discussion when the Major had said everything that needed to be said. He had turned a minor blip into a key topic of concern for the inner circle. Why? Because he was worried? Because he had a feeling about it that I didn't? Because he knew something that I didn't?

And then his quip about silencing those who create problems. Taken literally, it was pretty ruthless. I knew that neither of us tended to speak literally, but still. What was he trying to tell me?

If that had been the end of it, I probably would have forgotten his remark. But young Caligny and the Major wouldn't leave it alone.

"The vote could have been rigged," began Winston. "I don't know if it was, but according to my uncle, it was possible."

"Your uncle?"

"Yes, my uncle. He's an IT expert, among other things. I'll introduce you someday."

I was surprised. Just a day earlier, the party's IT guy had explained that the system wasn't hackable, and now here was the kid putting on airs with his uncle for backup to tell me he was wrong.

"First," continued Winston, "he explained very clearly that for anyone who knows anything about it, no system is impenetrable."

"I knew we should have kept the good old urn," I sighed.

"Because you think that can't be rigged?" said Caligny, his eyebrow raised.

"Of course not, but at least I would know how to do it . . . Explain what he told you, with simple words."

"In short, you need two things: the list of usernames, in other words, the party's member list, and the list of secret codes Droid assigned to each of them."

"That much I understand. That's what Froux said."

"Anyone who had both documents could potentially add fake votes to the system. To manage it, you'd need to have an inside man at Droid and another at the party."

"Fake votes . . . From real members? How?"

"That's where things get complicated: you have to know which members won't vote, so you can vote for them without their knowledge. I'm not entirely sure how you could know that, but I'm going to keep looking into it. Maybe by having dead people vote? People must do that in elections . . . In any case, someone clever could have rigged the vote."

"It's ridiculous to think it's so easy! Didn't the commission we established before the vote think of this?"

"To be perfectly honest, they did try to put safeguards in place. For example, they wanted to limit the number of votes that could be cast from a single computer."

"They could do that?"

"It's easy. Every computer has an internet address of sorts. The IP address. That's how we track down illegal downloading and kiddie porn. The commission had planned to make it so that each computer could cast no more than ten votes, which would prevent local apparatchiks from voting for all the little old ladies in their district."

"Sounds great. But I gather they didn't enforce it in the end?"

"The safeguard was rather discreetly removed at the last minute because we realized that many of our members don't have computers. And that quite a few don't even know how to use a mouse. So, if we wanted to ensure respectable participation rates, our members needed to be able to vote from the computers available in local party offices. That way someone could explain how to do it."

Bloody hell. When I think of all the trouble I went to for that election. If only I'd known . . .

"All the safeguards fell by the wayside when confronted with reality," the kid went on. "What would people have said if the oldest party members hadn't been able to vote?"

"I don't know what people would have said, but what I *do* know is that the Boss would have lost."

"Clearly. But the important question is who would have benefited from the crime," Winston said, thinking aloud.

So, it was possible. Now we needed to find out if it had really happened.

"We can't get much further without accessing Droid's data," he continued. "So, the moral of the story is that if we want to know if something untoward occurred, we'll have to go and ask them for their files."

I wasn't sure the word "moral" had its place in our discussion, but there it was.

"No, Caligny," I countered. "If I go and see Droid and start asking questions, someone will find out about it. And then the cat's out of the bag. My faith in those yobs has always been limited. I'm not going to give them the opportunity to compromise us when we're not even sure if there's a problem. That said, I've been thinking, and there aren't a lot of people who could have got their hands on both those lists. We should be able to find out who could have rigged the election, if it was rigged at all."

"Yes and no. We know for sure that they would need someone at Droid. That narrows things down a lot. But they would also need the members list, which would require major connections within the party. Or maybe someone who used to have connections, since the usernames never change."

"What do you mean?"

Winston paused. "Sometimes I wonder if you're playing dumb or if you're really completely lost."

"Don't start talking like an IT guy. You're better than that," I scolded.

"All right, all right. What I mean is that when a member joins the party, they're given a username. And it never changes: the first two digits are from the year they joined, the next two from the region where they live, then the district, etc. Someone who joined ten years ago still has the same username, even if they've moved since. So with a list of members from, say, five years ago, you would already have quite a few usernames. Because, as you might have guessed, we leave members in the file for a few years, even if they don't renew their membership. It inflates numbers, and many of them do end up coming back. And, to rig an election, you don't have to tamper with all the votes, just enough of them to change the outcome."

It was easy to do the arithmetic in my head. 302,638 members with dues fully paid, 229,817 voters, 115,204 votes for the Boss, 114,613 for Trémeau. 491 votes between them. 491 clicks of a mouse. Nothing at all.

More than enough to win, but not enough to preclude doubt.

"Thanks, Winston," I congratulated him. "Good work. Keep it to yourself for now. Did you tell your uncle about all this?"

"Just enough about the system for him to help me out."

"And he won't say anything? We can trust him?"

The kid smiled. "We can. He's quiet as the grave. No one could get it out of him . . . But there's one thing that's been troubling me: why do you think *I'm* the one they called?"

He was right on the mark. This was at the top of my list of unanswered questions. First, because there had been no press about him joining the inner circle. Old dinosaurs might have been able to link his name to his father, but few people even knew his name and all of them had forgotten his father.

"No idea, my young friend. But it's a good question, and we should try to answer it quickly, for the Boss's sake as well as yours."

"The person who called is a man. He chose me without knowing me, and the only thing that could have led him to choose me is the fact that I'm part of the Boss's entourage."

"How can you be so sure you don't know him?"

"Because I'm certain I've never heard that voice before. But mostly because I don't know anyone on Vital's team," he added.

"Caligny, you may not know anyone on Vital's team, but what makes you think the call came from there? Why would someone on the other side warn us that he has a bomb, when it would be in his best interests to set it off?"

"If it's not Vital or someone working for him, who is it? I mean, you have to ask who benefits from the crime here.

I realize it's a bit unorthodox to warn the enemy about what's coming, but then again, why not? Maybe Vital's people think we also have a bomb we could use against them and they're just letting us know they could retaliate so we'll keep it to ourselves. Or maybe we have a friend among them, who thinks such things have no place in a presidential race."

"And maybe someday there will be no budget deficit or public debt or unemployment or poverty," I gibed. "I'm not saying that it won't ever happen, but if I were you and I was a gambling man, I would keep the bets low, because given how things are going, we will undoubtedly feel the heat if all that ever comes to pass."

"I'm glad to see you're as sure of yourself as ever and that your pessimism is intact. But we still have to ask ourselves: who would want to warn us?"

Good question. I still didn't know who was behind the call. And I barely understood what the caller had said.

11

I was torn between satisfaction and anxiety.

Winston was a source of satisfaction.

Despite the worrying news that had been piling up over the past few days, I was pleased with myself for having asked him to help out. I wasn't sure he had realized it was a request. He probably thought it was an order handed down from on high by the Boss.

He had earned a fair amount of trust. For me, "a fair amount of trust" is already quite a lot. That's when I stop having someone else redo the work I give a person. In this profession, when you don't trust someone, you always make sure to assign the same task to someone else. When I explained this at dinner parties, people thought I was nuts. So, I stopped. Stopped telling people that is. That way I'm spared their shocked looks and mocking smirks while I carry on doing things my way, because I prefer not to pinch pennies when it comes to getting the results I need.

As for my anxiety, it stemmed from my natural paranoia.

Paranoia is a workplace hazard for politicians and apparatchiks. Miners get silicosis, diplomats fall prey to loneliness and alcoholism, teachers fight bitterness or depression, and politicians get paranoia. It's impossible to work in this field for more than a couple of years without succumbing. It's because, when you get down to it, to be in politics, you have to have a serious ego. It must already be well-established when you start out, and from there it only grows and strengthens its defences. Politicians—maybe even more so female politicians—have overgrown egos that make them believe that they are always better than everyone else, that they will be able to solve the world's problems, change people's lives, and achieve peace on earth.

This is no criticism. Paranoia gives people drive and, after all, why bother running for election if you don't truly think you'll do better than everyone before you? The natural consequence of these puffed-up personalities though is that you begin to interpret everything that happens around you through an imaginary lens, as simple as it is brutal: if it doesn't suit you, it was done to harm you; those who aren't with you are against you; there are no coincidences.

Everyone in politics is or will become paranoid, but to varying degrees. The Boss's case is quite moderate. He has managed to retain perspective, making him one of the sanest men I know in the game. As for me, I accept my full-blown paranoia. I know that a lot of people don't like me and would really love to hurt me. Besides, even paranoids have enemies. I may be paranoid, but at least I'm still alive.

Anxiety will always win out over satisfaction. The day when that is no longer the case is the day I'll need to consider a career change.

I sat pondering it all, wondering how the primary could have been rigged right under my very eyes without me realizing it.

The Major came into my office without knocking. I hated that.

When I saw him, I thought back to his insistence that we should adopt electronic voting and the worried look on his face as we listened to Froux try to explain. My innate paranoia, most likely.

"I think I know which Pinguet we're talking about."

Maybe my anxiety was about to make room for satisfaction after all. I gestured for the Major to sit.

"The senator is in good health," he explained. "They're talking about his son."

It was difficult to believe. When a senator's son dies, I hear about that sort of thing. The news would have found its way into specialist publications and party higher-ups would have called the Boss to get him to offer his condolences.

"Dead?" I asked. "When?"

"Monday morning. At the hospital in Grenoble. I asked one of my friends who works at national police headquarters to look into it, and he just called to tell me that Jean-Dominique Pinguet, the senator's son, died during an operation."

"What was wrong with him?"

"Car accident. Sunday night. Thirty-six hours before the anonymous call. He was speeding, from what I understand. It seems he swerved to avoid an obstacle and the car rolled. I don't know any more for the moment."

"And why is it we're only hearing about this now?"

"It wasn't his car, and he didn't have his ID on him, or on what was left of him. It took a while to identify the body."

It was 6:47 p.m. We had hit the Snag two days earlier, and ever since, there had been nothing but bad news.

Three things seemed very clear. First, the chances of this car crash being a genuine accident were as slim as my chances of joining the clergy. What had at first been a slightly irksome affair had now turned violent. That was an important distinction.

Second, there seemed to be an obvious link between Pinguet's death and the anonymous call. The caller had known about the death very early on, even before the police. How?

Lastly, my anxiety was growing and my reasons for satisfaction shrinking. The imbalance was getting out of hand. Another important distinction.

"Here's what we found on the son," stated the Major, handing me a file.

Pinguet, Jean-Dominique, business owner, born 22nd August 1966 in Grenoble to Pierre-Etienne Pinguet, politician, and Bénédicte Maupin. Degree in computer science from ENSIA, junior ski jump national champion in 1980. Interests: oenology and motor sports.

The photo that accompanied the *Who's Who* biography was a bit dated, but he looked just like his father. And, surprise surprise, he'd studied computer science. Now I had an issue with an online vote and a guy who'd studied IT. A coincidence was seeming less and less plausible.

"He was pretty successful," continued the Major. "He put together his first company with few resources at a time when no one really thought online sales would take off, and he capitalized on his father's contacts to make a name for himself in ski resort real estate. He sold the first company for a good price, and with the profits he founded a second company, still online, but selling wine this time . . ."

It occurred to me that his father's contacts must have been less useful in this department, but then again, I may have been underestimating the Senate's auditing abilities when it came to a good vintage . . .

"That's when he started making quite a bit of money," the Major went on. "Not because the company was particularly profitable, but because he sold at the right time, just before the internet bubble burst. He could have stopped there. He was young and almost rich. But he wanted to stay in the game, so he invested a small part of his earnings in a third company: 'D&M'. Any guesses as to what they do there, my friend?"

My friend. Since when were we friends? I shook my head.

"B2B consulting in online direct marketing. Internet yet again. He made a decent living. I'm not sure the company made that much money, but young Pinguet became pretty well known in the field of online commerce."

I listened to the Major's speech without interrupting him. When he was done, I nodded and congratulated him on the quality of his research. Then I encouraged him to get back to work.

I sat alone in my office perplexed and dismayed. I studied every detail of the documents the Major had given me and looked online for any information I could find.

It took quite a while. Nearly an hour. I'm still not very internet savvy. I think I've been quite clear about my feelings for IT personnel, and I must admit that for a long time to my mind computers were little more than televisions attached to typewriters. Luckily, though I don't know how they work, I do more or less know how to use them, which is the most important thing.

The name of one of Pinguet's partners caught my attention. There were three founders: Jean-Dominique Pinguet, Stanislas Dufourcq, and Paul Grulier.

I began researching these two other names.

Nothing on Google. Just fifty-seven pages of hits for Gruliers that had nothing to do with my man.

My Grulier was a partner in a business. An entrepreneur. So, I decided to look him up on websites that list registered companies. And that's where I found him. Paul Grulier, founding associate of D&M, also ran another company called "Electronic Voting and Direct Democracy" or EVDD. Though no one had ever heard of it, the company had been around for a little over five years. And during that time, I discovered that it had done something extremely interesting. It had changed its name.

It was now known as Droid.

12

I was standing to attention, like a riot police officer on duty, when Caligny received the second message.

I was waiting for the Boss. It might not seem obvious, but in this field, you have to know how to wait. That's something apparatchiks and riot police have in common. The older I get, the more similarities I discover. Lack of popularity for example. And celibacy, due to working nights, unexpected trips, shortened holidays, an overdeveloped esprit de corps, and intellectual fatigue. And let's not forget necessity. There is no democracy without riot police, because public order must be preserved between votes; and there's no democracy without apparatchiks, because they're the ones who keep political parties alive. And without political parties, there is no democracy.

Of course, there are always a few geniuses who argue that political parties are nothing but machines designed to fool voters, clans that only band together to conquer power while spending most of their time trying to stab their so-called friends in the back. Based on this assertion, which is true, they deduce that political parties are a danger, and that democracy would be better off without them, which is ridiculous.

I thought while I waited—the analogy with riot police had its limits.

Though most would claim the contrary, not many of us had thought the Boss would earn the party's nomination before the primary. The press, the public, political commentators—no one had believed he had a chance. Some said his career was over, and they were thrilled. Others said he was remarkable but had missed too many chances and wouldn't be offered any more starring roles. For the vast majority, he was both a household name and yet somehow already forgotten—like a football star who suddenly disappeared mid-career.

Even certain members of the inner circle had had doubts. Even me.

Experience has taught me that when you crank up the heat on a politician by subjecting him to a new type of campaign or a crisis that will impact the future of his career, the members of his inner circle always end up in a shouting match. It's a bit like binary fission: the more important the politician becomes, the more divided the entourage.

And though I hate to admit it, we had been no exception to the rule. All of us had hoped that the Boss would be able to run for president, but few of us had imagined it was possible, so when we had had to manoeuvre, particularly within the party, to make sure he became a candidate, we had been through some rocky times.

Once he had the party's nomination, I had put our disagreements aside like bad memories, blaming them on the sudden pressure and insufficient preparation. But since we'd hit the Snag, I could tell that the worst lay ahead.

13

Letting my natural paranoia run its course, I tried to construct a theory to explain this series of disturbing events. The questions were all tangled up, forming an inescapable labyrinth of hypotheses and alternatives. Had the primary been rigged? If yes, by whom? If not, who would benefit from letting people believe it had been? Had Jean-Dominique Pinguet been the victim of an everyday accident, or had he been eliminated, and by whom and why? It was hard to convince myself it was a coincidence because of the ties that linked Pinguet to Droid . . . Who would want to warn us? And why call Caligny?

I had reached the conclusion that it was all a conspiracy to keep me too busy thinking about something other than the Boss's campaign, when Winston came into my office looking rather upset.

"I just got another message. Same voice," he said.

Shit.

"What does it say? Let me listen!"

Caligny shook his head. "I can't," he explained. "He didn't leave a message on my voicemail. It was a pre-recorded message he played when I picked up. But I took notes right after to make sure I wouldn't forget anything. First, he explained that he didn't want to reveal his identity, but that his 'idea of honour is a cut above most people's'."

Right. Tipsters can be useful or dangerous, depending on your point of view, but they're rarely paragons of honour and panache.

"He really drove home the fact that 'the situation is urgent'. He didn't say whether it was urgent for him or for us, but his voice, even on the recording, sounded strained. He said that he was getting together some papers he wanted to hand over to us, and that we need to meet. He gave me a time and place."

"When? Where?"

"Under the Pont Neuf on Saturday night at ten o'clock."

"What did you say?"

"Nothing."

"What do you mean nothing?" I asked, outraged. "What's wrong with you? The guy wants to meet us under a bridge in central Paris and give us highly confidential documents and you say nothing? You must be out of your mind!"

Caligny just looked at me, wide-eyed. He was about to open his mouth to defend himself when I realized my mistake.

"Right, right," I said. "It was a recording. Sorry . . . So how are you supposed to let him know that you accept his invitation?"

"We're to publish a press release on our website saying a high-ranking official will be visiting Meylan next Monday."

"Meylan? Near Grenoble? No one would ever go there during a campaign . . ."

"Right, but it's in Isère. Senator Pinguet's region. I think it's a way to put us on the right path . . ."

"All right. Call the webmaster and tell him to put it up. But you're not going to this meeting, Winston. I'm going. With a guy from security. I have a few things to say to this Mr Anonymous—he's really starting to get on my nerves."

"That's right, so when he goes looking for a handsome young man with a full head of hair and healthy skin, you'll fit that description perfectly. Great plan. Wonderful idea."

There was one thing that bothered me more than anything else with this mess. I was worried it might impact the Boss and annoyed that I didn't understand, but the worst part was that I could feel I wasn't doing a good job. I was behind. My reflexes seemed to be dulled. Caligny, on the other hand, seemed to be keeping pace, and he was growing increasingly caustic to boot. The cleverer he got, the older I felt.

"One last thing," the kid continued. "He urged caution. He told me, 'Watch your step better than Pinguet did. He recently learned you can never be too careful'."

"That's how he said it?"

"It's a direct quote."

A rather ambiguous message. Caligny suggested it was a vague warning. I saw it as a threat.

We looked at each other for a long moment. There were now even more questions than before. Though the second message didn't shed any light on the affair, there was one positive outcome at least: we were going to meet the man behind the Snag.

14

Friday 19ᵗʰ February, 10:12 a.m.

Marilyn's office was a mess. Every surface was covered in newspapers, magazines, and dispatches. Any time she was in her office for more than fifteen minutes, Marilyn plugged in her mobile to recharge. When she wasn't on official trips with the Boss, handling yet another fit of journalistic hysteria, Marilyn spent her time on the phone trying to prevent them. An excellent spin doctor, she was always trying to set the tone and cast events in a way that played to our advantage. Spinning is about convincing people that what you have to say about the story is just as important as the story itself.

In a campaign, spin is crucial.

As soon as she had a spare second, Marilyn would call journalists to find out what they were working on or what stories they were thinking about writing to give them her take. And her take was almost always mine.

That's why I had a lot of time for Marilyn. She regularly consulted me about how to reply to this or that and informed me as soon as a relevant dispatch came through. I had developed a habit of going down to her office to go over things once a day.

But that wasn't the only reason.

I loved going down to see Marilyn because I liked her. She was attractive, of course, but that was nothing new. She was probably less beautiful than six or seven years earlier, when

I had hired her, but she was even more charming. Her sharp wit more than made up for the—minimal—marks left by the passage of time on her figure and complexion. Men who like the young bodies, spontaneity, and carefree nature of women under thirty would probably say her beauty was fading. But I was of the opposite opinion. Time had made her even more sensual. She was no longer impressed by the powerful men she mixed with, and she had successfully managed the more or less clumsy advances of all those who saw nothing but her physique. She had a remarkable gift for separating her private life from her professional one with an airtight seal, as I have learned first-hand.

The other reason I was always so keen to go down and see Marilyn was that I loved talking to her. I quickly realized that she helped me formulate my ideas. When we talked, she always asked the right questions, helping me to see things more clearly. In this area, she was the antithesis of Démosthène: she made those she was speaking to feel clever. So, whenever I was having a hard time expressing an idea clearly, or when I wanted to test out an argument I was planning to submit to the Boss, I went to talk to Marilyn.

Since my brain was still a whirlwind of questions and hypotheses, I thought speaking to Marilyn would do me some good. As usual, I stepped into her office with a perfunctory knock.

She wasn't alone.

The Major was sitting across from her. The Major looked at me and Marilyn instinctively glanced at her computer screen, where the AFP dispatches were constantly popping up.

They had been talking about me, or some other poor paranoid chap, and I had interrupted them.

The fraction of a second of silence following my entrance, the Major's surprised look, his very presence in her office, which was rather unusual, Marilyn's uneasiness—everything seemed to indicate they had been talking about me, or the Boss, or about a sensitive subject. In other circumstances I would have made them feel bad about it by asking what all the whispering was about, but I didn't want to upset Marilyn before I'd had time to benefit from her wisdom.

"I hope I'm not interrupting anything too important," I said, "but I wanted to know if we have any information about what Vital is planning to say on TV tomorrow."

A bit of irony and a reference to our shared enemy seemed like the best tools to disperse the awkward atmosphere that had developed since I'd stepped into the room.

Marilyn, who was probably grateful for my olive branch, replied right away. "We've heard a few things, yes. He's going to distance himself a bit more from his party and say he is for nuclear power. He's also going to back car-free zones in urban areas and maintaining the 35-hour working week."

"It's risky for him to say he's in favour of banning cars in city centres. He was the mayor of a major city once. The yuppies will be all for it, but his working-class base won't like it at all," replied the Major. Jumping into the conversation I had started with Marilyn was the easiest way to avoid talking about the topic of their previous discussion.

"Not necessarily," I countered. "In any case, if he's coming out in favour of nuclear power, he has to throw the environmentalists a bone. Green zones in cities are one of their obsessions. As for his working-class base, it vanished ages ago. Better to lock down the votes among those who are already inclined to vote for him rather than to make a desperate move that will displease them just to get a few ballots from lower-income voters. It's a good move. And if he plays his cards right, he can even paint himself as an independent."

This is the basis of politics: positions themselves matter little; what counts is the impact a position has on voters.

It's crazy how long a conversation can go on when people are trying to skirt another topic. I had already used this move at quite a few family dinners and after the odd row with friends.

As we exchanged trifling details about Vital's campaign and the best positioning for the Boss, it occurred to me that this little episode confirmed that I had made the right choice. Working with Winston to handle the situation was a good idea. After all, he was closest to the source of the rumour. He was also relatively unknown to the outside world, which meant I could use him to ask questions without making waves. Plus, if I kept treating him poorly, people were likely to open up to him, which meant he would be able to glean a lot of useful information.

I was going to have to get him to discuss the Snag with the Major and Marilyn. Those two weren't telling me everything, and I didn't like it one bit.

15

Friday 19ᵗʰ February, 1:15 p.m.

Having lunch with a political adversary is a sport that I had learned to love.

First and foremost, because I like to eat. But mostly because I had learned very early on that, to be successful in politics, you have to learn to love everything that seems repulsive to any normal, sensible person. Who would be delighted to have lunch with a man he hates? And think it perfectly acceptable to come to an agreement with someone who never keeps his word? And see nothing wrong with spending more time fighting with people from his own party than with those on the other side of the aisle? A politician, that's who. Or worse, an apparatchik.

Since I wasn't sure that my lunch with Texier would lead to anything other than his frustration with the Boss's refusal to visit his district, I had decided we at least needed to go somewhere where we'd be sure to be seen together. In our small world, the fact that we were having lunch together in public was a statement in itself.

Chez Françoise was the perfect venue given my goals. Just a short walk from the National Assembly, it's like a parliamentary canteen where MPs from all parties and lobbyists eager to invite them to lunch rub elbows and exchange smiles.

At Chez Françoise, our lunch wouldn't just be noticed; it would be talked about. The higher-ups in our party would realize we were doing whatever it took to get the job done, and Vital's troops would know we were a united front. At least, I hoped they would . . .

"So, what's next?"

The routine question. They must teach it in second-rate politics schools. It gives the impression that you care about the person you're speaking to. I know it all too well. It's become a linguistic tic for most of the MPs, who always pretend to be asking for your opinion on the political situation. I wasn't surprised to hear Texier use it. I was, however, a bit taken aback that he would ask *me* this question. Who did he think I was? A novice?

"Well, we're going to run a good campaign and we're going to win. And once we've won the presidential race, we'll move on to the legislative elections," I explained, reminding the little worm that the two subjects were linked.

"If your boss wins, he'll have to hold the majority, which is terribly divided, you know," he countered. "He'll need everyone he can get."

You don't say.

"He knows it and I know it. But I also know that a lot of people will need him too to remain where they are. I've never subscribed to the belief that legislative elections following a victorious presidential campaign are a cakewalk. Who knows what these parliamentary elections will look like . . ."

The answer was simple: the two of us. Texier and I were in the best position to know which seats were safe and which were marginal, which swing seats were sure to go to the other side, which seats would be decided by the presidential election, and which ones were hardest to predict. Not to mention which constituencies were facing a changed electorate and the resulting political upheaval. Like Texier's district.

He offered a small smile. We understood one another. I could see that he was about to show his true colours and slip back into being the apparatchik he had always been at heart.

He adjusted his face so that he was no longer wearing the bland, polite expression of an MP on autopilot. I had just finished my sole meunière, which is what I always ordered at Chez Françoise. He had gobbled down a steak in pepper sauce. And yet lunch was just getting started.

"We know each other well enough to tell it like it is," he said, going on the offensive. "Here's how I see it: your boss won the primary and is now the party's candidate. Will he win? I don't know. No one does. What I *do* know is that he needs to unite his party to win. And we're not quite there yet. In my camp, people are still pretty disgruntled by the primary. Too many blows below the belt. Too many personal attacks. You went after my boss too hard, and the MPs who supported her are angry about it."

"But the voters sided with us."

"Maybe. But the party's voters aren't the same as the country's voters, you know. Plenty of people are saying that you're sexist, that you have deprived France of a female candidate who embodies modernity and youth. We can't undo the primary. I'm just saying that the divide is very real."

This was the usual argument. I had heard it a hundred times since the end of the primary. A loser's argument. You won, but you need us so much more than we would have needed you . . .

"It takes time to breach a divide. We've only just concluded a no-holds-barred fight in which, need I remind you, you didn't exactly pull your punches. Your boss, who is always ready to paint herself as the victim of sexism, conservatism, liberalism, technocracy, or even the party's members, spent quite a lot of time calling my Boss a dinosaur."

"I admit we may have taken things too far. On both sides. But nothing irreparable, I hope. In any case, we still believe we can play a role."

Of course. But what role? The different positions and ministries weren't for sale just yet. It was too early. I wasn't going to start negotiating who would be the Minister of Puff Pastry two months before the election. The Boss hadn't given me the go-ahead, and he wouldn't until after the first round.

"Jean," I said earnestly, "neither of us is going to negotiate right here and now over dessert the makeup of the government if we win the election. That would be unreasonable. What I *can* tell you is that my Boss sees the past as the past. Everything will depend on the campaign. Those who put their drive and talents to work for the campaign over the next couple of months will have good chances, even if they backed your boss. We'll achieve unity through action and victory, not vulgar haggling."

Texier was listening carefully. He wasn't surprised by my answer. He would have said the same thing in my place.

"I understand what you're saying. Everyone understands. It's all very sensible. But the first step is always the hardest. If your boss doesn't extend the hand of friendship, who will take it? And now, frankly, he's the one who has the most to lose."

I stayed calm. What was he implying?

"We all have a lot to lose," I balked. "He could lose the presidential election, and you could lose your seat in parliament. And, without wanting to sound too dramatic, I think our country would suffer if it turned its back on us for a guy like Vital."

Texier smiled. He was drinking his coffee. Slowly, down to the last drop.

"You're right, we all have a lot to lose," he replied. "But we won't all lose the same thing: your boss will disappear, you'll find a new boss or retire, we'll be in the opposition for five years, and then my boss, who is young and popular, will take over our party. This defeat would be easier on me than on you."

In objective terms, he was right. His argument was rational, well-constructed, and most importantly, true. He was bluffing a little, of course, but like all good threats, this one was anchored in reality.

"Listen, Jean, lots of people told me the Boss would lose. They're still crying into their cereal. He's going to win this election. And when he does, everyone will be eating out of his hand. And anyone who goes against him will have to explain themselves to the voters in the parliamentary elections and to the media for the next couple of years. Your boss can play a central role if—and only if—she gets on board. It's your job to convince her. You can't keep playing the victims. I hear what you're saying about the importance of coming together. I'll see what I can do. I'm sure we can work something out for appointments after the election. Let's get together regularly to ensure everything goes to plan between our bosses. They both need our help."

He seemed to be listening. I had suggested meetings and discussions and implied that Trémeau could play an important role after the election. I wasn't sure I'd convinced him, but I was certain that my arguments were weakening his resolve and that he would take them to his boss.

"Marie-France will have candidates to put forward for support in the legislative elections. She won't understand if your boss doesn't back me in my district, as a peace offering."

"The best way to convince him to come is to stop threatening him. Your election is still a long way off. We should come together now. You know he'll back you if everything goes to plan," I countered, trying to put all my conviction into this evasive reply.

"So, you're saying he's not coming? Did you talk to him about it? He could come before the presidential election for a joint rally. Marie-France and him on the same stage. The voters in my district would love it."

If I suggested that to the Boss, he'd have a fit of rage and die of a heart attack.

"I'll see what I can do," I said, "but the most important thing is for us to come together, trust one another, and get to work."

Everything had been said. I paid the bill without so much as a glance at the amount. I didn't have a euro to my name, but I had a nearly unlimited budget for taking professional contacts out to lunch at nice restaurants. In politics, you rarely get rich, but it's hard not to end up fat.

As he was leaving, Texier shook my hand and came in closer, to ensure he wasn't overheard. "I get what you're saying about trust and fair play. Trust is important. But I've heard things I don't want to believe about your team playing less than fair. Only rumours, of course . . ."

I said nothing. As usual, the real topic of our lunch came up once we had left the table.

"It would be extremely difficult, of course," he continued, "to convince my boss to work with a campaign which got its start thanks to voter fraud. And it would be nearly imposs-ible to convince her supporters not to put together a counter campaign. She'd lose, of course. But so would you. And she's not afraid to lose, you know. If it's about embodying honesty and loyalty to our ideas, she'll do it gladly. In politics, the important thing, if you want to win someday, is to partici-pate whenever you can. And don't be fooled by her current silence; she's perfectly capable of taking the necessary steps if you back her into a corner. We expect a gesture from you, a grand gesture. Because, just between us, we both know it was entirely possible to rig the primary and I have enough respect for you to know you're perfectly capable of such a thing. Don't say you weren't warned!"

He probably said goodbye and shook my hand with a smile. I don't remember. But I do recall feeling the sole meunière sliding back up my oesophagus.

16

The Snag had got to me. I had doubts. Doubts about the Major and Marilyn. And even myself. The Boss was unusually agitated. Texier had shaken me, and Trémeau was likely to crawl out of the woodwork at some point. Vital's campaign was in full swing. I had a meeting with a madman under a bridge the next night. It was beginning to feel like things were spinning out of control.

Whenever I was down, I went to see Démosthène. Each member of the inner circle served a purpose for the Boss, but it was true for me as well. The Major was so stressed that he helped me relax. Marilyn made me a better man. Winston made me feel young again. And Démosthène, so far removed from the depravity I dealt with on a daily basis, reminded me that my worries were not the centre of the universe.

He was in his favourite spot: leaning so far over his desk that his chest almost touched the wood, his legs crossed to the left, and his head leaning to the right for balance. He was writing. His body was immobile except for his eyes and his hand, which moved over the paper as he scribbled down line after line of words. He was utterly absorbed by the page in front of him. No one knew why Démosthène adopted this back-breaking position and no one knew why he wrote by hand when the rest of his generation had adopted computers.

★ ★ ★

Among speechwriters, there are those who write well, those who write fast, and those who write a lot. Démosthène wrote fast and well. That made him a rare and particularly useful commodity. Especially during a campaign. For all of these reasons, no one ever suggested he should sit up straight or use a PC.

He was working on a speech about political engagement, which the Boss was scheduled to give a few days later to an enthusiastic youth caucus somewhere in Brittany.

When I stepped into his office, he raised his left hand towards me while the right continued jotting down an idea he didn't want to lose. Then his pen came to a stop, as if it had hit an obstacle. Démosthène's body relaxed as he uncrossed his legs, straightened his neck, and sat back in his chair. I had interrupted him. If I had been anyone else, I would undoubtedly have felt bad about it.

With an impassive look on his face, Démosthène continued his thoughts aloud.

"Do you know how Thatcher explained her political engagement?"

"The sheer thrill she got from breaking the spirit of Scottish miners?"

"She said she went into politics because that was where good and evil went head to head. Because she thought that, in the end, good had to win out. Admirable, don't you think?"

"Yes. But I do wonder if the widows of the Irish hunger strikers really think good won out in the end. It's so oversimplified it sounds American. Is the Boss really going to say that in Rennes?"

Démosthène laughed and shook his head. "If I write that for him, he'll end up explaining why it's so hard to make decisions, why it's normal to hesitate, that nothing is ever really good or evil . . . He's such a contrarian that he'd be tempted to say the exact opposite."

I wasn't convinced that the Boss would tank a speech just for the pleasure of contradicting Démosthène. But it's never a good idea to drag a speechwriter back down to earth. A hefty dose of vanity is absolutely indispensable when you're writing for someone else and live for the words he utters. I was not about to throw him into a fit of existential doubt when we needed him to start laying like a prize hen. Besides, that wasn't what I'd come for.

"Has he ever done something like that?" I asked, surprised.

"Oh no," Démosthène replied with a wink. "But I know him! It's only human to present yourself as something you're not. It's true for individuals, but it's even truer for nations. For example, the French have always claimed to be Cartesian. That's absurd! There's not a people on earth that is less logical and coherent than the French. Our grammar is full of exceptions. Our laws should be a cathedral—bright, simple, and solid—but instead they resemble a Byzantine temple; things are so muddled that it's hard to know whether it will hold or even what it means. There are so many inconsistencies in the French mind that we had no choice but to invent Cartesianism—without it we'd be a mess."

"Interesting idea . . ."

"And it's the same for the English, you know. The country of fair play! Do you really find the English fair play? They hate losing so much and are so likely to commit abominations when they do that they were forced—forced, I say—to invent the concept of fair play."

"Maybe, yes . . ."

"And as for the Americans, the fundamental value they defend above all others, in every possible way and throughout history, is freedom. A lovely idea. But have you ever gone for a walk in small-town America? Everyone is watching you. People will call the police if you do anything out of the ordinary. You can't move for social constraints. And don't get me started on political correctness! How can you suggest for even a second that a country where you can't even say what you think is *the* country of freedom?"

"Yes, but . . ." I protested vaguely. Démosthène's theory was just that, an intellectual theory: provocative, appealing, vague . . . There was truth in what he was saying, and it was all based on an observation with some merit, but why take it so far? But Démosthène was just getting started . . .

"Don't tell me," he continued, "that you've never thought twice about all those images of Kennedy putting on a show to prove what good health he was in while in fact his back was in such a state that he could barely move at all. And what about Chirac, who spent his time convincing people that he was a friendly if rather dull layabout? You knew him. You know as well as I do that he was a mean, devilishly clever workaholic, right? And Mitterrand! He went so far as to make people believe he was a socialist! That takes the cake in my opinion!"

I was amused and about to chuckle when a doubt suddenly popped into my head.

"What about the Boss, then? What does he say he is that he's not?"

"Ah, that's a hard question. I see that the apparatchik in you is on high alert. Always keeping track of criticisms of the Boss to ensure the right heads roll when the time comes. Saint-Just and Vyshinsky would be proud!"

Even people who hold two doctorates give in to the most hackneyed clichés. Every time I asked a question that might lead someone to say something unflattering about the Boss, they suspected I was setting a trap to take them out. The assumption was absurd, though. First, I didn't take people out that often. But most importantly, I didn't need any such artifice to get rid of someone and enjoy doing it . . .

Tickled by the direction the conversation was taking, Démosthène kept thinking, his mouth open and his eyes directed towards the ceiling. He looked absurd.

"For example," he suggested, "when he pretends to be entirely disinterested in political games, it's an illusion. You and I both know he loves all the scheming. When he paints himself as an intellectual, a man of integrity, and a statesman, that's sincere. But I'm not sure if the loyalty people attribute to him, loyalty to his ideas and to his friends, is real or a sham. But something tells me that we'll find out very soon, regardless of the campaign's outcome."

I burst out laughing now. "One thing I love about intellectuals is that you're never afraid to say the most ridiculous things. How could you possibly think that the Boss is faking his loyalty? Haven't you seen him with the chaps who have been living off him for ages? And how he goes out of his way to help people through rough spots even when it does nothing for him? The Boss is loyal through and through. If your whole theory is based on the fact that he laughs about rumours in private when in public he says he can't stand them, you've been wasting your time. I'll let you get back to work . . ."

"You can always keep your questions to yourself if you don't like me challenging your conformism," Démosthène replied with a frown.

He had reassumed his writing position, signalling that he intended to get back to it. In other words, I was no longer welcome—or perhaps I never had been. He needed quiet, calm, and intelligence—all things that my presence scared away.

I laughed loudly as I left.

Once in the lift, I stopped. Démosthène was wrong about the Boss's loyalty. But was he completely wrong? I suddenly realized that, for the first time since I had met him almost thirty years ago, I wasn't sure I really knew the Boss.

17

In politics, you rarely have to worry about physical violence.

The worst is usually a cream pie to the face. Or rotten eggs, or overripe tomatoes. In uncomfortable situations like that, you have to remain dignified. Not everyone has mastered the art of looking dignified with tomato juice running down their suit, but it's a necessary skill in an era when everything is caught on camera by TV crews, or worse still, by mobile phones, which upload footage in seconds. The number one rule is to never get upset. There's nothing worse than being angry on film. I remember a clip of a few high-ranking officials insulting several blokes because they thought no one could hear them. The commentators had gone to town with it for weeks and the voters had been shocked. If you absolutely must lose it, opt for something telegenic. A clean slap to each of a young pickpocket's cheeks and you're a statesman that embodies authority, when before everyone said you were weak.

Physical violence is rare, but fear is common.

You can't imagine what it's like to dive into a dense crowd. Shaking hands is nice but being swallowed up by a crowd is an experience that is both rare and terrifying. Nothing can prepare you for how it feels to be absorbed into a mass of people that want to talk to you, touch you, feel you.

Aided in part by his height, the Boss loved it. He felt there was nothing like mingling with a crowd to really understand the country. He was good at it, and people could tell he enjoyed it. How many times had his security team demanded he be reasonable and simply shake hands from the other side of the barricade or walk through a crowd surrounded by a circle of bodyguards? But it was no good. The Boss did as the Boss pleased. I knew he also loved pictures of himself awash in the crowd, his head sticking up out of a human tide. He knew that neither Vital, too short, nor Trémeau, too bourgeoise, could touch him in this area.

But I also knew that a lot of his peers were terrified of crowds. Afraid of a punch, a knife, a barrage of insults. Afraid of being crushed by the swarm. I remembered that I had been forced, more than once, to take the Boss by the arm and kick journalists and adoring fans in the shins to reach the exit.

For me, politicians who are afraid of crowds have no chance of climbing to the top. If you're afraid of voters, even in a crowd, it's best to do something else with your life. Business, poetry, whatever, but not politics.

That said, fear is not an easy emotion to overcome. As Winston and I approached the Pont Neuf, I felt my stomach clench. He was silent. So was I. But I was seriously wondering whether going to this meeting was a good idea. There were two of us and we were being discreetly followed by one of the Boss's bodyguards—the Cowboy to be exact—and we were in the centre of Paris, not on some cut-throat council estate. But, for the first time in a very long time, I felt I could be in physical danger.

If I had been less worried, I would have joked about the grotesque nature of our predicament. A meeting with a mysterious contact in the dead of night: it felt like a remake of a Hollywood movie. *All the President's Men*, with all those nocturnal encounters between Robert Redford and Deep Throat. That was probably a good sign, though: in the movie,

Deep Throat provided crucial information, and if we became the President's men then we'd have succeeded.

The sky wasn't black. You never experience anything resembling true darkness in Paris. The City of Lights has a reputation to uphold. We were crossing the Pont des Arts, a footbridge that offers a splendid view of the Ile de la Cité and the Pont Neuf.

It had been Caligny's idea. By approaching this way, we could study the meeting point and anything happening on the Pont Neuf without attracting attention. Nothing could be more normal than two men out for a stroll.

It was a good idea, but we couldn't see anything.

The Seine was dark and looked frozen. Even the lights seemed to drown in it. We crossed paths with several couples walking swiftly across the footbridge in the other direction. Nothing seemed to be moving on the Pont Neuf.

Winston saw the guy we were looking for first. From where we were standing, it was impossible to recognize him. The man in a hoodie and jacket with a messenger bag seemed to be staring at us. He had seen us, and he knew that we had seen him, and he wasn't running. Caligny had had the brilliant idea of announcing that not one but two national officials would be visiting Meylan. If our tipster had wanted to see the kid alone, he wouldn't have come. Of course, I had been forced to field a call from a furious local party representative, who hadn't been warned we were coming.

The chap had begun moving towards us along the southern bank of the Seine. He was just below us and we had almost reached the far end of the bridge when everything changed.

I didn't really see where the two shadows came from, but they must have been hiding somewhere nearby for quite a while. They had been waiting for our informant, who turned around and started running as fast as he could once he saw them. I broke into a sprint as though I were still in my twenties.

One hundred and fifty metres ahead, our stranger was taking a beating from the two guys, who were really doing a number on him. Shit. I ran as fast as I could, shouting and calling for help. The Cowboy couldn't be too far behind. He had a gun. On my orders, Caligny had stayed back.

I landed a solid kick to the stomach of one of the attackers. Our tipster was on the ground and didn't look good. I wouldn't last long against the two burly men in masks who clearly knew how to fight.

Filled with rage, I punched one of them, but I had left my thumb inside my fist, breaking every rule in the book. As a result, it hurt me much more than it hurt him. With my other hand, I grabbed the guy by the collar and ripped off his ski mask. I noticed he had ginger hair and a pallid complexion before I took a blow to the back of the head and blacked out.

18

I woke up on a blue sofa in a big, beautiful room, welcomed by the kind smile of a stranger, who seemed to be a doctor.

"Are you feeling better?" he asked.

"My head hurts, my right hand is sore, and my mouth is so dry I feel like I swallowed a hedgehog."

"Don't try to talk. You took several blows. I don't think it's too serious, but you should go to hospital to make sure. And you'll need to rest. Take some time off."

I nodded obediently. When a doctor tells me to rest and I agree, knowing full well that I won't, I already feel better. Rest, holidays, sounds great, but I have a campaign to run. In two months or five or ten years, when the Boss quits politics, then I'll rest. In the meantime . . .

"I'm fine, doctor, thank you. I can see you clearly, I remember my name, and I think I can stand up and walk. But can I ask you a question without you packing me off to hospital against my will?"

"Of course."

"Where are we?"

"This is Louis Caligny's flat. Or rather his mother's to be more precise. And as for mandatory hospitalization, I would have already signed the papers if the two people in the next room hadn't convinced me that my hands are tied. You're all being terribly reckless!"

Caligny's mother. The widow of Alexandre Caligny. I remembered her husband's funeral. She had been quite beautiful back then. I hadn't seen her since. She had completely disappeared from the public eye.

"Can I see them?"

"They're eager to talk to you. But let me remind you that you need to rest. You shouldn't talk too much."

I nodded again.

Winston and the Boss stepped silently into the room as the doctor left. I caught a glimpse of the Cowboy, who stayed in the corridor.

"If this is how you handle the things I trust you with," the Boss said with a smile, "I'm going to have to start worrying. You look like shit."

He always knows just what to say to get the loyal employee back on his feet. But I could see in his eyes that he was worried, and first and foremost about me.

"I'll be fine," I said. "What happened?"

The Boss rolled his eyes and Caligny explained.

"I told him why we were there and what you did when the fight broke out. When you passed out, the attackers threw our informant into the water. There was nothing I could do. The bodyguard pursued the other guys, but they managed to lose him."

Once again, the Cowboy had been useless.

"Afterwards, when I realized that things had gone south and that we would lose points in the polls if the press learned that the presidential candidate's lead advisor had been in a fatal fist fight, I decided we should bring you here to avoid explaining the whole thing at the hospital. I hope I did the right thing . . ."

"You did, Louis," the Boss said immediately. "Thank you for your quick thinking."

Now the Boss was handing out medals? I was shocked.

"*Fatal* fist fight?" I asked. "Who died?"

"Our tipster, I'm afraid," replied Winston. "I'm not sure he's dead, but there was blood everywhere when we got there. They had thrown him into the Seine, and, at this time of year, I doubt a guy gushing blood could survive in the cold water. There was nothing on the surface."

"Have you checked the news? What are the police saying?"

"Nothing yet. I'm fairly certain no one saw us. As for the police, if we start asking questions, we'll attract unwanted attention, especially at the Ministry of the Interior, where Vital would get wind of it before long, don't you think?"

The kid was right, of course.

"Do you realize what a risk we're taking?" I asked. "It's great to want to protect the campaign, but what if someone saw us? What happens if the doctor who examined me talks? And our security officer decides he needs to inform his superiors? We could be charged with failing to assist a person in danger, or worse!"

The Boss kept quiet and Caligny was the one who spoke. His voice was incredibly smooth and calm for a young man who had just been implicated in what was looking more and more like a murder.

"First, I'm sorry to say it, but we should have thought of that before going to the meeting. The doctor won't talk. He's a friend of my mother's and an especially close friend of my uncle's. I asked him not to say anything, so he won't. I can guarantee that. And I think we can all agree that it's not in the best interests of anyone here to talk. As for failing to assist a person in danger, that's ridiculous. You tried to help the man! He may or may not be dead, but you tried to help him. You could have been killed."

The kid was a kind soul.

"I know, Winston. I know. But the only people who could testify to that are in this room, and they're the same people who didn't call for help when they knew a man had been thrown into the Seine."

This remark made them both think. Caligny was finally realizing how grave the situation was. The Boss seemed to be lost in his thoughts.

"What about his messenger bag? The papers? Did you find anything?" I asked.

"Nothing. Either the attackers took his bag, or it went into the river with him."

After a minute, the Boss broke the silence. "This regrettable incident leads me to three conclusions. First, my dear Louis, I congratulate you for your sangfroid. I think everyone here is delighted to have you with us. Second, if someone died over this rumour, which started everything, it doesn't necessarily mean the rumour is true, but it does mean that we need to take it seriously. Very seriously. So, I want to know who's behind all this and what I should say if I'm asked about it. Lastly, I want absolute silence regarding last night. It's to stay between us. We'll find out what happened to your mysterious stranger and what the police have to say about it if they find him. And I think you should both be careful. One warning is enough, I think."

"Two warnings, Boss. Two," I corrected.

I told him about Jean-Dominique Pinguet's "accident", which had clearly not been one. Pinguet was dead and someone had tried to kill the stranger with the slow voice. Two troubling coincidences. And I'd almost been added to the list of victims, though my life hadn't been in any real danger. I knew that if they'd wanted to kill me, they would have done it.

"All that only lends more weight to what I've said," concluded the Boss. "Prudence and discretion, but I need answers now. Can I count on you?"

Of course he could. Who else was there?

The Boss left me alone with Winston, who offered me some aspirin and some other pills the doctor had left. I asked for a glass of port. I like port, especially white port, when it's nice and cold. It's the best remedy.

"So, Winston, what do we do now?" I asked.

The kid was trying to act calm, but I could see that the previous evening's events had shaken him.

"I don't know what you're planning, but I can tell you what I think. First, we have a problem: the attackers had been following the informant for a long time, so either he was bugged or I am. It's the only way they could have known about the meeting. Second, I think a man was killed last night. Which means there are people out there who are determined enough to murder someone just because he wanted to tell us something. And I think that the Boss is going to want to know what that something is, and that he's going to ask you to find out, and that you'll ask me to help you because you don't have anyone else you can turn to. So, I think we're in trouble. And when I'm in real trouble, I always do one thing: I call my uncle."

"Your uncle the IT guy?"

"Yes. My father's brother. Gaspard Caligny. You'll see. He finds politics and anyone who meddles in it terribly distasteful. He'll hate you. But if he agrees to help us, believe me, the guys from last night are the ones who will be in trouble. In the meantime, lie back and rest. I'll ask him to come round this afternoon."

I like people I know. And places I know. Restaurants I know. I don't like surprises, or new people, especially two months before an election. I don't trust new people. But I was too tired to fight.

I fell asleep almost immediately.

19

Sunday 21ˢᵗ February, 6:27 p.m.

Feeling weak from the sedatives, I spent most of the day sleeping. When I slowly opened my eyes, I found a man sitting next to me reading a book. He hadn't realized I was awake yet.

Winston's uncle looked a lot like his brother, and maybe even more so like his nephew. I guessed he was in his forties, rather fit with broad shoulders. His eyes weren't moving. The casual style of his jeans and velvet jacket contrasted sharply with his general demeanour. He wasn't tense, but he sat up straight, looking so solid nothing could move him. The kind of man who probably laughed when he got burnt and didn't get burnt often.

"Ah, you're awake," he said finally, putting down his book. "Louis told me you needed my help and that you'd explain the situation. I'm listening."

"You're the IT guy?" I asked.

"Among other things."

I tried to sit up in bed, but he had to help me prop myself up on the pillows.

"Do you know much about politics?"

"My brother was a minister. The little I know about politics doesn't make me want to learn more."

"What has your nephew told you about the campaign?"

"Nothing, because he's well-mannered and discreet. But he said he needed me. That's enough for me. If you have something to say, it's now or never."

* * *

Caligny's uncle didn't seem to be the type to waste time.

So, I decided to tell him about our problem. Not everything, just what Winston could have told him. After all, maybe he'd already spoken to him. Gaspard was perfectly still as he listened.

"My boss won the party's primary in September, with a very small margin, as I'm sure you read in the press," I began.

"No, but go on."

"Two months earlier, everyone had thought it was a done deal and that Marie-France Trémeau would be the party's candidate. But she made a few mistakes, and my boss came to embody the wisdom of the old guard. He looked like the only one capable of beating the left, which has been at the helm for the past ten years. It was the tightest primary race in the history of France and the first to feature online voting. The party organized the election, but my boss resigned as the party leader as soon as he became a candidate, at the end of August, so he couldn't be accused of interfering."

"What does that mean exactly?" he asked thoughtfully. "That you made the necessary concessions while behind the scenes you were actually organizing everything?"

He was a quick learner.

"That's one way to put it. We decided that the party members would vote and that they would vote online. And we made that decision because it was in our best interests. But an independent commission approved by both candidates organized the vote: the system, schedule, count, etc. Trémeau didn't contest the results in public, but she's waiting in the wings to throw a spanner in the works."

"Why do you suppose she didn't contest the results?"

I like it when people ask the right questions.

"It's Al Gore syndrome. In the world of politics, losing isn't great. But being a bad loser is a mortal sin. She wants to protect her chances for future elections, all while hoping my boss will lose so she can replace him at the head of the party and win the nomination next time. As you know, the first round is in two months, and it will be a tight race between Vital and my boss. A week ago, your nephew received an anonymous message on his mobile, informing him that a certain Pinguet had died and claiming that the primary had been rigged. The Pinguet he mentioned turned out to be the son of a senator in our party, a man who founded several successful IT companies. We went on to learn that one of his associates is a founding partner of Droid, the company that organized the online vote. We also discovered that he died in a mysterious car accident two days before we received the tip-off. A few days later, the tipster called back to ask your nephew to meet him under the Pont Neuf so he could hand over documents related to the affair, but the rendezvous was cut short when the man was thrown into the Seine by two unknown attackers. The documents disappeared and a muscly redhead knocked me out. We can't go to the police since the Ministry of the Interior is in the hands of Vital's friends."

Winston's uncle smiled.

"And now," I continued, "I'm not sure what to do. I'm used to political battles. I know how to handle myself. But this is different: a man died. This is beyond my skill set."

"I see," he said with a nod. "I'll help you."

Right. I already regretted confiding in him. He was probably good at whatever he did, but he clearly knew nothing about politics.

"Great, thank you," I said. "Please call if you learn anything. I'll look forward to seeing you again."

He stood up and came closer.

"I don't think you will," he countered. "If we ever see one another again, it will be nothing to look forward to. The only thing we have in common is Louis. He's a remarkable kid, you know."

"I absolutely agree. Clever, brave, and loyal."

"Precisely. Three qualities that lead me to believe he'll be disappointed by the world of politics. His father was in politics. He had the bug. The father died and the son caught the bug. What can I do? I have to let him live his life, after all . . ."

I didn't really understand where he was going with this, so I kept quiet.

"He lost his father ten years ago, and I've been looking out for him ever since. A bit like his father would have done, though I'm not doing as good a job, no doubt. My methods are a bit less civilized, I have to admit. So, I'm going to be very clear. Louis likes you. I don't know why, but he does. I, however, do not like you. I don't know you. I am perfectly indifferent to your fate. The only thing I know for sure about you is that if you ever put my nephew in a dangerous situation again or if you put him back in the path of the chaps you ran into the other night, *you* will be the body they find in the Seine. Got it?"

I could have told him to get off his high horse and reminded him that I hadn't chosen to implicate Caligny in this mess. In fact, I had insisted that he let me go with him to the meeting. I also could have told him to fuck off. But there are people who know how to hold your attention and inspire respect when they speak. And Caligny's uncle had delivered his entire tirade without raising his voice or picking up the pace, all while staring straight into my eyes. This was no joke.

I was speechless.

"I'll call as soon as I know anything," he said as he left, without shaking my hand or saying goodbye.

If I'd been in better shape, I would have made short work of the man. We all do what we must to reassure ourselves.

I was about to fall back to sleep when my mobile rang. It was Marilyn.

"Are you sitting down?"

"I'm actually in bed," I replied.

"At seven o'clock?!"

"I'll explain later. What's going on?"

"*Le Matin* is going to print the fraud rumour tomorrow morning. We need to prepare tonight. And we need to see the Boss."

I sat up in bed, and my head throbbed unbearably.

And I had thought things couldn't possibly get any worse.

20

Since the rumour was coming out the next day, we had no choice but to act. We needed to come up with a response. I say "come up with", not because we were making things up per se, but because we needed to find the right way to tell the truth. I'd seen too many politicians try to fend off slander armed with nothing but their good faith; you end up making matters worse by telling the truth without formatting it first. The format matters, just like on a computer.

What I wanted to do was draft our truth and broadcast it over every available wavelength in the hopes that people would be satisfied with it.

Setting the record straight can often be fairly simple. But stopping a rumour is another thing entirely. There are always certain political situations in which no one will listen, no matter what you say. Situations in which your word is dismissed out of hand, when everyone has decided you are in the wrong regardless of your arguments.

When you use taxpayers' money to rent a flat that costs more than ten times the monthly minimum wage, you can try to explain, but no one will care. When the situation can be summed up in a catchy, straightforward sentence, you're a goner.

Complicated problems are easier to handle: you just have to muddy the waters. No one will understand, and you have a chance to make it out unscathed. For example, if you're accused of money laundering through a Luxembourg clearing house, ninety-nine per cent of people will be lost, and the remaining one per cent will wonder why they didn't think of it themselves.

In this situation, unfortunately, the problem was horrifyingly simple: the rumour claimed that the Boss had cheated to win the primary. It was crystal clear and a serious accusation. Our response would need to be just as simple: the Boss didn't cheat, and here's the proof.

Unfortunately, I didn't have the proof yet. This state of affairs had only worsened my throbbing headache which hadn't let up since Marilyn had called.

"Those goddamn journalists are bloody bastards! They go on and on about their ethics and the unique and indispensable nature of their profession, and its critical role in democracy. Ha! But as soon as they have the chance, bam, they drag you down into the muck!" exclaimed the Boss.

Every member of the inner circle except for Caligny was gathered in the Boss's office for an urgent meeting. I had ruined his only free evening that week, and he was furious. Marilyn had managed to get her hands on the confidential article that would be published in *Le Matin* the next morning. Someday I'll ask her how she works her magic.

The entourage of the presidential hopeful has become concerned about a persistent rumour which claims that the close-run primary which led to his nomination was rigged.

Snags often start with a few lines on page five. From there, they're either forgotten or amplified. It seems like nothing, between the ads and obituaries, but you have to handle it, since it's usually hard to know which path it will travel.

But with this one, I was certain it would gain traction. And fast.

Just a few lines. No by-line of course. They mentioned the concerns provoked by the rumour, which gave them an in to talk about the rumour itself. They gave the impression that the information had come directly from the candidate's entourage. The jerk who'd whipped this up was good. The anonymous journalist had played it safe but hadn't tried to hide his eager curiosity. His colleagues would undoubtedly join him before long, asking us to comment. The Boss would have to be ready to respond the next morning. So, we needed to outline our talking points, preferably based on truth, and make sure we could stick to them, even when more comprehensive and concrete information was published. The heart of the matter would be decided tomorrow: the story would either be a frontpage headline in every major daily or would fizzle out on its own.

We had a rough week ahead of us, and the Boss continued his tirade.

"Some idiot working for Trémeau or Vital anonymously suggested to some scribbler that there might be a story worth telling, and without checking his source, the guy, who obviously remains anonymous as well, publishes the rumour! Tell them I said they can forget about any future interviews!"

I took note of the fact that the Boss seemed to believe the Snag was just as likely to have come from Trémeau as from Vital.

"We need to do exactly the opposite," Marilyn chimed in. "For the moment, it's still just a rumour. If we don't want it to get out of hand, we have to play nice with the journalists, give them something to go on or tell them another story to keep them busy and show them we have nothing to hide."

This is why I loved Marilyn. Not only was she the best at her job, but she also had the guts to tell the Boss the truth, even when it meant telling him he was wrong.

The silence that followed Marilyn's advice was only interrupted by Caligny's arrival. He apologized for being late. He had a piece of paper in his hand.

"Of course," the Boss finally said snarkily, "we must never upset the journalists. So, what should I say?"

This was my chance.

"Boss, Marilyn and I have given it a little thought, and we think you should say that you didn't organize the primary, that, to the best of your knowledge, it was legitimate, that no one has contested the results, that you're proud to have earned the party's nomination thanks to a democratic process that enabled more than 200,000 people to vote, that it's only a rumour, and that you fully intend to focus your attention on the important topics, the ones that are important to the French people. And then you move on to the next thing. For example, you could move up an announcement, something big, an issue you're committed to."

"Hmm. As usual, minimal thought and the maximum number of words," grumbled the Boss. "What about the rest of you, what do you think?"

No one dared move a muscle. No one but Caligny, that is, who had been trying to get my attention for three minutes. But it was the Boss who noticed him first.

"Louis, you don't seem to agree?"

The kid looked at me, then started talking as he stood up and handed me the piece of paper. "I'm no specialist," he said, "but it seems to me you could always use humour, at least in the beginning. For the moment, no one has read the article. And for a few days, no one will pay it any heed, unless you or a spokesperson give them a reason to. You could just laugh about it. Say it's a pitiful rumour and that you expected it, or something like that. You could say that if you start responding to every rumour, people will soon be asking if you think Elvis is still alive!"

It wasn't bad. I chuckled to myself as I unfolded the piece of paper. It was an AFP newswire. The body of a drowned man had been found at the tourist boat dock at the Pont de l'Alma. Unidentified.

"You disagree with Louis?" asked the Boss, staring at me.

"No, not at all. It's a good idea. Smart. If Marilyn agrees, we'll roll with that."

"If you don't mind, I'll make the decisions around here," replied the Boss, whose bad mood was still in full force. "Very good. Now we need to discuss a few things. First, I'd like to know how we got our legs cut out from under us with this mess. Second, I'd like to remind you that, in politics, loyalty is a cardinal virtue. You can be as clever as you like, endowed with good sense, quick on your feet, but all of those qualities will turn against you someday if you're not loyal. You're in this room because I decided you should be. I presume, therefore, that you are all loyal. And loyalty demands discretion."

The Boss's frigid tone was full of anger.

"I can't help but notice," he went on, "that just forty-eight hours after our last meeting, the press is saying that my entourage is worried. It's probably a coincidence, of course, but for that to be true, it mustn't happen again. I don't mean to place the blame on anyone, not yet at least, but be very careful with everyone around you, including your families and love interests. We've only just entered a difficult period during which we will be tested again and again, and this is most likely nothing compared to what lies ahead. Any questions?"

Everyone was quiet. Everyone was ill at ease.

"All right, then, in that case, if none of you minds, I'm going to go home and go to bed since you're packing me off to Pau at dawn, in exactly seven hours' time."

When the Boss left, there was a collective sigh of relief.

My head was killing me.

Before heading home, I took Winston aside. "Let your uncle know about the body found in the Seine. See if he can find out his name. That's as good a place to start as any."

21

Monday 22ⁿᵈ February, 10:33 a.m.

The next day, *Le Matin* published the rumour, and the wording was identical to the text Marilyn had obtained.

The Boss was finishing a tour of the hospital in Pau when someone asked him about it.

"An insistent rumour suggests that the primary wasn't exactly by the books. What do you have to say about that?"

"An insistent rumour? All I've seen for the moment is some anonymous and unfounded gossip in one newspaper. The rumour will become insistent if you decide it should be—that's your responsibility as a journalist. Was there a question in there?"

"Are you certain that the primary wasn't rigged?"

"I'd just like to remind you all that I didn't organize the primary. Why is it my responsibility to prove it wasn't rigged? Shouldn't the burden of proof be on those who have doubts? If I say, for example, that one of my fellow MPs has a thing for little boys or some other vice, will it be his responsibility to prove that's not the case? No, of course not, and I'm glad of it. It's normal that certain people want me to fail; that's politics. But I won't just let them walk all over me. To the best of my knowledge, this rumour is absolutely unfounded. Whenever there is a vote, this type of rumour can arise, particularly when using innovative new technologies. I've commissioned an internal inquiry to look into the voting conditions and results, and I'm sure that the investigation will reveal that everything was perfectly legitimate. In any case, I am proud to be our party's first ever presidential candidate to have been chosen by our members."

I muted the television. That would do. For now.

22

Marilyn was preparing a file for the Boss, as she did every time he had a meeting with one of the Fates. This included the most recent proclamations from the party's big names, in-depth analyses of the major topics in the news cycle, headlines, and so on. The Boss hated being caught out.

When he was going on the radio or TV, it was even worse. In addition to the press kit, which focused on the news, he would make Démosthène put together a ridiculous amount of information on current affairs, so as to be able to explain the tiniest detail, or cite precise figures. And, to make absolutely sure he was on top of his game, he always organized a meeting to hone his arguments the night before or on the morning of his interview.

At first, I had found it all exhilarating. I would smile proudly with satisfaction when I heard him use a particularly pertinent turn of phrase I had suggested just a few hours earlier. But now, after several years at this pace, the pleasure was fading. A single invitation to a TV show or radio studio could ruin an entire weekend for me . . .

Luckily, this time it was just lunch with one of the Fates. Like the Greek goddesses, the major Parisian editors held politicians' lives in their hands and seemed to be able to read their thoughts. With their editorials, analyses, and dinner parties, they could make or break careers.

★ ★ ★

Marilyn made sure that the Boss had lunch with at least one of the Fates once a month. Since everything was off the record at these lunches, the preparations weren't as intense.

During such a lunch, anecdotes and information would be exchanged, and many of them would end up in the "confidential" columns of magazines. It would be up to the Fate or their Editor-in-Chief to distinguish between real information and the rumours cobbled together by an unsubstantiated source to do as much harm as possible. There was a fine line between the two, and that line was about as watertight as a sieve.

Of course, it was quite likely that this lunch would lead to a discussion of the current rumour. How was the Boss reacting? Could he prove anything? Prove that the primary had been rigged or that it hadn't? Was the rumour merely an attempt to destabilize his campaign? These were all relevant questions that I had been asking myself since we first hit the Snag. Questions the Fate would undoubtedly ask the Boss. Questions to which Marilyn and I needed to formulate answers.

Marilyn was at her desk. She was printing out documents and gathering photocopies of the articles she had selected. I had sat down across from her before she could offer. I needed to talk to her.

I began by asking how she felt about the lunch.

"We couldn't put it off," she explained. "It was scheduled ages ago. Cancelling would have raised suspicions. Plus, he knows her like the back of his hand. He'll be charming, as always, and it'll be fine. I'm putting together a few talking points now. Listen."

They were solid. Safe, but solid. It was doublespeak, but it was spirited.

The more I listened, the more beautiful I found her. She was wearing a white blouse, only very slightly open at the neck. Marilyn wasn't the sort to highlight her physique. She had a gift for laying the charm on when she wanted to, and she could excite the desires of pretty much any human, male or female, but her innate dignity prevented her from crossing certain limits. She refrained from displaying an alluring décolleté in a workplace populated by men whose libidos had reached levels on a par with the radiation at Chernobyl, even though she knew it could have given her a leg up in her line of work.

But just a hint of cleavage is so terribly fascinating.

I could see the top of her breast. There was a small mole just above her right breast. I was captivated. I tried to be discreet, to look her in the eyes, to act like I was thinking, but the only thing that really mattered was that mole.

We had slept together twice. And both times I had regretted it. I didn't regret actually sleeping with her, not in the slightest, but I regretted my inability to make the occasions special and to handle the morning after gracefully.

The first time was in Nice, seven or eight years earlier. Marilyn had joined the team just a few months prior. She was as pretty as could be, enthusiastic, single, and she had the entire milieu at her feet. Everyone wondered which lucky man would win her affections first. Even the Boss, who is rather austere and has claimed ever since we first met that he no longer has any interest in passing flings, seemed to lust after her.

We got on well. I had been the one to suggest the Boss hire her, and she knew it. Even back then she was already one of the best in the field, and we were in dire need of someone like her.

The hotel we were staying in was completely devoid of charm, a convention centre by the sea. The rally had gone well. The Boss had left to spend the evening with some local friends, and Marilyn and I spent the rest of the night together: at the restaurant, then the bar, then in bed. It sounds a bit callous when I put it like that, but that's the gist of it. First, we had a nice dinner at an Italian restaurant that made a mean bacon crawfish risotto. Then we talked at the bar as we savoured a few glasses of thoroughly chilled white port. It was a lovely night, and I was delighted to have finally found a pretty woman who was happy to discuss political strategy for hours on end. I had had too much to drink, of course. So had she, I think.

Afterwards, two things stood out. For one, that was the first time I had ever invited a woman to come down instead of asking her to come up, since the pool bar at the Radisson was on the roof. Second, I remember Marilyn's total and utter lack of inhibition. She made love without a hint of self-consciousness, revealed her naked body with pleasure, and was very precise about what she wanted and felt. I had thought myself rather accomplished in these areas, but I had met my master.

What's really telling, after a night of sex, is breakfast. I'm generally repulsed by the idea of having breakfast with a woman I've just slept with. I go to sleep, then go home and that's it.

Sometimes I don't feel inclined to share breakfast, but I'm perfectly happy to go back to bed. That's the sign that though it won't last long, she's great in the sack and I should keep hold of her number for any future conventions or long winter nights.

If, after a night of sex, I want to have breakfast with the woman, then she's got everything going for her: pretty, smart, and presentable. In that order. I am who I am.

With Marilyn, breakfast hadn't been an option.

In the middle of the night, when we'd finished our third go, she had kindly but clearly explained that it was time for me to leave.

That had killed my buzz.

The next morning, we had run into each other at breakfast. She was talking to a journalist who must have been staying in the same hotel. With a look or smile, I don't remember which, she made it obvious that our relationship had gone back to being purely professional. She had pulled the number I'd been pulling for years. She'd behaved like a man, or at least that's how I thought of it, since usually women aren't like that. They can't want to just use a man for the night. If they start acting like us, humanity is doomed.

I still regret not trying to turn it into something real.

That mole took me back to Nice.

But I was clearly the only one reminiscing.

The more I listened to Marilyn, the better I understood where she was going with things, and the less I liked it.

"Are you sure you've told me everything about this mess?" she asked, staring me straight in the eye.

"You know as much as I do," I lied. No one had told Marilyn about what had happened under the Pont Neuf, and I had refrained from mentioning Caligny's uncle. Marilyn was the last person I wanted to tell. I know I *should* have told her: if I had been thinking in purely professional terms, I would have told her. But the mole, combined with the anonymous calls, the people dropping like flies around us, and the adrenaline of the campaign had dulled much of my lucidity and amped up my already well-developed paranoia.

"I hope so," she said. "For you and for the Boss. Because there are plenty of liberties you can take with the press: you can tell them soporific stories or make them believe the most absurd analyses and idiotic rumours, but you cannot give them information that could be proven false by the facts in the future."

I smiled, trying to convey that I understood and agreed with her, that I didn't know any more, and that everything was fine. The kind of smile that's not easy to pull off when you know more than the person across from you and you're certain that things are far from fine.

"The leak in the paper, any ideas where it came from?" I asked, trying to change the subject.

"Hard to know. Journalists never give up that kind of information unless I have something better to trade for it. Plus, even offering is risky, because if I attract attention to the rumour, my contacts will start thinking there's something to it. Which is only reasonable . . ."

Marilyn's relationship with journalists was admirable. She took them seriously without going so far as to respect them. She knew their job was difficult and that they had rules to follow, but she also felt they worked too little and were too quick to print superficial statements and let themselves be fooled by appearances. Whenever I criticized them, she defended them. When she criticized them, it was best to keep quiet.

"You don't have anyone over at *Le Matin* who could tell you where it came from? In the name of friendship or the promise of a future scoop?"

Marilyn looked at me intently, almost as if she was hesitating. "There's no such thing as friendship in this profession. And as for promises, you yourself have shown me how they're hardly binding."

Our seemingly amicable meeting was turning into a settling of scores. What was going on? Despite my predilection for tension and my very real passion for shouting matches during which I was capable of hurling cruel insults, thinly veiled threats, and my endless reserves of hypocrisy at my opponent, I decided there was no point continuing down this slippery slope.

But Marilyn wasn't ready to put down her weapons.

"You know what's wrong with these talking points?"

I didn't. Though I did see that they were designed to slow an attack of unknown origin and intent. I shook my head.

"They're completely off the mark," she explained. "They imply that it was possible to rig the primary and that no one knows if it was or wasn't. If I heard about this affair in the press for the first time, I would be inclined to believe something had happened. And since I know you and what you're capable of, I think that if something *did* happen, you were behind it. And the fact that you lied to me just now when I asked if you had told me everything seems to indicate I'm not entirely wrong."

I was taken aback.

"How can you really think I rigged the primary? What do you take me for?"

"An apparatchik who's been waiting for this presidential campaign for the past thirty years and who will stop at nothing. You know full well that if he asked, you'd do it."

"But do you think he'd ask?"

I had spoken too fast. I should have stuck to my first line of defence: I would never have done such a thing. I wouldn't have convinced her, but at least it would have bought me some time.

"I don't know," she said. "I don't think so. But if he didn't ask you to, then I don't understand why you did it. And I'm not alone!"

She had discussed it with the Major. They agreed that I was behind all this. I was furious.

"I didn't bloody do it!" I shouted. "You're both mad!"

Marilyn raised her hand in a definitive gesture.

Faced with this wall of incomprehension, I decided to leave her office, slamming the door with theatrical flair. In a pathetic fit of rage, I sent a pile of magazines flying across the room from a table in the corridor. The tight ship I had built to carry the Boss to victory was taking on water. And I was having to defend myself simply because the others knew I was capable of the occasional underhanded move: I was paying for my twenty years of dirty work.

Everyone was starting to have doubts. I had even started doubting the Boss. As for Marilyn, there was clearly no trust between us any more: we could work together when all was well, but at the first whiff of crisis, the bitterness of the past came to the fore.

I needed some air.

Just outside HQ I tried in vain to light a cigarette. The freezing February wind rendered my lighter useless, and my hands were shaking too much from cold and rage to do anything about it.

I angrily chucked my lighter across the street and tossed my cigarette to the ground as the surprised security guard looked on. My whole body was shaking now, preventing me from feeling my phone vibrating in my pocket.

I dialled Winston's uncle right away when I saw his missed call.

"Your drowned man is named Mukki, Paul Mukki."

"Well hello to you, too. How do you do?" I replied sarcastically, all the while thinking about the name, which I'd heard before.

"Does it ring any bells?" asked Gaspard, ignoring me.

"Maybe. How did you get his name?"

"A magician never reveals his tricks, you know."

For Gaspard's nickname, I couldn't decide between Mandrake the Magician and the Godfather. He'd given me a lot to work with.

Mukki. I knew that name. I started shaking even harder, from the cold and the rage, and now from fear.

Paul Mukki was a former party employee. He had not been in an especially senior role, but he had worked at the party HQ for a long time. If I remembered correctly, he had been in membership, where they recorded all member data.

Where he would have had access to the username file.

23

The Boss couldn't believe it either.

"First Pinguet and now Mukki. How did those losers get mixed up in this mess?"

"I don't think we should really lump Pinguet and Mukki together," I objected. "We didn't know Pinguet very well, but Mukki was a party employee, family really."

The Boss raised his eyebrows. "Family, eh? Let's not get ahead of ourselves. You say this Mukki left the party when I took over. It's difficult to see that as a friendly move, much less as a sign we're family."

"Well, it's not totally illogical. He got on well with the former team, who had hired him, and when they left, so did he. That said, the Major remembers him and says he was an all-right guy. Apparently, he's the one who hid the papers six years ago when the police first turned up to search party headquarters. When the detectives turned up at reception, he rushed to the Treasurer's office, grabbed the account books, shoved them in a bag, and took them up to the roof to wait it out. No one saw him do it, and he undoubtedly spared quite a few people indictments."

The Boss's lips began to curl into the first smile I'd seen on his face in a while. I was sure he remembered the search as if it was yesterday since it had been the first step in a plan that had led to him taking the reins of the party. But I could also see that this was the first time he'd heard about Mukki's role in it all.

"You know," he said, "in Turkey they say that though swans belong to the same family as ducks, they're still swans."

Caligny blinked nervously.

"What I mean to say, Louis," the Boss continued, "is that, for a member of our family, he sure did cost us a lot: his loyalty and quick thinking slowed us down by at least five years. If everyone had been convicted following that search, we would have been catapulted to the head of the party much sooner . . ."

His tone was lightly ironic and young Caligny was clearly struggling to understand if he was serious. Was the Boss really angry with Mukki for having slowed his rise to the top, or did he admire the way he had displayed his devotion to the party? Probably both. The Boss was perfectly at ease with harbouring conflicting opinions.

"So, what was his job before we took over?" the Boss asked now.

I knew the Boss well enough to know that he was feigning this carefree attitude. Behind the calm exterior and sarcastic quips, the Boss was looking to get to grips with the affair and was expecting specifics. Luckily, before coming to brief him, Winston and I had done our homework. I had questioned the Major at length, read through the HR files, and encouraged the kid to hang around the HR department to glean as much as he could.

"From what I understand," ventured Caligny, "Mukki was, to all intents and purposes, a dogsbody."

"What do you mean exactly?"

"He did data entry. But the data he entered isn't totally without interest. It was membership data, including names, addresses, professions, birthdates, membership dates, and the infamous usernames. Mukki entered all of this information into the main database."

I wasn't surprised. Dismayed, but not surprised. It had been clear to me for some time now that the Snag was not going to throw up any good surprises. If Mukki had been in charge of mailing stickers for local elections, he wouldn't have got mixed up in this in the first place.

"And how did he get hired?" asked the Boss.

"He wasn't hired to do that," I said, joining the conversation. "He was originally hired by facility services to carry boxes and set up new offices. Three years later, he was transferred to the IT department. His file is empty after that, right up until he left, a week after you were elected party leader."

"Who hired him then?"

The crucial question. In a political party, *who* hired you is often more important than what they hired you to do. I still remember the painstaking investigation I had carried out when the Boss and I had taken over to find out where everyone had come from—the political equivalent of an archaeological dig. When you know that, you may not know who will be loyal to you, but it gives you a pretty good idea of who won't . . .

"I don't know," I replied. "There's nothing in the file about it. He was hired twelve years ago. He spent eight years at HQ, then he left, but it's not clear where he went. His file is pretty thin."

That was strange, too. Could Mukki have been hired without out a reference? By a political party? By *this* political party? Impossible. But who would have an interest in hiding their association with such an obscure recruit?

I ran through my list of questions and doubts aloud. The Boss nodded and agreed. After a time, Winston suggested that I would get more answers if I asked the Major, whose job was to run this ship, including its most tedious administrative aspects. He wasn't wrong, but I didn't want the Major to know more than me. Not yet anyway.

"And how exactly did he go about leaving?" asked the Boss.

"We don't know much there either," I answered. "We have his letter of resignation, but there's no address. It's dated a week after your election as head of the party four years ago. He left before you even moved in."

Apparatchiks quit about as often as mussels willingly let go of their rocks. In political parties, the politicians come and go—though often too slowly—but the permanent staff stay, hence the name "permanent". Some of them spend much of their professional lives trying to limit the risk of being fired by an incoming team while at the same time doing their utmost to seize any available opportunity to move up, to a minister's cabinet or a big company in the private sector. But they're not exactly hot commodities.

Mukki's resignation had probably gone completely unnoticed or been viewed as a win-win situation. The Treasurer's office would have been relieved to have a departure to partially offset the arrival of the Boss's new team. I don't remember being informed that he had quit.

"Have you spoken to the people who worked with him? Do they remember him? Are they still in contact?" the Boss said, continuing down his list of questions.

"They remember him rather well and have mostly good things to say about him: nice colleague, hardworking, straightforward, discreet. But no one seems to have stayed in contact. Out of sight, out of mind, as they say," said Winston.

"All right," replied the Boss. "We need to find out who hired him and why we know nothing about his hiring. Something tells me the two are linked. Next, we need to know where he went from here and what he had been doing of late."

The Boss was worried. My job was to prevent that. I would have preferred to see him in one of his early morning rages than like this.

24

Friday 26th February, 12:59 p.m.

Marilyn stepped into my office with a sour look on her face.

"We're going to take a hit in next week's edition of *L'Enquête*. I hear they're going to publish a long article about the vote. They're going to talk about Droid."

"Are they going to level any accusations against us?" I asked.

"From what I've heard, they're going to suggest that even though the Boss wasn't the head of the party during the actual vote, he was the one who pushed for online voting and set out the conditions before he left."

She paused before continuing. "Which is true. We won't be able to deny it."

Indeed.

"Will they mention Pinguet?" I asked.

"I doubt it."

"We have until Monday?"

"Yes, unless it comes out online first."

I was in deep shit.

25

Since smoking has been banned in cafés, you can have your breakfast at the bar without feeling like you're eating in an ashtray. I may be a smoker, but I have to admit it's rather nice to be spared the smell of second-hand smoke in the morning.

L'Espérance was an ageless bar—in other words, it was old. They served black coffee in thick yellow cups. The bar stools, tables, and customers were all a little worn around the edges. When I turned up every morning, they served me my usual: coffee, toast with salted butter, and orange juice. The waiting staff were offhand with strangers, but the regulars with their established habits were always sure of a warm welcome. L'Espérance was, in all respects, an authentic Parisian bar. And it was my local.

The Godfather had arrived before me. Sitting at the back of the room, he was the first thing you saw when you stepped inside. His chosen seat also meant he could keep an eye on all of the people in the café and any new arrivals. For the moment that included me and the concierge from next door, who came over every morning to down his two beers before nine o'clock. Smoking had been outlawed in public places for health reasons, but you could still work on your cirrhosis before dawn in the land of Descartes. There had to be some sort of logic . . . I smiled as Démosthène's theory came to mind.

Caligny's uncle studied me sceptically. He probably thought I was trying to hide my nervousness. He wasn't entirely wrong.

Over the years I'd run into plenty of chaps looking to intimidate me. I'd learned quite a bit about power struggles. I'd lost my fair share, but with time and experience, I had come to win more and more. I had become increasingly good at my job, and people had started to fear the Boss. The weak no longer dared get in my way, and the strong thought twice about it. I had enemies, but in this profession that means you're doing your job right. Anyone who's been in politics for twenty years and doesn't have enemies is doing it wrong. Few could outdo me on that score.

Gaspard Caligny was different. He wasn't trying to impress or to intimidate. He seemed to be perfectly indifferent to me. He wasn't afraid of my power or my ability to do harm. He didn't need anything from me. I had nothing on him. I knew all too well what effect indifference could have on others, but this was the first time I'd been on the receiving end, and I didn't like it one bit.

"Louis will be here soon, but I have a few things to tell you before he gets here," he said as he shook my hand firmly. He held my gaze. I felt like I was naked. As a child, that had always been my worst nightmare: finding myself at school without any trousers or pants, pulling as hard as I could on my T-shirt to hide my privates from the other children.

"Well, hello to you, too," I said.

He sat back on the bench and sighed. "Let's get to the point."

"And here I was thinking you were going to share your life story!"

There was something juvenile about my need to prove I was relaxed. I knew that sarcasm and low-brow humour never managed to hide anxiety and inferiority for long. In a duel, the favourite rarely acts smart. The Godfather hadn't even smiled.

"I took a closer look at your team. Nothing worth mentioning for most of them, and definitely no secrets. The writer and the secretary seem to be totally clean."

I said nothing and did my best to remain impassive. I was sure there was nothing to find on Démosthène, except maybe a passion for books that bourgeois morality would frown upon. As for Régine, the secretary, the Boss was her entire life. There was room for nothing else. It occurred to me that the same could be said about me . . .

"Things are less clear for your friend the campaign manager."

My right eyebrow rose slightly. He noticed. Shit. I'd shown my hand.

"I'll know more soon," he continued, "but from what I can tell, he seems to have shifting loyalties. He goes out of his way to make himself look trustworthy and forthright, but I'm not convinced."

I didn't even try to hide my smile now.

"As for your friend in press relations, her life is as complicated as it is fast-paced."

He didn't give any more details, nor did his expression change, but I was certain he knew about Marilyn and me.

"She's dating a journalist, which means nothing in itself, though it is proof of a certain lack of taste if you ask me. But I suppose it happens to the best of us. The guy is younger than her. He has long hair and is named Maussane. You know him?"

I knew him. This was bad news. In so many ways.

"Not really," I lied.

"Me neither," he replied. "But I don't know many journalists. I don't like them. What's more interesting is the lengths to which these two have gone to keep their relationship a secret."

"A secret or quiet?"

"Did you know they were together?"

I shook my head.

"If it was just discretion she was worried about, she would have told you, wouldn't she?"

Touché. The Godfather was onto something. All of a sudden, I was dying to change the subject.

"What about Mukki? Did you find anything on him?"

"Yes, a few things that will interest you."

He paused for maximum effect. In politics I had learned to be patient.

"Guess who our friend Mukki worked for right up until he went for his little dip in the Seine . . . The local government. In Isère."

Bloody hell.

It wasn't the Isère area itself that was the issue. It's rather lovely if you steer clear of Grenoble. But the fact that the local government there was involved was a problem of epic proportions, for two reasons. First, Pinguet senior was among its historic members. Second, it had been chaired for nearly eighteen years by a real stand-up guy. A guy who had resigned a year ago to devote all his time to his newest challenge. A guy named Vital, who was running for president and hoping to beat my boss.

I swallowed hard. "And what did he do there?"

"Not much. He was hired to oversee maintenance of the area's middle schools. I suppose it suited him since it gave him time to go skiing in the winter and play tennis in the summer. His neighbours describe him as a loner and a bit of a grump, though he wasn't aggressive or outright rude. He lived in La Tronche. It's a sweet little town, an affluent suburb of Grenoble."

"I'm familiar."

I know every town in France with a population over three thousand. I know all the mayors of all the towns with a population of over three thousand. Not personally, but by name at least. I also know which towns are in which districts. For the district of Meylan, it's simple. There are only four towns. La Tronche is one of them. And I am, of course, familiar with the representatives from each district. Especially in Meylan. It was hard to forget, at that particular moment, that this was Senator Pinguet's territory. It was also hard to forget that Mukki had mentioned this very district in the message he had left before being stabbed and drowned.

In ten minutes, the Godfather had tied Mukki—likely the man behind the anonymous calls who had died before he could talk to us about voter fraud—to Vital, who was alive and well and who could possibly beat the Boss, and to Senator Pinguet, the inconsolable father of "accident" victim Jean-Dominique, who had played a role in organizing the primary.

"That's it for now," he concluded, "but I'm only just getting started."

By all accounts, it was a pretty good start. I tried to gather my wits while I asked a few more questions. I couldn't help but look at him differently now.

"And Mukki's attackers? Anything there?"

"No, nothing. No witnesses. Not very surprising since you and Louis were the witnesses . . . Besides knowing that one of them is a redhead, I don't have much to go on. But I'm not worried. I'll find the guys who did this. The investigation into Pinguet's accident hasn't turned up any leads either. The police are getting nowhere. I'll have to handle it myself . . ."

I thought I could sense disdain in his voice. I had seen plenty of experienced soldiers come back from abroad with nothing but contempt for the police, and the feeling was most often reciprocal. Now at least I knew a bit more about the Godfather's background. And that when he despised someone, he let it show.

"Yes, we need to know—"

His expression changed so quickly and profoundly that I stopped mid-sentence. He'd seen his nephew come into the café and had immediately stopped being the man I thought I knew. His eyes filled with affection and his body relaxed as he shed his ferocious demeanour. I had never seen him smile before, and the effect was astonishing. All of a sudden, he seemed friendly and warm. He even looked trustworthy. The lone wolf I had been talking to had made way for a respectable authority figure, someone who was used to giving orders and being obeyed.

This was the first time I had ever seen them together. Winston seemed to be this man's son as much as he was his father's.

I remembered Alexandre Caligny, with his indisputable charm and unabashed ambition, rather well. The son enjoyed his father's healthy complexion and frank smile, which made you feel like you could trust him immediately. But the way he studied people and things happening around him and refrained from opening up about himself reminded me of his uncle.

We made small talk for a few minutes.

Gaspard Caligny was charming when talking to his nephew. His voice was gentle and his tone reassuring. He gave the boy confidence. I could imagine how he must have helped the kid try and get over the loss of his father when he was still a child and overcome his fears growing up.

I realized, as they spoke, that I didn't know much about Winston other than that he was the son of a politician who had died young and the nephew of a rather aloof military man. I knew that his mother lived in a nice Parisian flat and that he had a brother and sister. I was aware that he had studied political sciences, and that he was clever, brave, and rather gifted. That wasn't bad, but it still wasn't much.

The kid brought us back to the topic at hand.

"So, what do we know about Mukki?"

I told him everything his uncle had told me, doing my best to be both concise and exhaustive. I thought I noticed a slight nod from the Godfather as I finished, which was probably the closest he ever got to wholehearted approval.

"You really need to talk to Senator Pinguet," he said. "He's at the centre of all this."

Winston agreed enthusiastically in the way only young people can.

"I'm starting to find these work lunches quite literally hard to swallow!" I objected. "Do you really think I'll get anything out of the old dinosaur? You clearly don't know much about the Senate. Getting a senator to share something he doesn't want to is like trying to get a donkey to drink on command. Actually, trying to get a donkey to drink is probably less dangerous . . ."

Winston laughed. His uncle smiled, though I couldn't tell if it was because of what I'd said or just because he was happy to see his nephew laughing so cheerfully.

"I'm sure you can do it," the kid told me. "The more I think about it, the more certain I am that he's the key to this whole story. It's rather simple, really: we know Mukki put together much of the membership file while working at party head-quarters, or at least that he had access to all the data. And we know that Jean-Dominique Pinguet's company organized the vote and handed out the passwords. To rig the vote, you needed the file and the passwords. In other words, together Mukki and Pinguet could have done it. And what's the most direct way to tie Jean-Dominique Pinguet to Mukki?"

"Senator Pinguet. Elementary, my dear Winston!"

Gaspard suddenly tensed. "Why do you call him Winston?"

I was reluctant to answer. I could see that the Godfather's sense of humour was relative when it came to his nephew.

"Everyone in the Boss's entourage has a nickname. It's the rule. Louis is Winston or just plain 'kid'. Winston because he'll go far and kid because—"

"I prefer Winston," his uncle interrupted.

Winston himself said nothing, but I could see he was enjoying this.

"What about you? What's your nickname?" he suddenly asked mockingly.

"If I had one you would know it, wouldn't you?"

"I could come up with one, it's no problem . . ."

"Yes, well, we're getting off topic, aren't we. Pinguet may well be at the centre of this mess, but first we need to find out if he even knew Mukki. And we need to understand Vital's role, and why Mukki tried to warn us, and—"

"First and foremost," the Godfather said, interrupting me again, "I think what we need to know is if the primary was actually rigged. It seems like no one is even asking that question any more, but it's fundamental. I'll take care of it."

He was right. And even if he'd been wrong, he wasn't about to ask for our opinion.

He hugged his nephew and shook my hand.

The day was off to a better start than the previous days. We finally had a lead. For the first time since we'd hit the Snag, I felt like we had figured out part of the puzzle. It wasn't much, but I felt slightly less helpless.

And now I was sure about at least three things.

First, the Calignys. I liked Winston and his uncle was useful. He seemed determined not to let his nephew go it alone, and in messes like this one, my friends' friends are my friends.

Next, the Major. Winston's uncle had doubts about him, and I couldn't help but share them. There was something amiss about the Major. He wasn't telling me everything, so he was hiding something. I was going to have to keep my eyes on him, and that was a real problem. When team members start doubting one another, the team rarely plays well.

And then there was Marilyn. Marilyn who had accused me of being the source of the problem. Marilyn and the lover she'd never mentioned. That would have been enough to annoy me if I didn't have more important things on my mind. I knew that she was under no obligation to keep me updated on her amorous encounters, but I had always thought that if she was in a serious relationship, she would tell me, out of respect for our friendship or something.

Nevertheless, the sadness I was feeling had nothing to do with jealousy, or not much at least.

I knew this Maussane, her lover. He was a journalist. At *Le Matin*. The paper that had published the voter fraud rumour . . .

26

Monday 1ˢᵗ March, 7:40 a.m.

As expected, the article came out in *L'Enquête* the following Monday.

I read it to the Boss early that morning.

It explained how the vote had been organized and included an interview with the secretary-general of the party. It went into the details of the online voting system and how it was managed by a company called Droid, which had "declined to comment". It also outlined the possible sources for error or fraud, and compared it to a few foreign systems.

The journalist cited a computer engineer who argued that there was no such thing as a tamper-proof system. It reminded me of when losing barristers did their best to make the experts on the stand admit that there was always an infinitesimal chance that they were wrong.

Then they interviewed Texier:

> *"People have suggested that Marie-France Trémeau's entourage could be the source of this rumour . . ."*
>
> *"That's absurd! We heard about it in the press, but it is rather interesting."*
>
> *"People also say that she's had a hard time accepting her defeat . . ."*
>
> *"Who wanted an online vote? Who organized it? It certainly wasn't Marie-France Trémeau, who expressed her scepticism very early on. People can't blame her for being right now!"*

"*What consequences might follow this revelation?*"

"*It's not quite time for consequences yet. We want to know what really happened. If there was voter fraud then that is a very serious offence, and my suggestion to Marie-France would be to do what she feels is right in those circumstances.*"

"*So, you would tell her to run for president?*"

"*She will have to make that decision on her own.*"

Furious, I threw the magazine across the Boss's office. He gave me a stern look.

"It seems Trémeau only felt compelled to uphold the results of the primary if she won . . ." I said.

"There are two possibilities," he said, cutting me off. "Either she has proof that the primary was rigged, and she'll go public, or she doesn't, and she gets nothing. Call your friend Texier," he added, turning towards me. "Listen to what he has to say. They've gone too far; we need to show them we mean business."

"That's not what I'm most worried about."

"Really? What could possibly be more worrying?"

"If Trémeau was willing to say that, it's because she's sure of herself. In other words, she has information about the primary being rigged. There's only one explanation: we weren't the only ones contacted by the tipster."

The Boss frowned. As long as this thing was hanging over his head, he could have the best platform in the world, save the planet, and eradicate unemployment, but no one would listen. The debate about the primary would tarnish the whole campaign. I felt sick.

"All right, well, we still need to proof this speech on the length of the working week. It's got me banging on about antiquity! I'd rather talk about real people," he grumbled.

Démosthène was at it again, unable to make a point without citing centuries of history. We sat side by side, red pens in hand, crossing out entire paragraphs and adding in the imaginary Mrs Y, who lived in, let's say Lorraine. She wanted to work more to earn more money but couldn't with the current laws. The kind of example that got people on board.

We were still at it when Marilyn came into the office. She seemed to have earned the privilege of entering without knocking like I had.

"Here, look at this," she said. "A dispatch with a quote from Vital about the working week for your speech tomorrow. He says the French people want more free time."

"Free time without purchasing power, what's the point?" I countered. "The truth is that work is freedom."

"Really?" replied Marilyn sharply. "Go say that to some poor man who's been working a production line for thirty years. You're privileged! All of us in this room are lucky: for us, our careers are fun. But how will those who see their work as an inescapable burden react?"

"Don't worry," said the Boss, "I'll make sure my argument is nuanced." He seemed surprised by our little run-in.

Marilyn gave me the dirtiest look she could muster, then left. The Boss kept quiet for a few seconds, then picked up his pen and mumbled something about his wonderful team.

Marilyn.

A vivid memory surfaced at that moment: the day the Boss had taken over the party. The day everything became possible. As the head of the party, the Boss had a chance to someday win a presidential election.

It all happened in the most legitimate way, at the party's national convention, where the stalwarts finally decided that it was the Boss's turn to take the reins since, after the legal difficulties we had been through, only someone whose integrity was unimpeachable could get the machine back on its feet. Of course, behind the scenes pressure had been applied to local leaders to get them to make sure their troops fell into line. And Marilyn had managed the media perfectly, successfully painting the Boss as the only sensible option. As a result, the press was nearly unanimous in its estimation that it would take a miracle—the Boss—to keep the party from imploding. We had all played our parts without a single mistake, as attuned to one another as the members of a professional orchestra.

Over the course of that day, Marilyn and I must have exchanged hundreds of text messages. At first to let each other know what we were doing, support one another, and share information. Then, though I'm not sure how or why, the tone changed. It became more intimate. Funnier, too. And our messages became more and more frequent. While the epic battle at hand was being played out, Marilyn and I had picked up where we had left off in Nice, enjoying the intimacy of occasional lovers united in a common cause.

At the end of the day, after the Boss's speech to the party officials, his appearance on the primetime news, and his arrival at party headquarters, where his political allies were waiting for him, Marilyn had come into my office. She had sat down across from me, in the spot the Boss usually occupied when he was around—in the chair he might decide to come and occupy at any moment, in fact—so we could chat. And we had talked. And laughed the cautious laugh of winners who know that victory lasts but an instant. That's when Marilyn had shut the door. She came over and took my hand and got me to stand up. Then she kissed me. A long, lingering kiss like in the movies. A kiss which seemed to represent the fulfilment of many different things. I held her close, vaguely aware that anyone could come into the office and that if the Boss chose this moment for our little chat, he would be surprised or maybe even angry.

Then Marilyn had pushed me down onto the sofa, taken off the white blouse she was wearing on that glorious Sunday, and smiled at me. The most beautiful smile I had ever seen. Nothing like the one she handed out on a daily basis. There was nothing perfunctory or fake about it. It was a smile full of self-abandon and simplicity, with a hint of tenderness and nostalgia in her eyes. A real smile.

She had sat down on top of me with immeasurable charm and we had made love. It all could have been very sordid, but instead it was calm, natural, and extraordinary. The office had disappeared. We seemed to be floating. Marilyn closed her eyes, lost in a world of pleasure I could hardly believe I was procuring. When she opened them, she smiled again, and I grinned back like a happy idiot unsure what to make of that day's second miracle.

The only thing that brought me back to reality every now and again was my fear of the Boss turning up. Something told me it was better if he didn't know what was going on between Marilyn and me. Because this wasn't about him, but about us, and I wanted to preserve this tiny sliver of freedom that had somehow fallen into my lap. But also because I knew, deep down, that for the Boss, loyalty had to be exclusive. He never would have said as much, of course. But I knew that the bond the Boss formed with the members of his team was such that he couldn't bear any form of competition. Loving Marilyn would mean putting him second. Building something real with Marilyn would, by default, be detrimental to the special relationship the Boss and I had forged together.

And then the phone had rung.

I'm not even sure I heard the first ring. I was thinking about something else. I was thinking about nothing. I was thinking about Marilyn, and that was enough.

I paused for a moment at the fourth or fifth ring. I don't remember. It was when I realized it was the Boss calling.

It couldn't be anyone else. Who would have let it ring for so long so late on a Sunday night? The journalists had my mobile number. The Barons had gone home to their fiefdoms. The person who was calling knew I was in my office. He was letting it ring because he knew I would pick up. It had to be the Boss.

So, I paused. And when Marilyn looked at me, her ecstatic smile disappeared, leaving behind the lesser smile she offered everyone else. The spell had been broken. I had unconsciously, almost instinctively, made my choice. Maybe fear had played a role, too.

Marilyn and I never spoke of that episode again. She had left with a tender kiss, claiming she had somewhere to be. I pretended to believe her. The greatest love stories sometimes go out with a bang. At least our story had been anything but banal.

There was nothing between Marilyn and me any more. We had almost been in love. We chose to stay friends. Or rather, I had chosen not to fall in love and had failed, was still failing and still in love, and we were about to stop being friends altogether. No matter how I looked at it, the truth seemed clearer than ever: I had made a monumental mistake.

This realization brought me hurtling back to reality.

"Hello? Are you with me?" asked the Boss.

I must have been lost in my thoughts for a few seconds.

"Sorry, I was thinking about Texier."

"Well why don't you go call him. I'll finish this on my own. Everything will be fine."

I was far from convinced.

27

Monday 1ˢᵗ March, 8:55 a.m.

In my world, it's customary to send a message when you feel you've been dealt a blow below the belt. You call and make your outrage clear. It's perfectly vain, but not doing it makes you look weak and leads others to believe that the attacker's actions were justified.

"What you said in *L'Enquête* is totally unacceptable," I began.

"Don't use that tone with me. You can't blame me for doing my job just because your boss gave you a talking to. You would have done exactly the same thing in my position, and you know it," retorted Texier.

He was right, of course.

"You're adding fuel to the fire; there could be serious consequences."

"Serious consequences? The serious consequences are due to the fact that now everyone doubts the legitimacy of the primary. Marie-France was an exemplary loser, if lose she did . . . But she won't turn the other cheek. You'd better concentrate on the question of voter fraud if you hope to preserve your boss's reputation."

"I'm not worried," I lied.

"Really? Then why are you calling?"

"I'm calling to tell you that you had better sit tight. It would be in your best interests to keep playing the good losers, because when this thing is all cleared up, many of our friends will hold it against you if you try to take advantage now. I'm also calling to tell you that we really are just as concerned as you are about your district. Obviously, if the Boss wins the election, you'll keep your seat, as long as you toe the line. But if he loses, you'll be carried off by the pink tide, and you know it. That's why I'm calling."

"My personal situation is of little importance," he spat. "And I don't much care for this little quid pro quo."

"Take it or leave it. I'm telling you loud and clear: if you keep taking shots at us, we'll leave you hanging in May. And believe me, though I'm not certain I can get you elected, I definitely know how to ensure you lose. And I'll handle it personally—especially if I have nothing better to do with my time."

"You know where you can stick your friendly warning," he said before hanging up. Politics is very like the theatre in a lot of ways. The show must go on.

28

When most people hear the word "Luxembourg", they think of tax evasion in a Grand Duchy that few of them can place on a map. In Paris, people think of the eponymous gardens.

But for me, it evokes the seat of the Senate—the Luxembourg Palace—and puts me on my guard, because I know the people inside far too well.

To be elected, MPs have to convince real people, like you and me. Well, like you. It's a difficult thing to do, and demands organization, energy, and real conviction. That said, the gullibility of those so-called real people is staggering. I'm not saying you can tell them whatever you like, but in all honesty, I know MPs who do, and they're re-elected time and again.

As for senators, they're not elected by people like you and me. They're elected by local officials. Their voters are a small portion of the French population, but a portion that knows politics. It's hard to fool local officials: they've been around the block and know a thing or two about campaigns and electoral promises. It's not easy to be elected by people who have themselves been elected. But that's the senators' job, and most of them do it very well.

Old Pinguet had been a senator for nearly twenty years. Two decades spent getting rid of contenders, fighting tooth and nail for the support of unknown, yet statistically relevant local mayors, and doing yet more favours.

And all those favours had taken a physical toll. Pinguet, who was always dressed in a three-piece suit, had the ruddy complexion of a bon vivant who never turns down an after-dinner drink. He wasn't very tall, but he had good posture, which made up for it. He had a pitifully inadequate comb-over.

I was early. You don't make an elected official wait unless you want to put pressure on them. I had used the time to stop by all the tables at the Senate restaurant, which is always a good idea in my line of work—particularly two months before a presidential election.

Pinguet arrived less than ten minutes late, which was fairly punctual by our profession's standards. His demeanour was sombre, and his black tie emphasized his grief. The dark circles under his eyes spoke volumes.

"My dear friend, I apologize for making you wait so long!" he said in a smooth tone, offering me a warm look and a handshake that almost felt genuine.

Pinguet knew what he was doing. Even at rock bottom, he could pretend to be happy to meet with someone who might someday be useful.

"Hello, Senator!" I said enthusiastically.

"How are you? How is our candidate?"

"He's well, thank you. He asked me to pass on his sincerest condolences. He was terribly sad to hear about your loss. I'd also like to say myself how sorry I am."

Senator Pinguet raised a hand skyward in a gesture that reminded me of a Roman emperor. I wasn't certain whether it meant that he'd rather not talk about it or that he was resigned to the fate the gods had planned for him.

"You can tell our candidate that I was touched by his call. He has so many things to think about and I was flattered he had the time for an old man in mourning," he said after a short pause, in a softer voice than usual.

I nodded. Nods come in rather handy when you have nothing to say.

"But let's talk about something else if you're willing. Tell me, how are you running things? Is our candidate ready? You know I'm among those who have never left his side, whatever the circumstances."

Of course you are, you old liar.

"I know, and so does he! He's counting on you to make sure Isère goes his way. And, given your experience in the Senate and the weight your opinion carries with your colleagues, he hopes you'll be able to unite our camp and motivate them for the campaign!"

I was expecting this to be the beginning of a good half hour of useless conversation, as is usually the case with lunches like this one. But I was wrong.

"It won't be easy," said Pinguet. "You overestimate my influence, and you can't imagine how reluctant the senators are to enter the fray."

I wasn't surprised that the senators were hesitant to join a difficult fight. At the Senate, they weigh, measure, and consider. The poetic flourishes and verbal jousting that make the National Assembly interesting on occasion are the prerogative of MPs. At the Luxembourg Palace, prudence and compromise are second nature. And, unlike the MPs, the presidential election has no bearing on the senators' re-election races. In other words, if they weren't convinced, they wouldn't campaign.

"What do you mean, Senator?" I asked.

"Our party is still very divided, I'm sorry to say. Many of us favoured our friend Trémeau. Her charm, her youth, and the new way she presented things was a breath of fresh air for the old men here."

"That's not enough to properly run the country, Senator."

"I agree with you, but I hear what they're saying—or not saying—in the Senate, and I'm telling you that these divisions, which should have disappeared after the primary, are more present than ever. Some of my colleagues, my friends even, aren't far from calling for Trémeau to run."

"That would be madness!"

"That's what I think, too, but they say that if the primary wasn't completely above board, then maybe it's worthwhile to have the public weigh in to decide between your boss and Trémeau. They seem to think that's what the first round is for."

At least things were clear. First, the rumour was spreading like wildfire, and if the senators were encouraging Trémeau to run, the Boss was about to find himself up against a dissenting candidate in the first round. Second, Pinguet was on the opposing team. When someone starts all of his sentences by telling you he agrees and ends them by proving the opposite, you know you have to be on your guard. When he goes from "our candidate" to "your boss", there's no longer any room for doubt.

I decided not to point this out. But since he had brought up the rumour, I might as well dig deeper.

"Senator, I see that you've heard these vicious rumours. I can't believe that you would lend them more than a curious ear. This primary was legitimate, and I say that with all the more conviction since we didn't even organize it. All of the necessary measures were taken, and the results were verified. No one contested them, and I don't see how this story of voter fraud can continue to make the rounds. It's pure slander!"

Pinguet looked at me and said nothing. I decided to take things even further.

"In fact, if I remember correctly, you have ties to the company that handled the vote, don't you? That's a guarantee that you could bring up with any of your colleagues who have doubts."

Pinguet still hadn't spoken. I must have been a bit aggressive. He studied his plate and carefully chewed his veal Marengo. I waited for him to finish his mouthful.

"Not me," he finally said, his voice weary. "One of my sons has . . . One of my sons *had* shares in the company, and in many others. The one who passed away."

"I'm sorry, Senator. I didn't know," I lied. "I didn't mean to—"

"Oh, don't worry about it."

Pinguet's features had grown more animated during our conversation, but now he looked drawn again. And he was agitated.

"He liked to drive fast, you know . . . Too fast, I guess. He must have swerved to avoid hitting something. Or maybe he fell asleep . . . I don't know."

Pinguet was beside himself. That was understandable. But I was surprised to see him so nervous. I felt bad about pushing a grieving old man, but I had a mission to carry out, and I had no doubt that if he were in my shoes, Pinguet would have done the same thing.

"Senator, I'd like to ask you something that's been niggling me since the beginning of the campaign. You spent quite a few years around Vital in Grenoble, didn't you? How did the two of you get on?"

Pinguet seemed surprised by the question.

"Well, he's polite and so am I, as you know. Let's just say that, like all of us, he's a different man when he's on his home turf and not in Paris. He left the regional government to campaign for president, of course, but I have to admit that we got on well before that. He was always good to the opposition. It's probably easier to be friendly when it's about repaving a road than when you're running for president, I suppose. But I have to say that whenever I needed a subsidy, I got it. In Paris, I don't see him much, but I know how he is: excessive and narrow-minded. But that's your problem, not mine."

"That's precisely the impression I had of Vital too."

I took note of the fact that Pinguet and Vital had a working relationship that could explain why the senator was campaigning for us with one foot on the brakes.

But none of that explained why Mukki had been hired by the regional government after he left the party.

"As it turns out," I ventured, deciding there was no point beating around the bush, "Vital hired a former party employee to work for the local authorities several years ago. A chap I knew and who came up again recently as the victim of a crime. I wondered how our guy fell through the cracks."

"I wouldn't know . . ."

"You probably never crossed paths, anyway. Mukki? Paul Mukki? Does that name ring a bell?"

Pinguet hesitated for a fraction of a second.

"Never heard of him," he said, "but we have so many employees these days. And the opposition rarely meets with civil servants, you know. You say he had an accident?"

"Yes. Well, sort of. He died. He was stabbed and drowned. A terrible tragedy."

"My God, how awful! The poor man."

Pinguet went deathly pale for a second, then quickly pulled himself together.

"All of that just proves that public safety must be a central theme of our campaign. Your boss needs to address crime levels. We live in trying times, as you know, and if we do nothing, the criminals will start coming into our homes. I'm telling you. We must do something."

Senator Pinguet had grown anxious and reserved. He seemed to want to change the subject. I wouldn't get any more out of him. I switched to autopilot for the rest of our lunch and resorted to the good old classics.

"So, Senator, what's next for your district?"

Pinguet almost relaxed. Neither of us was going to say anything else of interest.

29

Tuesday 2nd March, 3:30 p.m.

The taxi ride back to HQ was perfect. Friendly, quick, quiet. I tried to wrap my head around what I had learned. It wasn't easy.

Pinguet wasn't doing well. He had been hit hard by the death of his son, which was fair enough. Even senators are human. But it wasn't the grief which had stood out for me in his silences and frowns.

Pinguet was worried. About himself.

After a long career in the Senate, Pinguet now feared for his life. Probably for the first time. That was the most interesting piece of information I'd glean that day.

Or at least that's what I thought.

30

"The mayor of Eu is on the phone," said my secretary.

What did he want? Some sort of promise or favour from the Boss no doubt.

"Put him through," I said with a sigh. "To what do I owe the pleasure, Mayor?"

"My dear friend, thank you for taking my call. I just wanted to speak to you quickly because I was caught rather off guard."

"Off guard?"

"Yes, we've just received the forms to endorse our choice of presidential candidate. Until this morning, I had no reason to hesitate, but I took a strange call earlier and now I'm not sure what to believe. It was a call from someone claiming to be a member of Marie-France Trémeau's team and who asked me to endorse her."

I shot to my feet.

"I'm confused," continued the mayor. "Who is the legitimate candidate? Which one is the party behind?"

"Thank you for letting me know. I'm quite surprised by this move, which goes against the members' vote. Supporting Mrs Trémeau would mean turning your back on the party."

"Thank you," he said, "I'll do what's right. But many of my colleagues have the same questions."

Trémeau was preparing a breakaway candidacy. Our Snag was now of the utmost political importance.

31

Tuesday 2nd March, 7:54 p.m.

Normally, after lunch at the Senate, I plan for a quiet afternoon and try not to eat dinner out. Digestion requires calm and common sense forbids excess.

But since the beginning of this campaign, since the beginning of the primary, really, nothing had been normal. Every day I had a thousand things to do and just as many people to see. The campaign pulled me along at breakneck speed.

The Boss wanted to speak to the country, to France, but I was the one who actually had to manage the French people who lined up for a word with him. That said, it would have been a grave mistake to talk to them in his place. This was his campaign, and he had to make it seem like he was reachable and more or less available. He handled it all remarkably well. As for me, the further we got into the campaign, the more I felt like I was drowning in a sea of obligations and appointments.

And then there was the Snag, which was sapping what was left of my energy.

I did my best to conceal it, but it was becoming more and more difficult to focus on the campaign when I knew there was a plot afoot that could blow it to smithereens. The doubts that had taken hold among the Boss's entourage weren't making things any easier. I needed to bounce my ideas and theories off a critical mind, but I couldn't talk to

Marilyn, who was still in a huff, and my growing misgivings about the Major meant I wasn't inclined to talk to him either. Démosthène was busy writing up a storm and he was useless in this area anyway. If things had been calmer, I would have shut myself away with the Boss so we could think together, but things were far from calm.

Winston was the only option.

Increasingly, whenever we were both free, we had a drink together after work to go over everything. It wasn't yet friendship: we needed time to bridge the thirty-odd-year age gap. But deep down I knew that it could become friendship, and I was surprised to find myself confiding in someone his age.

The kid no longer lived with his mother. He had a studio in the 10th arrondissement near the Canal Saint-Martin. It was just across from the Citizen Hotel, a trendy but charming little hotel where I had spent many a delectable night, and was located in the heart of "Yuppy Land" as Winston called his neighbourhood, which was a microcosm of the capital's shifting social and political landscape.

Twenty years earlier, it had been full of hardware stores, garages, and cafés that didn't look like much—working-class Paris, where factory workers and low-level office employees lived and worked. The people hadn't been rich, but they had often voted for the right in the local elections because law and order were valued there, because they didn't want to be forgotten, and because they liked Jacques Chirac, who was mayor of Paris from 1977 to 1995. They hadn't been poor either, though. The Canal Saint-Martin had always been on the right side of the Number 2 underground metro line, which many will agree was the unofficial border between respectable Paris and the rest.

And then the yuppies had arrived. Stylish young singles and couples with fancy degrees and jobs had invaded the neighbourhood to escape the city centre, which was too expensive, and the outskirts, which were too far. Bars had gradually replaced the cafés, and bank branches sprang up where craftsmen had previously toiled. Next came the clothes shops and photo galleries, which completed the transformation. The new residents, though wealthier than the original population, continued dressing as they had when they'd been young and broke, which created an atmosphere that seemed to blend social and ethnic backgrounds. But behind the art portfolios, cargo trousers, and artfully neglected beards, the prices climbed, and the neighbourhood changed. People started voting for the left, too, for freedom, and tolerance, and culture, and against all the rest: poverty, obscurantism, inequality, racism, moral order, pollution, evictions and deportation, world hunger, illness, and pain.

That said, the neighbourhood had its charms.

We frequented several different bars and restaurants. When we were in a good mood, we headed to La Madonnina, a little Italian place that served incredible pasta. When we were feeling down, we would choose the Spanish restaurant on Rue des Vinaigriers, where the beer was excellent and the *jamon* to die for.

That night, we were having Italian. We had a lead—that was a cause for celebration.

"Senator Pinguet must know more than he's letting on," said Winston. "First, he must have the same doubts we have about his son's accident. And what you told him about Mukki must have convinced him that something unsavoury is going on."

"I couldn't tell if he knows Mukki or not. He claimed he didn't, but his face said the opposite. He visibly paled when I mentioned the name. I don't know if I did the right thing by warning him . . ."

"If he's scared, then he feels guilty about something."

"What's your guess?"

"His son died in a strange accident. Mukki met with a violent end. Maybe Pinguet's afraid he's next on the list. And if that's the case, then he definitely has something to feel guilty about . . ."

It's amazing how easy it is to admire someone for their brilliant mind when they think like you. That's exactly where I stood with this kid.

The alcohol and the satisfaction of having at last uncovered a lead went to our heads. Though he wasn't exactly drunk, Caligny was clearly a little tipsy. He started touching my forearm to drive home his argument. And he kept running his hand through his hair. He had been to the toilet three times to keep pace with the respectable rate at which he was drinking and to make up for an undoubtedly diminutive bladder. He was talking louder and, most importantly, much more than usual.

The kid was talking about everything, his childhood growing up in Brittany, and his father's friends, who had been a big part of his life before his father's death, but who had disappeared afterwards. He mentioned the law firm where his mother had restarted her career, what we needed to do to prepare the Boss for the next stages of the campaign, ideas he had about using the internet to mobilize voters, his uncle, who had taught him Foreign Legion songs and told him war stories. For the first time, I was seeing him relaxed, freed from the reserve and self-restraint he had put between himself and us since joining the Boss's entourage.

I must have been wearing a dumb smile as I sat there thinking what a nice guy he was, because he suddenly came to his senses, told me it was late and that we needed to get home since the next day would be a long one. We both merrily pretended to speak Italian as we paid our bill, and we left La Madonnina laughing.

★ ★ ★

The Canal Saint-Martin was at the end of the street, waiting impassively.

It wasn't alone.

Four men sitting on the steps of a metal footbridge over the canal were watching passers-by, hardened looks on their faces. A young couple crossed the street to avoid them. I noticed them right away. There was something strange about them. Winston kept talking, still under the influence.

I locked eyes with one of the four men and was sure I recognized the redhead from the other night, who was much more attractive with his ski mask on.

Neither the kid nor I were in any sort of condition to handle a tricky situation. I discreetly tried to get him to cross the street to avoid the threatening group, without making it obvious or worrying him.

But the tall redhead was watching us. He stood up just as we started to cross. He had been waiting for us, his eyes scanning the faces of everyone who walked past. He was on the hunt—his presence was no coincidence. At least that's how I see it now, but in the moment little was clear. When I saw him, I realized something was wrong, but I didn't know how things would go down.

He came closer, followed by the other three, and asked for a cigarette with a strong Eastern European accent. I must have replied that we didn't smoke and picked up the pace, pushing Winston along. But the redhead was faster. He barred the way. And then, without any hesitation, without a word, or any sort of warning, he rammed his fist into Winston's face. I saw him fall and heard myself shout, but the other three immediately started in on me.

I gave one a run for his money before falling to the ground, but the alcohol had me at a disadvantage, and there were four of them. Since there was nothing I could do but scream for help—and not for long—I protected myself like I had done as a child when the bigger kids had decided to take out their frustrations on the boy with the best marks in the school. I huddled in the foetal position and tried to keep them from hitting my head or balls. Both might still serve me yet.

I wouldn't have been able to hold out long given how hard and fast their fists were raining down on me. My shoulder and stomach burned, and a blow to the kneecap had left my leg numb. Caligny was lying motionless on the ground, so they ignored him. My vision started to blur.

Just as things were about to fade to black, I felt someone grab hold of one of the guys who had me on the ground. There was a pause in the punches. I looked up cautiously. The big redhead was on his knees. Another guy was passed out on the ground. The other two had backed off. The Godfather was standing over the redhead, twisting his arm behind his back. I struggled to my feet, my legs unsteady. I couldn't seem to find my balance. To keep from falling over, I sat back down. I was two metres away from the redhead, who stared at me with his dark eyes. He was in pain and couldn't move, but he was clearly dying to jump on me again.

And that's when I heard the cracks.

The sound of human bones breaking is very distinctive. When the bone of a living human breaks, there are two sounds, actually. First the crack, which you hear clearly if you're close enough, and then the scream of pain, which you can hear even more clearly, even if you're some distance away.

Gaspard must have broken the man's wrist first, then his forearm, no doubt in several places. First the radius, then the cubitus, because I heard several cracks. The redhead screamed. The other two fled. Then I distinguished a few more cracks—probably another bone in his arm, or his fingers. I heard another terrible scream, then whimpering.

After that, I passed out.

32

Waking up in strange places and wondering how long I had been asleep was starting to feel like a habit.

I was in a hospital room. Pale blue. Quiet. But odd. I had a headache.

Outside the window stood a huge, leafless tree. A muted television hanging on the wall broadcast the news, but I couldn't see it very well.

When I tried to read the names of the people who were speaking on the screen, I realized what was wrong. I could only see out of one eye. My left eye was working normally, but the right was not. Everything was black for my right eye, with just a small circle of light in the middle.

Anxiety washed over me immediately, along with a jolt of adrenaline. I must have tried to get up, but everything started spinning and I passed out again.

33

Wednesday 3rd March, 11:22 a.m.

Either I am particularly fragile, or American films are full of shit. That said, I suppose the two aren't necessarily mutually exclusive. In any case, after seeing the doctor, I wondered how Hollywood could so blithely show men coming to blows without ever getting truly hurt.

The attack I had experienced had lasted no more than thirty seconds. And yet, the consequences were pitiful: my inner ear had been damaged, causing a temporary loss of balance, and my partial blindness was due to retinal detachment. I was nearly blind and could barely stand—a wreck. And that's without taking all the bruises and other contusions I had into account.

Winston was in better shape. He was younger and would heal faster, and he had been spared much of the men's wrath.

"You look like shit," he said.

He was even up to making fun of me.

"The doctor just told me they're going to keep me for a few days to do more tests. And he ordered me to rest," I replied.

My vision was blurred, but I could still make out his smile. He knew very well that my fierce disregard for anything other than the campaign would make quick work of the doctor's orders.

Winston kept quiet. They must have told him not to wear me out. I hate it when people are quiet around me. If I don't want to be spoken to, I make sure I'm alone. It's more effective and more practical.

"I bet this isn't quite how you imagined a presidential campaign, is it?" I asked, clearing my throat.

"Not exactly, no."

"Me neither. My whole body hurts, I look like a zombie, and I can only see out of one eye."

"You could say your wife beats you."

"If only, Winston, if only . . ."

The kid smiled. Then there were a few more minutes of silence. It was hard for me to talk, and he didn't know what to say.

"Your uncle is a strange one. That said, we're lucky he was there."

"He's always been there for me when I needed him. When my father died, he helped us out a lot. He's always there when things get rough. He's not as present when things are good, but I suppose that's better than the other way around."

"Yes, it's usually the opposite."

"I know. He's a rare specimen. He follows a few simple rules in life. He's totally indifferent to what people think about him. He's the freest man I've ever met. And probably the most determined. When he was in the Foreign Legion, he did some incredible things. I always thought my mother embellished her stories, but after what I saw yesterday, I now think she was just telling the truth. He never talks about it."

"It's always better to have done something and not talk about it than the opposite. I know quite a few people who would do well to emulate your uncle."

A gallery of portraits instantly sped past my eyes. I saw all of the Barons from campaign HQ hounding me to offer their loyal services and make their pretentions for the future known . . .

Thinking about the mechanics of the campaign and its rhythm was exhausting. Campaigns were always physically draining, and I didn't see how I was going to handle it when I was missing one eye and feeling constantly dizzy. For the first time, I felt defeated.

Behind Winston, the door opened and the Godfather stepped inside.

"You look like shit," he said.

"You Calignys have a gift for cheering me up . . ."

At the same time, I couldn't help but think that if the Calignys hadn't been there, my room would have been empty when I woke up. And if Gaspard hadn't been there the night before, I may not have woken up at all . . . I suddenly shivered with a blend of despair and gratitude.

"You were following us?" I asked.

Gaspard smiled. "I'm not following you; I'm looking out for my nephew. There's a difference. Lucky for you, though, wouldn't you say?" he said in a mocking but not unkind tone. "I think they were there to scare you, nothing more."

"Well, they did a splendid job, if I do say so myself!"

Winston and his uncle laughed.

"I wasn't just there to scare them, though," continued Gaspard. "I got some information off them. First, they were speaking an Eastern European language, though I'm not sure which one. Next, I noticed a tattoo on the redhead's arm that I recognized: the 13th Half-Brigade of the Foreign Legion, based in Djibouti. The seven-flame grenade set under a cross of Lorraine. Narvik, Mers el-Kébir, that's them."

"You didn't catch them?"

Winston gave me a dirty look.

"I know I didn't really help much," I offered. I felt pathetic. Pathetic for failing to stand my ground and pathetic for being incapable of thanking the man who had saved me. "I'm sorry," I finally managed.

Silence.

I was stuck in a hospital room with a kid and a guy I hadn't known six weeks earlier, in the middle of a presidential campaign that was going pear-shaped. And I still didn't know who was pulling the strings. Things were unclear, in all senses of the word.

"There are plenty of things that don't add up in this mess. But there's one thing I understand even less than the rest," I said.

"What's that?" asked Winston.

"I don't understand this violence. The political world is a violent one, as I know all too well, but it's a unique form of violence. We fight, we hurl insults at one another. We betray, criticize, and take plenty of tongue lashings, but we're not usually physically violent."

"People have always died in politics," Gaspard said nonchalantly.

"That's true. Every twenty years or so, there's an assassination. People wondered about your father's death, Winston. There are always conspiracy theorists out there. But, generally, in politics, you die symbolically, you're not beaten to a pulp on a dark street corner."

"And?"

"And, things have been particularly violent of late, compared to what politics usually has to offer. Two deaths, two assaults. This isn't a presidential campaign, it's a western!"

Gaspard had been listening attentively.

"Maybe," he said. "But, in any case, there's one big difference between the two assaults."

"What's that?"

"The first time, Mukki was the target. The second time, they were after you. That means that our friends now see you as an enemy. Someone is going out of their way to scare you. That's a good sign."

"How is that a good sign?"

"When someone becomes worth scaring, it means they're in the way. And if we're in the way, it means we're on the right track."

The logic was sound, but I couldn't see how we were on the right track and had no idea where it was taking us.

"So, I should be happy I took a beating," I joked, though my face probably betrayed my inner doubts. "But what tells you we're on the right track, besides the fact that they're after us?"

Gaspard took a document out of his bag which lay on the floor at the foot of the bed. He waved it around in front of me. "This!" he said. "It's very interesting. A little technical, but worth a read."

"What is it?" I asked.

"A security audit of Droid's system. It's dated late August, two weeks before the primary. And you know where I found it? Among your friend the Major's things."

I was left reeling.

"In his office?" I asked, still taken aback.

"No, at his flat. You know, the place where you put professional documents you don't want to leave lying around . . ."

"You broke in?"

The Godfather shot me a condescending look. It didn't make sense: the Boss's campaign manager, a trusted confidant, was hiding a document of the utmost importance and hadn't mentioned it when we got wind of the rumour.

I had decided to keep trusting the inner circle, but it was getting more difficult with each passing day.

34

There was no chance of escaping insomnia given recent events. I had been reduced to watching a nature document-ary on water buffalo.

I had, rather unwisely, returned to HQ two days after the assault. I was weak but lying in a hospital bed was more exhausting than deluding myself into thinking I was being useful to the campaign.

Politics had made me paranoid, but this attack had pushed me into a new state. I had always had a sombre view of hu-man nature, but the violence to which Caligny and I had been subjected had darkened it even more, erasing any shred of doubt: the rest of humanity was either a threat, a miserable mob, or a confused horde of dangerous mis-creants. That might seem excessive, and I'm sure that if I had mentioned it to friends, they would have encouraged me to lighten up. But what friends? And would they understand the difference between knowing life is always hanging by a thread and actually experiencing the reality of that fact?

The physical damage was relatively limited. After kindling the curiosity of everyone I saw at campaign HQ, the bruises had slowly disappeared. Behind my back, people must have assumed they were a parting gift from a jealous husband or a bender that had ended badly. On the upside, my mysterious injuries had given me an excellent reason not to accompany the Boss on his official trips. I also went out less, but that was practical as well since the campaign was picking up pace as the first round drew nearer.

The detached retina was more problematic. The doctors argued that it wasn't serious as long as I had an operation quickly, but I still hadn't decided when to go under the knife. Losing two or three days during the campaign was a luxury I couldn't afford. I stewed in my indecision and worry, plunged into semi-darkness, which didn't make matters any better.

The most troublesome consequence, though, was the extreme difficulty I now faced when trying to concentrate. At first, I thought I was just tired—a particularly credible argument given the circumstances. In politics, you always find what you want to hear most convincing.

But it wasn't just fatigue. The questions people asked me seemed more trifling and the games played by the Barons and everyone else who gravitated around the Boss increasingly futile. The theatre that is politics was losing its hold on me. I was still determined to help the Boss win, but the rest bored me. I was disillusioned and cynical, like when you can feel that the end is near.

I could have seen the shift as normal, or even a good sign. After all, electing to step back from a job you've done for thirty years isn't so shocking. Some might even see the choice as enlightened.

For me, it was a serious problem. My growing inability to concentrate meant I was missing things. It gave the impression that I had nothing but disdain for the details, and even people. I smoothed things over, when it became necessary, by explaining that I was there to handle the big picture, not the fine print. I'm not sure I actually convinced anyone . . .

Especially not the Boss.

35

We were in the small lounge at HQ, which the Boss had had furnished as a meeting room. He was the only one to use it. Around him sat all the members of his entourage except Démosthène, a few barons who had been invited to stroke their egos, and the three Sorcerers.

For politicians, communicators are an inescapable part of the job. Whatever an elected official's path to office, they will need communicators. If they have their sights set on a national position, they'll spend a lot of time with them.

When you're running for a seat in somewhere like Charleville-Mézières, communicators come in the shape of a small agency, or a photographer who likes politics, or a campaign employee who has in-depth knowledge of the local press. They're not always professionals, but they do have set ideas about what colour tie you should wear and how you should say or not say this or that. Give them a little time and they'll soon be telling you what message to share. In their profession, style tends to precede content.

When you're a candidate in a national election, particularly in a presidential race, you find yourself surrounded by real, professional communicators—the Sorcerers.

The Boss's relationship with the Sorcerers epitomized all of the ambiguous feelings of the political world for communicators. He didn't like them. The Boss was a man of the written word and of direct contact with the people. He could never wrap his head around the codes and demands of a profession so focused on image. But he knew he couldn't do it without them. Because creating and preserving an image was a profession, and not his. Because the Sorcerers often said things that other people thought but never dared say. And because, as always with their kind, most of them are frauds, but when you find one that can make it rain, you keep him close.

As for me, I saw them as a necessary evil. I wasn't really in the mood for their jawing, but I didn't want to be left out of any decisions. I fully intended to keep them on track. For me, communication is the answer to two questions: what do we want to say and to whom? The rest is a waste of time.

There were three of them that morning. Three of the best Sorcerers Paris had to offer, and there are many in the capital. Especially during a crisis.

The first was in his thirties with an unkempt beard in a black suit and white shirt. His ostentatious glasses were supposed to signal his intelligence and originality. Neither one of those things seemed particularly obvious to me, but he was respected in his field, which is why the Boss had chosen him. At the ripe old age of thirty-five, he was supposedly the master of the newest means of communication: the internet, social networks, e-campaigns, and e-networking. To me, it seemed like he just added "e" everywhere. That said, I had to admit he had a gift for developing slogans and catchphrases and an above-average sense of humour.

The second was older, heavier, and not as funny. He spoke loudly and was rich. He was the majority partner in one of the biggest communications firms in Paris and had sold a bit of everything, from dairy products to lipstick, which had left him feeling he had an intimate understanding of the French people. He had advised many CAC 40 companies facing negative public opinion and believed he was the man to turn to in a crisis.

After the Boss's victory in the primary, his teams had been responsible for handling the campaign's image: the slogan, the poster, in short everything voters would see or hear. We had had regular meetings ever since to adjust messaging and adapt the communications tools.

The third Sorcerer was probably the most important of the three. Looking fit in his sixties, he had known the Boss for decades and people around town tended to say they were friends. I doubted it, since I'd never noticed any of the warmth friendship requires between them. But their relationship was based on mutual respect. The Boss listened to the Sorcerer and the Sorcerer didn't take advantage of the situation. Of the three Sorcerers, he was the most powerful. His authority stemmed from the questions he asked. Since his early twenties, he had been tirelessly surveying the French people. For big companies, unions, the government, and political parties on both sides. He asked thousands of French people questions to find out what they liked, believed, and feared. His analyses were persuasive, and, to his credit, I had to admit that he had an unrivalled talent for going beyond the raw data to find out what the results really meant.

Fifteen minutes into the meeting, I had lost track of the discussion, which centred on the image the Boss should project in the final weeks of the campaign. The young Sorcerer felt we should change nothing. In his view, we had already played our cards, and the slightest change in the Boss's message or the way he presented himself would be misunderstood and counterproductive. The rich Sorcerer protested. The powerful Sorcerer urged to be more cautious. Everyone had an opinion. Everyone was talking at once. It was a mess. A classic gathering of communicators.

The Boss was surprisingly quiet.

I knew him well enough to know why he was hesitating. It's always hard to make a decision when people disagree—but even harder when you yourself are the object of the decision. He let everyone talk, hoping they would help him make up his mind.

"Voters want a man of the people," argued the rich Sorcerer. "They need to know that the future president understands them and shares their struggles, tastes, and expectations. They want to put their trust in someone they feel close to. It's great to be a statesman who goes down in history, but the French people want to feel like they can talk to the president and be heard . . ."

Approachability versus grandeur. A dilemma every presidential candidate has to face.

"A statesman is just a politician who's been dead for at least fifteen years," the rich Sorcerer went on. "That's not worth fighting over. We need to take advantage of these last few weeks to meet with and talk to the people. The president needs to relate to their preoccupations. Vital is just an apparatchik—hiss party's man. You have to be France's man!"

He had made his point using the full force of his authority. It occurred to me that he may be right, but would have said the exact same thing if he were advising Vital.

The young Sorcerer refused to back down. "Yes and no," he said. "We sold the public a clearly identified product. The candidate is a family sedan—solid, reliable, comfortable, with airbags and all the bells and whistles to prevent accidents. When people see the candidate, they see a nice Mercedes. And now, all of a sudden, for no reason, we're going to start telling them that their Mercedes has turned into a Renault Clio? People who like Mercedes will be disappointed, and those who like Clios will smell a rat!"

Thirty years as a politician to be compared to a car. I didn't dare look in the Boss's direction. Then again, it was better than laundry detergent . . .

I was starting to understand the problem. No one dared say it, but there was a reason the Sorcerers were so worried about the Boss's image in the final weeks of the campaign. It wasn't simply to justify their fees or for the joy of telling the tale at dinner parties.

The Snag was with us.

The Sorcerers had heard the rumour. They were too afraid to mention it, but it was obvious now. Changing the Boss's image was a way to manage the rumour, which was picking up speed, and any bad news that might come of it. And the reason the Boss couldn't decide what to do was because he knew about the threat and didn't know how to handle it. I probably should have joined the fray, addressed the elephant in the room and then wound down the meeting. That's definitely what the Boss expected. But I couldn't do it.

So, Marilyn spoke up. She asked the Boss a few cautious questions to broach the subject without upsetting anyone. "I'm not sure I understand the debate here," she said. "Your image is clear in the public eye: you are associated with the ideas of experience, integrity, and responsibility. Am I wrong?"

No one objected. The powerful Sorcerer nodded slowly.

"In other words," joked the Boss, "I'm old, honest and a pain in the arse?"

Everyone laughed, though I couldn't help but feel it was forced, nervous laughter.

"Your words, not mine!" replied Marilyn. "But these three characteristics are precious assets. The first question we need to ask is: are they enough, and, if they're not, do we need to add others?"

Approving glances all around. The powerful Sorcerer was taking notes.

"The second question is more delicate," she continued. "We need to know what to do if any of these three essential characteristics is ever jeopardized. Should we fight to cling to these themes or choose new ones?"

No one dared look at the Boss.

Marilyn had concluded with a smile. I stared at her lips, feeling nostalgic.

I don't know who spoke after Marilyn. I wasn't listening any more. I couldn't even hear any more. I was fully absorbed in that smile.

When I came to, the atmosphere at the table had grown serious. The powerful Sorcerer was pontificating. "Need I remind you that when it comes to communication, what matters is not what you say, but what people hear!"

The weighty silence that followed this definitive affirmation would undoubtedly have gone undisturbed for at least a minute if Démosthène hadn't burst into the room.

As usual, his clothes were wrinkled and misbuttoned. But he was paler than usual. He had come into a meeting room reserved for the Boss without knocking. It was as though he was itching to be told off by the Boss or the Major.

"I was writing a speech for next week," he said unsteadily. "The one about unity in our camp. The one where you evoke the history of the various political families and talk about why unity is necessary today. The one we spoke about a few days ago . . ."

Everyone was staring at Démosthène, wondering where this was going and what had come over him.

"And I was watching TV. I like to watch TV while writing speeches . . ."

The Major was fuming, and the Sorcerers clearly wondered if they were in an asylum.

"And . . . Well, I think I'll have to scrap it and start over . . ." he said as he walked over to the television, turned it on to the all-day news channel and upped the volume.

We saw Trémeau leaving the maternity ward of a little hospital in the Doubs region that was on the verge of closing. It had been in the news a few weeks earlier when the staff, local officials, and residents had gathered to protest the government's decision.

Her voice was firm and clear. She came across as an angry and determined woman.

"I'm here to offer my support to these people who are simply trying to raise their children in acceptable conditions, people who work just as hard as the rest of the French people, who pay their taxes, and have every right to expect the same healthcare facilities. This maternity ward cannot close! I don't understand how the presidential candidates can even be in this race without considering what real people are going through!"

Well, that was a slap in the face.

The reporter asked her if she was critical of the Boss and if she regretted not being able to run herself.

"I'm not criticizing anyone. I say what I think because I believe it, and I don't much care for what other people want to hear. That's the way I do politics. If the parties like it, great. If not, too bad for them, because I won't change. As for my candidacy, it's too early to exclude the possibility. The legal deadline to file is 17th March. Until then, it's all up in the air."

A second slap in the face.

Delighted to be getting a scoop, the reporter asked, for her final question, if Trémeau was afraid she would be painted as a poor loser if she failed to accept her defeat in the primary.

"I've lost before. When defeat follows a clear debate and there are no doubts about the fair nature of the election, I accept defeat. That's democracy. But I would like to be absolutely certain that that was the case with this primary. It is my right as a candidate to ask for proof. And if no one can produce it, then it's my right to refuse to give in to what would, in that case, best be characterized as political manoeuvring. In fact, it would be more than my right. It would be my duty."

And three. That's a wrap.

Démosthène was definitely going to have to rewrite that speech.

36

Monday 8th March, 10:33 a.m.

The Boss took it better than the rest of us, which didn't surprise me. As a true master of politics, he liked crises. I wouldn't say that he enjoyed them, because that would have been the sign of a vice rather than a virtue, but low blows didn't frighten him.

I had often heard him say that great men didn't make history; history revealed great men. There was undoubtedly some truth to that, and since I didn't really have an opinion on the topic, I'd always agreed with him.

What I did know, however, was that Marie-France Trémeau's announcement was a very low blow—the kind we might not come back from. Those three short sentences of hers, broadcast on a loop by all the evening news channels, jeopardized the Boss's entire campaign.

But he was calm. The quick pace at which his fingers rapped on the tabletop betrayed his annoyance, but other than that, he displayed remarkable composure. When the segment ended, the Major uttered a few choice swear words, placing his face in his hands and his elbows on the table. If a meteorite had destroyed his country house, his face probably would have displayed the same look of disbelief and consternation. Marilyn pursed her lips and immediately reached for her mobile. She would be on the front lines for the next few hours with every political journalist in town asking for a response. Winston said nothing, which was clever, and watched everyone carefully, which was cleverer still.

The Sorcerers seemed uncomfortable. The young Sorcerer kept quiet while his powerful colleague seemed to be absorbed in his notes. The rich Sorcerer answered the Major's exclamation by affirming that Trémeau was an idiot, a frigid bitch in need of a lay, and a whore, which seemed all at once rather excessive, vaguely contradictory, and very risky in the Boss's presence.

"I can't accept your comments, my friend," the Boss said firmly. "Mrs Trémeau is none of those things. She is an elected official of the Republic, she is ambitious, and she's playing a bold hand. She's a real thorn in our side, it's true, but, for one, she's still in our camp, and one of us will need the other in the second round. Two, she's doing exactly what I would have done if I had been in her shoes. And three, please forgive me for being old-fashioned, but I will not stand for anyone speaking about a woman like that around me."

In an instant, the rich Sorcerer turned into a little boy caught red-handed by his teacher. I would have enjoyed the moment if the situation hadn't been so dire. After a quick survey of the table, the Boss realized that no one had any brilliant ideas, but that the general attitude was that we were ready for a fight.

He sent everyone back to work, telling us he wanted to think for a bit about how to overcome this obstacle, since those of us whose job it was to devise such solutions had come up empty.

I assumed the jab was aimed at me in particular, and I was right.

37

Monday 8ᵗʰ March, 12:15 p.m.

"It's unbelievable! First a rumour, then leaks in the press, and now that bitch Trémeau has stabbed us in the back, and you have nothing to say! Good thing you're handling the problem! I'd hate to think where we'd be if you weren't!" shouted the Boss.

We were in the car with Winston and the Boss's doltish driver Schumacher. The storm was raging.

The Boss was really laying in to me, but to be honest, that was only fair. The Snag had been ruining things left, right and centre for three weeks, and I still hadn't identified the person who was trying to put an end to the Boss's campaign.

I hadn't exactly been idle, and I could have told the Boss that I had made progress, not to mention that I had almost been killed not once but twice in the process, and all while working on the campaign as well. It would have looked like I was making excuses, and in my line of work, excuses are worthless. Results are what count. When you don't get results, you have to make it someone else's fault. It's not pretty, but that's the way it is.

I had elected not to answer. I might as well just let the storm pass. I knew the Boss well enough to know that this was just his way of letting off steam. A few hours later, he would forget the tone and content of his reproaches.

"Sir, you're being unfair," Winston suddenly said, having apparently decided not to let the Boss walk all over him.

This approach was probably due to inexperience, or maybe pride, or perhaps some sort of bravery.

"We don't know who is behind things, it's true," he said, "but we do know quite a bit. We know that it was possible to rig the primary, though we aren't sure it was. We know that Mukki and Senator Pinguet's son were mixed up in it, and let's not forget that they both died violent deaths recently, which places this situation squarely in another league, I think you'll agree . . ."

The kid was holding his own. The Boss was taken aback to see such a young man go up against him.

"But there are two important things we don't know," continued Winston. "First, was the election really rigged, and if it was, who is behind it? Second, who is pulling the strings? Who benefits from this business coming to light?"

The Boss gave the kid a stern look. I let silence fill the car to give them both time to calm down. Schumacher was focused on the road. Even he had realized it was best to keep off the Boss's radar for the next few hours.

"Winston is right," I finally said. "We aren't far from the truth now. We'll find out who committed voter fraud. We're on the right path. And I hope we won't come across any surprises when we get to the end."

"What are you insinuating?" the Boss asked in a biting tone.

"Well, if the primary was rigged, it was done to benefit you, so it was most likely someone who is close to you, or who could be portrayed as being close to you . . ." I said, walking on eggshells.

"You are unbelievable!" he replied, outraged. "You can't even tell me if it *was* rigged, but you're already making accusations!"

"I'm not accusing anyone," I objected. "Not yet, not without proof. But I'm looking, believe me. I'm looking."

The heavy silence that followed was only broken by a few short grunts from Schumacher, who couldn't help but express his delight when he overtook other cars. The guy was a loser despite his suits and playboy look. The idea that he would be able to tell everyone about what a tongue-lashing I'd taken disgusted me.

"Our current problem," said Caligny, breaking the silence, "is as much about the rumour as it is about the possible fraud. Even if the fraud is a fabrication, the damage caused by the rumour is real. We need to find the source of the rumour to find the person who rigged the election, if they even exist. Who could have started the rumour?"

"Look into Vital's people, Louis," said the Boss. "Don't overlook Vital. You should reread your classics. *The Enemy's House Divided*, for example. Vital knows all too well that he improves his chances of victory if we're divided in the first round and unable to come together for the second. And this is just the sort of thing he would use. He doesn't even have to mention it himself; we're tearing each other apart from the inside. With his contacts at the Ministry of the Interior, he's in the perfect position to manipulate anyone he likes. And he's more than capable, believe me."

The Boss was right, of course.

But something was bothering me. I couldn't help but think that Trémeau had thrown herself into the fray rather quickly. She had jumped right in when the rumour had yet to be substantiated, and she was putting herself in a position to divide the party long term. It was a risky move, even for an ambitious woman, and she was leaving herself open to ridicule and criticism if we managed to prove that the election had been fair, or worse, that Vital was behind it all. That said, I was far from being able to prove anything.

"Unfortunately," said the Boss, interrupting my thoughts, "I can't wait for you to figure it out. Trémeau's little speech has forced my hand. I think I know how to handle it, but I need to think. Tell my friends not to attack Trémeau in the meantime, all right? And organize a campaign committee meeting as soon as possible, tomorrow night if you can. We need to show the public that the party is united, and we don't have any time to spare. Now, gentlemen, I think a bit of a stroll will do you good. We'll pull over to let you out. See you later."

38

Tuesday 9th March, 5:01 p.m.

It was a full house.

Meetings at campaign HQ don't tend to be particularly useful. Campaigns are all about organization and decision-making. The Boss delegates both to his team—mostly to avoid having to ask the Barons for help.

The Barons. The former heads of this or the ex-councillors of that whom people listen to thanks to their past glory. Especially when they're badmouthing the campaign and the candidate. Which is exactly what happens if they're not consulted and invited to pop into campaign HQ at least once a week. Some of them had even asked for and obtained permanent offices—that they never used.

That's why we created the campaign committee, which met every Thursday afternoon. This was the first time the Boss had ever called an emergency session. Everyone knew Trémeau's statements would be discussed, and the smell of blood had attracted every predator within range.

The committee comprised twenty-two members. The members themselves probably thought it was useless, while all those on the outside looking in were dying to be included. We had set criteria that were as objective as possible. We included: former prime ministers, the heads of the parties that supported the Boss, and the leaders of our group at the

National Assembly and the Senate. I had also added a few promising young MPs whom we would need to build a stable government if we won.

The Boss had also insisted we include Marie-France Trémeau as an important candidate from the primary, but she had never turned up, claiming she was no apparatchik. She had sent Texier each time instead, whom no one had ever dared to turn away. The Major, Marilyn, and I were silent observers.

As it turned out, it was surprisingly difficult to get important MPs from our camp and notable local officials to actively participate in the campaign. In the beginning, I had thought that everyone simply fell in line behind their party's candidate. Boy, was I mistaken. Between those who hoped for defeat so they could take the Boss's place, those who were already working on what came next, those who were most focused on damaging their rivals' reputations, and those who were mostly campaigning for themselves, the Barons spent very little time doing the one thing they were there to do: help the Boss get elected.

So, though meetings with the Barons were rarely productive, tonight the stakes were high. I hadn't said anything when he'd decided to summon the committee, because he was in no mood to listen and because I could see that he had something in mind, but I knew how risky it was. Bringing all of the Barons together during a crisis to demonstrate our unity obviously left us exposed to the exact opposite. Any Baron under Trémeau's thumb could turn the meeting into a car crash. I had a hard time imagining Texier would deny himself that pleasure.

Managing such a gathering was a true art form—one that the Boss mastered perfectly. Nevertheless, he would still need to be on the top of his game to get through this meeting.

Eager to ensure things went smoothly, I had met with all of the Boss's partisans and encouraged them to come and to speak up about their support for unity and for the only legitimate candidate: the Boss. Texier must have done the same thing, but he had the advantage since he was a member of the committee whereas I was only allowed to attend because the Boss wanted me there. In other words, I had to keep quiet. Even the most powerful apparatchik in France was reduced to silence at such historic events . . .

Outside HQ, the news cameras had filmed as everyone came inside, on the lookout for tension and snide remarks. There was nothing like a civil war within a party to get the political press all hot and bothered. If Trémeau was going to show at one of these meetings, this was the one.

But she wasn't there.

The mood inside seemed relaxed as the attendees exchanged smiles and hellos. Winston probably thought this horde of wild beasts was really just a gang of old friends delighted to see one another again in Paris. I knew better.

The agenda was concise. A review of the political situation and of the campaign. The real topic on everyone's lips didn't appear on paper at all. But there was absolutely no risk it would be forgotten.

The Boss was late. He was generally on time, though on occasion he waited until everyone was in place to make his entrance. A joyful din made of forced laughter and seemingly friendly pats on the back filled the room.

Then the Boss arrived and the room quickly fell silent. In his dark-blue suit, pinstripe shirt and blue tie, he looked like a president: serious, focused, and intelligent, but also friendly, with a broad smile on his face. His stature and penetrating yet kindly gaze made it seem like he was always entirely in control of himself and his surroundings.

For the first time in a very long time, I had no idea what he was going to say.

He began gently, thanking everyone for taking the time to come and apologizing for the short notice they had been given. His voice was steady. At the end of the introduction, after a quick glance around the room (I was always in the back so he could see me throughout), he dropped the first bombshell.

"Please forgive me for being late," he said, "but I was on the phone with our friend Marie-France Trémeau, and our conversation lasted longer than planned."

I was taken aback. I hadn't known that he had spoken to Trémeau and had no idea what they'd discussed. I had rarely felt so left out.

A sideways glance at Texier reassured me a little. I knew him by heart, and, though he was outwardly calm, I could tell from his face that he had had no idea either.

The Boss had obtained the desired effect. Both his partisans, who were the most ferociously opposed to Trémeau, and his declared adversaries were terrified. No one dared speak first. The meeting had taken a surreal turn. The Boss opened the floor to several vigorous calls for unity that danced around the real questions: Had the election been rigged? Would Trémeau run?

At last, someone stepped up. I was surprised because it was one of the youngest members of the committee. He had been serving as an MP for five years and had always been prudent, campaigning equally for the Boss and Trémeau, which was the sign of real ambition and a desire to stay the course. Indeed, without this second ingredient, ambition is just a vain flash in the pan. The talent and grit he had demonstrated at the National Assembly, his pretty face on TV, and his remarkable eloquence had earned him his seat at the table. I had, in fact, insisted we include him despite his reservations about the Boss because I felt it was best to win over the young wolves with bright futures.

"We're all talking about unity, friends, and I wholeheartedly agree with you about its importance. But, at the same time, unity is like love—it's more about actions than words."

The older members nodded fervently; others smiled.

"And over the past three days, our actions have been confusing," he went on. "I'm sorry to put my foot in my mouth, and I hope you'll excuse me for my inexperience which has probably led me to express myself too bluntly, but our voters, our party members, are disconcerted by what's going on at the moment. I am, of course, referring to these rumours of voter fraud. The primary was a brilliant democratic experience. It may have been imperfect and a tight race, but it enabled us to choose the party's candidate. We fought to explain that to our members, and I genuinely believe it. But now we're hearing that it was rigged? What are those who are relaying this rumour after? Defeat?"

The debate was underway now, and under favourable conditions for the Boss. I almost wished I had been the one to speak up.

Feeling attacked no doubt, Texier stood up. All eyes turned towards him. He could feel it, and I could tell how much he enjoyed it. "Acts of love are all well and good. But when they go hand in hand with shady betrayals, it's worth asking a few questions . . ."

Those who were reading between the lines might have seen an attack on the Boss who had once been known for his insatiable appetite for extramarital flings.

"No one here can question our devotion to unity within the party," Texier continued. "Marie-France Trémeau and all of those who campaigned for her during the primary, myself included, conceded the race to the current nominee."

I had to admit that he had balls. The choice of the term "current" was a thinly veiled barb. The murmur that arose was proof that it hadn't gone unnoticed.

"But I meet with party members, too," Texier went on. "I also talk to our voters. And what do they say? That they don't understand; that this whole affair is rather murky; that if we had used good old-fashioned paper ballots, we wouldn't be here. So, what would you have me tell them?"

"You could tell them the truth," the young MP replied with a smile. "That the vote was legitimate. Marie-France Trémeau lost. We have a candidate, and now we need to help him win."

There was a burst of laughter. He was good. I would definitely be using him for the campaign. If it continued . . .

"Of course we want our candidate to win," said another. "But *was* the vote legitimate? Are we certain of that?"

Everyone had turned towards the man who had just spoken, and they all seemed to be listening attentively. I could only see his back, but I recognized his voice. It had been a constant in my first years in parliamentary politics. He wasn't a Baron but an old wiseman, a former prime minister who commanded additional respect given his lengthy residence at the Hôtel de Matignon.

I couldn't believe he had spoken. He almost never did, to such an extent that people seemed to think that though he still attended meetings at over eighty years old, it was only to combat the boredom of his long retirement.

But I knew my political history well enough to know that his faint voice and friendly demeanour belied the talents of a first-rate orator that MPs from all parties had learned to fear.

"Unlike our young colleague, I am speaking to you with the wisdom that comes with old age. So, if my questions seem blunt, well, you know how old men get . . . I'm asking them myself because no one here would dare suggest that I have any sort of personal interest in the answer . . . You see, I don't plan to run in the next election. Unless, that is, you all think I should?"

Everyone laughed. The Boss smiled broadly, and I couldn't help but enjoy the moment.

"I'm asking these questions here," he continued, "because we're among friends and nothing that's said here will be repeated beyond these walls, right?"

Amusement all round.

"So, I'm asking you, my dear friend," he said, turning towards the Boss. "Was the primary legitimate? It's up to you to answer and to convince us, because you are our candidate and because you may soon be, I certainly hope so anyway, our president. You must answer because, by avoiding the topic, you're letting it get out of hand, to the point that it's not even about the question any more."

"You're asking me to prove that something didn't happen," objected the Boss. "That's not easy to do. If I remember rightly lawyers call it 'an impossible proof'."

"Your reply, old friend, is undoubtedly legally sound. But it's politically insufficient. You must find a way to ease the doubts of our political family first and foremost and of the French people, who won't allow you to hide behind legal precedents. If I may, when things get heated, no one gives a hoot about the law."

The wiseman was right. I was angry with myself for letting the Boss get bogged down like this. Texier was looking around the room as if to underscore the former prime minister's words. I didn't know if he was behind this speech, but he would certainly owe the old man.

The Boss had nodded. Without tensing up, he had jotted down a few words on the notepad in front of him, then continued calling on those who wished to speak. Since the most serious attendees had already spoken, it was now up to the remainder to split hairs. They seemed more committed to demonstrating their loyalties than to convincing anyone. Some of them were probably jockeying for whatever ministry they hoped to run after the election.

After what felt like an eternity, I realized it was time to wrap things up in some sort of positive way. It wasn't all-out war, but if the members of the committee left now, many of them would be happy to tell the press about the party's struggles and the current leadership's inability to stabilize things. The issues of dissension and doubt would dominate and unity would take a back seat.

Sensing better than anyone where things were heading, the Boss spoke up. "All right. I think everyone has had the opportunity to express themselves. I thank you for your honesty and your advice. They are more valuable to me than you know." He paused for a sip of water. There is no better way to captivate an audience. "I accept what some of you said so clearly: we need to talk about this rumour. I believe that the primary is beyond reproach. To the best of my knowledge, and until someone proves otherwise, the vote was legitimate and gave a clear result. Until I have proof to the contrary, that is the truth. And I believe that all those who spread rumours of this kind are—unconsciously, I hope—helping Vital."

The Boss's determination was magnificent. Each attendee felt like he was looking right at them.

"That said," he continued, "I've heard you this evening. We need to prove that there was no fraud. I would like to re-mind you that I didn't organize this election, and that I even took steps to exclude myself from the oversight committee. You should also remember that when it was decided that the vote would take place online, no one objected. I didn't select the companies in charge of the vote either. And no one con-tested the makeup of the organizational or oversight com-mittees. I'm going back over the facts, because I don't want anyone to get a biased picture of the events . . ."

The room was silent except for the Boss's calm, firm voice.

"But I understand that we still need to do more. That's why I have made two decisions, which will, I believe, unify our party. First, I'm going to prove that our primary was irreproachable. My team is working on it as we speak, and I would like them to present their findings at our next meeting to prove that nothing suspicious took place."

The Boss's eyes landed on me and, though my vision was still blurry, I could tell that we were going to need to come up with something concrete very quickly unless I wanted another tongue lashing.

"The second decision is, I believe, an important one. I have decided to ask Marie-France Trémeau to be my running mate. If I'm elected, she will be my prime minister. She has the necessary abilities, qualities, and talent. It has become very clear that we need to come together now to ensure the first round goes smoothly. Marie-France and I were adversaries in the primary, but we have always retained respect and esteem for one another."

I couldn't believe it. I wasn't sure who this was most humiliating for: the Boss, Trémeau, Texier, who was clearly in a state of disbelief himself, or me since I was realizing that the most important campaign decisions were now being made without me.

"I believe that this ticket will unite our organic electorate and reach many voters beyond as well. Of course, none of this is official yet, and I must ask you to keep it to yourselves for now. Marie-France and I need to think about the best way to announce what is, I believe, a first for our party, but I think we have started to build a solid foundation upon which we can win this election together."

The silence that followed the Boss's announcement was quickly broken by a burst of applause. The committee members were delighted. They had feared we were heading for civil war, but instead they were getting a sacred union. Reassured, they could go back to their districts, where they would tell anyone who would listen how much they had contributed to this brilliant solution.

The Boss had brought the meeting to a close. At least half of the participants had made their way towards him to congratulate him, while the others had quickly left the room to optimize their time in front of the cameras outside. MPs are drawn to news cameras like moths to a flame.

I was still dumbstruck, but I tried to hide my surprise as I smiled and had a friendly word with each of the MPs I passed.

Outside HQ, the MPs were commenting on the evening's events. Behind the cameras, I could see Marilyn talking to a few reporters. She hadn't been in the room for the announcement, but there she was chatting calmly with the journalists who were undoubtedly peppering her with difficult questions. I realized she had known. The Boss had told her. He had let her know before the meeting. Probably so she could lay the groundwork with the press outside. Definitely because he trusted her.

As for me, I was alone in the lobby, thinking about going up to my office, where Winston was waiting and working, when the young MP who had been the first to speak up clapped his hand on my shoulder.

"In times like these," he said, "it's easy to understand how your boss is *the* Boss."

I smiled warmly and patted him on the back in return. What else could I do?

39

Tuesday 9ᵗʰ March, 6:35 p.m.

I was annoyed with myself and annoyed about being annoyed with myself.

I had been paralyzed after the committee meeting. Furious about being kept out of the loop, furious that the Boss had trusted Marilyn enough to tell her, and even more furious to be so hung up on it when, in the end, the Boss had come out on top.

I had managed to hide my anger until everyone had left HQ. I couldn't bear the thought of making a spectacle of myself, and it would have cost me dearly. But, as soon as I could, I went out for a walk.

After all, it was almost spring.

Paris was about to enjoy the marvellous season where the terraces are full of flowers, skirts get shorter, and necklines lower. Strolling through the streets on the lookout for pretty women with whom I would exchange little more than a flirty glance generally helped me to forget the less glamorous aspects of my profession. I forbade myself to take a closer look at the mechanism that led me to turn to strangers for the approval that the person who knew me best seemed to have refused me.

The Boss's tactic was bold. It had the advantage of shifting some of the pressure on us over to Trémeau and her entourage. No official announcement would be made for the time being, of course. I saw right through his intentions. He would dangle Matignon in Trémeau's face, share the news with a few people while swearing them to secrecy, and count on a few leaks, which would avoid any formal commitment on his part. Then he would choose the best time to make the official announcement—or not—depending on what I uncovered in the meantime.

It was brilliant.

If she kept hinting at a possible candidacy, *she* would be cast as the divider and the dissident. She was now in a position where she had no choice but to campaign for the Boss, prove her loyalty, and keep a low profile.

People would forget all about the fraud rumour, moving on to the perfect ticket created by the unlikely alliance of the Statesman and the clever politician, between the wise old man and the ambitious young woman, the cultured intellectual and the somewhat populist maiden.

But his strategy also had drawbacks. First, he had been forced into it. I'm sure that he would have gladly kept Trémeau at a healthy distance during and after the campaign if he'd had any choice in the matter. He had only included her to neutralize her. It would be difficult, now, to give her nothing after the election.

Moreover, once it had leaked, the Boss's announcement would place Trémeau in the limelight for a few days, allowing her to capitalize on the campaign and paint herself as an official candidate for prime minister. But what was worse, I worried that Trémeau might present the offer as a concession granted under pressure. For an ambitious woman who wanted to be number one someday, ostentatiously refusing an offer to be number two in the name of virtue and conviction would be a magnificent play. Once the seven days that separated us from the candidacy deadline were up, I was afraid the Boss might find himself handling an even more damaging political crisis than before.

As I pondered all this, I tried to convince myself that he must have considered the risks before moving forward. He wouldn't have called Trémeau and made the offer without thinking long and hard about it. But with whom? I knew him well enough to know he did his best thinking when he could bounce ideas off someone else. That was one of the things I liked best about my job, actually: knowing I was behind his ideas or had helped to refine them or, more rarely, had encouraged him to put them to bed.

But maybe he had done it all on impulse. I knew he could be rash on occasion.

I found myself staring at the Louvre. Lost in my thoughts, I had walked aimlessly to the heart of Paris, to the very place where much more brutal political intrigues than this one had shaped the history of France. Great flocks of tourists invaded this part of the city as always. I was suddenly desperate to sit down and watch the world around me. I noticed a promising café whose outside tables, located beneath the Palais-Royal and across from the Comédie-Française, seemed like the perfect place to enjoy the show. I sat down and ordered a glass of Chablis.

40

Tuesday 9th March, 8:11 p.m.

I could have spent hours on that terrace. Though the sun had set, it was still relatively warm outside. The suited waiters were the best part of the show. Feigning the cynical arrogance Parisians are known for every time a foreigner sat down, they were clearly invested in embodying the best aspects of café culture. They were friendly with the regulars, unimpressed by the powerful, rude with slow or impolite customers, and flirty with pretty women. The Chablis was perfectly chilled and the people around me seemed happy. The tourists commented on the marvels they'd seen at the Louvre as they rested their weary feet and the members of the Constitutional Council, which was just around the corner, studied the finer points of the decisions they were considering. Much of it was in foreign languages and none of it was comprehensible, but the din it created was not without its charms.

The Chablis was working its magic. I wasn't happy, but my bad mood was lifting as I enjoyed the hustle and bustle of Paris at night.

Two tables away, an elegant woman was enjoying a drink alone. She was reading a book, but it hadn't captivated her enough to keep her from glancing insistently around her, and then, I thought, even more insistently at me.

Maybe she had noticed I was watching her.

She was beautiful in the way women over fifty often are. Elegant, intelligent, classy. Her greying hair betrayed her age but framed her fine features. She was wearing an extremely understated dark-green skirt suit that contrasted starkly with her quirky heels. I couldn't make out the title of her book.

I also couldn't tell if she was smiling or if the slight folds at the corners of her eyes and mouth were due to something other than my handsomeness. Maybe I was seeing what I wanted to see in the encroaching darkness.

I was hesitant to strike up a conversation with her. My ego had taken a beating over the past few days, and I wasn't sure I would be able to come back from a brush-off.

But I was certain she was smiling at me now. And it was a lovely smile. An inviting smile that encouraged me to make a move.

Still firmly seated at my table, I checked my mobile. As I feared, everyone on the planet—or at least everyone who was somewhat interested in the upcoming presidential election—had been trying to reach me. I was going to have to get back on my horse and make up for lost time. This break couldn't last.

But at the same time, I tried to discreetly make out the physique of the beautiful stranger. I quickly compiled a list of nearby restaurants where I could take her for dinner. There were plenty of cosy places in the neighbourhood where we could talk quietly. My flat wasn't far, but I couldn't just invite a woman like her over without any preamble. I knew far too well the impression it made on normal, sane people. It was big and usually clean, but it was very empty. I didn't live there, really. I ate out and slept elsewhere—either at campaign hotels or at the flats of occasional mistresses. No memories. No storied objects. Empty.

She was really looking at me.

What could I offer? A dinner during which I'd tell her the tales of an apparatchik on a campaign? A drink at hers, if she lived in Paris, or at mine, amid the emptiness, which I found both comforting and terrifying? A night in a hotel room? What would I say in the morning? Or even later tonight?

I needed to boost my confidence, not my anxiety. I needed something simple. Not a serious relationship. I wanted commitment but needed freedom. I didn't know what I wanted.

But she was gorgeous. And she was definitely smiling at me.

In another life, I could have lived with a woman like that. I would have had to choose another profession, using my talent for tactics for something other than politics. Corporate banking? Strategic consulting? I would have been bored, but I would have made much more money and I would have been able to build something. A family maybe. A love story, certainly. Maybe with someone like her, who knows?

It was too late. The beautiful stranger had grown weary of waiting. She was gathering her things and putting them away in her bag. In a few minutes, she would be gone. On her way to her dinner, her friends, her family, or her own lonely flat.

It was too late for me, too. I had chosen politics. I was married to the Boss.

And I had lost my appetite.

41

I had been at HQ for nearly an hour already. I had taken a sleeping pill the night before, but I had turned to them too often over the course of my life to expect it to work on demand. It would probably start working in the middle of the day—a ticking time bomb that would strike when I needed to focus the most.

Noticing my open door, Winston stepped into my office. He had a big mug of coffee in his left hand and the morning papers under his right arm. There were already allusions to the content of the "confidential" debate from the day before.

"Do you think Trémeau will accept?" he asked.

"I really don't know," I said. "And I'm not even sure that's the right question . . ."

The kid let it slide. He knew I was in a bad mood.

"What she wants," I continued, "is to be France's president, tomorrow, next week, next year, someday. The only real question is what will she do now to move one step closer to that goal, given the context created by the Boss's brilliant offer."

"In other words," Winston said dryly, "will she accept or not? I don't mean to sound cocky, but that's exactly what I said."

"Hardly," I retorted. "What I mean is that her answer is of little importance. What matters is that she wants to be president and that she won't give up on that. If she can be president tomorrow rather than waiting five or ten years, she won't pass up the chance! I would bet that, whatever her answer, she'll keep campaigning under the radar. I'm sure of it. I can feel it. I know her and Texier. They're perfectly content to say one thing and do the opposite!"

"A bit like you?" he ventured.

"Not at all!"

I was annoyed again. It was harder to laugh off the kid's sarcasm after being subjected to the Boss's contempt.

Winston left to get back to work. I turned on the radio to listen to a scheduled interview with Marie-France Trémeau.

> *"There are rumours that you plan to run as a maverick candidate, without the party's nomination . . ."*
>
> *"Maverick? I can't say I care for that term. And who's the real maverick in this whole thing? Many of my friends have encouraged me to share my ideas with the French people and let them decide, and that plan has its merits. If I were certain that my ideas would be at the heart of the elected candidate's agenda and that I would play a pivotal role, things could be quite different."*
>
> *"But, Mrs Trémeau, you can't organize a presidential campaign at the drop of a hat!"*
>
> *"Don't you worry about me."*

Even on the radio I could see her smile. As I turned it off and sat back in my chair, the Boss dropped in unannounced.

"Where did you disappear to last night?" he asked with a smile.

"I went for a walk, to think."

"Are you angry?"

"Angry? No. Since I couldn't think about it beforehand, I had to think about it after the event, that's all."

"So, what's your conclusion?"

"I think the ball's in your court. Everyone sees you as the president now, and her as number two. Paradoxically, you used the situation to take her down a notch. It's a brilliant trap. If she refuses, everyone will blame her. If she accepts, she'll be muzzled. Of course, I would have preferred for you to choose a prime minister you can trust, someone you could work with. But it is what it is. If she accepts Matignon, it's a de facto acceptance of her defeat in the primary."

The Boss smiled. "Precisely."

"What bothers me is that our hands are tied now," I continued.

"But I can still roll things back. If she goes too far, it will be easy to say that she's putting herself before the country. If she still decides to run, she will be weakened. I suspect she's had her signatures for quite some time. I certainly would have had them in her shoes. But you know what bothers me? It's that, in the meantime, Vital is campaigning away, focusing his attacks on us. He's already got his sights set on the second round and we're not even sure about the first yet. I'm afraid we might not be able to make up his lead. In any case, we'll know for sure about Trémeau very soon: 17th March is just around the corner. After that we'll be able to focus on what really matters. Once that date has passed, she can do all the sabre-rattling she likes, it won't make any difference.

17th March. The deadline for gathering the five hundred signatures from local officials and handing them in to the Constitutional Council.

17th March. One week to go.

42

Thursday 11ᵗʰ March, 4:03 p.m.

It may have felt like spring in Paris, but in the mountains, it was still the depths of winter. The snow and cold persisted, and I wondered if I had been right to advise the Boss to choose the Glières Plateau as the destination for his first campaign trip after the emergency campaign committee meeting two days earlier.

Ever since a former French president had chosen this site of a major stand by the Resistance during World War Two as the destination of his annual pilgrimage, Les Glières had become even more symbolic. For some people, it was the most iconic place associated with the Resistance and their heroism and courage in the face of German occupation. For others it was that and more: a reminder of our duty to disobey unjust orders and a call to a new kind of resistance. That said, for most French people, Les Glières was the Alps, and the Alps meant skiing and the Tour de France.

To each his own.

The emergency speech drafted by Démosthène was understated and elegant. The Boss could hardly turn up and hope to appropriate the image and spirit of the Resistance and the bravery of the four hundred maquis fighters who had stood their ground against over three thousand German soldiers and several hundred Vichy militiamen. Despite his many decades of experience, the Boss had maintained a fair amount of restraint, which served him well.

"Malraux said everything there is to say about Les Glières. Today, those men's courage should inspire silence, consideration, and respect rather than agitation and revendication," the Boss began solemnly.

A bit pandering, maybe, but well chosen for those on the other side of the aisle who were openly accusing him of appropriation.

"No one knows what they themselves would have done back then," he continued. "No one can be totally certain that they would have made the right decisions. No one can claim to have belonged to the Resistance. For each of us, the moment of truth is the moment when we have to make a choice. Faced with the Occupation, the men of Les Glières chose to fight. They weren't necessarily all French. They didn't necessarily all hold the same political beliefs—indeed some of them had been targets since long before the Germans barrelled into France. But in Les Glières, they were not communists, not Spaniards, not former French soldiers nor Savoyard men on the run from STO forced labour camps. In Les Glières, there were only free men and their choice to fight—a choice which will define them for all of eternity. We are all the product of our choices when faced with events we may or may not understand, may or may not accept, and may or may not fear . . ."

The five hundred supporters who had welcomed the Boss were hanging on his every word as they tried to keep warm. Marilyn was shooting me dirty looks, apparently worried that the Boss might catch a cold. With every word, a column of condensation rose slowly from his lips. The image was even more striking since he was just in his suit, having refused his coat. Standing tall in the crisp air, he looked young and determined. Those around him who had chosen to bundle themselves up looked a little ridiculous in comparison.

"We owe the men of Les Glières something. Like them, we must make our choices. That's why I wanted to come here to say to you all that I take full responsibility for my choices. I can't hope that everyone will agree with them, but I can guarantee you that, regardless of the events I come up against, I will make coherent, transparent choices that I will stand by. Now is the time to act!"

The audience was moved. The press had all the images and quotes they needed. They would return to Paris frozen to the bone, but at least they had got their material. Everything was going to plan.

Now that the speech was over and the flowers had been laid at the foot of the monument, things were about to get real. The journalists would start hurling questions at the Boss any second. They were all dying to get something from him on the latest political news. I could tell Marilyn was ready to pounce.

The Boss had climbed down from the stage and was making his way towards the crowd to shake hands. The photos would be fantastic. Schumacher was standing a few metres back, ready to hand the Boss his coat.

The first question rang out as soon as the Boss had finished his stroll among the crowd. He was still smiling.

"Rumour has it you reached out to Marie-France Trémeau to join your ticket?"

The Boss smiled broadly at three local officials who couldn't believe he was walking towards them much less speaking to them. He pretended not to hear the reporter. You can't refuse to answer journalists, but you have every right to act a little hard of hearing around them. You just have to know how to put on a good show. The Boss had a real gift in that area.

"Is the offer you made Marie-France Trémeau an admission of the fact that the primary was rigged?"

The Boss smiled warmly at the mayor of Entremont's twelve-year-old granddaughter and asked her if she had studied the Battle of Les Glières at school. The girl's mother and grandfather both teared up with pride. The Boss knew exactly what he was doing.

"Are you worried Mrs Trémeau might throw her hat in the ring?"

The Boss still apparently hadn't heard the question and had turned towards the nearest mountains, to the west, as the low late winter sun shone brightly over the plateau. I heard him ask the name of several peaks, which provided the perfect opportunity for the photographers to snap a few fantastic pictures of a candidate of the people in the golden March sunlight, holding out his arm towards what could easily be interpreted as the future. The Boss's mastery had reached new heights. For a man of letters, he had quite a flair for showmanship.

The questions kept coming, but the Boss still wouldn't answer. Marilyn seemed calm as she stood next to him. This little game continued for nearly ten minutes, after which he turned towards the cameras. All of the questions had been asked, so he could now choose which ones to answer.

"I came here," he said, "because I admire the men who fought during the war. I came here because these men gave their lives for our country, for our freedom, and for our democracy. I came here, because the people here have a better understanding of the fact that, when faced with great challenges, we must be brave and united. I didn't come here to play politics. That would be disrespectful to those who fought in the battle of Les Glières . . ."

He glanced at Marilyn, who nodded to let him know he had done well and that he could wrap things up.

"The Glières Plateau reminds us that France needs all of its talents. I fully intend to welcome and support all of the talented people who join me. My friends, of course, but others as well . . ."

They had their declaration. The Boss had managed to make it seem like he was saying something meaningful without really committing to anything. He had simply opened the floor to his friends, enemies, and all the rest to comment and explain his words. In any case, he was once again at the centre of the campaign.

"As for the rest, you really must let me keep a few surprises for the weeks ahead! Otherwise, you'll stop listening to me and following my every move . . ."

Everyone laughed as he concluded his short speech.

The operation was a success. Now I could get on with the real goal of our little jaunt to the mountains.

43

Thursday 11ᵗʰ March, 5:44 p.m.

I was sitting in the back seat of the roomy sedan we had rented for the occasion with Marilyn on my left. A local party official was driving. The Boss had stayed back with the Haute-Savoie MPs and would fly home to Paris.

To leave the plateau and drop Marilyn off in time for her train, we took a winding road back to Annecy. Our driver was so used to hairpin turns and treacherous cliffs that he seemed to be enjoying himself speeding and overtaking the ridiculous tourists who felt it necessary to keep under the speed limit. He kept saying again and again that we'd be on time for the train.

Marilyn was taking the train back because she hated flying.

I had claimed I was staying in the region so I could stop in Lyon and prepare for an upcoming campaign visit and for the legislative elections. The excuse was more than plausible since the city had just become a powder keg for our party. Everyone knew that the intraparty animosity there was so deep-rooted that it dated back to before the primary, before the Boss, and, as far as I could tell, before the party itself.

"Coming here just shows the Boss following in previous presidents' footsteps when what he needs to do is innovate. He needs to come off as a new man, not just another cog in the machine," said Marilyn. Her bad mood hadn't lifted. She grumbled on without even looking at me. I wasn't looking at her either. I was busy keeping my one good eye trained on the road to keep from getting sick. "And if he comes down with a cold in two days, where will that leave us?! I just don't understand why you suggested this place. There were barely five hundred people in the audience. It still feels like the dead of winter here! People will think the pictures are from months ago!"

"I can't say if he'll get ill in a few days, but I can tell you that if our friend keeps driving like this, neither of us will be around long enough to find out."

I could feel my stomach churning and my pulse starting to race. My salivary glands were on overdrive. Marilyn's presence could have explained all that, but given our current situation it was more likely a sign that I was about to vomit.

"You could have given me a heads-up!" she continued.

She certainly didn't lack cheek. I should have stayed calm, but the pressure that had built up over the past few weeks had to escape somehow. I was tired of letting people walk all over me.

"Christ! You've got to be kidding me! Like you ever tell me anything! Did you let me know before the Boss made a major announcement? Did you tell me what your buddy the Major is up to at the moment? And what about your cosy friend, the journalist at *Le Matin*, where incidentally you claimed you knew no one—did you tell me you were sleeping with him? Jesus!"

That made me feel better. It startled our driver, though. He sat behind the wheel, his mouth agape, unsure whether to look at us in the rear-view mirror or keep his eyes on the road. As for Marilyn, she was furious. Still and silent, she pursed her lips and clenched her fists. Out of the corner of my eye, I could see her clenching her jaw as well—a sign of extreme tension.

No one dared say anything else, so we drove on in silence until we reached the train station in Annecy.

★ ★ ★

As Marilyn got out, she turned to me and said, "You're such an arsehole. When the Boss asks me not to say anything, I don't. It's a straightforward rule, and one that applies to everyone. If you followed more rules, maybe the Major would still tell you things, and maybe you could explain your role in this whole mess. As for my love life, that's none of your business and never will be again!"

I didn't have a comeback. The driver, who had heard everything, waited until she was out of sight, then turned to me. "She's a fiery one!" he said enviously. "Never a dull moment with her, I bet!"

I was rarely bored, that much was true. But I was starting to feel rather tired.

44

Thursday 11th March, 11:04 p.m.

A few hours earlier, I had been fighting the urge to throw up as we hurtled down the mountain. Now my throat was parched, and I would have given a year of my life for a cool beer.

Luckily, Winston was stationed in the car as our lookout. If we got caught, at least he would be in the clear.

My legs were shaking and I felt like there was a rock in the pit of my stomach. I didn't dare think about what would happen if Gaspard Caligny, the brother of a former Budget Minister, and myself, the right-hand man of a presidential candidate, were apprehended breaking into the flat of a guy who had died a few days earlier.

Deep down, I knew perfectly well that I shouldn't be there. Every ounce of reason in my body was shouting at me to leave and take Winston with me. There was no need to worry about his uncle—he knew how to handle himself.

He was the one who had insisted we do this. I had come up with the idea of a trip to Grenoble, because it was clear that the Snag had come from this strange city. I hate Grenoble. Located deep in its valley, the city is too cold in the winter and too hot in the summer. Its only redeeming feature is that it produced Stendhal and Champollion. In my mind, the trip was just about gleaning more information regarding Pinguet's accident and the reasons that had led Mukki to begin working for the local government here. Since Mukki had wanted to talk to us before he died, we were starting with him.

Winston had left the day before, officially to help with the logistics of the trip. He had gladly accepted his mission, though he did complain a bit when I told him his uncle would accompany him. As I saw it, no matter what happened, Gaspard would have his nephew's back, and given the violence that had plagued the campaign since we'd hit the Snag, I felt teaming up with a man who was significantly stronger than the kid and me put together was the right move.

Yet another ingenious idea! As I should have anticipated, the Godfather ran things as he saw fit, and, after exhausting legal options for getting information on Mukki, he had moved on to more unsavoury techniques.

I had argued weakly that there wouldn't be anything worth our time at Mukki's house, and that the detectives working his case had undoubtedly already cleaned the place out. I must not have been particularly convincing since here I was, on a cold March night in La Tronche, just steps away from Mukki's house, whispering with Gaspard, who, I could tell from his bright eyes and precise gestures, was not embarking on his first break-in.

Mukki had spent the last years of his life on a soulless housing estate like thousands of others in France. This one was in La Tronche, but it could have been anywhere given the identical architecture of the houses all squashed in together side by side. Housing estates. If I ever decide to get my doctorate in political science, I'll write my dissertation on the political impact of these detached homes from the 1970s onwards, and their role in the decline of communism and the simultaneous rise of the far-right National Front.

The small, white or beige stucco houses sat in tidy lines. The only thing that changed from one to another was the colour of the letterbox—where the owners were clearly free to channel all their creativity.

It was dark outside. The streetlights were dim. Inside, lights were still on behind a few shuttered windows—proof that a shameful minority went to bed after eleven o'clock.

We couldn't see anyone, but we felt like everyone was watching us from their kitchen windows through the white lace curtains.

As we walked quietly down the deserted street, Gaspard suddenly pointed to a narrow path that ran along the side of one of the houses to the gardens. "This way," he whispered firmly. The Godfather was as comfortable breaking and entering as most people are in their own lounges. He moved stealthily, silently pushing aside branches and noiselessly stepping through flower beds. I did my best to follow him, but I was about as discreet as a team of majorettes at a parade.

When we reached a set of French doors, Gaspard stopped. In his hand, he held a small instrument which he used to quickly and silently cut a hole in the glass. And then, as if it was the simplest thing in the world, he slipped his hand inside and opened the door to Mukki's house. I couldn't believe how easy it had been. In less than five minutes, we were inside.

My eyes, or rather, my eye, was getting used to the darkness. I couldn't see much, but at least I could make my way through the rooms without bumping into the furniture.

The house was full to the brim. Piles of books, DVDs, and magazines covered much of the floor space. The table hadn't been cleared.

Gaspard had a tiny but powerful torch. He was methodically exploring the house, beginning with the drawers and then moving on to the piles of papers. He told me not to touch anything. The house wasn't at all what I had expected. In my imagination, Mukki lived surrounded by material things. I was surprised to learn that his "things" were mostly books and culture.

The sound of a car outside pulled me from my thoughts. The rock in the pit of my stomach felt like it had just doubled in size. I stopped instantly, hardly daring to breathe. Gaspard did the same, accompanying his silence with a firm hand gesture for me to keep quiet.

The white car drove slowly past the kitchen window. Probably a neighbour out late. Drops of sweat were starting to pearl on my brow.

Gaspard had returned to what must have been Mukki's desk. I saw him jot down a few lines.

"Did you find something?" I asked.

"Maybe. Phone numbers. We'll check," he whispered back as he continued rifling through Mukki's things.

I was pretty useless. In fact, I wondered why I had decided to accompany the Godfather in the first place. A taste for risk? My conscience, which kept me from letting Winston's uncle take all the risk when it was my responsibility? A gut feeling that going with Gaspard myself was the only way to keep his nephew out of it?

Reassured by the false alarm, or maybe encouraged by Gaspard's example, I made my way into the master bedroom alone. A large television sat across from Mukki's bed. There wasn't much on the walls: just a few photographs of snow-covered mountains and a bulletin board loaded with pictures of people whose faces I couldn't make out.

I didn't immediately realize that the reason I started to recognize them as I moved closer was mostly because a light from outside had brightened the room. The car had pulled up so quietly that I had neither heard nor seen it.

I was completely absorbed in the photographs. Mukki was in every picture, standing alongside notable politicians for the most part. The pictures must have been taken at campaign or party events. In each one, Mukki stood smiling, his arm around a minister's or MP's waist or shoulder. I had seen tons of photographs like these: the Boss had always graciously agreed to pose with his fans and party members—with anyone who asked, really.

I stepped closer and then stood stock still.

In the centre of the board, two photographs stared back at me. I gaped at them. My heart began to race and I felt my legs try to give out.

Suddenly, something landed on my shoulder. I stifled a cry of terror, which would have been silenced by the hand plastered across my mouth anyway.

Gaspard had silently followed me into the bedroom.

"The car from earlier. Colour, make and model?" he asked.

How was I supposed to know? I tried to think, but I could hardly breathe and all my muscles were tense.

"White," I replied. "Big and white."

Gaspard's hand had loosened only long enough for me to answer. I felt like I was suffocating, but at least I was quiet.

"We have to go then," he ordered. "We have company."

On the way out, I quickly removed the two pictures from the board. I was afraid that my legs might not obey my orders. Gaspard had a knife in one hand and used the other to guide me.

We were still in the lounge when I heard a key in the lock on the front door. My heart stopped. This was it. The Boss was history. His campaign would never recover. Gaspard pulled harder on my arm.

A second later, we were in the garden and he told me to run. I sprinted like a chased rabbit, without even checking that he was behind me. The light in the lounge came on just as I climbed over the hedge. Gaspard jumped through it.

We were silent again. I was standing behind a tree and Gaspard lay on the ground. The men were looking for something in the house, and clearly weren't trying to be discreet. They would see the hole in the window soon enough and figure out that we had searched the house, too.

Gaspard stood up without a sound and came close. "When they scream, we make a mad dash for the car, okay?"

How could he know they were going to scream? I didn't understand, but immediately nodded. I was eager to show him that I would do exactly what he told me to do to get out of there.

He offered a relaxed smile and I noticed that he no longer had his knife.

I was just starting to breathe normally again when I heard someone inside the house cry out in rage and pain.

Gaspard tapped me on the back, and I beat my personal best for the two hundred metre sprint. I didn't even know I was capable of running that fast. I should have smoked less and taken my chances as an athlete when I was younger.

The car where Winston was waiting for us felt like Noah's Ark at that moment. Surprised to see us running for our lives, the kid put his foot down, and we raced back to Grenoble.

Focused on the road and on the rear-view mirror to check we weren't being followed, he said nothing for at least five minutes. Meanwhile I tried to gather my thoughts and catch my breath.

Gaspard was in the passenger seat. He wasn't even breathing hard. For him, it was over.

"What did you do with the knife?" I asked.

He smiled as he turned around, his eyes bright. "Nothing too terrible. I knew that they would make sure the kitchen was empty and no one was behind them before moving deeper into the house. So, I left them a little practical joke I learned in the Foreign Legion. You place a knife in just the right spot and the guy who opens the door cuts open his hand. It works every time."

Gaspard chuckled to himself, and Winston was laughing outright. What a family of nut jobs. I was angry with them for putting me at such risk.

At the same time, I now held a photograph that was proof that Gaspard had been right.

It was a lovely picture. Mukki and Senator Pinguet's son, both tanned and smiling in matching aprons. Behind them I could make out the mountains and the Grenoble cable car.

I was trying to analyse the implications of my discovery when Gaspard pulled a piece of paper folded in three from his pocket and held it out to me. It bore the local government letterhead and was addressed to Mukki and signed by Vital: *Senator Pinguet let me know you were interested in a position. He praised your professionalism, which you consistently displayed during your time at your previous positions. I am pleased to inform you . . .*

Senator Pinguet also knew Mukki. That deceitful old man had lied to me. And if he'd lied about that, he could have been lying about everything. He didn't only know him—he had got him hired by the local government. The question was why?

"Just an hour later and we would have been too late," said Gaspard.

"Too late?"

"Yes, they were quicker than usual, but still not fast enough!"

"Who?"

"The police, of course."

"The police?"

"Yeah, you know, the guys who are running the investigation for the Ministry of the Interior. For your friend Vital essentially . . ."

The race against the clock had begun.

In my jacket pocket, I could feel the other picture I had found. A picture whose existence I had shared with no one. I had removed it from the bulletin board and taken it with me. I didn't want anyone to see it. Honestly, I would have rather not seen it myself. It was a picture of the Boss arm-in-arm with Mukki.

45

In a French presidential campaign, garnering five hundred signatures from local elected officials is an inescapable first step.

This sponsorship procedure was introduced to keep dilettante candidates from diluting the vote, though experience quickly revealed that handing this responsibility to local officials was a rather pointless endeavour. With nearly 500,000 local elected officials (here's at least one area where France was and will be for quite some time world champions), the process narrowed it down further, so only about 45,000—mayors, MPs, and regional and départemental officials—could sponsor a candidate. The 36,000 mayors (yet another world record) held a significant majority in this exclusive club, and among them, rural mayors (over 30,000) accounted for two-thirds of the potential signatories. As a result, people started incorrectly referring to the "mayors' signatures".

Of the 30,000 rural mayors, the vast majority were independents, which made some of them highly influenceable (for any candidate willing to drop by to see them in person and avoid talking policy) and others perfectly intransigent (refusing to compromise their political neutrality by supporting any candidate).

The "major" candidates had no trouble obtaining their five hundred signatures. We had had them for quite some time.

Nearly four thousand, actually, not including the ones that were sent directly to the Constitutional Council despite our suggestion to send them to us. The official procedure called for local officials to send their signed sponsorship forms directly to the Constitutional Council, which counted and verified them. Nevertheless, we had asked our friends to send them to HQ so we would know who had signed and who hadn't and be able to thank or remind people accordingly. But some of them had undoubtedly ignored our suggestion and sent their forms directly to the Council. We would never know their names, and they would go on to complain that they hadn't received a thank you letter from the Boss.

But smaller candidates never knew if they had enough signatures to compete in the first round until the last minute. Those who had been out in the field collecting them one by one from village to village for the past year brought them to the Council themselves, but they still didn't know how many signed forms had arrived without their knowledge.

The total number of sponsors obtained by a candidate was never published. Nor were the names of all of the sponsors— only five hundred randomly selected from among each candidate's partisans. It was another anomaly of the system to allow certain sponsors to remain anonymous and not others, depending on chance. But the potential for anonymity was probably important in convincing sponsors for certain "undesirable" candidates.

Over the years, I had learned all of the tricks relating to the five hundred signatures. This year, I had asked several of our trustworthy supporters to sign blank forms so I could use them at the last minute to help my young right-wing environmentalist and my eccentric leftist get in the race, to take a few votes from Vital.

I had also added a check or other markings to a few sponsorship forms that had arrived for the Boss from extremists or other unsavoury characters. This would invalidate them and prevent their names from being associated with the campaign.

And then there was my masterstroke. Since there was no formal declaration to be made to run for president, nor letter, nor anything at all from the candidate, I decided to sow the seeds of chaos on the left by introducing a silly but problematic candidacy: that of a former socialist presidential candidate who had left the political scene and would undoubtedly be very surprised to find his name on the list of official candidates.

I had managed to get five hundred blank sponsorship forms signed by friendly elected officials who weren't worried about their names being published since they were not planning to run for office again. I then filled in the name of the candidate that I wanted to include in the first round without his knowledge. The manoeuvre would be easy to counter in practical terms (no campaign, no ballots in polling places) but it would cause a media frenzy for a few days. The press would have to cite his name every time in the list of candidates, and Vital's team would be forced to explain it again and again. Nothing decisive, but a sizable obstacle nonetheless.

The Boss had found my move hilarious.

Four hours before the deadline for handing in sponsorship forms, I stepped out of a car in front of the Constitutional Council on Rue de Montpensier behind the Palais-Royal with my stack of four thousand forms. I had warned the civil servants I was coming, to make sure they would have time to count the forms and give me a receipt. It took nearly forty-five minutes while I waited in the antechamber. When it was done, the man who handed me the receipt told me that the Boss was the candidate with the most sponsors. He would never share that information with anyone else, but I fully intended to make sure the anecdote was leaked. There is no such thing as a small victory. My only worry was that he may have said the same thing to Vital's guy . . .

Some of the other candidates' representatives were there, and some candidates had even come themselves: the simple fact that they had garnered enough signatures was a victory in and of itself, which gave them access to unimagin-able publicity completely at odds with their real level of influence.

I smiled as I saw my eccentric leftist parade down the steps for the press. He walked past me and pretended not to recognize me. He was a smart eccentric, and I was rather pleased with my move. When you spent an hour with him, he was convincing, but when you spent two it was hard not to take him for a madman. Luckily, most people would never get that far. He would steal tens of thousands of votes from Vital—maybe more.

My young environmentalist was there too, trumpeting for all who would listen that environmentalism was not an issue for the right or for the left, but a cause to unite all of society. But I knew all too well that the voters she managed to convince for the first round would have a hard time voting for Vital in the second. Good enough for me.

My sources at the Constitutional Council led me to believe that the other expected candidates had all succeeded too: the Green Giant, the Lefty, the Radical, the Centrist, Vercingetorix, the Fascist, and of course Vital. There were also a few cause-based candidates: a young woman fighting for animal rights and an idealist who wanted to do away with countries and replace them with a global government (I would probably have voted for him if I didn't work for the Boss). There were thirteen candidates in all.

Twelve men (and women) to beat.

46

Pleased with myself for pulling it all off, I left the Constitutional Council and made my way to the bar I had enjoyed the previous week. It was a bit early for a glass of Chablis, but a coffee would do.

On my way there, I suddenly jumped behind a column. I had just spotted Texier sitting on the terrace of the same café with a pile of documents on the table in front of him and his mobile glued to his ear.

It made my blood boil: Trémeau had the signatures and Texier was about to hand them in. For a moment, I was tempted to snatch the precious forms off the table and run off with them. But the satisfaction of an unlikely success in this perilous endeavour seemed small in comparison to the ridiculousness of a probable failure.

I opted for confrontation.

"What are you doing here?" I asked.

"I'm waiting for you to keep your promise," replied Texier.

"Our promise?"

"Yes. Everyone is saying that Marie-France will be prime minister, but no one has officially announced as much. If no one does, I'll hand in her signatures. It's that simple."

I had two hours ahead of me. For the moment, regardless of my feelings, I had to appease him somehow. I asked him for an hour and managed to reach the Boss almost immediately.

"She has the signatures," I informed him. "I'm outside the Constitutional Council and Texier is here, too, ready to hand them in."

"And you can't restrain him on your own?" asked the Boss.

"No I can't," I answered, surprised by his reply. "It looks like it's decision time."

"I won't let her force my hand. I will not make any announcement without having time to think things through. Tell your friend to go ahead and hand in her signatures. We'll see if he has the guts to do it when he knows very well that my fall would take both of them down with me."

"Maybe there's another solution," I suggested.

"Do whatever you like, but I won't give in to this. It's hard enough for me to accept her as my prime minister. I refuse to shout it from the rooftops two months before the second round. I'll announce it when I see fit. The later the better."

Then he hung up, leaving me alone with my doubts. I was proud of his reaction: we weren't going to give in easily. But if Trémeau was a candidate, our chance at victory would be significantly decreased. Our defeat would be honourable, but it would still be a defeat.

So that left my idea. Still watching Texier out of the corner of my eye, I called Marilyn. "I have an emergency."

47

Wednesday 17th March, 3:52 p.m.

Half an hour later I sat down next to Texier.

"What do you say we listen to the radio for a bit, eh?" I said.

"We can do whatever you want," replied Texier, giving me a confused look. "But time's a-ticking."

"Let's just listen, okay?"

I used my smartphone to tune in to the station Marilyn had recommended. The frail voice of the wise old party stalwart who had spoken up in favour of Trémeau during the campaign committee meeting was on air.

"We unanimously advised our candidate to give everyone—and particularly his principal adversary during the primary—an important role in the campaign and beyond. And I am delighted to say that our advice seems to have been taken to heart."

"So you confirm that Mrs Trémeau will be prime minister if you win?"

"It's up to our candidate to outline the optimal process for implementing the principle we suggested. It is obviously not up to me to determine when or how he goes about that. What I can say, however, is that I am very optimistic and that I am delighted with the spirit of unity within the party which this solution has fostered."

Texier frowned. "That's not enough."

"It will have to be for today," I replied.

He was clearly thinking through his options.

"Marie-France asked me to hand in her signatures if she felt that the guarantees provided were not enough."

"I see. I imagine you are fully aware of the implications of your decision?"

"If we'd had five hundred more votes in the primary, you would be in my shoes right now."

"Maybe. And if I were in your shoes, I wouldn't go ahead with a candidacy that could blow up our party and lead to our loss of the presidential and legislative elections. Of course, it would mean you earn your place in history . . . For the rest of eternity, sabotaging your team and ruining your own prospects at the same time will be called 'pulling a Texier'. I'm sure you'd have plenty of job offers after that . . ."

We were both quiet for a moment.

Texier picked up his pile of signatures. I would have paid a lot of money to see the names of those who had sponsored Trémeau, so I could send them back to the salt mines for the next twenty years.

When he was a few steps away he called his boss. Who else could it have been? I would have loved to be able to lipread in that moment. But there was no need for such techniques to understand that the discussion was a lively one. I had really stirred the pot with my most recent move.

Texier hung up and came back over to me. "I'll let you get this," he said, nodding towards our coffees. Then he walked determinedly towards Rue de Montpensier.

I was speechless. I could feel my legs giving out. My bluff hadn't worked. I took my head in my hands. We were going to have to deal with Trémeau as a rival candidate. It was a disaster.

I had just endured the worst failure of my career, and now I was going to take the Boss down with me.

Bloody politics.

48

Wednesday 17ᵗʰ March, 6:22 p.m.

In an attempt to forget my failure, I had had a bit too much Chablis. I now had one blind eye and the other was seeing double. I staggered over to a taxi.

For a minute, I was tempted to go home, swallow two sleeping pills, and disappear from the face of the earth for fifteen hours or so. What had just happened was bad. So bad that I would undoubtedly need to disappear for much longer than that.

In the end, I gave the driver the address of HQ. Before going to sleep, I had a letter to write. A letter of resignation. A letter which I would write reluctantly but that had to be written. Someone had to pay to make sure that the Boss could continue his campaign and hope to maybe escape the difficult situation I had failed to help him avoid.

I opened the window and breathed in the cool, fresh air. When I reached HQ, I made my way straight to my office. Without taking off my coat, I drafted my two-line letter, starting over three times. I signed it, folded it, and put it in an envelope.

The Boss wasn't there. Régine gave me some serious side eye and told me he wouldn't be coming back to HQ that night. I could tell that she knew something was wrong. Without explaining the state I was in, I gave her the envelope and told her it was crucial that she give it to the Boss first thing the next morning.

On my way out, I ran into the Major. He seemed cheerful and almost impressed. I wouldn't have expected him to be so ironic.

"Excellent work! How'd you do it?" he asked.

The idiot apparently thought it was okay to poke fun at a time like this. Everyone seemed to be delighted by my fall. I almost punched him in the face.

I took a deep breath to calm my nerves.

The Major's face immediately tensed. He frowned. "Have you been drinking?"

I was speechless, torn between exhaustion and anger.

The Major offered me a confused smile. He seemed to think I was taking the piss out of him.

"Come into my office and tell me how you kept Trémeau from filing her signatures," he said. "You are the master of dirty tricks. None of us measure up to you!"

It took me a couple of seconds to reply.

"Right, yes . . ."

The Major was relaxed and talkative.

"Two hours ago, Marilyn was sure all was lost. You had told her that Trémeau was about to file her signatures, but at six o'clock, when the Constitutional Council published the official list of candidates, she wasn't on it. How did you do it?"

I slumped down into his armchair. Texier had backed down. My bluff had worked. The weight of the world I felt on my shoulders suddenly evaporated. I wasn't sure whether I should laugh or cry. I decided not to share my doubts with the Major, though, so I told him about my conversation with Texier in the most confident, virile voice I could muster. Deep down I knew that I had narrowly escaped being sent to prison and that the Boss's campaign had nearly been sunk.

The Snag had left some casualties in its wake, but not us. Not yet anyway.

I chatted a bit longer with the Major, then left. Behind his sincere praise and admiration, I could sense an equally strong distaste for what he called my "dirty tricks". Distaste mixed with unhealthy fascination. My "exploit"—also his word—probably reinforced his conviction that I was behind the voter fraud. Or maybe he was simply justifying the fact that he too had given in to such base actions?

It was seven o'clock. I went back to Régine's desk to get my letter of resignation. I didn't rip it up, though. It might still come in handy before long.

Sunday 9th May, second round of the presidential election, midday

My eighty-year-old mother hates politics. Actually, she's never liked it. She votes, of course, because it's her duty, and as a true aristocrat of the Republic, she would never fail to accomplish her civic duties. But she doesn't like the people who live off her vote. As a retired teacher who spent most of her life educating young minds and elevating souls, she despises the games and deceit of my profession.

She loves me, though. In a demanding, worried sort of way. She has always felt that my career did me more harm than good: too stressful, not meaningful or fulfilling enough, too little sleep. I think she still holds out hope that I might someday do something else. That I'll finally choose a real job and who knows, even settle down and start a family, as she says. She doesn't mention it any more, but I know that she would love to have a grandchild to teach to read in her final years. I'm not against the idea, but I've never found anyone I could commit to like that. Marilyn, maybe. In another life . . .

The problem with my mother is that I can't hide anything from her. I can lie to her, of course, and I would never share the details of my professional life. But when it comes to my state of mind, I am an open book. She can sense my anxiety and disappointment better than a lie detector test. Every time I mention this to her, she rolls her eyes and says in a tone that is both tragic and banal, "You're my son."

Despite all the love I have for my mother, our ritual election day lunch has become harder to stomach over the years. I hate talking politics with my loved ones. I can go on for hours about the topic at the office or at a dinner party, but I've always felt unnerved when my family asks me about what I do, see, or believe. Over the years, my answers have become increasingly terse. I'm not far from single-syllable grunts.

As I had feared, my mother said I looked thin. A problem she tried to remedy in a single meal. Over the years she had grown used to seeing me tired, pale, and irritable. But not thin.

Worse still, she immediately understood that the weight I had lost and my morosity were a sign that something unusual was going on. She asked a few questions and I told her not to worry. I blamed my condition on the fact that this campaign had been the most exhausting of my life, not only physically but also emotionally. I explained that I was worried about the operation on my eye, which was coming up in a few days. I suggested that at my age, it took longer to recuperate. I hid behind every excuse I could imagine.

She didn't believe me.

Unable to deny that I had doubts, I went on to admit that the campaign had been much harder than I had anticipated. I had expected an extended crescendo with a beginning, a middle, and an end, but instead I had weathered terrifying storms followed by anxiety-inducing periods of relative calm. There had been three incredibly intense moments in the campaign: the September primary, the defeat of Trémeau's candidacy, and the final sprint. The rest of the time, I had simply managed routine matters.

Once Trémeau had backed down, the Boss had picked up speed with a jam-packed schedule of visits and speeches. Trémeau had reluctantly joined the campaign by his side, and we devoted all our energy to beating Vital.

As the first round approached, we were no longer discussing strategies and ideas. We were simply rehashing the key messages in a bid to reach those who still hadn't understood without troubling those who had. Our days were punctuated with the daily polls, which had us neck-and-neck with Vital in both the first and second rounds.

Then, around mid-April, we picked up the pace again.

I obviously omitted the criminal aspects of the campaign in my conversation with my mother.

I hesitated, though. No one else understands me like she does. And what would she have done with the information? Who would have believed her? She would find out someday. Secrets are like bubbles in treacle: they always eventually find a way to reach the surface. Too many people knew. And regardless of how the election panned out, there were too many people who would want to find out exactly what had happened.

I didn't say anything. It was too soon, or maybe too late.

And how could I tell my mother, who believes in hard work, probity, reason, merit, and the power of education—in short, in the Republic—what the end of the campaign had really been like?

PART TWO

PART TWO

49

Thursday 22nd April, 5:44 p.m.

Comfortably installed in the back seat of the Boss's sedan, which was parked in the hospital courtyard, I knew I was in the eye of the storm.

It was a beautiful day and the radiant sunshine confirmed that spring had arrived. For the first time in months, I didn't feel rushed. The courtyard was silent. Inside things were undoubtedly hectic, but none of that showed out here.

The soft leather upholstery of the seat was reassuring. I had planned to read a few files and make some calls as I waited for the Boss, but as soon as he had got out, I had rolled down the window, turned off my mobile, and closed my eyes to take advantage of the sunshine.

Schumacher and the Cowboy had got out to smoke.

It was a perfect opportunity to catch up on my reading. I pulled out a long article on the relationship between the Boss and Trémeau which had been published in a reputable weekly. The article went back over the primary, the power struggle surrounding Trémeau's potential maverick candidacy, and the mysterious nature of their reconciliation.

Though it included a rather long list of the problems in their unnatural alliance, it also underscored the way visible tension had disappeared, leaving behind a spirit of cooperation undoubtedly motivated by the possibility—continuously mentioned but never officially confirmed—of a ticket that would make Trémeau prime minister if the Boss won. Though she was actively campaigning for him, she never completely backed his positions, and always implied that she remained a free agent. But at least she wasn't criticizing him any more.

Trémeau was now in the limelight almost as much as the Boss, and she was doing a good job of it. She had made progress since the primary. She now knew how to control her words, tone, and effect. She wasn't quite as solid as the Boss, but she somehow reconciled her refreshing energy and her newfound stature. The party stalwarts had noticed, and their behaviour and declarations over the past month had lent more credibility to the possibility of her inheriting Matignon than the Boss's invitation had.

What the article didn't mention was that the Boss knew all too well that over time it would become increasingly difficult to manage Trémeau. We were brewing intraparty turmoil for after the election that would be hard to dispel, and we knew it. For now, the main thing was to win. We would have all the time in the world to take her down a notch once the Boss was sitting comfortably in the Elysée Palace.

The Boss was holding up admirably despite the pressure and exhaustion. I had never seen him as fit and full of energy as he was during that month of grace. He triumphed at every rally and hugged old women and children with the same enviable simplicity. He was fantastic on TV. He had a handle on every topic and successfully distilled his thoughts into sentences that were both short, which ensured they wouldn't be edited, and clear, which meant we could hope people would understand them.

Though we never said as much, we could all sense that he was taking things to a new level. As we watched, he was becoming a President. It wasn't a transformation so much as the fruit of thirty years of hard work. During his entire political career, the Boss had thought about this election three times a day. He had developed a personality, forged ties in a wide range of fields, and grown a thick skin to keep from feeling the sting of criticism while still remaining accessible to new fans—those who had only just found him and who wanted to believe in him.

Even for those who had known him for decades, he was no longer a person. He was the candidate: a thing, a product, a concept, an idea, an embodiment.

In all honesty, the inner circle no longer talked about serious things. There was so much to be done that we could avoid asking ourselves too many questions. The atmosphere between us still looked good from the outside, but the trust and friendship that had united us before the Snag had now dissolved, leaving behind an ostentatious cordiality which fooled none of us.

The inner circle had been undermined by suspicion. Other than Winston, I trusted no one. The Major had hidden the existence of a crucial audit from me and could very well have rigged the election—for the Boss or someone else. Marilyn had hidden a lover, and I wasn't completely convinced she had played no role in the leaks that had almost ruined us.

The Boss had been acting strangely, not talking to me or consulting me, or including me in his decisions, as if he was hiding something. As the weeks drew on, we no longer spoke as often. Of course, I could have assumed that it was because of the campaign, his trips and extremely busy schedule. But deep down I knew there was something else. Before, the Boss had always found the time to come and talk to me, to get me to confirm his intuitions and to try out his messaging, or just to talk shit about people. But for the past few weeks—the most crucial weeks in his entire political career—our exchanges had become rarer and more formal. I was starting to regret giving up my role as campaign manager, which would have given me a thousand pretexts to talk to him.

But none of this slowed us down. The machine the Boss had patiently built over the years—a machine in which we were the most important parts—had too much momentum to let the Snag stop it in its tracks. Our dedication to our jobs made it possible for us to put aside our disillusionment and distrust.

But I was still worried. There was always a ball of anxiety in the pit of my stomach, eating away at me. The rumour had gone quiet, but it hadn't disappeared; it could come back to haunt us at any moment. Thanks to Winston and his uncle, I knew that someone had played dirty in the primary and that a few people were willing to kill over the rumour. But who was manoeuvring behind the scenes? Would they come at us again? And if yes, when? Just before the second round? Or after?

I was mulling over my doubts in the sun when something caught my eye and pushed me to consider the whole thing in a different light.

A few steps from the car, Schumacher and the Cowboy were sitting on the steps smoking and chatting. Without them noticing, a patient walked by with a young woman. The man looked to be about fifty and his daughter (or very young wife) was helping him along. She was talking and he simply nodded in response. He couldn't talk. Even at a distance, I could see that he must have had an operation on his throat or been intubated, because there was a plastic lid right in the middle of his neck above his collar bone. *He couldn't talk*.

Maybe the people who were willing to kill weren't trying to bring the rumour out into the open after all. Maybe they were trying to snuff it out. I had always thought that the invisible enemy wanted to spread the rumour, but maybe it was the opposite.

Maybe I needed to look at the whole thing the other way around. That's where I was, completely stunned by this change in perspective, when I saw Schumacher and the Cowboy suddenly stand up and stub out their cigarettes. The Boss had finished. And he looked paler than before.

50

Thursday 22ⁿᵈ April, 6:42 p.m.

"How is she?" I asked.

The Boss had sat down in the car without a word, and we were now making our way down the boulevard. I had hesitated before speaking. Maybe he needed silence more than he needed support from a colleague, even me.

"She's dying and she knows it. She's so strong," he finally said solemnly.

You had to be strong to live with the Boss. But I imagined it took even more strength to look death in the face.

I knew she had been ill. And I'd gathered, from the Boss's sombre, clinical tone when he first mentioned it a few months before, that it was more than a cold. But the rhythm of the campaign and handling the Snag worked like a drug on me. Everything outside the election was secondary, and I had so many priorities to deal with that life itself had taken a back seat.

The Boss's wife had always hated politics. But as a widely respected barrister, she was interested in issues facing the country, and the Boss always took her opinions on his positions to heart. What she hated with a passion were political games, his frenzied entourage, schoolyard-style stand-offs, overinflated egos, and fake friends—everything that lay hidden beneath the public debate of ideas. She never participated in events and had felt no pressure to start a foundation or contribute to a good cause. She was off living her own life, and that was all there was to it. We had grown used to it—she wouldn't be an asset for the campaign, plain and simple.

When I started working for the Boss, she had been wary of me. I was the embodiment of everything she hated, and of her husband's drive to see his ambition through to the end. But gradually our relationship thawed. I took her aversion for the phony aspects of politics seriously and made sure she was kept out of the limelight. Over time, I came to appreciate her quick and biting wit, infinite charm, remarkable talents in the kitchen, and discreet but authentic kindness.

Knowing she was dying of cancer, that she was now thin and diminished when she had always burned so brightly, left a bitter taste in my mouth. Maybe I should have taken the time to go and see her myself. But I wasn't sure she would like that, much less the Boss.

He had asked Schumacher to turn on the radio as we made our way slowly through the Parisian streets. I was almost intimidated to be by the Boss's side at such a difficult time. I had always planned to take him all the way, to get him to the Elysée Palace—into the annals of history as Winston put it. But now I found myself with a man who was about to lose the love of his life.

"I asked you to come with me because I knew that you wouldn't say anything. And because I know I can always count on you," he said after a few more minutes of silence.

In other circumstances I would have been overjoyed at this proof of his trust. But now it was coming from a man who was alone with his grief and the absurdity of the fact that he was finally reaching his lifelong goal while losing what really mattered.

"I'm sorry, Boss. Truly sorry."

In answer, he squeezed my right knee with his left hand. He was overcome with emotion, and this was his way of showing it.

After that, there was nothing else to say.

51

Thursday 22ⁿᵈ April, 7:05 p.m.

The road along the Seine on the Rive Gauche side was free of traffic. I watched the Trocadéro as it rose up in the distance on the other side of the river. The Boss had recently moved into a building near the Musée de l'Homme. It was an elegant flat full of books from which he enjoyed a magnificent view of Paris.

As the car pulled up in front of his place, he offered a shy invitation. "I think I'm going to have a drink," he said. "You busy?"

Are you kidding? Like I would ever say, yes, sorry, I have to wash my hair while you mope around all alone . . .

"No. And I'm thirsty," I said. "But I'm buying."

"No. I'd rather not see anyone right now. I want to show you a place few people know about."

Several minutes and many stairs later, we found ourselves on a tiny roof terrace on the top of the Boss's building with a bottle and a pair of glasses. It was a stone balcony just wide enough for a café table and two chairs. We could see all of Paris and much of its suburbs to the south, west, and east. The setting sun lent an orange hue to the stone. The whisky was slightly smoky.

I kept my mouth shut. The Boss had asked me to have a drink with him, not to blather on about my life or feelings. I could tell he wanted to tell me something and intended to take his time.

After a few minutes spent admiring the view and engaging in light conversation about the merits of peated whiskies over the others, he paused. This was it.

"I'm going to win this election, you know. I can't say for sure, of course, and a lot could still happen, but I can feel it in my bones," he said in a calm, almost resigned voice. He believed what he was saying. He wasn't trying to motivate his staff or convince himself. He realized that after the election, he would have to prove himself worthy of the French people's faith in him. He was just beginning to understand what was waiting for him once the campaign was over.

I said nothing for a long while. Then, unable to hold back any more, I said, "I don't know if this is the time, but you should know, for what comes next, that the circumstances surrounding last month's rumour are still very murky."

No reaction.

"I'm worried about a few things, and I think you should know. First, it's no accident that the story fizzled out. The people behind it have certain goals, even though they have made themselves scarce for the past month, so I seriously doubt they've given up on them out of the goodness of their hearts."

No reaction. Neither surprise nor annoyance.

"What's more," I continued, "people have been hiding things. The Major, for starters. Just before the primary, he had a security audit performed on the online voting system. The audit explains exactly how to rig it. And yet, he told no one about it. Not me, not you. Odd, wouldn't you say?"

The Boss was listening closely now, but only raised his eyebrow at this last bit of information.

"And that's not all. God knows I'm fond of her and she's fantastic at her job, but for the past few months, Marilyn has been sleeping with a reporter who works—wait for it—at the paper that published the leak."

A discreet but noticeable smile.

"Last but not least, I think we need to look at this whole thing from another point of view. We've always assumed that we were being threatened by someone who wanted to spread the rumour. But what if we're really under attack by someone who wants to keep it quiet?"

No reaction.

"In any case, Boss," I concluded, "I'm afraid this mess is far from over. No one's talking about it for the moment, and that's great, but it's hanging over our heads, and I don't want everything to come tumbling down because of it. You can count on me to try to get to the bottom of it, but I need to be sure I have all the information as I go forward." I didn't dare venture any further.

After a long pause during which he was perfectly still, the Boss picked up his glass and emptied it in a single gulp. He looked me straight in the eye.

"All very interesting points," he said. "Not all of them are true, but they are interesting. You're right to believe that things are far from over and that the rumour could still hurt me. You're also right when you say we don't communicate enough. Marilyn doesn't tell you everything, it's true, but she did let me know about her relationship with Maussane. She wanted to be sure that I didn't mind and that I wouldn't hear about it from someone else. She must have been thinking of you. In the end, she wasn't wrong . . ."

Great! Now I looked like a paranoid, suspicious lover. I was speechless. On the upside, this did clear Marilyn: she wouldn't have been stupid enough to leak the rumour in her boyfriend's paper.

"The Major's omission is more problematic. We need to look into this audit business. That said, is it really such a big deal? I bet you don't tell him everything. Do you even tell *me* everything?"

I didn't like where things were headed. I had started us down this road, of course, but I was starting to regret it. Maybe I should have just stuck to a glass of fine whisky in silence with my Boss.

"I think I tell you everything that's important for our work together," I said earnestly.

"Maybe," he countered, "but you're the only judge of what qualifies as important . . . If you had a fling with someone close to me, someone close enough that such a fling could impact our objectives would you tell me?"

It takes years to earn the Boss's trust. Loyalty has to be proven. I had earned the Boss's trust by proving my loyalty again and again. After a while, he felt certain that what he told me didn't leave the office, and I was sure that he truly confided in me and no one else. But, like with any old married couple, problems arise when you start taking things for granted. I knew all of his weaknesses and doubts. I had been by his side when no one else was. I had supported him, carried him even, when he thought he was finished. And yet, despite all of those years of loyal service, all that proof, a single moment could still undermine my loyalty—a single doubt could call everything into question. Trust, like reputations, takes decades to build, but can be destroyed in an instant.

And maybe that instant was now, when I least expected it. And yet the Boss had a smile on his face.

"You see," he continued, "you *don't* tell me everything. And I don't hold it against you. That said, you had hundreds of opportunities to come clean . . ."

I kept quiet, feeling awkward about this reproach from the Boss and unsure of how to reply. Deep down, I knew that I was under no obligation to share the details of my love life with him, even my short—too short for my taste—dalliances with Marilyn. If things had become serious between us, then maybe I would have, but as it was I considered the Boss was being slightly unfair.

To spare me my uneasiness and the embarrassment of a blunder, the Boss changed the subject. "What you said about changing the way we look at the situation is most interesting of all. It almost sounds, though, like you think I rigged the primary. With the Major's help, maybe . . . After all, I am in a position where I could easily have the witnesses bumped off . . ."

The Boss was staring at me. It took everything I had not to look away, but I knew I couldn't back down now. As the sun disappeared beyond the horizon, the temperature dropped.

"I'm not really sure how to interpret the fact that you think I could do something like that," he went on. "I suppose I could take it as a compliment. I could reassure you, but the seed of doubt is there, and denying it won't be enough to change your mind. To be absolutely certain, you'll have to get to the bottom of it yourself. But as it turns out, that's good for me, too."

He went quiet for a few minutes. I didn't dare break the silence.

"That reminds me of a quote by Benjamin Franklin," he said finally. "'Three can keep a secret, if two of them are dead.'"

52

Saturday 24ᵗʰ April, 8:42 p.m.

Cherbourg. This was a first for Winston, but for me, the trip and the dinner that went with it were a pilgrimage.

In the beginning, it had been just me and the Boss. The night before the first parliamentary election he ever won, he suggested we have dinner together to go over a few things and enjoy a good meal. Only after I had gladly accepted, did he tell me he would be waiting for me in Cherbourg. And ever since, on the eve of every election he had run in, we had made the trip to Cherbourg.

For years I had truly enjoyed the ritual. The number of participants had grown, but the ambiance had never changed. It was always a place for sincere camaraderie among a team of people that had fought tooth and nail to get the man they believed in elected. We were never short on campaign anecdotes, and we spent the evening laughing, drinking too much, and saying nasty things about our adversaries—and sometimes even nastier things about our political "friends".

Winston had driven since my torn retina meant I couldn't get behind the wheel. If I had followed the doctors' advice to the letter, I would have had to stay home altogether since the vibrations in any vehicle were dangerous in my condition. But they would have had to chain me to my bed to keep me from attending the Cherbourg dinner.

The restaurant was always the same provincial jewel with somewhat tacky décor but a warm welcome and a beautiful view of the sea. Seafood was their speciality, and we enjoyed it at a table that was now round, to accommodate all of the members of the inner circle.

The Major had arrived first, on time, as usual, but early in relative terms since being late is the norm in politics. Démosthène, who had preferred to travel by train since his mother had died in a car accident a few years earlier, was due to arrive any minute. Marilyn was expected momentarily with the Boss, after they'd met with a few local journalists.

Despite Winston's smile and his enthusiasm for the view, by the time the sun set, the atmosphere was already morose. No one had wanted to back out, but no one looked happy to be there. The winter campaign and final spring sprint had left us looking pale and exhausted. But more than that, the tensions between us had worn us down. We didn't want to spend time together any more. No one dared say as much, but that's where we were.

"So, Major, did you drop by Omaha Beach?" I asked. Given his strict demeanour and *pater familias* status, I had always imagined the Major on the D-Day beaches explaining to his grandchildren how the Germans had been defeated by the Allied attack.

"No time," he replied. "I spent the whole drive making calls. Did you take the car, too? You should have told me. My driver could have brought all of us."

Right. As if the Major would have wanted to spend four hours trapped in a confined space with me.

"Shame," I said simply. If everyone else was going to be hypocritical, I didn't see why I had to miss out on the fun.

We wouldn't sit down at the table until the Boss arrived. It looked like the pre-dinner drinks—accompanied by more than their fair share of small talk and cruel jokes—were going to drag on for a while.

When Marilyn finally appeared in the private room the restaurant had reserved for us, I noticed three things. She was beautiful, as always. She was annoyed, as she often had been of late. And she was alone, which had never happened before.

"The Boss isn't coming," she announced.

For the first time ever, the Boss had decided to skip the Cherbourg dinner.

53

A single person was missing, but the place felt deserted. Without its centre, the inner circle lost its cohesion. That's how I felt at least amid the falsely carefree exchanges between a group of people who had once been so friendly.

I watched us. Marilyn, across the table, whose eyes seemed to be shooting daggers of disgust at me. Démosthène, who was lost in his thoughts as always. The Major, sitting ramrod straight, inviting everyone to speak and confidently summarizing the points made. And Winston, who said nothing but saw everything. If he had been there, the Boss would have provided the glue we so sorely needed, but, though he had decided to spend the evening in Cherbourg, he was spending it with his daughter. Without us. His wife's health had undoubtedly prompted his desire to take better care of the family he had left. He probably also wanted to spare himself the unsavoury tensions that were eating away at our group.

I knew that, with him gone, it was my responsibility to run things. I ordered the good old sole that had got me through so many of my difficult professional dining experiences.

"I'd like to take advantage of this dinner to get a few things out in the open," I said.

I wanted silence, and that's what I got. All eyes were on me.

"First, I'd like to apologize if some of you have found my behaviour strange since the beginning of this campaign.

I'm getting old, and I suppose I don't handle the stress as well. And I'm not at all used to losing the use of an eye. Let me tell you, a retinal tear changes the way you see things— and not in a good way."

"But you're part of a very exclusive club!" offered Démosthène whose smile suggested he was about to start pontificating. "There is a great tradition of one-eyed warriors, you know. Beginning with Odin. Then there's Hannibal. Antigonus the One-Eyed. And Moshe Dayan, of course. Napoleon's two greatest military adversaries both had only one eye, and—"

I wasn't about to let this dinner get bogged down in the cobwebs of history when what we really needed to discuss was the upcoming election.

"What I mean," I continued, cutting in, "is that this campaign has been difficult. Harder than any of the others. Harder than I expected. Overall, we've done pretty well. I don't know what the ballots will say tomorrow, but the Boss has a real chance at winning the second round. And to make sure he wins, there are a few things we need to do . . ."

They were all wondering where I was going with this. To be honest, I wasn't totally sure myself. I was taking my time, carefully cutting up my sole. I was about to go on when the Major beat me to it.

"To win," he said, "we need to do two things. First, we need to give it our all for the next two weeks. I think we're all experienced enough to know this and to give it everything we've got in the final straight. Next, we have to avoid the kind of mistakes that often plague campaigns late in the game: unforeseen smears, or the Boss or one of our guys taking the election for won and going off the rails. It comes down to hard work and discipline. With that, the Boss can win."

Winston was staring at me in disbelief. The Major had pre-empted the topic to give himself a central role in the discussion and avoid any delicate subjects. With a smirk, I let him know that I wasn't inclined to leave things there.

"There's another thing we need to do, though, Major," I said. "We need to tell each other everything. Because if we don't, hard work and discipline mean nothing."

The temperature in the room had suddenly dropped ten degrees. The brewing tension was palpable. A seemingly endless silence descended on the gathering, each of us waiting to see what the others would do.

Marilyn finally spoke up. "Funny *you* should be the one to say that." The smile had disappeared from her face and her tone was gentle but ironic.

"I don't see why it's funny, but I know it's true. We all almost failed the Boss because of a rumour that caught us off guard, if I remember correctly. Ever since that rumour surfaced, I've noticed that things between us aren't like before."

"What rumour?" asked Démosthène, who had clearly decided to play the fool, in spite of beingthe smartest man in the room.

"*The* rumour," I replied. "The rumour that the primary was rigged and that our win over Trémeau was suspect."

"Do you really think it was possible to rig it then?" Démosthène asked again.

"Yes!" The Major and I answered in unison. We looked at one another, surprised by the certainty with which the other had spoken.

Winston was so taken aback that he dropped his cutlery. Marilyn seemed to be increasingly interested in the turn the dinner was taking. The Major had never been closer to confessing that he knew how to commit electoral fraud.

"Okay, *was* it rigged?" said Démosthène.

I hesitated and glanced at the Major, who was watching me in prudent silence.

"Hard to say," I replied eventually. "But it wasn't impossible. And given what's happened since the rumour reared its ugly head, I'm rather inclined to believe that it was."

I remained cautious. Only Winston and I knew about how Mukki had died, and we had kept the Canal Saint-Martin encounter to ourselves.

The Major nodded in agreement with what I had just said. Everyone around the table was quiet now as they took in the information. They had all wondered about it, of course, but tonight, for the first time, the Major and I had publicly agreed that the primary had most likely been rigged. That changed everything.

"Do you have any idea who's behind it?" Marilyn asked, trying to sound disinterested so people wouldn't think she was accusing me. But I knew that deep down she believed I was behind it. She'd never said as much, but I could read between the lines.

"No," I said. "But there's something I have to say. I'll only be saying this once, so I want it to be crystal clear: I am not behind the voter fraud or the rumour. It wasn't me. The Boss didn't ask me to do anything. I can't say for sure that I wouldn't have done it if he'd asked me, but he didn't. It wasn't me."

I had tried to put the full force of my conviction into my words. I wasn't sure I had convinced Marilyn, who was staring straight at me, seemingly probing my soul with her gaze. Maybe she had noticed that I had only said that the Boss hadn't asked *me*.

Démosthène, who had obviously decided he'd be the one to ask all the questions, let things sink in for a minute, then said, "Okay. It wasn't you. So, who was it then?"

I instinctively glanced at the Major. As did Winston. The others' eyes naturally followed. In any case, since it wasn't me, the next most logical person would be him.

I didn't expect a revelation, of course. I couldn't see the Major giving in to pressure like that. But I was expecting *something.* He had admitted that it had been possible to rig the primary. Maybe he had regrets. Maybe he wanted to tell us something.

"It wasn't me either," he said. "I wouldn't be capable of such a thing. I believe that something shady went down during the primary, but that kind of dirty trick isn't my thing . . ."

I believed him. Not completely, but almost. I had a hard time imagining the Major getting himself into something so technically risky, politically twisted, and morally bankrupt. Maybe he had participated somehow, by making it possible—voluntarily or unbeknownst to him—but I couldn't see him as the brains of the operation.

I noticed that the team seemed to accept the Major's denial more readily than mine, and this left me feeling regretful and a little jealous.

"Great, so no one did anything. That's fantastic," Marilyn said sarcastically.

"In any case," Winston said suddenly, changing the subject, "I've learned so much from working alongside all of you."

We all turned towards him.

"Really," he continued. "Now I know that a candidate can campaign admirably even when his entourage spend their days tearing one another to pieces. I didn't know that before. I thought that it took a united team to win. But it turns out that's just not true. We can still win despite all that. It's surprising."

The kid had given everyone some food for thought.

"But I'm afraid that if the Boss loses by a just a little bit, it will be easy to blame it on the dissension between us," he went on. "Something tells me that none of you would be able to forgive yourselves for that. So, even though I know you all have various bones to pick with each other, as is always the case in any group, I think we should put all that aside for the next two weeks, just long enough to ensure the Boss's victory." Winston turned his attention back to his plate.

He was probably the only one who could bring us all back to our senses with so few words.

"You're right, Winston," I finally said. "In two weeks, we will have completed our mission. Our shared cause has to come before everything else until then. We don't have to go on holiday together or anything, but let's try to hang in there for two more weeks and revive what was once one of our strengths: good communication."

Though it still didn't compare with what we had enjoyed at past Cherbourg dinners, the atmosphere slowly thawed. At least we were talking. Maybe the team wasn't broken after all.

The Major seemed relieved, but he was still rather glum. He listened to the others' stories, giving the impression he wouldn't speak again.

As for me, I was lost. I was happy that our small team was going to try to regroup, but also disconcerted by the dead end I now found myself in.

I hadn't done it. The Major hadn't done it. The Boss had told me he hadn't done it. Either one of us was lying, or someone else had rigged the primary. But who?

As I listened to Démosthène talk and watched Marilyn laugh, I tried to silently answer the question that had been gnawing away at me since my conversation with the Boss on his rooftop terrace. Did I trust him? Could he have blatantly lied to me?

He hadn't come out and said, man to man, that he wasn't behind it. Nevertheless, I had to believe he wasn't. I wanted to believe it. Maybe I even heard him deny it. But I couldn't stifle my doubts. Since the beginning, his reaction to the rumour had surprised me. The strange blend of casualness and concern was unlike him. The others hadn't said so, but they had to have felt it as well. The Boss had changed.

And then there was that picture of the Boss with Mukki. It didn't mean a thing on its own, of course. The Boss had probably posed for photos with half of the party's members over the course of his political career. A coincidence. A troubling coincidence though. I hadn't thought much about it since I'd been so focused on the ties between Mukki and Pinguet, but in Cherbourg that night, when the Boss chose not to participate in our ritual dinner, I couldn't help but come back to it.

What did it mean that the Boss was always casting himself as a statesman and a man who put the public good first when, in fact, he loved a good political intrigue? Was he pretending to be something he wasn't? Could he have cheated? Could he have done something so risky and unethical just to gain the party's nomination for the presidential election—the election he had always been after and the race which was likely to be his last?

Because it was fairly clear that something underhand had happened during the primary. And the Boss had won. Up until this moment, I had always told myself that he couldn't have been involved in it because I wasn't. I had cleared the brain of wrongdoing because the right hand hadn't moved. But the question that was starting to torment me was whether the brain had wanted to. And to be honest, I wasn't sure.

My inability to answer this question with any degree of certainty didn't mean the Boss was guilty, of course. But it did tarnish the image I had of him. The relationship we had built was underpinned by mutual trust. He was sure of my loyalty, and I was certain he would make the right choices: for himself, for us, and for France.

Since the Snag, my certainty had slowly but surely been worn away.

What with the unresolved rumour and my torn retina, I was finding it hard to look to the future with any sort of confidence.

54

I had never seen the Major in such a state. He was made of much sterner stuff than most people. He was rarely funny, but you could count on him. He slept little, never forgot a detail, and could handle a multitude of complicated tasks at the same time.

I can't say that we were ever friends. I have few of those. But I had always taken him seriously, even over the course of the past two months when I had had my doubts about him. I respected him for what he knew how to do and for the fact that he still had his spine. There weren't many people in our profession who could say as much.

And yet, here he was, on the verge of falling apart.

Not physically, of course. He was standing up straight. His eyes were unblinking. But his gaze was less direct and darted subtly to and fro. I only noticed because I knew him so well. A stranger would have had no idea. I don't even think the others picked up on it.

He was falling apart from the inside out.

He had managed to wait until almost everyone had gone back to their hotels for the night. We were alone. He invited me to have a drink with him. Now we'd really seen it all during this campaign.

"Is something wrong?" I asked.

"You see, don't you?"

I said nothing and waited. It's the best way to get someone to say more than they intend to.

"It was possible to rig the election. Simple even, for someone who knew what they were doing."

I remained impassive.

"I had an audit performed on the system before the primary. Last summer, I ordered a third-party audit to assess the system we had chosen for the vote. I thought that it would be proof of our good faith if there was a problem. I took advantage of the occasion to have the party's IT system, which I found rather lacking, audited as well. We did it in August since most people would be on holiday then, making things easier for the auditors."

I kept my eyes focused on him.

"I hired a consulting firm I trusted: the owner is an old friend and I knew nothing would ever get out. The audit provided a detailed analysis of the voting system, which an attentive reader could use to figure out how to commit voter fraud. As long as they had access to both the list of party members and the passwords attributed by Droid. That said, even having read it, I don't understand how to vote for people without them knowing or change their votes. The audit isn't a how-to manual for fraud, of course. It says the system is imperfect, but it doesn't provide instructions for rigging elections."

Having scanned the audit report myself, I knew that the Major was telling the truth. But I had no intention of revealing to him what I knew. I was a few steps ahead for the first time in a while, and I had no intention of helping him catch up. First, because I wanted to see if the Major would tell me the rest. And second, because I didn't want him to know that the Godfather had discreetly searched his flat.

"Did you tell anyone about it?" I asked.

"Not a soul. At the time, no one even cared. If I had come to tell you that I was about to have an IT audit done, you would have dismissively waved your hand and moved on to something else."

I couldn't really argue with that. But, at the same time, we both knew that such reasoning was unacceptable given the gravity of the situation. Keeping my expression neutral, I signalled for him to continue.

"I should have told you about it anyway, but sometimes I get discouraged by your disdain for logistics. When I received the final report, it was too late to stop everything. I tried to let the oversight committee know what to look out for, but I remained cautious. I would have done something if we had lost, of course. But really, what was I going to say? That it was possible to commit voter fraud? If I had, you would have gone to war with everyone a month before the primary, and we would have found ourselves in a situation where no one from the party would have been able to run."

The Major's naivety was startling.

"And did we actually avoid all that infighting in the end?"

He looked down at his feet, overwhelmed. I almost felt bad for him.

"I understand why you didn't mention it at the time," I offered. "You were captain of the ship, I get it. And honestly, if you told me today that you had talked to me about it back then, I would believe you since I know I have a real tendency to forget things like that. So, I follow your reasoning from last summer. I accept it. What I don't understand is why you decided not to bring it up when this bloody rumour surfaced. That, I really can't grasp."

"I didn't bring it up because the audit incriminates me!"

What was he talking about?

"It points the finger at me because our IT system is not watertight and I'm the one responsible for it. Because I am the one who pushed for online voting, and it was my job to make sure it was reliable. I didn't mention it because I didn't take the audit's conclusions seriously enough at the time and I did nothing to fix things. Weeks passed, the election oversight committee took over, we were no longer in control, and I forgot about it. I forgot about all of it right up until the rumour emerged in February. And in that moment, I had ten seconds to decide whether to admit all of that or not: I made the wrong decision. And after that, it was too late."

The Major had blurted this all out so fast that he was now struggling to catch his breath. He was wringing his hands in dismay and annoyance at himself.

"Who knows what you've just told me?" I asked after a short pause.

"No one. No one saw the audit, no one had the information. I go way back with the consultant. He has nothing to do with politics. Honestly, I'm not even sure he would be able to make the connection between his analysis and the rumour if we told him about it . . ."

I had a hard time believing that—even if he was an IT guy. I decided to push on.

"You realize that what you've said could also lead people to believe you were behind the fraud, right? You and your old friend were in the best position to rig the primary."

The Major's desperate expression was painful to see.

"In your shoes," he conceded in a quiet, almost other-worldly voice, "I'd think the same thing."

"I don't think anything," I countered. "I'm thinking about the future. I want to see the audit. I'd like to have it reviewed by experts. I want to know exactly how feasible it was to rig the primary. That's what I want."

"You'll have it tomorrow morning. And the Boss will have my letter of resignation."

Now his naivety was almost touching.

"Absolutely not," I replied. "The last thing I need is a pile-up on my hands between the first and second rounds."

"A pile-up?" asked the Major, who was now officially lost.

"You know, when one accident causes several others."

"I'm not sure I follow . . ."

"Your mistake is one accident. The resignation of a campaign director between the first and second rounds of a presidential election would be the resulting pile-up. And its consequences in the media would be far worse. So, you'll stay put, keep doing your job for the next two weeks, and after that, it'll be up to the Boss. One mistake doesn't erase ten years of good work, especially since you came clean."

The Major gave me a strange look. He suddenly realized, though he wasn't entirely sure, that I had already known about everything he'd just told me. He also realized that he owed me one now.

After a short silence, he finished his drink. "I think the primary was rigged. And then someone was murdered."

Now it was my turn to be surprised.

"Pinguet didn't die in a car accident," he continued. "I'm sure of it, no matter what the police say. And Pinguet is at the heart of this whole mess. As for Mukki, I'd be surprised if his death wasn't related as well. So . . ."

The Major had done his homework. He understood part of the puzzle. I wondered if he was telling me everything he knew.

"So, what?"

The Major seemed not to know how to put what he had to say into words. After a short pause, he said, "I'm sorry to put it like this, but doesn't it seem obvious now? A rumour surfaces that inculpates the Boss, or at least his team. Then the two people tied to the voter fraud suddenly meet with violent ends. I guess what I'm saying is: who benefited from the crime?"

There was fear in his eyes. Not fear of any sort of physical threat, but the fear that he had been terribly wrong, the fear that he had been an accomplice to something really bad without even realizing it.

He didn't dare say as much, but I knew he now thought that the Boss had rigged the election and silenced all those who knew about it.

The Major smiled at me sadly as he left.

I looked at my watch: one o'clock in the morning. It was late, but I had a call to make. The Godfather answered on the first ring.

"I need you to make a copy of the IT audit and take the original back to the Major's flat before we return tomorrow morning. He's just come clean, and I think he's innocent. I don't want him to know we searched his home."

"You're calling me in the middle of the night for *that*? The original never left the place. I photographed every page where I found it. That way he never suspects a thing. And it *usually* spares me the inconvenience of being woken up from my beauty sleep by a guy who wants me to do the exact opposite of what he asked me to do the day before."

He hung up.

Despite the night I'd had, I couldn't help but smile.

55

Politicians always run the same campaign.

Campaign managers think that they're devising the strategy. Sorcerers believe that they conjure up its messages. The volunteers believe they're making the big ideas a reality. And they're all right. But when it comes down to the fundamentals, all of a candidate's campaigns are the same.

And that's as it should be. Candidates don't change much over time. How can you change someone after forty years in the same profession? Candidates, along with their reflexes and preferences, stay the same. The modern technology around them—the 24-hour news cycle and the rise of the internet—has added new campaign tools to the fold, but the gist of it all is unchanged: it's about saying who you are and what you want. And between campaigns, candidates usually stay the same and want the same thing . . .

I don't change much either. Since I've known the Boss, I have always spent my Sunday mornings on election day driving home from Cherbourg—usually at the crack of dawn. After that, I get on with the rest of the ritual.

Winston and I had left at five o'clock. I had talked to him the whole way home to help him stay awake. At his age, it's always hard to wake up. At mine, you're afraid to go to sleep.

When we reached Paris, I made my usual rounds: a stop at my neighbourhood café followed by a trip to my polling station. I always voted at ten o'clock on the dot so that I could compare the turnout rates in my polling station year after year. For the past thirty years I had been hoping to stumble upon a system that would allow me to predict national voter turnout or even the national results based upon this one metric. I hadn't found it. But I still politely asked the poll manager how many of the registered voters had cast their ballots by ten o'clock. 11%. Not bad. It was no record, but not bad. As I left, I wondered what it could mean for the Boss.

HQ would probably be empty, as it always is on election Sunday. The morning of the vote was the only quiet moment in the life of a place which was home to such intense but ephemeral activity. It was a tacit rule that no one was expected to come in until four o'clock in the afternoon. The people who had worked so hard—or pretended to do so—to get the Boss elected were allowed a moment's rest.

The Thing was guarding the entrance to HQ. He was a short but stocky man whose face was so craggy that he looked like the Fantastic Four hero from my childhood. He was so massive that I imagined a normal pair of scales couldn't accommodate him.

He shook my hand with a blend of respect and simplicity. The security team was all right. We spoke for a minute, and his threatening appearance seemed to soften under the effects of his sing-song south-western accent. My mobile vibrated once in my pocket. Once meant an email. Text messages vibrated twice and calls six times.

The Thing, who was delighted to have someone to kill a bit of time with, had started telling me about his life. He had played rugby and worked for all of the Boss's campaigns because he felt the Boss was "a good guy but also really smart". He argued it was unusual for statesmen to also be so friendly.

My phone vibrated again. Another email.

I was about to leave my superhero to go up to my office when a noise coming from inside HQ caught my attention. I paused for a minute. The Thing seemed equally surprised. He had thought the building was empty.

My phone vibrated again. Twice this time. A text. The Thing clearly felt like he had made a mistake. It was his job to guard the entrance.

My body suddenly started pumping adrenaline. As it turned out, the security team wasn't so great after all . . . But I could see there was no point telling him off. He had the kind of physique people with my physique prefer not to piss off.

I gestured to him to keep quiet and follow me.

As noiselessly as possible, I made my way to the part of the building the sound had come from. I peeked my head through a door which was slightly ajar into an office where the light was on. Two men were standing where our legal and financial teams usually worked. In other words, the office where they make sure the campaign team hasn't made any mistakes. The office where they know which cupboards have skeletons in them. Thinking of skeletons set my heart racing. I thought of Mukki in the Seine.

One of the men was speaking a strange language I had never heard before. One with lots of "a" sounds. The other replied in German. I took a few slow, deep breaths as I decided what to do. The Thing, who was standing next to me, would scare just about anyone. There were two of them in the office, but I was pretty sure my superhero could take them. We would have to handle them together since I couldn't call for reinforcements: Winston wasn't there and Gaspard wouldn't pick up.

My phone vibrated again in my pocket.

I whispered in the Thing's red ear that on my mark we'd burst into the office. I hoped that I'd seen enough Hollywood movies to know what to do after that. In any case, the Thing kicked the door open and bravely strode into the room.

What happened next could have been a disaster. The two guys shouted and jumped in surprise. If they had had any heart problems, they would undoubtedly have died on the spot, which would have been a shame since I knew both of them. Young senior civil servants who had been working the Boss's campaign since the beginning, probably hoping to follow him to the Elysée Palace or a minister's cabinet, where their love of politics and personal ambition would have free rein.

"What the hell are you doing here?" I shouted before I realized, from their pale trembling faces, that they weren't dangerous.

The Thing glared at them, ready to pulverize them if need be. I would have been terrified in their shoes.

"We're working! Just working!" they said. "On the policy statements! We haven't done anything!"

Despite the context, it amused me to know that well-educated senior civil servants could claim in the same sentence that they were both working and doing nothing.

"Who told you to do that this morning?" I asked. "What were you saying just a minute ago?"

Silence. What were they hiding?

"Campaign management told us to take care of it. We were reading the candidate's policy statement in Tahitian. We have to finalize the Tahitian translation for Tuesday at the latest so we can print it and send it to Polynesia. It's a legal requirement. Sometimes they even have to parachute them in because the boats don't have enough time to reach all the islands."

The taller of the two calmed down a bit. "And I was reading the German. We also have to translate them into German for Alsace because of a law left over from the Occupation, you know."

The Thing looked at me, clearly confused. He seemed unable to wrap his mind around the fact that a candidate hoping to become president of France would need to translate anything into German and Tahitian! I had to admit, I was struggling myself . . .

I couldn't believe it. It was all perfectly ridiculous. But things seemed to be in order, and I really couldn't see those two spying on us. I told them off nonetheless, warning them that they'd better inform security next time they came into the office. They were young and ambitious enough not to mind. And there's nothing like giving a good lecture to bring your blood pressure back down. I told the Thing to call a colleague to come and help him watch the building more thoroughly and went up to my office.

My mobile started vibrating again. When I finally checked it, I found that Winston had tried to reach me three times. He had sent me a text message telling me to read my email. And when I saw the heading on the second most recent email in my inbox, I understood why. Adrenaline started pumping through my veins again. It was a Google News alert. An article mentioning one of my chosen key words had just been published.

Google Alert—'*Droid*': Le Dauphiné: *Break-in at a company near Grenoble*

56

I could only read the title of the article on my mobile, but I instantly realized that the rumour had just popped up on our radar screens again.

My computer was slow. IT services had claimed it was due to the firewall when I had complained. Right. My faith in the same chaps who had certified the online voting system as tamper-proof had its limits.

I cursed computer geeks across the globe but had to admit that these Google alerts came in rather handy. I decided that at my age I was entitled to have contradicting opinions. The alerts had changed my life, or at least my way of working. All you had to do was enter a word and wait for the search engine to send you an email whenever an article used it. Thanks to Google, I knew instantaneously whenever someone wrote something about the Boss, me, or Bruce Springsteen.

But the alerts had their drawbacks. Not everything they unearthed was useful. Thanks to the alert I created for my name, I had discovered I had a namesake who was a Quebecois ice-racing champion. I regularly received notifications about his performances. Lately, they hadn't been stellar. Maybe he also occasionally received alerts pertaining to statements I'd made. He probably didn't find them stellar either.

Luckily, the Boss didn't have a namesake.

Since the beginning of the campaign, I had added four new key words: Trémeau, Texier, Pinguet, and Droid.

The article was laconic. The kind of brief news piece you see every day without really noticing them. An accident, a fire, some sort of terrible event that's quickly forgotten in the 24-hour news cycle. Unless there's a photo or video, most of us skip over them, simply happy to have avoided other people's bad luck.

Google Alert—'Droid': Le Dauphiné: *Break-in at a company near Grenoble. La Tronche: There was a break-in at IT company Droid on Friday night. According to the company's COO, who called in the crime, the burglars don't seem to have had time to finish the job since nothing was stolen. Several computers were damaged, however. The police have opened an investigation to find the culprits.*

While I realised that I had to keep my paranoia in check, I also knew, deep down, that the break-in at Droid was hiding something. The article said nothing about the ties between Pinguet, the primary, and Droid, but someone would eventually put two and two together.

I called Winston.

"Did you read it?"

"Yes, of course. I even sent you a text and called three times! Were you sleeping?"

"I never sleep, you insolent youngster! I was studying the policy statements. In a campaign, you have to handle everything yourself. Even translating them."

Silence. Winston seemed confused.

"I'm worried," he finally said. "I thought that maybe . . ."

I cut him off immediately. Yet another chatterbox who was about to broach a sensitive topic on the phone. If people knew how easy it is to listen in on mobile conversations, they would stop paying so much for them and start making appointments to discuss serious matters in person—like we used to do before mobiles existed.

"I have lunch plans." "I'll meet you at HQ at three o'clock," I said.

It was time for the most difficult of my election day rituals: lunch, with my mother.

57

Sunday 25ᵗʰ April, 2:50 p.m.

One thing was certain: I could make it to the second round without eating another thing. My mother had insisted I try some of everything she had made—enough for an entire regiment.

Back at HQ, as I waited for Winston, I started thinking about the second round.

The second round of a presidential election is a wonderful time.

First, because after the results of the first round, there would be only two candidates left. A head-to-head between two heavyweights. A binary choice for voters: one or the other. All the other candidates disappeared. That said, the higher the failed contestants' scores, the more they could impact the final outcome by endorsing one of the remaining candidates.

Another particularity is that there are two weeks between the rounds. Two weeks is a long time. Over the course of those two weeks, the candidates change their tune. Before the first round, they're talking to their base to make sure they get all of their expected votes. But for the second round, they're hoping to reach people who voted for someone else in the first. They're trying to bring people together. It's a race to the centre: their messaging becomes more presidential. In other words, it's more poised and encompassing and loses its hard edges. Both candidates make this move, which must be both real and discreet to avoid putting off hardliners in their own camps.

Much of these two weeks is also devoted to thinking about the upcoming legislative elections in light of the first round results. It's a time for wheeling and dealing. It's a time for apparatchiks. It's the best time.

The last wonderful thing about the second round of the presidential election is that it provides an incontestable result. There's a winner and a loser. It's clear, clean, and definitive. Even though, in politics, things are rarely clean and never definitive.

I was deep into my review of the swing districts for the legislative election when Winston came in.

"You're late," I said, looking at my watch.

"I don't know what's going on with them," he replied, clearly winded, "but the security guys are on high alert. I had to take a taxi home to get my ID so they'd let me into the building."

I smiled to myself. "They're just doing their job. At least we won't be burgled here . . ."

"About that . . . I think I know what the thieves were after . . ."

I stared at the kid, whose awkward demeanour didn't bode well for what would come next.

"I mean, my uncle . . ."

Shit. I understood. The Godfather had struck once again. He was behind the break-in. How could I have been so stupid as to involve him! If he was caught, it wouldn't take long for them to tie him to his nephew and our campaign. A wave of rage, surprise, and dread washed over me, then settled in the pit of my stomach. I pursed my lips to keep from shouting and was about to slam my fists into the desk when I realized something strange.

I looked up and noticed that Winston seemed quietly pleased with himself, not stressed or terrified. He was taking the piss.

"As I was saying," he continued with a smirk, "my uncle did pay Droid a visit. But he didn't touch anything or break anything. He did it three nights ago, and the offices have been open since and no one noticed. So, he's not behind the break-in, or at least not this one. Did you really take him for such an amateur?"

I said nothing, but I could breathe easier.

"I think he found something worthwhile," he continued. "He mentioned encrypted documents but wouldn't say more. In the meantime, what we know for sure is that someone else broke in just after him, and discretion wasn't their forte."

My breathing was easier than before, but my chest still felt tense.

"Do you think it could be the police? Like at Mukki's?" he asked.

"Why would they have smashed the computers?"

"How should I know? Because they don't give a shit? Or because they're not especially bright?"

I had to admit that we couldn't completely exclude the possibility. But I could also see that there was another possibility as well. One that was just as worrying.

"Maybe it wasn't the police at all," I ventured. "Maybe the people who broke into Droid were looking for something or looking to destroy something. You think they were idiots because they made it obvious that they had been there. But maybe they did it on purpose to cover up whatever they were really doing."

There was a long silence. The kid seemed bewildered.

The fact that whoever was behind the voter fraud might now be trying to clean up after themselves was not good news. It meant that they were still active, and it didn't augur well for the future.

"When will your uncle be able to tell us more about the encrypted files he found?" I asked.

"He told me it would take a while. He's on it."

"Tell him to pick up the pace. And ask him to come by tonight. I need to talk to him, and maybe it's time for him to meet the Major as well."

Winston looked worried.

"Are you sure that's a good idea? I imagine there will be loads of people here tonight. Journalists, apparatchiks, and more. Do you really want him to be seen here? With the Boss?"

It was my turn to smile now. I wasn't sure exactly where I was headed, but I had decided to go on the offensive. I was tired of having whoever it was run rings around me.

"Maybe it's time to let the people behind this know that we have a few cards up our sleeves as well."

58

HQ was steadily filling up. Security had placed barricades at the entrance to hold back the growing crowd of young, impatient party members, journalists, curious passers-by, and a few optimists who were hoping to get a free glass of champagne out of the evening. The atmosphere was relaxed. The Boss's partisans were outwardly confident. As for the curious passers-by, their sincere nonchalance seemed to indicate that the election results would have no impact on their mood, much less the rest of their lives.

Inside, however, things were tense. For those who had made it past the bouncers at the entrance, tonight was so much more than an election night party. All of them had something to gain: a ministry for the most important or cleverest among them, an easier race for a parliamentary seat two months down the road, or a job in a ministerial cabinet or at the party for the rest.

Ever since a former prime minister, who had been ahead in all the polls, had failed to make it into the second round, it had become more difficult to be confident about the results of the first.

None of us let our imaginations wander to the worst case scenario, but we all wondered which of the two major candidates would take the lead: the Boss or Vital? Would the total number of votes on the right be greater than those on the left? And would each camp be able to pick up the pieces of their political family and unite them before the second round?

Participation was in line with the most recent presidential elections. Though that meant nothing, when it came down to it, the commentators were all discussing it. They weren't allowed to give any indication about the results until after eight o'clock. But we all knew that they already had estimates based on exit polls in the districts most representative of the country as a whole. The best institutes could provide relatively reliable figures around four o'clock and nearly definitive numbers around a quarter past six.

At HQ, everyone knew that if numbers were circulating, I would have them.

And they were right.

I would know soon, or in any case before they did. I was waiting for a text message any second now from a friend at the Ministry of the Interior who would be among the first to be able to cross-reference the estimates from the different institutes.

In the meantime, I paced the halls to channel my excitement and anxiety and to encourage and thank those who had worked so hard to help the Boss. I was also trying to avoid spending any time with the Barons, who were pontificating in the meeting room on the first floor as they enjoyed a buffet that was quite a cut above what the volunteers and journalists would enjoy downstairs after eight o'clock.

People kept asking if the Boss would make an appearance. Politics is a tactile profession. Candidates have to make themselves physically available so their supporters can touch them. If they don't, they risk coming off as distant and disdainful. I avoided the question and let the uncertainty grow. Real leaders are always shrouded in mystery. It heightens their charisma and always positively impacts the feeling in the room.

★ ★ ★

The Major was upstairs managing the Barons. Marilyn was dazzling journalists and the rest downstairs. Démosthène was nowhere to be seen—probably holed up in his office drafting the speech he would pitch to the Boss at seven thirty. Démosthène didn't have any results to go on, but he didn't need them. He always prepared a dozen different versions. Victory, defeat, surprise, a call to arms . . . Depending on the results and the Boss's mood, we would cobble together the best parts from each at the last minute.

Winston was at the bar with his uncle. Even from a distance, I could see the complicity they had forged over the course of several difficult years. The past few weeks had undoubtedly strengthened it as well.

I walked over. To my great surprise, the legionnaire smiled broadly at me. "So, I hear you thought I had got clumsy? Louis really scared you earlier, eh?" He spoke quietly so that he wouldn't be overheard and followed his question up with an affectionate tap on the shoulder. Winston laughed openly. The kid was terribly endearing. Just seeing him happy alongside his uncle, so different from the boy's overbearing father, brought a smile to my face.

"I almost passed out," I replied. "But it was nothing compared to what I did earlier to two young guys who work here." Drawn in by the warm, friendly atmosphere, I told them about my adventure with the two young technocrats and how they had narrowly escaped heart attacks that morning. Everyone laughed, including the bartender, who had probably only seen me in such a good mood a few times. I'm not sure why, but his relaxed demeanour set off alarm bells in my head. I looked around the room as subtly as possible and noticed everyone was watching us.

Maybe it was my good humour when everyone else was stressed out? But the teams knew me well enough to know that I was perfectly capable of putting on a smile when things were heading south just to fool my enemies. I could also be unbearable when things were fine. In short, anyone who assumed there was any sort of correlation between my mood and the results was sorely mistaken.

It was probably Gaspard Caligny who intrigued them. Maybe some of them noticed the resemblance with his brother. A few of the campaign staff must have known him. Or maybe the legionnaire just stood out in this company. Like most former soldiers, Gaspard wasn't exactly at ease among civilians.

And then there was the fact that everyone had to be wondering who this man could be. A man who was so close to Winston and so direct with me. New people turn up all the time at the party and even in a candidate's entourage, but when they do, the people already in place get straight to work. They need to know where the newcomer came from: their pedigree, their relationship to those in power, and their ambitions. All information they use to judge the newcomer and, in most cases, start undermining him or her.

Though I had been discreet, Gaspard had, of course, noticed me scanning the room. Without interrupting his conversation with Winston, he changed the way he was sitting to make himself less conspicuous.

I was about to tell both of them to be careful when Gaspard said in a breezy tone, "Come on, you should have known those blokes in the office were no danger!"

I looked at Winston, trying to gauge if he understood what his uncle was saying. He didn't seem to.

"What I mean," continued Gaspard, "is that the best way to hide is often to be in plain sight. If they had wanted to steal anything, they would never have done it on a Sunday morning when no one was in the office. They would have waited until the place was bustling. That's how you go unnoticed . . ."

He was probably right. It felt counterintuitive and yet true. The best way to avoid drawing attention was, of course, to act natural. After all, no one knew why Gaspard was there or what he had done for us.

I nodded and smiled.

"And there was no need to worry about my visit to the site," he continued. "I dropped in, of course, and I even brought back a few souvenirs we need to discuss. But I saw no one and no one saw me. Those who came afterwards were either careless or had other objectives. Don't tense up, people are looking . . ."

I nodded again, but my smile was forced this time. Gaspard had said all this as if he were talking about last night's dinner. Nothing in his body language or expression had changed. Anyone watching must have thought he was telling me about his holidays.

I was about to reply when two things happened.

First, Trémeau made her entrance. I hadn't expected her to turn up at HQ so early in the evening. Her presence when the Boss was absent was incongruous, unsettling even. She made sure to stop and say hello to everyone she crossed paths with, making ample use of her ability to simultaneously and convincingly feign interest in others, devotion to a higher calling, and an approachable personality. She really knew what she was doing. A few steps behind her, Texier was taking even longer with the party members. He had a lot of ground to make up. He had been so brutal with the Boss during the primary that many of his unconditional supporters considered that Texier had crossed a line. He knew it and was trying his best to backpedal. He was considerably less gifted in this field than his boss.

Just as Trémeau started up the steps, the Major came down to meet her and give her a proper welcome. Their encounter seemed friendly. I watched as they exchanged a few

words. Texier followed his boss. He had given me a mischie-
vous look to say hello and also, it seemed, to challenge me
somehow. He was shaking the Major's hand with the over-
the-top affection only arch-enemies within the same party
can muster.

The three of them talked for a while, and then I suddenly knew Texier was talking about me. You don't have to be
paranoid to know when people in the same room are talking
about you. Texier was probably asking where I was, pretending to look for me in the crowd. What he really wanted to
know was who I was talking to.

That's when the second thing happened, once again interrupting my train of thought. The phone that I had been
clutching all evening finally vibrated.

I turned my gaze from the Major to my mobile to consult
the first estimates.

I had rarely seen such ambiguous results.

59

Sunday 25ᵗʰ April, 6:34 p.m.

The results weren't bad, but they weren't good either. They were disappointing.

The Boss led the pack with 28% of the vote, but Vital was right on his heels at 25%. The total for the left was around 46%, with the Green Giant at 11% and the Lefty at 8%. My eccentric had secured 2% of the vote, and though he would endorse Vital as well, votes would be lost in the process—he had served his purpose.

The total for our camp was slightly lower. The Centrist had taken nearly 8% of the vote and had already unofficially endorsed the Boss for the second round. The Radical, at 4%, would do the same. Vercingetorix and my young environmentalist both took 2%. That made for a theoretical total of 44% of the vote for the right.

The Fascist had seduced 9% of voters and the weirdos had taken 0.5% each.

This election would be decided in the final stretch. It would mostly depend on the candidates' ability to draw voters from the extremes—those who disagreed with both the Boss and Vital.

The Boss could say he was confident that coming top in the first round would undoubtedly create additional momentum that would carry him to victory. And Vital could reassure himself with the fact that there were more voters on the left. Either way, one thing was for sure: the race was still wide open.

The pressure was on, and I loved it. I loved the idea of an old-fashioned duel between the left and the right. Man to man.

It took ten minutes to agree on our suggestion for the Boss. We had been focused, efficient, and on the same page. I was going to call him to share the forecast and present the speech Démosthène was finalizing. Marilyn would try to sell the journalists on the idea that the most important thing in the first round was taking first place.

The inner circle seemed to be working in harmony again. A miracle made possible by our dinner in Cherbourg?

In a bid to further strengthen our new entente cordiale, I invited the Major to stay while I called the Boss.

"Thanks, but no," he replied. "I don't have time. I have to go and mingle with the Barons, and I don't want to leave Trémeau and Texier unsupervised for too long."

He had a point.

"Who was that guy with you and Caligny earlier?" he asked before leaving.

I smiled. Even the Major got curious when someone new turned up at HQ.

"Winston's uncle," I replied. "He wanted to see where his nephew works."

"The legionnaire?"

I didn't hide my surprise. No one had ever evoked the existence of Caligny's uncle in front of the Major, much less his role over these past few weeks.

Now the Major smiled. "I do my due diligence as well, you know. Did you really think I would let someone get that close to the Boss without doing a little digging? Do I look like I was born yesterday?"

That was the second time I'd been asked something along those lines today. I stammered as I tried to formulate a reply, but the Major waved his hand to let me know the question was rhetorical. He was off to join the Barons.

"I'm not the only one though!" he said from the doorway.

"The only one who what?"

"The only one wondering who he was. Texier also seemed very interested. He tried to get something out of me—fairly discreetly, but still. He must also think I was born yesterday . . ." And with that he closed the door.

I sat alone at my desk, taken aback by this last piece of information.

Texier's interest in Gaspard Caligny didn't bode well, but I didn't have time to think about it. The moment had come to call the Boss and share the news. I had dreamed about this call. All apparatchiks dream of being able to tell their boss that he's come out on top in the first round of the presidential election. As is often the case, my expectations didn't exactly coincide with reality. I had imagined our exchange would be exciting and light-hearted, a certain victory. Instead, I felt worried and stressed.

Victory was within reach, sure, but defeat wasn't far off either.

60

Sunday 25th April, 7:59 p.m.

As soon as the TV presenters announced the Boss's score and his position in first place, a roar of applause rose up from the ground floor making the whole building shake. The volunteers saw his edge as a harbinger of victory, and they were delighted to express their joy and faith in their candidate. It made for great pictures—that was the main thing for now.

The volunteers' reaction contrasted dramatically with the ambiguous restraint that prevailed among the Barons. They had immediately understood that the results of the first round didn't give either candidate a solid advantage. Their faces remained reserved. Many of them had been pleased to see the Boss come in first if their smiles and audible congratulations were to be believed. But since he wasn't there, I think the goal was more to publicly voice support than to express any real satisfaction.

Among a few of them, I had caught a glimpse of a doubtful look that conveyed a fairly widespread concern in our camp. If the Boss hadn't managed to solidly outperform a candidate who had to justify the extremely middling results obtained by his party over the past five years, how could we be sure he would beat him in the second?

I agreed with the Barons' analysis but preferred the volunteers' enthusiasm by far. The former thought like the officers in a general staff. As spectators of a fight that they understand but have not themselves experienced, they suggest, suppose, infer, and relativize. As for the volunteers on the front lines, they knew deep down that it wasn't over yet, but they had won a battle and were celebrating that victory. There would be plenty of time to cry later if they lost the war.

The cleverest reaction came from Trémeau. She knew she was being watched, particularly since the Boss had decided to stay in Cherbourg. Her strategy focused on occupying any space the Boss left her.

In the wake of the announcement, she remained perfectly impassive. She had simply nodded measuredly, to express her satisfaction. Everything about her demeanour said she believed the Boss could win but that she knew it wasn't over yet. It was the perfect reaction, even I had to give her that. Too much enthusiasm would have been suspicious. Too much confidence would have come off as indifference. She knew the next two weeks would be difficult, but for her that was a good thing: if victory was uncertain, we would need her. The more the Boss needed her, the more powerful she became. It was as simple as that.

To set himself apart from Vital, the Boss hadn't wanted to wait for the results in Paris. He wanted to send a message about his commitment to the rest of the country. Speaking from the headquarters of his party in the capital, Vital would come across as a cog in the Parisian machine. The Boss would jump on a private plane to come straight home right after his airtime.

His reaction, when I had shared the ambiguous results, had been remarkably calm. Even on the phone, I could sense the self-control he had learned to channel by this point in the campaign. In moments like this, I couldn't help but think that if he was elected, he would rise to the challenge.

He had approved Démosthène's speech for the most part but had informed me that he would make a few changes himself. Then he told me he wanted to see me the next morning at eight o'clock at HQ to discuss our next move.

He was scheduled to speak at quarter to nine this evening from the campaign's regional headquarters which were based in an ultramodern farm about six miles from Cherbourg. I smiled as I thought about what sort of impact the visuals of the Boss there would have. He would definitely come across as a man of the people . . .

Winston had joined me. He wanted to know how the Boss had taken the news. All while watching the scene around us, I told him about our exchange. I may have delivered a slightly more enthusiastic and optimistic version than the original, but sometimes the troops needed motivating. That was part of my job, too.

I didn't take my eyes off Trémeau. Texier was following her around the room. He had noticed I was watching them. He stepped closer to his boss and whispered something in her ear that made her laugh heartily. They were making fun of me. I decided not to get upset, but I wasn't about to take it lying down either.

"Winston," I said, "your uncle won't get a real feel for HQ if he stays downstairs. He should come up and join us."

The kid looked at me, incredulous. "Are you sure?"

"Of course. Tell him to come up and listen to the Boss's speech with us. He'll learn a lot. And I'm rather eager to up the pressure on that arsehole Texier."

After all, if Texier wanted to know who Gaspard was, maybe I should help him out. I was impatient to see if he made Texier as uncomfortable as I expected. It's the little things in life . . .

61

Sunday 25th April, 8:25 p.m.

The arrival of Gaspard Caligny in the Barons' lair had a noticeable effect on its occupants.

Conversations dwindled and eyes, which had been trained on the television screens until moments before, now strayed. Someone new, a man no one really knew, had just entered an extremely exclusive club.

The Baron from Brittany nearly suffocated. Gaspard Caligny must have seemed like a ghost to him. As I watched the Baron cough and splutter, I remembered that he had experienced the rise of Winston's father in his region as a threat and his death as a blessing.

Texier had tensed as soon as he had seen Gaspard. It was more than curiosity. I didn't know what, but I could see that there was something between them—tension, fear, something . . .

I would have to look into it.

By the time I had introduced Gaspard to an old friend of the Boss's, Texier had moved on. He was standing with another MP watching the screen. Trémeau was chatting with a group of Barons who were fawning over her to such an extent it was almost indecent. Since the man who could become president was away, they might as well get on the good side of the woman who could soon be prime minister.

As for me, I once again told the story of how the Boss had reacted to the results and summarized what he would say in a few moments. All of the Barons within earshot diligently agreed with our approach. Texier was still in front of the screen, making calls.

Gaspard was talking to the Baron from Brittany, who was doing his utmost to appear friendly and warm despite the sweat pearling on his forehead from fear. Winston, alongside his uncle, was smiling happily. I had no idea what they were talking about, but the kid certainly seemed to be having a good time.

And just then, I saw Texier close his flip phone, scan the room to make eye contact with Trémeau, and share a conspiratorial smile with her. Not the smile of an employee checking in on his boss, no. There was something twisted in it, something unhealthy. Those two were working on a low blow.

I cut my conversation short and made my way over to Winston and his uncle. Gaspard was putting on a real show. He was asking the Baron all the questions one might ask before going into politics. The Breton Baron was doing his best to convince them that he saw Gaspard's ambition in a positive light, suggesting that he could even advise him and introduce him to people. But his entire being betrayed his apprehensions about this charming young man whose name, in the region, evoked talent and hope cut short by fate. The poor old man had come out for a fun night and now found himself entertaining a Kennedy.

I was taken aback to see Gaspard indulging in this little game. Once again, I had to admit that behind the rude military man exterior, he really was very witty with a fine sense of humour. Winston was clearly as much the product of his uncle's upbringing as his father's genes.

Taking advantage of my arrival, the Breton Baron retreated to the buffet table.

"So, when will you start your campaign?" I asked teasingly.

"Tomorrow," Gaspard replied with a smile. "I'd like to know how long you think it'll take me to beat that guy. You think I can do it?"

"Easier said than done if you want my opinion. If you get started tomorrow, it'll be too late. As soon as he's done at the buffet, he'll be setting up a Breton Defence League to protect the region from the return of any Caligny, and believe me, though he doesn't look like much, he's tough. He's seen plenty of rivals come and go. Politics are no laughing matter in Brittany!"

Winston laughed openly, followed by his uncle.

"Shame, guess I'll throw in the towel, then. But I'm not sure I'll recover . . . I felt for sure this was my path . . . Democracy in action, the greater good . . ." he said sarcastically.

I rolled my eyes but said nothing. I turned my attention to the screens. On every channel a handful of Barons were commenting on the results without saying anything of interest.

With nothing else to do, I asked Winston to go and check with Marilyn what time the Boss would be giving his speech in the end. When his nephew left, Gaspard came closer.

"Speaking of which, we still need to talk about what I brought back from my visit," he said in a near whisper.

"You have something new? I thought everything was encrypted?"

"Encryptions can be decrypted," he replied. "This isn't the time or place, but I have things to tell you. Alone."

"I can't leave until after the Boss's speech. Can we get a drink right after?"

Gaspard nodded to let me know he'd wait.

I watched him slowly make his way to a corner of the room where he could see everyone. What had he found out? And why did he want to talk to me alone? What did he want to hide from his nephew?

62

Sunday 25th April, 8:39 p.m.

It would be at least an hour before I could join Gaspard
Caligny, and I could tell I wouldn't be able to properly focus on anything else until then. Texier was still there. He had
moved closer to his boss and the small group that had gathered around her.

When I saw them this time, I suddenly wondered: why was
Trémeau here and not in a television studio? I seemed to remember that we had decided she would participate in one of
the televised debates. Politicians generally fought tooth and
nail for TV appearances, not to avoid them. And yet here she
was. It made no sense.

Unless it did, and I had somehow missed it, which was not
a good sign. If she wasn't on live television at the moment,
it was because she didn't believe it was in her best interest.
What could possibly push her to turn down a national television appearance when this evening's results had left her in a
relatively favourable position?

The Radical's face on all the screens, the way Texier had
signalled to Trémeau that something was about to happen,
and the smiles I had noticed between them suddenly hit me
like a freight train.

They were up to no good. The Radical was about to take
a shot at the Boss.

The Radical was a young man who had made a fortune in
business before nurturing his passion for politics. His money,

people skills, and charm had rapidly made him a favourite among the political press. A year before the election, a few journalists had predicted he could actually win.

The truth was that he had a real gift for speaking to journalists and explaining to them how he was different from other politicians. The problem was that only journalists ever fell for his act. During his campaign, he slowly realized that the French people weren't listening to him—in fact, most of them didn't even know who he was. Only beginner politicians and ministers are silly enough to believe that being in the Parisian papers is enough to win a presidential election.

With his 4% score in the first round, the Radical had just learned his lesson.

On screen, he looked pretty good for someone who had just been slaughtered. He was calm and spoke well. He was proud to have defended the ideals and values of his party, one of the oldest in France. A movement had begun to take shape and would continue to grow and spread. The rhetoric was rather biblical for a candidate who shouted his disdain for the Church from the rooftops, but the Radical's number one asset was that he was under no obligation to respect the usual constraints of political coherency. Even the name of his party defied logic. The Radical Party wasn't radical at all.

The Radical went on to thank his friends, party members, and those who had voted for him. At 4%, I couldn't help but think that they were all probably one and the same.

Everything could have gone splendidly. He could have invited his electorate to vote for the Boss in the second round, which would have been expected given that the radicals were part of the same opposition group as our party at the National Assembly. He could have at least encouraged voters to come together without even citing the Boss's name. That would have been interpreted by those in the know as an invitation to start negotiations. The Radical had only accounted for

4% of the vote, but we needed that 4%. He could have used the promise of an endorsement as leverage to get what he wanted: a ministry and a few districts, for example. That was all part of the game.

But nothing went at all as expected. His tone was aggressive. He questioned the conditions surrounding the campaign and harped on the fact that the French people must be able to trust their political representatives. He denounced old-school politics, which, he said, still ran the show. He concluded by announcing that he would not be endorsing any candidate for the second round, because he wasn't even sure who he himself would vote for.

The Barons gasped in unison. Nothing could have predicted such a virulent pronouncement. Our messaging was focused on opening up to other voters and uniting, but now we would also have to manage this imbecile who had apparently decided to shoot his closest allies in the foot.

I was dumbfounded. I had to warn the Boss immediately so he could change the speech he was about to give. Since the Radical had spoken first, he had stolen the Boss's chance to deliver a victory speech and forced him instead to respond.

Texier and Trémeau had smiled. It had been discreet and fleeting, but I didn't miss it. They had known. They had known all along that the Radical was going to cross us. And something told me that Trémeau and Texier also had something to do with him choosing that path. If that was true, it meant that they were willing to betray their own party if it was in their long-term interests.

I immediately started thinking about our next move. The situation was incredibly complicated. I had to call the Boss for the second time tonight. And I wasn't looking forward to it.

63

Sometimes I wondered if they were trying to kill me.

It had started the night before with the Boss. He had stayed calm on the phone, but I could tell from his tone that he was doing his utmost to stifle his simmering anger. After a few laconic but biting sentences, he told me to be in the office at seven thirty the next morning, reminding me that it was my job to anticipate and prevent the sort of unpleasantness the Radical had just inflicted. I had kept my mouth shut. He was right.

After that, I had spent my night trying to come up with solutions to get the Boss out of this mess. I hadn't slept. I could tell I was seeing things less and less clearly as the campaign drew to a close. I wasn't sure I'd make it out in one piece.

The next morning, when I opened the door on my way out, I jumped and shouted. The Godfather was standing on my doorstep. Given how little I had slept, I was lucky my heart didn't give out. For a second, I actually wondered if Gaspard was there to settle some score. I didn't think I had done anything to deserve his wrath, except maybe standing him up the night before, but if he was angry about that, he could take it up with the Radical. After all, he was the one who had forced me to cancel.

"We need to talk," said Gaspard.

I sighed and gathered my wits. "Right, I'm sorry about last night. I had an emergency to handle. I don't have much time now either. I have to meet the Boss at HQ. There's a taxi waiting downstairs and I want to get there early so I can read the papers before he gets there."

"I'll ride with you. We need to talk."

I didn't have the strength to argue with a former soldier so early in the morning.

I tried to get the conversation going in the taxi, but with a commanding gesture, Gaspard let me know it was not a topic to be broached in the presence of a third party—even one as disinterested as our driver, who was fully concentrated on the news that he had turned up full blast.

When we reached my office at HQ and before I could even pour our coffee, Gaspard pulled a USB key from his pocket.

"What's this?" I asked.

"A USB key."

Why did they all seem to assume I was a moron?

"I can see that," I replied sarcastically. "What's on it?"

"Something very educational. Something that I'm pretty sure will worry you. Something I managed to decrypt after my visit to Droid."

"You've decrypted it all?" I asked. "I thought it would take time."

"It does. Whoever encrypted the documents had some serious equipment. I haven't cracked it all yet, it'll take a while longer, but I have this so far."

"Go on."

"I have proof that the primary was rigged."

I sat there with my mouth open wide. There were better ways to start a Monday morning.

"This file is a compilation of data related to the vote. A kind of vote meter, if you will, which recorded the number of votes cast every minute during the whole day of the election."

"I see. Like a digital version of the old-fashioned counters on top of ballot boxes?"

"Exactly, but this one counted all of the votes cast in the primary, not those for a single polling place. It's an overall counter, okay?"

Winston must have told him that I wasn't exactly tech savvy. He was treating me like an idiot. That said, if he had used more complicated language, I probably would have asked him to simplify . . .

"If you take a look at the file, and I think you should, you'll see the number of overall votes over the course of the day. You'll note that it doesn't increase in regular intervals, which is normal of course."

"Right. Even with physical ballot boxes, there are always many more voters in the late morning, between eleven and one. We call it the 'after Mass effect' or the 'aperitif effect' for the non-Catholics."

"The day of the primary, there was a slight increase in voters at that time as well. Which doesn't make much sense."

"Why not?"

"Because the voting took place online, so from people's homes. If we know people tend to go out around eleven o'clock, then that's not when voting should peak in this scenario."

I understood where he was coming from, but he was wrong.

"No, it makes perfect sense. First, because young people probably wake up around noon on Sunday, and they were the ones voting from home. But the many, many old people with no computer at home—and there really are a lot, believe me—went into party offices to vote. And it makes sense that they would turn up after going to church or just before lunch. Your peak can be explained the same way it always is."

I felt surer of myself. Gaspard had misinterpreted the data.

"Okay," he agreed, "but that doesn't explain the other peak."

"What other peak?"

"The one that happened at 5:50 p.m."

5:50 p.m. I still didn't see why that was particularly surprising. Polling places were always busier just a few minutes before closing. It was the "latecomer effect".

"And don't talk to me about latecomers," said Gaspard. "This peak is huge. And most importantly, it was buried."

What was he on about? Realizing I was lost, Gaspard grabbed a pen and a piece of paper.

"There were 302,340 party members who could vote in the primary. 229,817 of them actually voted. You with me?"

Of course I was. I knew those numbers by heart.

"The vote was open from eight to six. That means about 230,000 people voted over the course of ten hours."

"That's an average of 23,000 per hour." I could do maths, too!

"But voters didn't stick to averages, of course. During the first hour of voting, only 17,372 people cast their ballots. And during the second, it was 22,107."

"And during the first peak?"

"From eleven to noon, 32,000 people voted. From noon to one, it was about 26,000. After that, things calmed down. But can you guess how many people voted between five and six o'clock?"

"No idea. 35,000?" I suggested, guessing that the two peaks had probably been about the same size.

"Not far off. 36,364 to be exact."

"What's so shocking about that? You think it's strange that 36,000 people in the entire country waited until the last minute to vote? Gaspard, I'm sorry, but I think you might be more paranoid than I am."

"Maybe . . . But the counter I mentioned earlier doesn't just measure votes per hour. It also records the number of votes *per minute*."

I didn't see where he was going with this.

"And?"

Gaspard smiled. "Well, between 5:49 p.m. and 5:51 p.m., 27,482 people voted. That's a lot of people in two minutes. Too many people. So many it's hard to explain. Impossible, even."

He was right.

"But why did you say this peak had been buried?"

"Because it was. The file I decrypted is not the file that was sent to the primary oversight committee. The official file looks perfectly normal. It includes the midday rush, but not the 5:50 p.m. peak, which was spread out over the last two hours of voting to be less noticeable. The primary was definitely rigged. That much is sure. The problem remains that we still don't know who is behind it or who benefited from it, really."

"I'm not sure I follow."

"Well, we don't know who the fraudulent votes were for. In other words, we don't know if those votes led to your boss's victory by taking him over the top at the last minute, or if they simply reduced his lead, which would have been even greater three minutes before voting closed."

I had been telling myself since the beginning of this mess that we were in for a nasty surprise, but this was still a blow. Supposing that there may have been voter fraud is quite a different thing than knowing for sure that there was.

I sat silently across from Gaspard. I didn't know what to say. I was angry with myself for missing the signs, for not knowing that it was possible to rig the election and that it had in fact been rigged.

"What did you do with the original files?" I asked hoarsely. "Did you destroy them?"

Gaspard gave me a scornful look. "Why would you ask me that? Are you trying to get rid of all proof of the fraud? To cover for your boss or for yourself?"

I opened my mouth but no sound came out. Gaspard thought I was behind it. And I could tell from his eyes that if I was, that meant I had deliberately involved his nephew in a dangerous and twisted series of events which I had myself set in motion. And I knew the Godfather well enough to know that if I didn't change his mind quickly, things wouldn't turn out well for me.

That's when the Boss, early for our meeting, stepped into my office. He looked to be in a foul mood. On top of that, he seemed surprised to find me with someone he didn't know just a few minutes before our meeting.

He instantly recognized Gaspard Caligny, though. If you knew Winston and had known his father, the resemblance was so striking that there could be no doubt.

"You must be Louis's uncle," he said.

"Indeed, I am."

"I'm delighted to meet you. I didn't know you were busy," he said, turning to me. "I apologize for interrupting." Then, beaming, he returned his gaze to Gaspard. "Your nephew is just wonderful. He's a big help. You should be proud of him. Really. I'm not sure I've ever met someone so promising at his age. And I hear he owes much of that to your advice and support. You've done a great job with him. Well, I have a lot to do today, so I'll leave you two, but I'd love to talk another time."

Before leaving, the Boss had put on his most radiant smile and warmest tone. I was certain that he really thought everything he'd just said. I'd never heard him so full of praise for anyone in this profession.

Gaspard nodded without a word. He felt awkward since he was both intimidated by the Boss and suspicious of him, though only I could discern the latter.

"Listen, Gaspard," I said when the Boss was gone. "You haven't known me for very long, and I know you don't much care for the world I live in, but I swear to you, on everything I hold dear, that I am not behind the voter fraud. I swear."

Gaspard remained impassive.

"I didn't ask if you had destroyed the originals to get rid of any proof," I continued earnestly. "I asked because I wanted to know who else might know what you know. My goal is not to cover for anyone, but to take my boss to victory and prevent that from becoming impossible because someone leaks this file."

Still no reaction from Gaspard.

"I swear I had nothing to do with it. And I'm almost certain that the Boss didn't either. Gaspard, you're the only person I can say this to. I'm almost sure that he isn't behind it, but I'm not completely sure. But until I have hard proof that he was, I trust him. Do you have that proof? If you show it to me, if it exists, then . . ." I trailed off. I couldn't bear to think of what it would mean for me and the man I had chosen, the man to whom I had devoted nearly my entire professional life—and much of my personal life—the man in the big office on the other side of the corridor who might be president of France in two weeks.

Gaspard put the USB key back in his pocket.

"I didn't destroy them, because for now it's better that those behind the fraud don't know I know. But I have all the files. I haven't deciphered them all yet, but I will. I will find out who rigged the election. I want to believe it wasn't you. I'll give you the benefit of the doubt. But if it is you, I'll know soon enough."

"I'm sorry, but I just don't understand. Vital could hear about it from the police . . ."

"First, they may never find it. I didn't steal the file, but I re-encrypted it, which has multiple advantages: if they decrypt it, they'll think no one else has ever seen it, and if they can't manage it, we'll be the only ones. Either way, they'll have no idea we have the data."

"That's all well and good, but we won't know if Vital is on the right path."

"No, we won't. The police have a lot of information—everything we have and probably several things we don't. But they're missing one crucial thing: the link with your ginger friend, whom I'm about to get my hands on."

Just thinking about the redhead who had roughed me up not once but twice made my jaw clench.

"All right," I conceded. "Work as fast as you can to decrypt the rest of the files. And to find out whoever is behind this. This is more than a rigged election; people died. And others could die too. I won't tell Winston any of this. I think it's better to put a little distance between him and this mess."

Gaspard nodded and stared me straight in the eye as though he was looking into my soul. His eyelids narrowed. He had just given me my final warning.

64

Monday 26ᵗʰ April, 7:28 a.m.

The Boss was going over his files, red pen in hand, briefly annotating each document. I knew that as tension mounted, he found this daily ritual soothing. Some people smoked. Others drank. He worked.

Before I could say a word, he laid into me. "I can't believe no one saw that arsehole coming! I'm surrounded by a team of people who think they're the best in the business, and yet, on the night of the first round of the presidential election, a loser with 4% of the vote throws me under the bus and no one saw it coming. What the hell have you all been doing?"

His voice was calm, but his anger still palpable. I decided to keep quiet and let the storm pass.

"Did you see how that turned out? I was forced to change tack at the last minute. I had to try and dig myself out of a hole on live television instead of capitalizing on my victory."

"You did a good job of it. Really."

The Boss nodded anxiously. He was starting to calm down and get back to thinking.

"What happened? Why attack me now? Let me be very clear, if he's hoping to get a ministry with tactics like that, he's got another thing coming. I'll show him who's boss."

"I really don't understand," I replied. "I tried to call him last night, but he didn't answer. I spoke to his right-hand man. He doesn't understand either, actually. At least that's what he says, and I generally find him trustworthy. I guess he just lost it. Or . . ."

The Boss stared at me, waiting for me to finish.

"Or, someone told him something that *made* him lose it. The Radical is an arse, to be sure, but he's no idiot. If he's refusing to play ball, it's because he thinks that you're going to lose, or that he'll get more out of playing with someone else."

"Who? Vital?"

"I have a hard time imagining him in bed with a candidate who belongs to the majority he has been fighting for the past five years. The radicals are twisted, but not even they would go that far . . ."

"It's happened before, you know. A major ministry goes a long way in convincing people."

"I know, but I don't think Vital's behind it. Did you notice anything strange on the televised discussions last night?"

"Besides the plethora of platitudes our beloved commentators enjoy spouting? Vital was pretty good. Confident. That said, *he* didn't have to handle a defection in his own camp just five minutes before speaking . . ."

I wasn't sure I would ever hear the end of that one.

"Our guys were good, too," continued the Boss. "And I noticed once again that my lovely running mate didn't bother to even . . . Actually, I didn't see her at all last night. She called me around nine thirty to congratulate me and tell me we were off to a good start, but I didn't see her . . . What channel was she on?"

"None. Not a single one. Which I find strange. And in my experience when two strange things happen in a single evening, there's often a link between them."

Deep in concentration, the Boss looked up at the ceiling. After a few seconds, the fingers on his right hand began fiddling with his wedding ring. Between the presidential race and his wife's illness, I couldn't imagine the pressure he was under.

I didn't dare move or speak.

He finally broke the silence in a calm voice. "That conniving bitch is going to use this to get ahead. She'll secure her position as prime minister by casting herself as the protector of a united majority. She stayed off the air last night so she wouldn't have to respond to that bastard. She's going to let him criticize the campaign, then make a show of bringing him back into the fold. And it will be a win-win for her because she'll be playing a central role if the radicals manage to put together a parliamentary group after the legislative elections."

Bingo. I had been right about her being behind it, but the Boss had been quicker at figuring out why and how.

"I'm afraid you're right," I said. "But I don't understand how she got the Radical on board. It's risky for him."

After thinking for a moment, the Boss slammed his fist into the desk. I jumped. My heart couldn't withstand much more if they kept this up.

"She won't get away with this! First, the Radical, as you know, is nuts. He'll never be a minister under any prime minister I name. Do you hear me? That's final. Can you think of anyone who could sow a bit of chaos within the Radical party? Some up-and-coming young chap with a bright future? Or someone with solid experience?"

"There's Roumert. The MP from Moselle for the past two terms. Serious. Nice guy. Ambitious but reasonable."

"Perfect. He will be our token radical minister. And we'll give him a good ministry, too. But first I need him to do something for me now. He needs to divide his party. Shouldn't be too hard, right?"

That was a euphemism.

"Second, I want you to negotiate with our nationalist friends this morning. I'm open. I need them. They need us, too. They have legislative elections to finance, and I doubt they have a single cent left after their poor performance. I can agree to ten or so seats at the National Assembly. And we'll reimburse all of their debt as long as they join our parliamentary group. Let's do our best to be inviting. If they need more, we'll think about it. But I don't want them breaking off and creating an independent group, okay?"

"Got it."

"I imagine the Centrist is going to act like one?"

"Given yesterday's events, I prefer to be cautious, but I think things should go to plan. As troubling as it may be, I'd venture so far as to say that I trust him—it's the first time I've ever said that about a centrist."

"Things change. I hope you're not wrong. Make an earnest and inviting appeal to him, too. Together we stand, divided we fall and all that. Lay it on thick."

"They're going to want guarantees."

"Go ahead and give them, then. Go out on a limb, but make sure to leave me some wiggle room. Get the Major involved."

When he noticed my surprise, the Boss smiled. "Since people will soon know about the dissensions within my team, we'll blame any changes of direction on poor communication. That's how I'll keep my voters and rally new ones to us. Get to work."

The Boss had handed down his orders and could get back to his notes. I stood up, somewhat troubled by his final remark, but reassured by the clear orders he had given.

I had my hand on the doorknob when he looked up and asked, "Where are you with the voter fraud business?"

Should I tell him that I knew for sure now that the primary had been rigged? That I would soon know who was behind it? That Caligny's uncle thought *he* might be behind it? That I was almost convinced myself?

"I'm making headway, Boss. Slowly but surely. I'll know soon."

"Soon it will be too late."

The Boss had also just given me my final warning . . .

65

Wednesday 28ᵗʰ April, 12:22 p.m.

Usually, after the first round, the final outcome has been decided.

It's a basic calculation which all apparatchiks can do in their sleep. You learn on the job, through experience. All you have to do is take whoever's in the lead, determine where the tipping point is between votes on the left and the right, compare it with the last several elections, and you've got your winner. Give me the results from any first round and I can predict the winner of the second with ninety-five percent accuracy.

Everything's decided, unless . . .

Apparatchiks also learn this second basic principle over the years. Unless the second round is between three candidates who garnered enough votes in the first. Unless something serious happens between the two rounds. Unless there's an extra-terrestrial among the remaining candidates, someone whose fame and charisma can turn a trend around. The list goes on and on, and there's a never-ending store of surprises to be added to it.

One rule and many exceptions. So many things in France operate under this system. Grammar. The law. Politics are no exception. It's a rule.

Despite all this, three days after the first round, I was sure of one thing: the outcome of this presidential race was terribly uncertain. The final showdown had rarely been so open-ended.

The Boss was in the lead, and that gave him good momentum. But Vital wasn't far behind, and he *theoretically* had more reserve voters on the left. Ah, the transfer of votes between the rounds. Incomprehensible electoral arithmetic that kept the political analysts talking for the full two weeks.

The Boss had earned 28% of the votes and needed to reach a little more than 50%. We had to turn our attention to voters who had cast ballots for the candidates closest to us: the Centrist who had garnered 8% of the votes, the Radical, who was turning out to be more difficult than expected, at 4%, Vercingetorix, the impassioned, anti-European nationalist at 2%, and my right-wing environmentalist at 2%. That made for a very theoretical total of 44% on the right, and again, that was only if we managed to convince everyone. Getting all of them to endorse the Boss was a prerequisite for victory, but it wouldn't be enough to get us over the top. And we had to avoid angering the Fascist while we were at it.

In other words, at the very least, the Boss would need to take all of the centrist votes without upsetting the far-right voters, win over the Catholics without antagonizing the anti-clericals, and unite the pro-Europeans without enraging the nationalists. A seemingly impossible feat, but one that many had successfully accomplished before us. Every president ever elected actually.

My young right-wing environmentalist would enthusiastically rally to our cause: she was my puppet.

I knew Vercingetorix well. His convictions were as solid in the first round as they were negotiable for the second: for a minor ministry for him and a few districts for his friends (the Boss was offering eleven, but I was sure I could make a deal for five or six), he would fall in line.

The Centrist and the Radical were a different story. We hadn't tried to dissuade the former from running, and we

had made the right decision: he had swept a portion of the
centrist vote that could have gone to Vital if he hadn't been in
the race. But we had created a monster that was beginning to
realize the extent of its power and fully intended to capitalize
on it. I had a meeting with his right-hand man that afternoon.

As for the Radical, his tirade on Sunday night had surprised everyone, and I was afraid he might be uncontrol-
lable . . .

I was preparing for my meeting with the centrist's man,
thinking about all the tricks he would try to play, when Marilyn came in without knocking. I smiled instinctively. Sin-
cerely, like before. She was ice cold in return. Fixing our
relationship would have to wait. She was working and had
no time to lose.

"The Sorcerers want us to talk about his wife," she said
bluntly. "Bloody bastards."

"He'll never agree to it. And he'll send them packing if
they so much as mention it."

"*If* they talk to him about it . . . One of them seems inclined
to leak his wife's illness to the press, to make him seem more
personable and play on undecided voters' heartstrings . . ."

I said nothing. The Sorcerers were all about image. That
was their job. But I knew the Boss well enough to know that
he would disapprove of this strategy.

"Do *you* think we should leak it?" I finally asked.

Marilyn shrugged. She wasn't totally sure. "I don't like it,
but I can see their point. Cancer patients, their families, and
little old ladies will feel sorry for him. Widowers will identify
with him. That's a lot of people."

"Try thinking about it this way: a poor sick wife abandoned by her husband who's too busy with the campaign
and his political future to take care of her. How will that go
over?"

Marilyn looked at me, taken aback. "Not bad. Good argument. Too bad you're such an arse." And with that she stood up and left.

I sat alone in my office, smiling. In her own way, Marilyn had just given me a compliment. Coming from her, that meant something. Maybe it would even pave the way for a truce between us. Maybe. Just a few hours before entering negotiations with the centrists, the moment was too precious not to savour.

66

Wednesday 28th April, 12:44 p.m.

I had taken out the file I had compiled on the Radical over the years, to prepare an attack and convince him to endorse the Boss.

My files. What would I do without them?

The inner circle mocked my old paper files on the country's major political figures. Despite the rise of the internet, they were still filled with yellowed press clippings and handwritten notes on napkins. Over the years, I had gathered information on about a hundred politicians.

Every morning I had my secretary add new documents to them: articles, announcements, and rumours to check up on. It had become a habit, and I had never been able to go digital. I trusted my little safe more than I trusted any digital security system. Recent events had strengthened my conviction that paper was best.

I had pulled the Radical's file from my safe. There had to be something in there that I could use to pressure that stubborn bastard . . . I dusted off the cover and started reading everything inside from the oldest documents to the most recent. The general feeling I got from reading the file was negative, but there was nothing I could turn into a real scandal.

If I had seen this coming, I could have dug deeper or made up my own rumour to take him down, but now I was out of time.

I was feeling discouraged.

* * *

I was going to have to go above board in my dealings with the Radical. Morally speaking, this was a good thing, of course. As for my immediate future, I wasn't so optimistic.

How had I—a man whose reputation was rooted in a propensity for dirty tricks and brutality—found myself in a situation where I was the only one playing by the rules?

67

Wednesday 28th April, 5:06 p.m.

"So, we're in agreement?"

"For the most part."

"Centrist voters won't go and cast their ballots for Vital?"

"I should hope not."

"You're on board with the platform we rolled out during the campaign?"

"Yes."

"And we can count on a joint campaign for the legislative elections?"

"Not joint. Coordinated. In the districts where we can't agree on a single candidate for the first round, the runner-up will step down."

It wasn't quite as good as I had hoped, but it would do. We just had to avoid running important candidates against one another.

"Great. So, your boss will endorse mine now?"

"No."

Despite the fact that I was comfortably seated in a leather armchair drinking a really good whisky and the fact that I had already been subjected to all of the snubs a centrist can inflict on another politician, I was surprised by his cheek.

"You're *not* going to advise your voters to vote for us? I don't understand. What are you going to do then? Go fishing? Refuse to join the parliamentary majority? You said yourself that none of your voters would follow you in an alliance with Vital!"

"I see you expected us to fall in line without a fight."

"What do you want? Ministries? You'll have them, but we can't decide how many and which ones right now."

The man could smile through any situation.

"I'm not worried. You'll give us ministries. You can't do it without us. You might manage a majority in the National Assembly without us, but not in the Senate. You'll need us. I'm glad you're offering ministries, thank you, but you haven't really given me anything since I already knew we would have them."

"Ministries come in all shapes and sizes . . ." I countered.

"Because you were planning on leaving us nothing but crumbs? That would be rather unreasonable . . ."

It was true that the centrists carried more weight in reality than the 8% of the vote their candidate had taken in the first round. Like the communists on the left, they had managed, defying all logic, to maintain a tightknit network of local officials and MPs who made them much harder to ignore than one might imagine.

In my world, strength is measured either by your ability to lead or your ability to cause trouble. Few people had ever seen a centrist lead anyone anywhere, but everyone knew that they were great at causing trouble. As a younger man, the Boss had often said that a good centrist was a dead centrist . . .

The nationalist's lackey had been much easier to convince. He had just two demands. First, I promised him that no one would have to use their own money to pay for the campaign if the Boss won, though I wasn't exactly sure how I was going to pull that off. Second, he wanted his boss to be a member of the government. That was easy. We could always come up

with a position for him. Just look at all of the past govern-
ments in the Fifth Republic and every French Republic before that and you'll see from the collection of eccentric job
titles that it's an easy demand to meet.

He left my office happy, and we had agreed that his boss
would attend the Boss's final campaign rally to announce his
endorsement with great pomp and circumstance.

But he was small fry. Across from me sat the real prize,
and this was a whole different ballgame.

Lost in my thoughts, I let the silence between us draw out as
my adversary enjoyed his Strathisla. Lovers of fine whisky
know it's best to keep quiet when enjoying a masterpiece.

I went over what could be behind his refusal again and
again.

"What's standing in the way? Really. I don't see it," I said
finally.

"Trémeau. Trémeau as prime minister."

"You're joking."

"Do I look like I'm joking?"

"Do you want guarantees she *will* be prime minister or
that she won't?"

There was a long silence as he continued to smile. I would
have to figure it out on my own. I did the best I could with
what was left of my brain after the primary and the campaign.

It seemed that the centrists didn't want Trémeau to be
prime minister. But why? I could see that the centrist leader
might not want to see the woman who would most likely be
running against him for president in the future sitting pretty
at Matignon. But that said, serving as prime minister didn't
actually help candidates win the presidential election. Under the Fifth Republic, a sitting prime minister just before
the election had never managed to take the presidency.

I excluded the possibility of an affair gone wrong. It happened all the time but rarely led to such lofty political demands. And I had a hard time imagining Trémeau getting it on with this Bible basher. That said . . . Now that it had occurred to me, true or not, the rumour would be a fun one.

After thinking a bit longer, I realized that Trémeau's manoeuvre to shepherd the Radical and his party into the majority could handicap the centrists. If, thanks to Trémeau, the radicals took up too much space in the majority, they would threaten the centrists. A radical is a centrist who doesn't believe in God. If Trémeau became prime minister, the centrists feared that their candidate would be forgotten in favour of the Radical. All he would have to do is take the anticlerical rhetoric down a notch and he could quickly become the leader of the centrist party, too. And so doing, the Radical would help Trémeau, who would also be eliminating a serious adversary in the next presidential election. It was terribly clever.

"You know," I ventured, "the Boss will teach the Radical a lesson. He's an idiot. If I were you, I wouldn't worry too much about him . . ."

My adversary's face remained for the most part impassive, but I noticed his lips purse ever so slightly and he blinked meaningfully. I could see I had guessed right. I hadn't reassured him yet, but at least I knew what he was after now.

"That's not the only problem," he said.

Bloody hell. This time, it would be up to him to explain himself. I wasn't going to keep solving riddles all evening.

"We don't understand why you let people announce unofficially that she would be prime minister. Why didn't you ever deny it?"

I was taken aback. As if not understanding someone's motives in this profession was a justification for anything.

"What I mean," he continued, "is that we don't understand why you chose her. You beat her in the primary. You don't trust her. She spews insults about you whenever she gets the chance. She's worth much less to you than we are, but you gave her Matignon before the first round. There's something fishy about it."

"As you know, in politics we're rarely surrounded by people we like and trust. If we were, you wouldn't be sitting here with a guy like me."

He nodded with something that looked like regret. The assertion was indisputable but rather dismal.

"You're right," he said. "But I know you're not telling me everything. Don't take me for a fool. After a bloody primary, your boss comes out on top in a narrow victory. We start hearing rumours of voter fraud and then, bang! Before the election, before the first round even, when you're under no obligation, you let people believe that Trémeau will be prime minister. You threw yourselves on her mercy by doing that. And it's not like you. You or your boss."

I kept quiet and held my breath. He hadn't finished.

"The only logical reason is because you were scared. Scared of her undoubtedly. So, my question is: does she have you by the balls or not? Because if she does, *she* will have all the power, and if that's the case, why should we back you? And be conned by Trémeau for the next five years?"

"I get what you're saying, but I'm not sure that justifies your refusal to back the Boss in the second round. That would mean taking a considerable risk for your leader. And Trémeau will screw you over even more if you're not willing partners from the beginning."

"If you win."

"If we lose and it's your fault, your boss doesn't stand a chance in five years."

"Five years is a long time. People forget . . ."

"Not that. It would take them much longer than five years to forget something like that. And if you look at it the other way around, since five years is such a long time, you can count on the fact that the Boss will find a way to handle Trémeau. You know him. He has a lovely collection of trophies on his wall, and I'm sure he would be delighted to add Trémeau and Texier's heads to it as soon as possible."

I knew I wouldn't be able to convince him tonight, but I had sown the seeds of doubt. His boss would have to back mine. I would have bet my life on it.

There was another strange silence as he emptied his glass. Mine was still full.

"I know you think my boss will endorse yours in the end, and I understand why. We centrists aren't known to hold out for long. But my boss is determined to run again in five years. He's sure he can win, and he's right to hope. As long as he thinks that Trémeau as prime minister is the worst possible situation for him, he won't fall in line. If you say that nothing's been decided or that anything is possible, maybe he'll endorse you. Otherwise, no dice. He'll leave the job to the second string, and you won't get his support. And given your situation after the first round, you need him. He's worth more to you than Trémeau!"

He was wrong, but I couldn't tell him why. If we side-lined Trémeau now, she could blow everything up. If I knew that the primary had been rigged, she might, too. I couldn't take that risk. With her we weren't sure we'd win, but without her we'd definitely lose.

My counterpart's bright eyes and fixed smile had the same effect as ellipses at the end of a sentence you don't know how to finish. They said more than any speech. Maybe he knew things and wasn't letting on. Maybe he wanted me to think he did. There was no way to know with him. Like a poker player, he would never admit he was bluffing.

Unless I came up with a brilliant plan very quickly or Gaspard found us proof of who rigged the primary, I was going to have to give the Boss even more bad news.

68

Tuesday 4ᵗʰ May, 10:37 a.m.

"So, you want to lay off civil servants to lower taxes? Tell me, then, where will you be sacking police officers? Which hospital will be losing nursing staff? Lille? Lyon? Montbéliard?"

"I must admit, Mr Vital, you have a real gift for criticizing other people's ideas. Unfortunately, when it comes to your own ideas, your talents are less obvious. Your attack on our suggestions is pitiful, really. Let's not forget that over the past five years, the government you belonged to increased taxes and the number of civil servants, but during the same period, the quality of the public services you mention—healthcare, law enforcement, education—all declined. All of the international rankings say as much. And the French people have noticed."

"Our fellow French citizens will be expressing their opinions in four days' time. I trust them to make the right decision!"

"As do I, Mr Vital. As do I. I trust them to ask themselves if they think it's possible that by some miracle your agenda—which hasn't worked over the past five years—will suddenly start working. I trust them to know that it's time to do things differently. I have new ideas; you are still peddling the same old criticisms and solutions that have yet to produce a positive impact. And yet you expect the French people to believe you?"

"Excellent!" said the Major, who couldn't help but comment on the practice debate out loud.

The Boss stopped for a second. He didn't like distractions.

He and I were sat facing each other. The set was as similar as we could get to the venue where the Boss would have to win the real presidential debate, with the same timer and dimensions. But what we couldn't reproduce was the tension, which would grow exponentially over the next few hours.

The next day, at the real debate, the Boss and Vital would be afraid. Not for themselves, though. At their level, neither was afraid of losing any more. They had both lost plenty of times over the course of their careers and knew that it was part of the game. Since each of them was thoroughly convinced that he was the best man for the job, they weren't afraid of one another either.

If the Boss and Vital were afraid of anything, it was themselves. They feared they might not perform well, that they might miss an opportunity or be unable to contain their irritation, or worse, that they might misspeak, take too long to reply, or say something incomprehensible. I was sure the Boss was afraid of those things, and I would have bet my life that Vital was, too.

This morning, after days of preparations, we were running a dress rehearsal. Like in a theatre, we were doing a full run-through under performance conditions. The audience wasn't there, but for a televised debate, that hardly mattered. Vital was missing as well, which was, I had to admit, the biggest hurdle to a lifelike rehearsal. But it meant that I got to take his place for a couple of hours.

There was something wonderful about playing Vital.

For two hours, the Boss and I were on the same level. I could question him, interrupt him, and contradict him. A rare opportunity—of which I was taking full advantage.

"Let's carry on, gentlemen," said the journalist, an old friend of the Boss's who had agreed to pitch in. "We have discussed international politics as well as social and economic policy. The third part of this debate will focus on domestic policy, and I'd like to start by asking you what kind of president you hope to be. We know that presidential leadership styles can be just as important as policy, so how will you lead the French people? Mr Vital?"

My answer to this question was completely devoid of interest. Vital might be elected president, but I never would. I was mumbling a truism about the importance of taking the position seriously and following republican traditions when an idea popped into my head.

"And I think," I said, changing tack, "that a president must never stop being the President. Wherever he is, whatever he says, he embodies France and the Republic. And yet, it's important to keep from becoming too distant from the French people. The best way to stay close to the people is for the president to explain his choices and the challenges he faces as often as possible . . ."

The Boss looked at me, clearly wondering where I was going with this.

"I firmly believe that a presidential candidate is duty-bound to explain his choices to the French people. I am willing to do so. I hope you are, too."

"I couldn't agree more, Mr Vital," said the Boss. "At last, something we agree on."

"In that case, maybe you could explain the choices made during your campaign. We've been hearing that you've already chosen your prime minister should you win the election. You've let the rumour circulate, but you've never made an official announcement. Is that what you call explaining yourself?"

The Boss's stare darkened, and I could feel the team's ears prick up around us.

"What exactly are you insinuating?"

"Nothing at all. I'm simply asking a question. You've let people say that you have chosen your prime minister. Why not? But you should have the decency to explain your decision!"

"Mr Vital, I share your opinion that a president should explain himself—his choices and decisions. Not rumours."

Marilyn pursed her lips and the Major frowned.

"I suppose that's your idea of responsibility and transparency. You're all for it until you're asked questions you don't want to answer. Then you simply cast them as rumours . . . The French people want to know whether you intend to name Marie-France Trémeau prime minister if you win. Asking that question is not spreading rumours. I'm simply asking you to be open and honest."

The Boss was visibly tense. "Marie-France Trémeau is a remarkable MP. We have known each other a long time. She defends the ideas of my political family with talent and passion. She would undoubtedly make a very fine prime minister—"

"That's not what I'm asking—"

"And if you would stop interrupting me, you would get your answer," the Boss cut in dryly before pausing for a moment. He was still smiling, though, since he knew that the most important thing was to never seem angry, but I could tell that he was on the verge of betraying his feelings.

Everyone was watching him. The powerful Sorcerer was scribbling furiously in a notebook—observations he would share in the debrief.

"Marie-France Trémeau and I," he continued, "were adversaries in the primary. Each of us defended our own style and agenda. Neither one of us are the kind of person who gives up when faced with a challenge. That is one of the many things we have in common. But at the end of the day, the party chose me—"

"In a primary election that lacked transparency—a value you just claimed to defend!"

The Major exhaled sharply as if he'd just been punched in the stomach.

"Mr Vital, I won't let you get away with dragging this debate down into the mud with your insinuations. We are here to debate in front of the French people. If you have something to say or criticisms to get off your chest, come out and state them clearly!"

"I'm not insinuating anything. I'm asking questions, and the French people want answers. They're the ones who read in the papers and heard on the news from Mrs Trémeau and her partisans that the primary was run in less than ideal conditions."

"My party's primary designated me as the winner. Marie-France Trémeau has played a major role in this campaign and will play an important role over the next five years. She is perfectly qualified to serve as prime minister. And I maintain that our debate should be above insinuations."

What seemed very clear to me was that the Boss refused to come out and say that Trémeau would be prime minister. That meant I had some room to manoeuvre in my final negotiations with the centrists. I was delighted on that account, but I was there to push the Boss, not to hear what I wanted to hear.

"In other words, you refuse to answer my question . . . I think the French people have noticed your inability to express yourself clearly. It seems to me that the very least you could do as a presidential candidate, is answer questions about what you will do if you're elected!"

The Boss was furious. He was about to answer when the tension within him suddenly disappeared. His shoulders slumped and he seemed to have shrunk an inch or two. His voice went soft. "This isn't working. We're done for now."

I couldn't believe it. The journalist looked at me in surprise. The Major held his head in his hands. Winston was clearly trying to decipher the Boss's sombre expression.

I had never seen him cut a session short like that in all the time we'd worked together. He had just let himself be boxed in, which was terribly unlike him. I knew the extent of my own talents well enough to know that it wasn't really me. He had stumbled on his own. I had pushed him, of course, but Vital would never miss such an opportunity. I was just doing my job.

The Boss stood up without a word. After pacing the room for a moment, he left, mumbling that we'd pick up again later.

Marilyn looked worried. "You just couldn't help yourself, could you?"

I stared at her. What did she want me to do? Play a friendly Vital who did his best to protect the Boss's feelings?

"I didn't push that hard," I objected. "Vital can be much more aggressive than that."

"And the Boss can do much better than this! The idea behind a rehearsal is to build him up ready for tomorrow, not shoot him down!"

Marilyn could complain all she wanted; I had only been doing my job. No one else agreed with her. She was usually so lucid, but she seemed to be making one of the worst mistakes an apparatchik can make: swearing to her boss that he had done well when he had really crashed and burned.

There are two kinds of apparatchiks. The kind who obey without discussion, and those who obey after discussion. The former aim to execute orders as quickly and efficiently as possible. Little by little, they become lackeys, or even whipping boys. And when their boss makes a mistake, they blame fate or other people.

The latter naturally have more complicated relationships with their bosses. Disagreements can be shared and accepted.

For them, absolute loyalty is a prerequisite, particularly when it means implementing decisions they may have contested. They have more qualms than their counterparts and enjoy longer discussions and closer bonds with their bosses.

When I was honest with myself, I knew that we all moved between the two categories on a regular basis. Even I had a few examples of times when I had spinelessly agreed to a bad idea from the Boss. A moment of indecision, the path of least resistance, the desire to please or protect the Boss . . . Even the best of us could be lackeys at times.

In the end, the main thing wasn't belonging to one category or the other; it was choosing the right boss. Some of them wanted nothing but a smile and a nod from their employees. For them, questioning their decisions was treason; thinking was synonymous with betrayal.

Luckily for me, and for him, the Boss had nothing but disdain for such despots. Nevertheless, even he occasionally enjoyed a bit of fawning when he was down . . .

I looked around and realized that everyone was feeling as awkward as I was. The Boss hadn't come back and no one was certain he would. The thought of returning to the debate was intimidating. Even though I knew I hadn't strayed from my role, Marilyn wasn't totally wrong about what the actual goal of the rehearsal had been.

Winston, who hadn't left his seat and who was clearly heartbroken to see the Boss in such a state, now came over to try and comfort me. Such an endearing kid.

"Interesting turn of events," he said.

"Indeed. The kind of rehearsal that's best kept between us. Not what you expected, I imagine?"

"Not at all. But you know what struck me most?"

"The Boss leaving? Don't be too surprised. He may be the Boss, but he's still a man who loses his temper and makes mistakes sometimes. And he hates realizing he did a poor job. Tomorrow he'll be great. He'll eat Vital alive."

Winston stared at me intensely. "That's not it at all. I'm aware the Boss isn't a god, you know. He can't be perfect all the time. What struck me was his answer when you mentioned the voter fraud rumour and the way the primary was run."

I didn't remember what the Boss's reply had been. I knew he hadn't been convincing, but the rest was a blur. "What did he say, exactly?"

The kid's eyes widened. "Nothing. Nothing at all. It's what he didn't say . . ."

I was starting to see where he was going with this.

"Can you believe that he didn't even say that the primary was legitimate? You basically accused him of fraud, and he didn't deny it! Don't you think that's a bit strange?"

I did, of course. The Boss's attitude had been strange since the beginning.

"Maybe he forgot?"

"Maybe. Or maybe it's a confession . . ."

Winston had come to the same conclusion as his uncle. He had doubts about the Boss.

I was taken aback. It was impossible. There was no way the Boss could have been mixed up in something so sordid. Two men had died. I had almost been killed myself. Impossible. The Boss wasn't like that.

Unless maybe I, too, had migrated to that first category of apparatchiks.

69

Thursday 6ᵗʰ May, 5:31 a.m.

The huge venue had the feel of an empty cathedral. At the far end, there was a bit of light and activity around the altar.

I had slept three hours. I was tired, irritated, and unable to rest—like all those who have ever been truly exhausted. Too tired to sleep. I had to hang on for a few more days, but I honestly wasn't sure I'd make it.

The last campaign rally was scheduled for tonight at the Parc des Expositions in Paris, much to the dismay of the Barons. They had all pleaded for the climax of the campaign to take place somewhere else. Somewhere besides Paris, anywhere else, and if possible on their home turf, where they all promised record-breaking levels of attendance and an unbeatable atmosphere. For most of them, the choice of the location for the final rally was just another step in the fight to get closer to the Boss, gain influence, and make a show of their importance. Traditionally, at campaign rallies, the first speaker is always the mayor of the hosting city or town—as long as he or she falls on the same side of the aisle as the candidate. Speaking in front of forty thousand people, a slew of cameras, and all the other Barons was a rare privilege. No one wanted to miss out on such an opportunity.

This final rally was the political equivalent of high mass and always had an air of mystery about it. You had to believe in politics to understand the appeal. For cynics and abstention-ists of all backgrounds, campaign rallies are vain, grotesque, and hypocritical. For devotees, they're the highlights of pol-itical activism.

Everyone goes to church for different reasons, but they're all guided by the same faith.

As for me, I've never experienced the same type of en-thusiasm as the volunteers. I understand the magic of com-munion without really experiencing it. Like many of my counterparts, I fall into the category of people who see these events as operations or professional exercises. But over time, and with experience, I'd grown to enjoy the work that went on behind the scenes: the organization, the absurd amount of logistics required, the negotiations about the order of ceremonies, the tensions they create, and the tangential issues they inevitably bring to light.

I took a deep breath. Tonight was the last campaign rally. Maybe the last rally of the Boss's career. Maybe mine as well. I might as well enjoy it. As I neared the gigantic stage, I could make out Winston's silhouette. He was standing perfectly still in front of the stage, enthralled by the assembly work. I was impressed that he was already there.

The giant screens were going up. They were huge, but it was the bare minimum to ensure that those seated in the back would be able to see the Boss's face. Below them, on the stage itself, were the first rows of seats where the lucky few would take their places: young people, women, smiling, happy faces symbolizing the diversity of the France the Boss claimed to represent. The images would help to make up for the fact that he was a white man of a certain age.

But the most impressive feature by far had been chosen by the Major and the Valkyrie to really showcase the Boss's arrival and his speech.

While the other speakers would address the crowd from a podium off to one side of the huge stage, the Boss would deliver his speech from a mobile dais that would extend out towards the audience on nearly invisible rails. The symbolism had seemed a bit extreme to me at first, but the Major had convinced me with photographs from the most recent Republican convention in the United States. The Boss had agreed as well. Now, seeing the real thing, I couldn't deny that the mobile dais, complete with a podium and transparent teleprompters, was imposing.

"Impressive, right?" I said.

Winston jumped. He hadn't heard me walk up to him.

"It's incredible! But do you think they'll finish in time?"

Up close, I could see that the kid was just as tired as I was. He hadn't slept much either, of course. We had been together just four hours earlier at a restaurant where the Barons had wanted to take the inner circle after the debate to celebrate the Boss's performance. I had to admit he had done a good job. Neither arrogant, nor effacing, he had managed to place two well-worded quotes that would be broadcast by every media outlet in the country over the coming days. His demeanour had made it perfectly clear that he was ready, serious, comfortable, and capable. He had demonstrated that he could take the debate to a higher level when needed, but that he could also express himself in simple terms. At no point had he lost his temper. I wasn't sure that he had really won the debate, but he certainly hadn't lost, and he had definitely scored a few points. The contrast with the failed dress rehearsal was so striking that the inner circle had felt a wave of relief mixed with the anticipation of impending victory.

A few years earlier, I would have been proud of myself. I would have believed that the Boss's success was due to the preparations I had put him through. Maybe Winston still believed this. It wasn't totally impossible, of course. But I knew deep down that the Boss, like all truly gifted politicians, knew how to go above and beyond when the circumstances demanded it.

"Everything will be ready at the last minute," I replied. "These guys only work under pressure. You'll see. An hour before the event, it will still be a mess, with people rushing to put down the carpet and complete the finishing touches. It's always like that."

It was true. Over the years, I had determined that two golden rules invariably applied. First, no matter how unorganized things seem, everything turns out mostly okay. Second, regardless of how organized things are, there's always something that doesn't go to plan. As a result, I had decided long ago that there was no point worrying about any of it. However, choosing the right stage manager was paramount. With the Valkyrie, I knew I could rest easy.

"He was really good last night," said Winston.

"Vital wasn't bad either. Maybe a little less incisive, but a little more open to undecided voters. This race is going to be incredibly close."

Next to me, the kid watched wide-eyed as the workers continued to build the stage. I was certain that he was wondering which of them would vote for Vital and which for the Boss. Given the abstention rate in their professional category, it was unlikely many of them would vote at all . . .

"Any news from your uncle?"

"No, nothing. He's not at his flat and he's not at mine."

"Does he often just take off and leave like that?"

"Fairly often, yes. But I'm still surprised that he's left now . . . So, I went by his place. And guess what I found."

I couldn't help but wonder when he'd found the time to go by his uncle's flat. He had slept even less than me, apparently, but his eyes shone bright with excitement. He wanted to tell me something.

"All of the IT data from the primary," he continued. "I didn't know that he had it, but he had left everything out. Can you guess what I learned from reading it?"

"That the primary was rigged."

The kid's face suddenly darkened.

I told him about my last meeting with his uncle, the day after the first round, and how Gaspard had stressed the importance of keeping the information between us.

As I had feared, he was furious. He was trying to stay calm, but I could see that his anger was eating away at him from the inside.

"Winston, your uncle made me promise not to tell you. And you know as well as I do that crossing him is a bad idea. He's not exactly a forgiving man—especially when it comes to you. What would you have had me do?"

"Trust me," he said before turning around to watch the workers and avoid looking me in the eye. I had disappointed him. I regretted it.

Disappointing people was usually no problem for me. In fact, I spent much of my time disappointing people. Politics is often about kindling hope: hope for a better world, for real change, a promotion, a job, an outcome, a medal. But when the dust settles, you have to be ready to manage disappointment when what you promised takes longer than expected to become a reality. As Churchill once said, politicians need to be capable of foretelling what is going to happen tomorrow, next week, next month, and next year. And equally capable afterwards of explaining why it didn't happen.

And yet, disappointing young Caligny was almost physically painful. I didn't have many allies left in the campaign, and now I had upset one of them. I kept quiet.

"Did he tell you if he had managed to figure out who was behind the voting peaks?" he finally asked.

"He told me he was about to find out, that he was waiting for more information. You know as much as I do."

"Maybe. For now. How can I be sure?"

What did he mean by that? Things were getting out of hand. I decided to change the subject by taking Winston backstage, where things were getting busy as well.

The Boss would have his own office with a little sitting room complete with secure phone and internet connections. Here, he would prepare his speech, meet with the faithful, hold a meeting with the most important Barons, have his makeup done before going on stage, and receive visitors when the rally was over. The party photographer would be responsible for capturing these crucial campaign highlights. Then, a few days after the election, if the Boss had won, we would send the lucky few who had been by his side tonight a signed photograph with a little note from him. Well, the Boss would do the signing, but his secretary, Régine, would write most of the notes. After their many years together, her imitation of his illegible handwriting was flawless. Tonight, access to the Boss's temporary office would determine the pecking order among the Barons.

Trémeau had also demanded an office, and I knew why. She wanted to send a message to the world about her importance in relation to the Boss. The battle had begun. The Boss wasn't even elected yet, but Trémeau was already demanding to be treated like the prime minister.

I had given in. It would have been silly to argue. And, in some ways, it was better for her to be in her own office than in the Boss's. I also made sure her office was smaller than his and as far away as possible from the press room.

Just as we were about to step into the press room itself, which was really a second stage of sorts, I glanced at Winston.

He was still cross. I silently cursed Gaspard for getting me into this mess.

"Here we are," I said. "You'll have to come back tonight to see what happens here. It's quite a show! All the Barons will drop in to deliver their comments, predictions, or analyses in a desperate bid for a little airtime or a paragraph in the printed press. Really, Winston, it's essential that we have one of ours in here at all times to ensure the right messages end up in the media."

I was about to continue when he blew up. "I don't give a shit about the press room! Marilyn will handle it brilliantly, and it's not my job! You know the primary was rigged, you know that it's possible the Boss was behind it, and you're just getting on with things as if nothing has happened? What the hell is wrong with you? We were almost killed!"

I looked around quickly to make sure we were alone. This early I knew chances were slim any journalists were around, but I didn't want any apparatchiks to hear what the kid needed to get off his chest.

"For the moment," I replied calmly, "I have no proof the Boss was involved. None. And until I do, I will continue to assume he's innocent and do my job. Do you have any proof?"

"No. But the primary was rigged!"

"So what! Maybe it was organized without his knowledge by someone else, by someone who wanted to set a trap for him or help him. There are quite a few people in the party who are twisted enough to do that, believe me!"

"Right, sure. You really think I'm an idiot, don't you?"

"Hardly. If I did, I wouldn't be giving you the tour of the Parc des Expositions at the crack of dawn or talking to you about the Boss. I need proof. That's what I told your uncle. And he agrees. It's not my fault he hasn't figured out who voted and for whom! I'm waiting for proof, and he just takes off!"

As I said this, young Winston's face lit up. I was about to continue, but he cut me off.

"All right, okay . . . Earlier you said that there was an internet connection back here, right?"

"Uh, yes . . . I mean, there will be later . . ."

"Is there somewhere I can plug in two or three computers and enjoy some serious bandwidth?"

Great, he was an IT expert again. It was too early in the morning for me to deal with this. "You'll have to ask the Valkyrie," I said. "Should we go see her now?"

"No," replied Winston. "I'll do it. You go and manage your journalists and whatever else. I can take care of this alone."

He was about to leave, and I could tell that there was no point discussing it further. I felt guilty, which surprised me—it had been a long time.

"Take this badge," I said. "It'll get you through any door backstage."

"Thanks. I'm going to need three more though. For some friends of mine. They'll be helping me."

I was taken aback, but I could tell from his determination that he had an idea and intended to see it through.

"Ask the Valkyrie," I answered. "And if there's a problem, have her call me for confirmation."

Winston seemed reassured. That made two of us.

70

Thursday 6th May, 11:32 a.m.

"A high-stakes rally! A rarity these days!"

My centrist counterpart looked like he was salivating at the prospect. He was feeling sorry for me, imagining all the difficulties I would have to manage today and all the delicate situations I would have to defuse. But I could see that, deep down, he envied me. I was at the centre of everything three days before a presidential election that could take my boss all the way to the Elysée Palace. He was out in the cold. He realized he might never be in my shoes, and, as a good apparatchik, he realized the full extent of my accomplishment.

The Centrist still hadn't officially endorsed the Boss. Three days before the vote, it was now too late to hope he would change his mind. And in any case, I didn't need him: the majority of his party's MPs had already fallen into line. The Centrist would pay dearly for his refusal to endorse the Boss. His party might even crumble after the second round. If we won, a few of his closest former allies would become ministers. He would be isolated. I was also certain I could count on eighty per cent of his voters. We could do it without him.

And yet, it wasn't enough for me. First, because the Centrist was a man with values, and I thought it a shame that the Boss should go without the support of a talented politician in a milieu of mostly mediocre pretenders. Second, because I would have preferred to have all of his voters rather than eighty per cent.

"Indeed! So rare it would be a shame to miss it, don't you think?" I said.

A broad smile appeared on my counterpart's round face.

"We aren't invited. And it's rude to crash a party."

"You could be. Why shouldn't your boss be here tonight?"

"Because he's decided not to endorse yours for the second round. Because you've given Trémeau too much. Because, thanks to her, you've brought that bloody Radical into the game when he's worth nothing at all!"

"Okay, but all that is settled. Trémeau will play an important role. I'm the first to regret it, but that's the way it is. She didn't run against the Boss, and she campaigned for us. You can't expect us to treat her worse than those who took shots at us during the first round."

"Not worse, no, but not quite as well as you have done. You don't even know what she's worth. You know what we're worth."

"What's done is done, I'm afraid. You can moan about it, or you can do your best to mitigate the impact. If your boss comes tonight and gets friendly with the Boss, it could stymie the Radical's influence and pave the way for a different future."

"You want my boss to come tonight despite the fact that he refused to endorse yours? You want him to endorse him tonight without any promises? Dream on!"

My counterpart may have laughed in my face, but I knew he was thinking about my offer. When you don't want to negotiate something in politics, you don't talk about it. Simple as that. Moreover, I could see that he didn't really have a choice. Refusing to endorse anyone for the second round was a bold move, but it meant he would find himself between a rock and a hard place for the entire five-year term. He would always be less critical than the left and less loyal than our allies. It was a lose-lose situation for him.

"I'm not dreaming," I countered. "I'm offering you a deal. Your boss comes tonight. He gets a prominent spot and some face time with my boss. If he decides he wants to endorse him at the rally, he can. If he doesn't want to, that's fine, too. All he has to do is make an appearance in the press room to say he respects the Boss for his integrity, his statesmanship, and so on. In return, I promise you the Radical will not be a minister. We'll put him in a corner right after the election. You have my word. I don't give it often. And we'll keep your boss in mind for after Trémeau."

"You won't be able to keep your word."

"When it comes to today's rally, you better believe I can. I can make sure he gets some time in the spotlight. The Boss will showcase his involvement. As for the rest, we both know I can't guarantee anything, but that's how things work in our world. The end of the first term will necessarily involve a move towards the centre. If the Boss runs again, you'll play a pivotal role. Your boss will be prime minister. And if the Boss doesn't run . . ."

Making promises to another apparatchik is no easy feat. It's a bit like two telemarketers trying to con one another into buying their useless products. It makes for a great show, but the results aren't always there.

"I hear what you're saying."

In the language of apparatchiks, that meant that he himself agreed with me overall but couldn't say as much because his boss might not. Nevertheless, he wanted me to know we were on the same page.

"Talk to your boss," I urged. "See what he says. And keep me in the loop."

"I can't promise anything. It's a bit of a long shot."

"If we manage it, we'll have done our jobs and helped both our bosses. That's what we're here for, isn't it?"

My counterpart smiled. He was probably already thinking about how he was going to pitch it to his boss. Maybe he was also already imagining taking out Trémeau and the Radical if his boss agreed to come tonight. They could turn the event into an offensive . . .

"I'll let you know by mid-afternoon."

"No later. I need enough time to make the arrangements. I'm counting on you. It's in our best interests for both of us this time."

Though our handshake didn't seal the deal by any means, it was the beginning of an understanding. If we were successful, Trémeau would be unhappy. And Texier would be furious. I felt more cheerful already.

71

Thursday 6th May, 11:53 a.m.

Back in my office at HQ, I smiled as I thought about the face Texier would make if my discussions with the Centrist paid off. I hadn't told the Boss about my plan yet, of course, but there was no reason for him to be against it. He would commit less than I had, as usual, but the deal I had hammered out with my counterpart was a good one. The only thing that dampened my good mood was the fact that I wasn't certain I could read the Boss as well as I once had. Maybe he would be angry with me for going out on a limb. He had been the one to suggest the ticket with Trémeau, after all; maybe he would refuse to change his mind. At the same time, he still hadn't officially announced that she would be prime minister, so I had some leeway.

My good mood ended abruptly when I saw a bloke loitering in Marilyn's doorway. With his long hair and young face, I instantly recognized Maussane.

He saw me and nodded.

"I'm honoured that such a great investigative journalist has decided to pay us a visit!" I said.

"I was hoping to speak to the press office, but I guess they're on the road with the candidate," he replied softly.

I noticed that he was going out of his way not to mention Marilyn. He probably knew all about our little tryst. She had to have told him. The idea made me sick.

"They were in Strasbourg for breakfast. They must be on their way to Metz by now."

Maussane nodded again silently. "That's not really why I came, though," he said. "Do you have a minute?"

I didn't have a minute, and if I did, it certainly wouldn't be for him. "Of course. Come in. We'll have coffee."

I had to admit he was a good-looking man. Not my type, but handsome. Clever, too.

"Will your candidate be announcing tonight that he'll be naming Marie-France Trémeau prime minister if he wins?"

No beating around the bush with this one. I did my best to stay calm.

"I have no idea."

"I seriously doubt that."

I would have doubted me in his shoes, too. But I really didn't know if the Boss would go that far. Why hadn't he done it during the debate? The fact that no one had asked him the question remained a mystery to me.

"Seriously," I replied. "I really don't know. The idea comes up regularly, but he's never spoken of it publicly."

"He did, in a meeting here with campaign management!"

"We say plenty of things in those meetings. That's a far cry from a public announcement. I don't know if he'll make one tonight."

"I hear Trémeau demands it."

"She may. But is she really in a position to demand anything?"

"I hear she is."

Shit. Maussane was asking questions, but he was really trying to tell me something.

"In other words?"

"I hear that she plans to give a long interview tomorrow and that she could . . . say different things depending on the candidate's attitude towards her . . . Especially since she says she was given assurances . . . The word 'revelations' has been used a few times . . ."

He chose his words wisely. He was good at what he did. I looked him in the eye, doing my best to remain impassive, but I couldn't help but think about the fact that his paper had been the one to go public about the Snag in the first place. Was he warning me that it was about to surface again? Or was he just trying to lay the groundwork for an article on an upcoming press conference Trémeau would give if the Boss came out and said it? And who had put him up to it? Someone in our office or an outsider?

"I honestly don't know what the Boss will say. If I find out more before tonight, I'll call you I promise, as long as you don't write anything before an announcement. As for the rest, no comment. I'll just say that Marie-France Trémeau has already been given all assurances that she will play an important role after the Boss's victory. No one has ever said anything to the contrary."

"An important role as prime minister?"

"An important role. I'll call you if I find out more."

Maussane pulled a face and stood up to leave.

72

Thursday 6ᵗʰ May, 2:12 p.m.

I hate answering the phone while I'm eating lunch. It's rude for those you're dining with, but not only that, it's also a sign you've given in to the prevailing culture of immediacy that disgusts me more and more with each passing year. The young people around me don't seem to have the same principles as me. Or maybe it's just that the older I get, the less suited I am to the current era.

Nevertheless, as soon as the caller's name appeared on the screen, I knew I would answer. First, I was alone, wolfing down a so-called Italian sandwich purchased from the bakery across the street from HQ. Second, it was the Major, and on a day like today, I knew it had to be important. He was also doing his utmost to make sure the final rally went off without a hitch.

"So, Major, shall we go ahead or cancel the whole thing?"

"Don't try to be funny. I'm with the Boss and he just got a strange call. Your friend the Centrist rang him to ask if he would let him speak tonight. Are you the one who offered him the possibility?"

Oops. Usually this kind of thing is handled between apparatchiks. That's what we do. When the bosses start calling one another directly to talk deals and logistics, things tend to get messy.

"Yes," I answered. "He might come tonight. It would be useful for Sunday. The visuals would be great, and it would give us a leg up on Trémeau. I'm certain the Centrist is considering it." I gave the Major a few seconds to digest what I'd told him. "What did the Boss say?"

"That he'd be delighted to see him tonight."

"That's all?"

"Yes."

"So, will the Centrist be there?"

"I don't know. Neither does the Boss. That's why I'm calling."

The train had already come off the rails. The conversation must have ended in such a way that neither of them knew exactly what the other thought or was planning to do. Exactly the opposite of what I needed.

"I'll handle it," I said. "Tell the Boss to call me as soon as possible. I have a few things to talk to him about and ask him."

As I hung up, I couldn't help but notice that the Boss had asked the Major to call me. He apparently thought that we needed a middleman to talk to one another now.

Thursday 6ᵗʰ May, 2:37 p.m.

As I read the text message, I stifled a yelp. But the three other people in the lobby of the building where the centrists had their offices noticed nonetheless.

Found the redhead. Will call when I get him talking. Keep an eye on Louis.

I shivered as I read it.

Given what Gaspard had done to him the last time they'd met, I thought the redhead might give it up voluntarily. If not, I was certain Gaspard had the means to convince him . . .

In any case, the redhead had killed Mukki and beaten me up. I didn't care much about what happened to him as long as Gaspard didn't get caught and it was never tied to me or the Boss.

As for Louis, I was happy to keep an eye on him, but he seemed uninclined to let me. Luckily, he was at the convention centre at Porte de Versailles under the dual protection of the security team and the Valkyrie. The former could, perhaps, be got round, but the latter was impassable. Nothing to worry about there, at least.

Thursday 6th May, 3:01 p.m.

My centrist counterpart seemed troubled.

"My boss still hasn't made up his mind."

Hardly unexpected. A centrist who has made up his mind has changed parties.

The Boss hated their hesitancy. He agreed that taking the time to think before acting was well and good, but he'd never been able to stand the way many centrists seemed to never reach a decision at all.

I said nothing. I had made a clear offer that morning, and now he owed me an answer. I wasn't going to change my offer just because the Centrist couldn't make up his mind.

"I know he's tempted," continued my counterpart. "His place is by your side. He's always respected your boss, admired him even . . ."

Could have fooled me! During the first-round campaign, the Centrist had pulled no punches, painting the Boss as an old dinosaur unsuited to his time, a relic from another era. And that was a man he respected—what would he have said about someone he didn't?

"But, he's hesitant to commit. He trusts you but is afraid that endorsing your boss at the last minute will tarnish his image."

He wasn't wrong. Shouting your independence from the rooftops and then falling in line just before the election wasn't exactly a good look. That said, many politicians had come back from worse. It had to be something else.

"I understand that your boss is concerned," I said, "but we need enough time to properly organize his appearance. If it's just about his image, you know we can find a solution."

"I know. I wish that was the only problem . . ."

Here we were at last.

"There's also Trémeau. For some reason I don't entirely understand, my boss has a real bee in his bonnet about her. He refuses to be there if she'll be named prime minister tonight. He doesn't want to appear to endorse her as well. He's convinced that she's contemptible and swears he'll never support her."

The rhetoric was a bit over the top. The world of politics was full of quarrels between different personalities, but they had never taken precedence over the logic of figures and power struggles. Trémeau was in our party and played an important role in our majority.

"I doubt I need to remind you that the prime minister is named by the president of the Republic. The Boss isn't president yet. It's too early."

"And I doubt I need to remind you that though I'm just an apparatchik in a small party, I'm no novice. I know that Trémeau has demanded that your boss announce that she will be prime minister *before* the election. If he doesn't do it tonight, something tells me she won't take it sitting down."

That was the second time I'd heard that threat today. Two times too many for my taste.

"I've heard that before," I said. "During the primary, throughout the campaign, and since the first round, people keep saying that. I'm still waiting. What I know for certain is that the Boss has no desire to be played by her. He hasn't sacrificed his entire life to become president so he can be at her beck and call. You know that's not like him."

"I know he doesn't *want* to . . . But in this profession, you have to have the means to get what you want."

"Listen, my offer still stands. Trémeau will be more powerful if you're not there to offset her. The ball is in your boss's court now. I have to get over to Porte de Versailles to arrange everything before the Boss gets there. Call me asap. We're running out of time."

As I left the building, it occurred to me that if both Maussane and my centrist counterpart had mentioned retaliatory measures from Trémeau today, it meant someone was shaking things up. Someone who wanted to put pressure on me and the Boss. Someone who had carefully avoided all contact with me for several days, but who would undoubtedly be in the front row at the rally tonight: Texier.

75

Thursday 6th May, 3:30 p.m.

There was already a dense crowd outside the building. The party members' smiling faces were an early glimpse of victory. The bullhorns were still quiet but above the gathering horde I could already see signs and banners in our colours.

The first thing I needed to do was find a new badge. I had been silly to give mine to Winston. I wasn't sure that all the members of the larger security team put together for the occasion would recognize me. And even if they did, they might be stubborn enough to refuse me access without a badge.

I elbowed through the crowd towards the VIP entrance where the staffer in charge of badges would be. On my way, I crossed paths with several dozen party officials who had welcomed me and driven me around during the campaign. We shook hands or clasped shoulders and said hello as if we were best friends. For them, high mass had begun.

My phone rang when I was about fifty metres from reception. The Boss had finally decided to call me himself.

"Hi, Boss. Did it go well?"

"Yes, we're about to take off. We're running late, but I'll still be on time for the rally. Or at least I hope we will. If not, just start without us. No, but seriously, where are things on your end?"

As concisely as possible, I relayed the content of my conversation with my centrist counterpart and the deal I had offered his boss. To give him the full context, I also mentioned the rumours about Trémeau's intention to retaliate if he didn't announce her as his prime minister that evening.

"You went out on a long limb," he replied. "I'm happy to welcome our centrist friend tonight, and we'll give him the VIP treatment if he does, but I don't see how I can get out of my agreement with Trémeau."

"But, Boss, you've never made a public announcement!"

"Nevertheless, I came to an agreement with her. I'm bound by that. And I'm afraid that she may have enough to go through with her threats . . . I'll tell you more when I see you . . ."

My already compromised vision blurred, and the Boss's words weighed heavily on my chest. Trémeau would be prime minister. Texier was going to win. And the Boss was within an inch of admitting he was behind the fraud.

Suddenly, high mass was starting to feel more like a funeral.

Thursday 6th May, 4:10 p.m.

Distraught, I held my badge in one hand and my phone in the other. The backstage VIP area was still empty. The MPs and important guests wouldn't arrive until after six o'clock. The higher you got in the political hierarchy the less you had to wait around.

Behind the movable partitions, I listened as the huge venue filled up.

The text message made me jump.

Where are you?

I had almost forgotten about Winston. I was going to have to tell him. And his uncle, too. I had no idea how they would take the news.

VIP area. You?

I was glad to be communicating with him via text message. I didn't have the courage to talk to him face-to-face just yet.

In the control room. Come quick. I have something.

I had something, too. But I was in no hurry to share. To reach the control room, I would have to cross a huge room full of volunteers and party officials who would be dying to celebrate with me.

When I was on my game, I loved playing Moses parting the human sea. But today the very thought of struggling through the crowd felt like climbing Calvary hill.

Thursday 6th May, 4:22 p.m.

When I finally reached the control room, I felt like I had stepped forty years back in time to an era when smoking was something everyone did. It reeked of cigarettes, and I couldn't see five metres ahead of me. The hardened face I finally made out at the back of the room through the clouds of smoke was the Valkyrie's.

"I thought smoking was prohibited in the workplace," I said.

"I live here. Have you forgotten? Are you really going to keep me from smoking in my own home? You really are fascists in this party."

I couldn't help but smile. I had long believed that the Valkyrie probably didn't vote for us. She liked the logistics and atmosphere of the big rallies, but she didn't necessarily ascribe to our party values. Maybe she was right . . .

"All good here?" I asked, changing subjects.

"They would be better if I had a finalized list of tonight's speakers. It's not easy to schedule everything without knowing who will be speaking."

"I know . . . All of the party leaders who have endorsed the Boss will be giving speeches, in order of increasing importance. The Centrist may come but I don't think he'll speak. Trémeau should deliver her speech right before the Boss. I have to finalize that with Texier. I haven't been able to reach him."

And I had no desire to. I knew he would smother me in phony concern and camaraderie. The very thought was exhausting.

"Just so you know," said the Valkyrie, "I'm not changing anything after six o'clock. I need a little time to add the finishing touches and get the Boss's mobile dais hooked up to the teleprompters."

I nodded vaguely. Further into the control room, I spotted a group of young people gathered around Caligny, their eyes glued to their computer screens. Without looking up from the lists of names and numbers he was studying, Winston spoke.

"Let me introduce Paul, Khalid, and Juliette. My best friends. Paul and Khalid were at uni with me. Juliette made the wrong decision and decided to follow in the footsteps of all those presidents and Nobel prize winners and attend the Polytechnique. But we try not to hold it against her . . . You can speak freely in front of them. I trust them and they trust me. And working together, we've found something that will interest you. Come and have a look."

I walked over to the computer as Winston began describing the information on the screen.

"These are all the documents I got from my uncle's place. We started by isolating the IP addresses used during the voting peaks."

"Wasn't the data encrypted?"

"It was. Juliette managed to decrypt it."

Juliette was a young woman of many talents, it seemed.

"Well, I didn't really break the code myself," she explained. "I set up a challenge for the IT addicts at the Polytechnique. They're convinced they're the best in the world. Encryptions are really just algorithms, maths. I told them that whoever cracked it first was the winner."

Juliette was barely twenty years old, but her voice was incredibly sensual. I was totally fascinated by her. If they had told me at the beginning of secondary school that girls like her attended the Polytechnique, I would have tried a lot harder in maths and physics.

"And?"

"They did it. They're very competitive, you know. The desire to win is a powerful motivator," she replied.

"In any case," Winston cut in, "we got access to the data. What comes next is a bit complicated, especially since we decided to work on both the official data handed over to the oversight committee and the real data which my uncle found at Droid. We wanted to compare them."

"How?"

"Once we cracked the code, we used several computers to generate a list of the IP addresses behind the votes."

"Right, a sort of ID for every computer connected to the internet," I ventured. I didn't want to look stupid in front of them, especially not in front of Juliette with her hypnotic blue eyes and half-smile.

"Exactly," confirmed Winston. "You seem to have a better handle on IT basics today. It's amazing how you can have a real aversion to something, and then it just disappears when you have the right teacher . . ." He glanced at Juliette, then back at me.

"Right, so, what do these IP addresses tell us?" I asked.

"Well, having them is great, but it only gets us as far as the computer."

"Is that useful?" I asked again, giving Winston an imploring look. We were really testing the limits of my tech savvy now.

"Yes and no," Juliette said, jumping back in. "What you want to know is where the computer is located and who is sitting behind it. But to get hold of physical names and addresses we have to cross reference the IP addresses with the records of the service providers. That takes time, and you have to know what you're doing."

"Ah. Unfortunately, we don't have much time."

"Yes, but we really know what we're doing."

"Great, well, this is all fascinating, but I have a rally to finalize. What did you find in the end?"

"Two things," said Caligny. "First, in the official data, there are a lot of strange IP addresses. Many of them belong to foreign addresses or are no longer valid. It looks like they may have been compiled from addresses listed on a commercial website. Our feeling is that they were included in the official list because whoever was behind the fraud didn't think anyone would ever check to make sure the IP addresses matched the registered primary voters."

Now I was listening. Things were finally getting interesting.

"So, the primary was definitely rigged!" I exclaimed. "Does this mean we can prove it?"

"It seems to indicate that the primary was rigged, yes. But I'm still not certain we can prove it. We'll need to make sure that the IP addresses that are no longer valid were already invalid on the day of the vote. And we'll need to compare the number of voters abroad with the foreign IPs. We might be able to do it, but let's not get ahead of ourselves . . ."

Great. Winston still hadn't given me any more than his uncle.

"However," he continued, "our work on the real data found at Droid is more enlightening. It shows that there were fewer computers than voters during the peaks, which corroborates the fact that whoever is behind it added made-up IP addresses to the official results."

"But, as I already explained to your uncle, that's perfectly normal!" I objected. "Most of the party members voted from computers located in local party offices."

"Right. But there are *way* fewer computers than votes. Way, way fewer."

"How many exactly?"

He smiled and paused for maximum effect. "Four."

"Four what?"

"The peaks came from a massive number of ballots cast in less than a minute from just four computers. The first, we've just discovered, is at Droid. We're trying to identify the three others, but it's not easy because they all took precautions."

I stared at the four young people, trying to understand.

"So, you're saying that once you've identified the three remaining computers, you'll know who rigged the primary?"

"Precisely. Shouldn't be long now. Maybe an hour or two. I'll call you when we know."

Caligny was about to unravel the mystery. The Boss was going to be caught out by a twenty-year-old kid that he himself had brought onto the campaign. I smiled at Winston benevolently. The irony of the situation still escaped him.

78

Thursday 6th May, 5:15 p.m.

I had stepped outside for a bit of fresh air and a think.

An uninterrupted flow of compact groups converged towards the entrance to the venue. The huge banners floating above them sometimes indicated which part of the country they hailed from. The younger attendees were particularly enthusiastic: some of them were in costume while others were making noise on drums and horns. The atmosphere was perfect.

Usually, at high-stakes rallies where internecine strife can be a problem, I draw up the seating chart. I carefully place the Boss's loudest supporters in strategic positions around the venue to ensure that natural applause is always there when and where he needs it.

This time the stakes were different. The only thing I had to do was make sure that Trémeau didn't get more applause than the Boss. This performance indicator was always highly subjective, but I didn't want the last rally to be tainted by a faux pas.

Texier still hadn't called me. I still didn't know if Trémeau would speak.

The Boss would be here in two hours and the details still weren't ironed out. He wouldn't like that.

In two hours, Winston might have finished analysing the data he stole from his uncle. Gaspard would be furious, and the kid would be outraged when he discovered the turpitudes of the man to whom he had devoted his waking life since the beginning of the campaign.

The Centrist hadn't called back either. We were running out of time. After all, the second round was on Sunday. Three days was a long time given everything that was going on. For the moment, my priority was to ensure the rally went off without a hitch. As for the rest, I'd cross that bridge when I came to it.

It was time to talk to Texier.

79

Thursday 6th May, 5:50 p.m.

"You still haven't given us your answer. Is she coming or not?"

"Of course she'll be there. I'm surprised you still thought it was up in the air. She always planned to come. No one can accuse her of being disloyal to the candidate."

Ah, Texier. I struggled to keep calm.

"I suppose she'll want to speak as well? Right before the Boss?"

Silence on the line. What did he want? For Trémeau to speak *after* the Boss?

"Marie-France has decided not to speak tonight. The last rally should be about the candidate. She thinks it's better that way. I think that was the original plan anyway, wasn't it?"

Now it was my turn to pause. What were they up to?

"Are you sure?" I asked. "I wouldn't want the press to drum this up into a story about tensions within the party."

"She's sure. And I don't think the press will do anything with it. Marie-France Trémeau will be in a coveted position, just to the right of the candidate, I imagine. And since he'll be announcing her as his choice for prime minister tonight, I doubt there's any risk . . ."

Ah, here we were at last. Just shy of a threat.

"Of course," continued Texier, "if the candidate forgot to keep the promise he made to her, she might be surprised and be tempted to manifest her displeasure. You know her. But there's no need to let things get out of hand. That said, to be completely frank, a little more trust between them would have been nice."

"What are you getting at?"

"You could have sent us the speech so we could give you our take on a few paragraphs . . ."

Texier was getting on my nerves even more than usual. He had the upper hand, of course, but I wasn't about to let him tell me what to do.

"The Boss has never submitted his speeches to anyone. Ever. I don't see why he'd start doing so now. And you've never given me one of Trémeau's speeches to read. I would never even ask for such a thing . . . But don't worry, it'll be a great speech!"

"All right, all right. Marie-France and I will arrive around six thirty. She wants to meet with a few party members before the speeches. She has such a close relationship with the grassroots activists, you know . . ."

I ignored the allusions and contradictions and wrapped up our conversation. Wanting to be close to the party members but turning down an opportunity to speak before forty thousand of them? Trémeau and Texier were definitely up to something. They wanted to make sure that the Boss would announce her as his running mate and ensure they could retaliate if he didn't.

I couldn't see any way out.

Thursday 6ᵗʰ May, 6:10 p.m.

The Centrist finally reached out.

"We're coming. We'll be there at seven o'clock. He won't speak, but he will make an appearance in the press room. Just make sure your boss doesn't mention it to any journalists beforehand. Let us surprise them. Everything else as agreed?"

"You have my word. He'll be sitting on the Boss's left."

"Could he be on his right?"

"That's Trémeau's place. Nothing I can do. But he'll be just on the other side of him. The photographers won't be able to miss him, believe me."

"All right, I trust you."

The centrists may have taken their time, but at least they'd come to the right decision. This was the first good news of the day. The photos would be great and would help get momentum going for the second round. Maybe it would even help to loosen Trémeau's vicelike grip on the Boss.

Saved by a centrist. Who would have thought it . . .

Thursday 6ᵗʰ May, 6:11 p.m.

The Valkyrie had many flaws, but she had one crucial strength. The more pressure she was under, the calmer she got. It's a welcome quality in anyone, really, but for someone who spends her days managing big egos and the logistics of political rallies with audiences of up to forty thousand, it's priceless.

"So, do you finally know who's speaking?"

"Everyone who was already on the schedule, in the planned order," I replied. "The Centrist will be here, to the left of the Boss, but he won't speak. I need a spotlight on him when he arrives and when he sits down. Trémeau won't be giving a speech in the end. So, the Boss should be on stage around seven thirty. It will be perfect for live streaming on the major channels."

"Works for me. The Boss's dais will start moving out over the audience at the end of the speech before his. It will take a minute, but by the time he comes on stage, it will be ready. I'll send the speech to the teleprompters as soon as he reaches the podium."

"Are young Caligny and his friends still here?"

"Yes. Working hard by the looks of it. Haven't heard a peep from them. What are they working on?"

"I can't explain it in detail, but it's important and they need peace and quiet. And I need them to have no contact with the outside world. Can you make sure of that?"

"Are you asking me to spy on them?"

"No. I'm asking you to protect them. I'll explain later. If I can . . ."

82

Thursday 6th May, 6:40 p.m.

The Boss still hadn't arrived.

Over the course of the day, the delays had added up. Everyone wanted to shake his hand, talk to him, have him kiss their babies, and it was hard to cut things short with such jubilant fans. The lunch in Metz had started late and gone on for too long. And last but not least, a thunderstorm in Lorraine had kept the Boss's plane on the ground for longer than expected.

He would land at Le Bourget airport, where a helicopter would pick him up and drop him directly at Porte de Versailles. He would still make it just in time for the beginning of the rally. He'd take ten minutes to freshen up, change shirts, get his makeup done, and concentrate on his speech. After that he'd be on stage, next to Trémeau.

I was quietly reading the speech in the Boss's office. Démosthène had done a good job. It was full of warmth and energy. It had the Boss talk about himself and about the France he hoped to build. It was clear, clever, and moving.

But it didn't mention the Centrist or Trémeau.

If the speech wasn't changed, the Centrist would be angry with me for centuries. And that would be nothing compared to the wrath of Trémeau, who would take out the Boss and our campaign right after the rally.

I would only have five minutes with the Boss to take care of all this. It would be last moment and stressful. I closed my eyes and took advantage of the final seconds of calm before the storm.

Thursday 6th May, 6:45 p.m.

It was hard to stay calm, though. To distract myself from my anxiety, I called Winston.

"How are things going?"

"Not very fast. The IP addresses pass through layers and layers of VPNs and servers. We're having a hard time getting to the bottom of it. We have something on the second computer, but I'm not sure we can use it."

"What have you got?"

"It's the server of a company in the Ain region, in Ferney-Voltaire to be precise. SCI Carlier. I can't find anything else on it."

"Doesn't ring a bell. And the others?"

"We're working on it. I'll send you a text as soon as I know more."

Young Caligny was clearly absorbed in his research. I might as well let him get on with it.

To make a little headway, I started editing Démosthène's speech so I would have a version to submit to the Boss which mentioned the Centrist and Trémeau.

The part about the Centrist was fairly straightforward. All the Boss needed to do was build him up a bit, underscore his bravery, and call for unity. But Trémeau was more complicated. Coming up with something nice to say about her was no small feat. Writing it would already be an act of heroism. Saying it out loud would be unbearable.

Thursday 6th May, 7:01 p.m.

I was waiting for the Boss behind the building.

The Major had called just five minutes ago to tell me that the helicopter had landed and the Boss was on his way. I had run to be there when his car pulled up. He would have no more than ten minutes in his office before the car picked him up again and took him to the main hall for his big entrance through the back of the venue so he could mingle with the audience and let their applause carry him up to the stage. It was a classic move, but it was tried and tested.

I had less than ten minutes to get him up to speed. I had to tell him what to say to the Centrist, what I had promised, what Texier had told me, and submit the changes to his speech. And while I was at it, if the opportunity arose, I would need to mention that I was nearly able to prove that the primary had been rigged.

There was no room for error. The next ten minutes were crucial.

And at precisely that moment, Gaspard sent me a text message asking me to call him back. His timing was impeccable as always.

Urgent. Don't reply. Call me on +421 2 5954 XXXX in 15 minutes. The 4 Xs are: Winston's address and Marilyn's age.

Had the Godfather completely lost it?

I wasn't sure what to think. My first reaction would have been to laugh at this mysterious message, which felt like a parody of a bad spy film.

But I knew Gaspard. I knew what sort of stuff he was made of. He wasn't the type to try to impress me with spy nonsense. If he had sent the message, it was because he couldn't talk but needed to get in touch. But via whom?

+421 2 5954 XXXX. A foreign phone number. What was he doing abroad? And the use of Winston's and Marilyn's nicknames. Anyone who happened upon the message would most likely assume it referred to Churchill and Monroe.

No one else would be able to find the number he had sent me. Marilyn was forty-two. I couldn't remember young Winston's address, but I could ask him.

The Boss's car pulled into the alleyway. I had just enough time to send Winston a text. He would no doubt wonder why I was asking where he lived . . .

85

Thursday 6th May, 7:07 p.m.

The Boss was both calm and tense.

When he was focused, he always gave this contradictory impression. He had little time and he knew it. He was sprinting down the home stretch, forcing his team and his opponent to keep up.

With a glance, he invited me to speak as soon as he got out of the car. I didn't have much time; I had to make the most of it.

"The venue is full. Forty thousand people. The atmosphere is perfect. You're on in twenty minutes. The Centrist is here. He'll be to your left . . ."

"Will he give a speech?"

"Not on stage, but he'll talk to the press to say only good things about you. You'll need to return the favour."

"Return the favour . . . How much is this going to cost me? What did you promise him?"

"Nothing. I just explained that if he wanted to limit Trémeau's influence, he would need to get closer to you. And he came. You'll have absolute unity on the right."

No "thank you". No "congratulations". I was used to it. I didn't do the job for my own personal glory. That would come after the Boss's victory. Maybe.

"And Trémeau?"

"She's here. She'll be sitting on your right. But . . . She won't be speaking."

"I'm sorry?"

"She won't be giving a speech tonight. Texier says she thinks only the candidate should speak tonight."

"Fair enough."

"But *I* think that she expects you to officially announce her as your choice for prime minister."

We had reached the Boss's office. Without a word, he stepped behind a curtain to take off his shirt and put on a robe. His features were set. Without so much as a glance at me, he sat down at the mirror and the makeup artist got to work.

"Boss," I ventured, "I've read your speech. It's great. But there's no mention of our friend the Centrist or Trémeau. And if I've understood correctly, she seems to believe that you've promised to announce it tonight . . . They're getting a little worked up . . ."

The Boss had started flipping through a press review. He was focused on what he was reading.

"I've prepared a few lines. If you approve, I'll include them in your speech now and you'll have them on the tele-prompter."

No reaction. He needed to emerge from his torpor so I could really talk to him.

"Boss . . ."

It wasn't working.

Every apparatchik on the planet likes declaring that they can look their boss in the eye and tell it like it is. Everyone who's ever been close to a politician says they can tell him or her the truth, claims they're not like everyone else.

But the truth is that that's a lie.

It's a lie because telling complicated truths to someone you're close to is always difficult. Just imagine telling a friend he drinks too much, or telling your spouse something's really off between you, or telling your children that you're dying. Not so easy. With the Boss, who had a public life, whose intellect was far superior to mine, and whose wife was dying, I could contest his decisions and express political disagreement, but I was having a hard time telling him that I thought he had rigged the primary, that Trémeau knew it, and that now he was stuck.

The din from the audience was growing louder. The atmosphere was growing even more electric as everyone waited for the Boss.

In a few minutes, he would give his last speech as a candidate. Maybe his last speech as a politician.

I was waiting for him to answer me, but he was silent.

"Boss, I have to get moving . . . Should I incorporate these lines?"

"How long until I'm on?"

I checked my watch. Vercingetorix was on stage, and he had orders not to go over ten minutes. Then a young MP from our party would give a five-minute speech and introduce the Boss. If I included time for applause and making his way to the stage from the back of the room, he had at least half an hour before his speech, but he had to be ready to enter the venue in less than ten minutes.

"We have to go," I urged, "but I have enough time to do it if you give me the green light now. I'll run to the control room and incorporate the changes."

"Okay," he finally said in a somewhat defeated tone. "None of this is like I imagined it. But I guess power never is . . ."

The die had been cast.

As I left the Boss's office, my mobile vibrated. It was a text from Winston. Even at such a low point, he managed to make me smile.

23 rue Lancry. Thought you'd be asking for Juliette's address

86

The Boss had just entered the venue. The crowd's reaction was incredible. Bullhorns barked triumphantly. Forty thousand fans put their hearts and minds behind a single man standing among them in the centre of the room.

I had let the Boss make his way to the stage alone with only a discreet security team which was struggling to get him through the crowd.

I didn't have much time. I had to change the speech and call Gaspard.

Urgent. Don't reply. Call me at +421 2 5954 XXXX in 15 minutes. The 4 Xs are: Winston's address and Marilyn's age.

I dialled the number as I climbed the stairs to the control room. After a few rings, a recorded female voice pronounced an incomprehensible message. A beep followed, and then we were on.

"Is it you?" asked Gaspard.

"Yes. Were you expecting someone else?"

"Okay. I can't talk long because they're looking for me, but I'll be fine. When they figure it out, I'll already be back in France."

What was he on about?

"I got your redhead to talk. It took a while. Tough cookie, that one. But he talked . . ."

I closed my eyes and tried not to imagine how Gaspard had managed it.

"He killed Mukki. He says it wasn't premeditated, though. He panicked when he saw two chaps running towards him. Must have been you and Louis . . ."

The thought that I had contributed, even indirectly, to a man's death, was uncomfortable.

"He says he didn't kill Pinguet, though. He was supposed to scare you off. His orders were not to hurt Louis and to rough you up just enough to get you out of the game."

"You can't be serious."

"His words, not mine."

"Who put him up to it?"

"Not your boss, if that's what you're asking."

"Are you sure?"

"Absolutely. Our ginger friend says a woman is behind all this."

"A woman! Who?" My thoughts turned immediately to Trémeau.

"He doesn't know. But he's sure it's a woman. In any case, it's definitely not your boss."

"Can you ask for more details about the woman?"

"I'm not going to hang about," replied Gaspard with a laugh. "Bucharest is lovely, but I got what I needed. The red-head has friends. They know that someone wanted to talk to him and that he disappeared. When they find him, I'm the one they'll want to talk to. As for him, I doubt he'll ever be able to answer another question again . . . I'll call when I can."

Gaspard hung up and I was alone on the stairs leading to the control room.

Trémeau?

87

Thursday 6th May, 7:25 p.m.

The smell of stale smoke had reached every corner of the control room. It was silent, and the Valkyrie's concentration was absolute. The many screens displayed images of the audience, the stage, and the Boss from every possible angle. I didn't know how many cameras were out there, but guessed there were at least fifteen.

On the screens and out in the venue, everything seemed to be going perfectly to plan. The audience was jubilant, and we were right on schedule.

In my head, however, things were less rosy.

If Trémeau was behind everything, why had the Boss won the primary?

Why had Trémeau wanted to get rid of Mukki? To get revenge for the voter fraud that led to her loss? To keep him from talking? Why would she have wanted to scare me? I had nothing to do with it; I was just trying to get to the bottom of things!

The Boss was still crossing the room. It had been nearly ten minutes, but the stage was still quite a way off. Everyone wanted a piece of him. On the control room screens, I saw the smiles of the people who managed to touch his hands or enjoy a proper hug. I saw his smile, too—natural, sincere, such a contrast from the austere concentration that had been written all over his features just a few minutes earlier. He was ready to speak to them.

I needed to change the speech to ensure the right text appeared on the teleprompters.

But should I?

The Valkyrie had noticed almost instantly that something was amiss. She was much more attentive and attuned to others than most people thought. I trusted her but couldn't talk to her about this.

If Gaspard was right, one of the biggest political scandals of the last few decades was about to come to light. And a number of crimes had been committed to uncover it— including a few on my watch. Not to mention the redhead's fate . . .

Winston was still with his friends at the back of the control room. They were so focused on their computers that they hadn't heard me come in.

Like a centrist, I hesitated.

In the end, I chose loyalty. The Boss had asked me to modify the text, and I had said I would. The goal was to win the presidency. And to do that, we needed absolute unity on the right. We needed the rally to go well and for the Boss to announce Marie-France Trémeau as his choice for prime minister, as expected. We'd handle everything else when it was over.

"Where's the text for the teleprompter?" I asked. "I have to change it."

The Valkyrie sighed through clenched teeth. "Now?! He's about to speak!"

"I've still got at least five minutes. Everything's under control."

If only . . .

88

Out of the corner of my eye, I watched the Boss slowly make his way towards the stage. The crush of people around him was in a state of elation. Even the most worldly-wise journalists had to have noticed that something extraordinary was happening.

I had just finished correcting the text. Now all I had to do was swap out the file in the computer and the Boss would be able to give his speech. I could breathe a bit easier.

The Valkyrie looked at me, her eyes frenzied. She was used to the last-minute changes, erratic schedule modifications, and more or less controlled blunders that were generally part of these big events. But this time she had sensed there was something else—a blend of worry and urgency, doubt and importance.

The quiet control room contrasted dramatically with the exultation out in the room. As I came back to myself, I looked around. The members of the Valkyrie's small team were all focused on their screens. Winston and his friends were also still glued to their computers.

It was time for me to tell Winston what Gaspard had just learned. I was sure the kid would find out eventually, and I didn't want to disappoint him again.

I walked over to the small group.

Winston had moved off to the side. He was alone in front of his computer, his mobile in hand. He was concentrating so hard that I doubted he noticed anything else.

"How are things going?"

"I'm wrapping up. I've got the information, but I'm afraid it might not be useable. It might prove nothing. How about you? Anything new?"

I knelt down next to him to quietly tell him about my conversation with his uncle. The other three were his friends and the Valkyrie was loyal and discreet, but I didn't want anyone else knowing about what Gaspard had been doing in Romania, let alone what had gone unsaid.

As he listened, Winston ran his hand through his hair. He couldn't believe it either.

"Do you think it's her?" he whispered, his voice barely concealing his excitement.

"I don't know. I don't know anything any more. But who else could it be?"

The kid took a moment to let it sink in. Without a word, he returned to his computer. A table popped up on his screen.

"This is all you've got?"

"We've managed to identify the four computers, but we don't know who used them."

He seemed disappointed. He had been looking forward to solving the mystery.

"All I can tell you," he continued, "is that the last two computers are registered to a company and a guy no one has ever heard of. The company is located in the Somme region, but I can't get anything else on it. As for the guy, it's a certain Mr Bruno, who lives in the Alpes-Maritimes. Ring a bell?"

Not at all, unfortunately. The only Bruno I knew in the Alpes-Maritimes was . . .

"Wait, what's his first name?"

Winston leaned in towards his computer. "The contract with the service provider says Bernard Bruno."

I couldn't believe my ears.

"Does he live in Grasse or somewhere near there?"

"Yes, Mougins."

I had them dead to rights.

I didn't know any Bernard Bruno, but I knew a Bruno Bernard rather well. He had been the party head in Grasse for many years. A real arsehole whom I had held back at every opportunity. It was no surprise when he had joined the Trémeau campaign since she had gladly offered him appealing prospects.

If Bruno Bernard turned out to be Bernard Bruno, then Trémeau and Texier were behind the voter fraud. Those bastards! They had rigged the primary. And killed Mukki. They had wanted to keep us quiet.

Feeling a sudden a rush of adrenaline, I stood up. I had to warn the Boss. He couldn't give Trémeau what she wanted now. He could wring her neck instead.

The din grew even louder, bringing me back to reality. The Boss had made it to the stage. He was about to speak.

89

Thursday 6ᵗʰ May, 7:40 p.m.

Standing before the euphoric audience, the Boss was the picture of serenity and power. The standing ovation that had accompanied him through the room and onto the stage was now such a tumult that it seemed the rules of politics had faded away to make room for the kind of hysterical frenzy more often found at rock concerts.

He was alone before the crowd, and he was about to speak.

In the control room, the Valkyrie was about to feed the text into the teleprompter. I watched in dismay as the first two paragraphs appeared on the screen nearest me.

The cogs turning more slowly than usual, I tried to piece together Trémeau's machinations. How had she managed to rig the primary, and why had she still lost if she was behind it? Had she knowingly chosen to eliminate anyone who could tie her to her misdeeds by getting rid of Senator Pinguet's son and Mukki? Or had her lackeys taken liberties? Nothing was clear, except that she was behind it and her goal had been to put pressure on the Boss. She had succeeded.

In just a few minutes, the Boss would announce that she would be his prime minister. By changing the text, I had laid out the hot coals for him to walk across myself. Everything I had sworn to accomplish was falling apart. I hadn't protected my Boss.

I gently placed my hand on the Valkyrie's arm.

"Can I still change the text?"

Silence. She must have been wondering if I was kidding. I might have done something like that under other circumstances.

"Are you joking?"

"No. I need to change his speech. I need to delete the two paragraphs I just added. I've never been so serious about anything in my life. It's crucial. For him. I'll explain later."

The Boss started speaking. The Valkyrie gestured at me to be quiet. She had to scroll through the text, taking care to stay a paragraph ahead of what the Boss was saying. The task wasn't intellectually demanding, but she had to concentrate. If she didn't, the text might scroll past too fast or too slowly, impairing the Boss's gifts as an orator. She did not need anyone messing with a speech that was already underway and could no longer be changed.

"We can't change the text any more," she snapped, keeping her eyes glued to the screens in front of her (on one side a close-up of the Boss, on the other the text). "We'd have to stop the teleprompter. And to do that, he'd have to stop his speech. Impossible. The only solution is for someone in the audience to warn him when he reaches the part you want him to skip."

I turned to Winston. "I need you to do it. Go stand in the front row if you have to, and when he's about to mention the government after the election, find a way to make him understand he mustn't say anything."

The kid stared at me with his mouth open.

"But, how do I—"

"Find a way! We have no choice! Try to get him to understand. I'll be here trying to find a way to change the speech! Go!!"

After a second's hesitation, Winston glanced at the screen and rushed out of the control room as if his life depended on it.

"Now all we can do is pray that the Boss takes his time and Louis doesn't waste any," said the Valkyrie.

I watched on the surveillance feeds as Winston ran across the room, bumping into security guards and flashing his badge, roughly pushing aside anyone in his way. I still wasn't sure that security would let him reach the front row or that the Boss would see him if he made it. You're really elsewhere when you're on stage. You don't always see people right in front of you. You have to pretend, but it's a bit like the theatre: you hear the audience more than you see them.

The Valkyrie was still as a statue now, fully absorbed in the text. The captivated look on her face was almost moving. Orders occasionally barked in her hoarse voice were the only indication of her otherwise explosive personality.

"Do you still want to change the speech?" she asked.

"Do you have an idea?"

"Get on another computer, delete what you want to delete, then save it to a USB drive. When he's interrupted by applause, we'll swap it out. He'll have to manage without the prompter for thirty seconds, but he should be okay, right?"

We were playing with fire. I could easily imagine how the Boss would feel about the prompter cutting out on him as he stood alone in front of forty thousand people and every television camera in France just days from the second round of the presidential election. It was the kind of thing that could take him over the edge. But given what was at stake, it was the only option.

I tried to stay calm. For someone who hates messing with computers, I'd had a rough day. I was about to get to it when I saw the Valkyrie frown. My blood froze in my veins.

"What is it?"

"He's gone off-script. He's just skipped a paragraph and now he's digressing. It's good but I'm having a hard time following!"

The digression was met with thunderous applause. The Boss was bringing the house down and seemed inclined to let himself get carried away. For the Valkyrie, however, every change he made to the speech was a trap. How could she scroll through the text if he wasn't reading it?

As a seasoned professional, the Valkyrie soldiered on without even a hint of annoyance. Whenever the Boss went off-script, she stopped the text, hoping that he would eventually get back to it. It was the only thing to do, and she did it all while radiating an otherworldly calm. As for me, I was in a sweat.

The Boss was improvising. The audience was utterly captivated. Unlike most politicians, he wasn't just adding asides to explain himself in a less formal tone. He was going into greater detail and incorporating anecdotes. The crowd was at his feet. It was like a conversation between a single man and every person in the room. The silence while he spoke was absolute. It was nothing short of magical.

Even I was hanging on his every word.

The Valkyrie sighed softly as she waited for him to come back to the text. "You would have had enough time to make the change."

Shit. She was right. I sat down at the keyboard. Deleting all references to Trémeau was profoundly satisfying. I'd been so enthralled by the Boss that I had almost lost sight of the task at hand.

With a quick glance at the surveillance screens, I suddenly realized that the text wasn't the only thing I'd forgotten. Winston seemed to have disappeared, lost in the crowd or held up by security. I couldn't see him in the front row, and I knew deep down that the Boss wouldn't see him either.

90

Thursday 6ᵗʰ May, 7:50 p.m.

My text was ready.

I had the USB key in my hand ready to go with the finalized version, purged of all mention of Trémeau.

The audience was still enthralled.

I had never watched a rally from the control room before. I usually spent them in the press room or backstage or at the very back of the venue, to get a better understanding of how the show played out for the audience. This was a first for the control room. Quite the experience!

I had attended hundreds of rallies, but I had never felt what the crowd and I were experiencing now. The Boss seemed to be floating on stage. He was speaking to each and every one of us. He had somehow created a magic bond based on reason, intellect, and arguments that reconciled ideals with reality.

The Valkyrie had relaxed. She sat back in her seat listening attentively. She was so fascinated that she had let go of the joystick she had been using to scroll through the speech. The Boss didn't need it any more.

He was taking a considerable risk. His speech was incredible, but a speech like this one only worked on the people in the room. The television networks would repeat a few excerpts, but they would never be able to capture the spell he had woven on the live audience. If he went too far, however, and accidentally misspoke, that would be the one thing everyone in the country would hear about. And two days from the election, it would be impossible to come back from a mistake like that.

In the close-up shot, I could see that the Boss was fully inhabited by the idea he had of the position he was hoping to earn. He was giving it everything he had. He wasn't just trying to convince people or to win any more. He wanted to show them who he was and what he would do to live up to the presidency.

There wasn't a single sound in the control room. Winston's friends had stepped closer to a screen. They were all under the Boss's spell, too. The few cameras that were not trained on the Boss showed images of his fans, utterly captivated, open-mouthed and bright-eyed. Winston had been stopped by security at the entrance to the MP rows. For once they had done their job, and this time the Boss was going to pay the price. It was terribly ironic, but the Boss's performance, which had absorbed the entire room like a black hole absorbs matter, made everything else seem trivial.

He would eventually mention Trémeau. Sooner or later, he would talk about how he saw the future, his government, its composition, its priorities. That's when he would mention Trémeau. And neither Winston's gesticulating nor my USB key could keep him from falling into the trap that awful cow had laid for him. It was all too much.

My phone vibrated in my pocket. Marilyn. A text message asking me if I knew what the Boss was doing and if she should give the journalists the original text as planned since it didn't have much in common with the speech he was giving now.

I had no idea. I had become a spectator.

91

Thursday 6th May, 8:20 p.m.

I'm not certain paranoid people can believe in miracles.

When you are convinced that all your problems are the product of the ill-will you suspect others bear you, you're more likely to believe good surprises are due to the incompetence of your enemies than to a benevolent higher power.

In any case, up until this rally, I had personally never believed in miracles.

However, I had grown increasingly convinced that perfection was attainable. Maybe it was my age? Or maybe I just needed to reassure myself that my life's work wasn't in vain? Perfection never lasted long, except on those rare occasions when human genius managed to capture eternity in a work of art, but I was sure there were fleeting moments.

And right now was one of those moments.

It was as if the Boss's natural talents, polished and faceted over years of hard work, were taking the world by storm.

The speech Démosthène had written was but a vague memory. The messaging the Boss had mechanically repeated throughout the campaign had disappeared, and there wasn't a truism in sight. This speech was complex, radiant, moving, and stirring.

I was fascinated as I watched the Boss evolve right in front of me—and without my help. He had left this world to join the ranks of those who would go down in history.

That's when my intuition told me that he wasn't going to talk about Trémeau. He hadn't just taken liberties with his speech, he had abandoned all the political games and contingency plans to focus on what really mattered. Now I understood why he hadn't really been listening in his office. He wouldn't see my changes on the prompter, nor Winston's gesticulations. He wouldn't mention Trémeau.

I was ready to put money on it.

And I decided that if we won, I would reconsider my position on miracles.

92

Thursday 6th May, 8:30 p.m.

The explosion of applause that followed the end of the Boss's speech was so intense that the windows in the control room shook.

The fog horns, the trumpets, the brass bands from the southwest, and the hoarse voices of volunteers full of hope and energy came together in a deafening but joyous din unlike anything I had ever heard before.

Stately as always, the Boss brandished a determined fist in the direction of the crowd, perfectly aware of the effect he was having on them.

The Valkyrie had promised an American-style ending to the rally, and she had delivered. As soon as the Boss had finished, thousands of balloons held up by nets in the ceiling fell onto the stage and the audience. There were firecrackers, dry ice, and lasers—"the works" as she said.

The Boss hadn't talked about his future government. He hadn't mentioned Trémeau or any of the Barons present. Sidestepping the meaningless platitudes candidates typically showered on their supporters, the Boss had spoken to the crowd and the crowd alone.

The first notes of "La Marseillaise" had filled the air and the Barons had, instinctively it seemed, climbed onstage to sing alongside the Boss.

On the control room screen I could see the sweat streaming down his face. An hour-long speech under the scorching spotlights was trying for even the coolest politician.

Next to him, Marie-France Trémeau had plastered on a smile. Given the distance, it probably fooled the audience, but the close-up I had before me on a screen revealed her true feelings. She was furious. I imagined the cogs turning in her mind as she pretended to sing the national anthem. Should she attack now and risk looking overly emotional, or wait until tomorrow to go on the offensive under conditions she could control? In any case, one thing was certain: unlike her colleagues who had joined her and the Boss on the stage, she would have been only too happy for "impure blood to soak the fields" as the national anthem would have it.

I shuddered at the thought. She had already demonstrated what she was capable of. We couldn't expect her to throw in the towel now.

The standing ovation from the crowd continued and the Barons remained on stage to bask in the glory. Some of them were doing their utmost to get closer to the Boss in the hope that they might figure in some of the images broadcast on a loop by every network in the country for the next few hours. Others seemed determined to make the magical moment last as long as possible. Trémeau had decided to stay as well. She was standing tall and proud at a bit of a distance from the Boss. Her eyes scanned the room.

She was looking for someone. She was looking for the pawn she needed for her next move. Texier. He wasn't on the stage or in his seat.

My anxiety, which had evaporated during the Boss's speech, made a swift comeback.

"Where's Texier?!" I shouted. "Has anyone seen Texier?"

The Valkyrie jumped. The rally was over and had been a major success from a logistical point of view. She had finally been starting to relax.

"Where do you think?" she replied with a laugh. "Where would you be in his shoes?"

I was about to start shouting again when I realized she was right. He had to be in the press room. All of the journalists would be going straight there to gather quotes for their articles. That's where he would be able to do the most damage.

"Call Marilyn and Winston and tell them to hotfoot it to the press room and keep Texier from getting anywhere near the journalists!"

The press room was at the other end of the venue. I would have to push through the slowly dispersing crowd. There was no way I could make it in less than twenty minutes.

"Take security with you and go around the outside!" urged the Valkyrie.

My adrenaline was pumping. I forgot about my age, my exhaustion, my barely functional eye, and all of the doubts I'd had since we'd hit the Snag. I grabbed the two bored security guys outside the door to the control room and started running.

93

Thursday 6ᵗʰ May 8:40 p.m.

The press room was a hive of activity.

The print journalists were all typing furiously on their computers, and the television teams gathered and dispersed around each new Baron who came in to comment on the Boss's speech.

I was out of breath. The two brutes I had brought with me were big, but they ran fast. It had been difficult to keep up.

When I burst into the room, I saw the Centrist from behind. The Boss hadn't complemented and thanked him as I had promised, but he hadn't mentioned Trémeau either. The Centrist was probably delighted. I was counting on him to sing the Boss's praises.

Marilyn pounced on me. Without worrying about drawing attention to herself, she led me to a corner of the room. "What's going on? I thought he was going to announce the ticket, Trémeau as his prime minister! I've already been asked the question twice. The journalists are all talking about a press conference tomorrow. Everyone will be there. What should I say?"

I hesitated. I noticed several reporters looking our way. Marilyn was so rarely worked up that people were bound to take notice.

"Nothing," I finally said. "Play it cool. A campaign rally is no place to announce a prime minister. There's a time and place for everything: a time for campaigning and, from Monday, a time for governing. Elaborate on that."

"You're out of your mind if you think they'll accept an answer like that. They'll move on to Texier, who will be taking digs at us left and right. Did you know the Boss was going to freestyle it like that?"

If she ever found out just how little I knew . . . I looked at my watch. Quarter to nine. I couldn't tell Marilyn any more. I didn't have time, and I didn't know who was completely trustworthy.

I needed to see the Boss. And keep Texier away from the press. And take down Trémeau.

There are times when the best option is to take a risk.

"If you see Texier," I replied, "do whatever you have to do to keep him away from the press."

"But how?"

"Find a way. And if all else fails, grab him by the scruff of the neck and tell him that the Boss wants to talk to him in person. Remind him that he'll be president in three days, and that he never forgets. You get him in line. Got it?"

No. She didn't. But I could see that she would do as she'd been told.

"Another thing," I continued. "Tell them Trémeau will be putting out a press release tonight."

Marilyn somehow looked even more incredulous now. "What do you take me for, her press secretary? And how do you know that? What the hell is going on?"

"No time to explain. You'll just have to trust me. For the Boss's sake. If you've ever thought I knew what I was doing or that I was good at my job, now's the time to remember that and trust me. Okay?"

Marilyn stared at me. "Okay," she said hesitantly.

"I'm off to find the Boss. See you later!"

Now it was time to take down Trémeau.

94

Thursday 6th May, 8:50 p.m.

The corridor outside the Boss's office was as busy as a Broadway theatre on opening night.

All the Barons were trying to get inside to say hello, congratulate him, express their admiration and undying support, or just to be seen with him. They all wanted to get close.

Trémeau and Texier weren't there. A quick glance at the far end of the corridor led me to believe that she was in her office, where she was probably finalizing the plans for her attack with her own inner circle.

I pushed through the crowd to reach the security man guarding the Boss's office. I was lucky; it was the Thing.

I gently tapped his shoulder as if to say that unlike the others, I was allowed in.

But the Thing had orders, and I wasn't an exception. He awkwardly explained that no one was allowed in and that there was no point making a scene in front of everyone. I pulled a piece of paper from my jacket pocket and jotted down a short note.

"Give him this and tell him I need to see him. Now."

I didn't need to be an eminent psychologist to imagine the storm that had to be brewing in the Thing's head. A request from the Boss's right-hand man, whom he liked, versus orders from the head of security.

With a meaningful blink, he invited me to wait. He stepped quietly inside. I was reassured to see I still had some clout in this party.

Just thirty seconds later, the Thing beckoned me in. I imagined the Barons' faces and, under any other circumstances, that would have made me smile.

The Boss had just stepped out of the shower. His office was empty. His immaculate white bathrobe, the soft sounds of bossa nova, and the drink he held in his hand made for a surrealist scene. The Porte de Versailles convention centre had turned into a luxury beach hotel in Brazil.

The Boss looked exhausted. With the note I'd passed him still in hand, he started asking questions.

"You know who's responsible for the fraud?"

"Trémeau."

The Boss was a force to be reckoned with. I had just dropped an atomic bomb on him but he had hardly blinked. I had to admit I was impressed.

"Can you prove it?"

"Yes, well, I think so. But not tonight, and I'm not sure that my evidence would be accepted in a court of law. But I'm absolutely certain, if that's what you're asking."

The Boss put down his drink. He was thinking, trying to put the facts together in light of this new information. I knew him well enough to know that he was making a list of all the possible solutions he could choose from.

"Are you sure?"

I nodded. Trémeau was behind the rigged election and, directly or indirectly, behind the murders that had accompanied it.

"Tell me what you know," he said.

In less than five minutes, I told the Boss everything Gaspard, Winston, and I had learned, though I refrained from detailing our methods. At this point, there was no need to frighten the Boss or unnecessarily expose him.

"Who else knows?"

"Winston, his uncle, and me. For now. We're the only ones who know that Trémeau rigged the primary. The Major, a few of Winston's friends, and maybe Marilyn know that the primary was rigged but no more. And I'm afraid the list is at least as long on Vital's side since the police are on the case."

"You're forgetting the culprits. Trémeau didn't do the dirty work herself. Who helped her?"

"I have a hard time imagining Texier was completely in the dark. He's in on all her dirty tricks. But I'm not sure."

Sitting in his armchair, the Boss seemed entirely indifferent to the din coming from the corridor. Through the door, I could hear the conversations and fits of laughter of all the important people hoping to get inside. The Thing was in for a long evening.

I glanced discreetly at my phone, which kept vibrating. Winston was looking for me. He had sent me a dozen text messages. When I looked up again, I locked eyes with the Boss, who had been watching me.

"I'm exhausted, you know," he said. "Reading a text takes much less effort. But something happened tonight. I decided to say exactly what I wanted to. That's the first time I've ever felt like that in front of an audience."

"You were extraordinary, Boss. Truly outstanding. But now, I'm sorry to bother you with this mess, but we have to put it behind us. We have to act. Trémeau doesn't know that we know. She's going on the offensive. We have to take her out now."

The Boss frowned. "She's despicable, but we still need her. And since you can't prove anything, we have to play our cards just right. Do you know where she is?"

"No. In her office maybe. I've heard she's organized a press conference for tomorrow. Do you think she'll opt for a confrontation?"

"That's not what I would do. But as I hope you now know, I'm nothing like her. Go and find her. I know what to do."

I ignored the Boss's insinuation. He knew that I had suspected him or at least had had doubts. I wasn't certain our relationship would ever recover, to be perfectly honest. But at that moment, it didn't really matter because, after a brutal primary and a bloody campaign, I was finally about to put Trémeau and the Boss in the same room. And I had no doubts about which one of them would come out alive.

95

Thursday 6ʰ May, 9:10 p.m.

When I had left the Boss's office, all the MPs had hurried over to ask me when they could see the candidate. I had replied mischievously that the Boss had asked me to find Trémeau and bring her to him so they could talk first.

The hundred or so people hanging around outside the Boss's office probably took this for as good as an official announcement. Some of them hoped that with Trémeau at Matignon, it would be easier for them to ask for a ministry.

I kept an air of mystery about me, but on the inside, I was overjoyed at the thought that Trémeau was finally about to get what she deserved. Her career was over. Texier would pay dearly, too.

In that corridor, as I travelled the few metres between the enraptured crowd outside the Boss's door and Trémeau's office, I realized just how close the Capitol is to the Tarpeian Rock.

But the scene which greeted me when I stepped into Marie-France Trémeau's office was still a shock.

Texier was bright red with anger. "Ah! There you are! Thank goodness! I've never seen such a thing! I'm holding you personally responsible for this! Your intern here behaved in a way no one in this party has ever dared to behave!"

He jabbed his finger in Winston's direction again and again as he spoke. The poor kid was as white as a sheet. I didn't know how long this had been going on, but Winston seemed to be taking the tongue lashing of the century.

Trémeau was sitting alone in a corner of the room. She was clearly furious but had kept her distance. Her anger was different, colder. She was much more frightening than Texier.

"What's going on?" I asked. "Why are you yelling at my employee? If you have something to say about this campaign, you take it up with me. And if I were you, Jean, I'd be careful not to threaten Louis. He's only ever done what I asked of him. If you mess with him, you mess with me. And with someone else whose methods and arguments are a whole different ball game!"

I tried to stay calm but seeing young Caligny so pale got me worked up. After all, I'd almost been killed by the lackeys of the two evil bastards who were now giving Winston a lesson in manners. I almost envied Gaspard and his more direct methods for handling people who crossed him.

Texier and I were seconds from coming to blows. Winston was silent.

"Jean is annoyed with this young man," interrupted Marie-France Trémeau. "And he has every right to be. The youngster's attitude is quite simply unacceptable. He bumped into party members from my constituency and hurled unspeakable insults at me. I didn't come here tonight or decide not to run for president to be treated like this. I want to speak to the candidate immediately. Right this instant. Do you hear me?"

I heard her. I could hear the rage in her voice. She was taking it out on Winston, but it was the Boss she wanted to kill. And since I'd learned just what she was capable of, I knew not to take that word lightly. The kid looked at me imploringly. Texier was so tense he looked like he might explode.

"Well, that's just perfect, Marie-France," I said obsequiously. "I came over to tell you that the Boss wants to speak with you in his office."

96

Thursday 6ᵗʰ May, 9:20 p.m.

"You're going to pay for this. No has ever dared cross me like this. I'll never forget it. I'll bury you!"

Trémeau had exploded as soon as the Boss's door had closed behind her. In the corridor, she had done a remarkable job of pretending as she smiled at everyone and shook hands. But now, like a forgotten pressure cooker, she could no longer contain herself.

The Boss remained perfectly impassive. As she spoke, he poured her a glass of water.

"Here Marie-France," he said. "Drink this."

"I don't want your water! Who do you think you are? You think you can dangle Matignon in front of me and then cast me aside when you still need me to win? Do you really think you can win alone? Thanks to your fancy speeches? And fancy degrees? Because you're smarter than everyone else? I'll show you!"

The Boss stood tall, his hands clasped behind his back, calm and steady.

"My dear, dear Marie-France . . ."

"Don't 'my dear' me! You wanted to go behind my back, fine! I guess that's all your word is worth. You see, Jean," she said, turning to Texier, "he says he's a statesman, but he's really a lying creep. I can hit below the belt, too, you know. You won't have the last word."

"I'm afraid I will, Marie-France."

Caught off guard, Trémeau lost her momentum.

"You see, Marie-France," he continued, "I know everything. I know about the voter fraud. I know who was behind it and about the criminal acts committed to cover it up."

Utter silence.

Seeing that his boss was struggling, Texier cut in. "Well, aren't you bold! We can prove that the primary was rigged and that your IT system had holes in it."

I couldn't believe it. Either Texier had bulletproof poise or he didn't know. Could Trémeau have really kept him out of her machinations? It seemed so unlikely. That said, I myself had thought for a while that the Boss might have used the Major instead of me to rig the primary . . .

The Boss kept his eyes on Trémeau, barely acknowledging that Texier had spoken.

"Go right ahead," the Boss replied. "It will prove that the primary was indeed rigged, but that the people behind it aren't those you would suspect. Isn't that right, Marie-France?"

Trémeau said nothing. Her already light complexion was now so pale I could almost see through it. All of the blood had left her face. Her rage had been washed away, replaced with a mournful look.

"Not to mention the . . . incidents, if you will, which led to the deaths—accidental, I'm sure—of at least two French citizens. I hear a friend of yours from Bucharest is inclined to share his story. What do you say, Marie-France?"

The Boss had gone out on a limb. I doubted the Romanian redhead was in any sort of condition to talk. I wasn't even sure he was still breathing.

Texier was dumbfounded as he watched his boss grow small and silent. He was beginning to realize he had made a mistake. A big one. I wasn't sure he'd ever get over it.

This plus Trémeau's defeat. The night was turning out too good to be true.

"Here's what we're going to do," said the Boss. "To keep this episode from harming your career and staining our party, you're going to sign this press release which I've written for you. And you're going to pass it on to the press within the hour. I think it will preserve the future. My future. France's future. And probably yours, too."

With a firm hand, he held the piece of paper out to Trémeau, who hesitated a few seconds before reaching out a trembling hand to take it.

97

Thursday 6ᵗʰ May, 10:15 p.m.

BREAKING. AFP—Paris—10:12 p.m.: Marie-France Trémeau declines to serve in government for "personal reasons".

Marie-France Trémeau, the MP from northern France, who has been presented as the most likely candidate for the position of prime minister should her party win the election, explained after the final campaign rally this evening that she would decline any and all positions within the government for "personal reasons" on which she preferred not to elaborate.

"I am fully committed to the campaign and to ensuring the victory of my ideas and my candidate, who is clearly the candidate best suited to lead our country," she explained in a press release. "The rumours about us running together on an American-style ticket are absurd and unfounded. They go against the logic of our country's institutions and my own values. Serious personal reasons have led me to temporarily decline any position within the government. It would be perfectly useless to try and interpret my decision in political terms."

Marie-France Trémeau was defeated in a particularly close primary last September, which led to the nomination of the party's presidential candidate.

Sunday 9th May, 5:33 p.m.

My boxes are packed.

There's nothing left on the table that was my desk until last night. I'm ready for the ecstasy of victory or the emptiness of defeat. The campaign is over. Tonight the Boss will know: he'll be president or he'll be finished.

I should be tense, impatient, and excited. I probably am somewhere deep down, and maybe it will surface as the evening draws on. Maybe once the results are in, my joy or rage will explode. Or maybe, as usual, I'll remain impassive, whether the news is good or bad.

But for the moment, alone in what was once my office, I find myself somewhere between apathy and distress. The series of facts, calculations, reactions, doubts, and decisions made have left me literally speechless.

Since the rally, I have tried to piece everything together and shed light on the details that remain in the dark. I've been trying to understand. And I feel like I'm the only one.

The Boss doesn't want to talk about it. Trémeau's press release is all the explanation and reparation he needs. It's all behind him now. He won't forget it, because he never forgets anything, but he doesn't want to make a big deal out of it. It's in the past. Its impact has been contained, at least for now. Maybe he has decided to look the other way because he suspects how far we went beyond the bounds of legality in our quest to find answers. Maybe he's already forgiven the culprits, though I admit I doubt it. The Boss is a pure politician: he's moved on because that's the job.

It's up to me, the apparatchik in the shadows behind the scenes to make sure this scandal is cleaned up but never forgotten. It's my responsibility to keep a few carefully chosen pieces of evidence to ensure that those who wanted to take down the Boss will never resurface unless he deems them useful—at which point he'll decide the ground rules. It's also up to me to cover up enough to avoid putting the Boss in a difficult situation if anyone comes sniffing around.

Since the rally, I have devoted most of my time to clean-up. First, I had to give Marilyn enough ammunition to justify Trémeau's about face. No small feat given the sudden nature of her change of heart. Luckily, Texier was quite helpful. Once he'd been fooled by his boss, I almost found him likeable. Since I'd thought for a while that the same misfortune had befallen me, I couldn't help but make excuses for him. And, despite it all, he was still a professional: clean-up came first. We spread a good old-fashioned rumour about a horrible disease so no one would ask any questions. Texier was remarkable: upstanding with his boss, who had been anything but with him, yet efficient and vicious enough to protect himself. His seat at the National Assembly isn't lost as long as the Boss wins tonight.

Marilyn had realized something strange was going on behind all the last-minute manoeuvres, but she hadn't tried to learn more. She was focused on the end of the campaign and the results, which will be in in a few hours now.

I never really spoke to the Major about it again. He had doubted the Boss, which was serious, and he'd admitted as much to me, which was worse. I don't hold it against him, though. I doubted the Boss, too. But the Major doesn't know that, and I'm sad to say he's been avoiding me. He'll never be comfortable with me again. And he knows very well that complicates his future with the Boss.

We cancelled the second Cherbourg dinner, the one that would have taken place last night. Everyone was pleased, except maybe young Caligny, who had developed a taste for the ritual.

Instead, Winston and I got together in Paris. He was the only one who knew as much as I did. His uncle had come home from his little Romanian escapade and had remained perfectly discreet regarding the conditions under which he had obtained the information we needed from the redhead. He hadn't said a thing to Winston, who feared the worst. With me, he had made a few allusions, which led me to believe that his nephew was right.

Winston and I weren't in total agreement about the events and the motivation of the people who set them in motion. Young people tend to oversimplify, ignoring the intangibles and inevitable human error. They see premeditation and never the possibility of a simple blunder. For Winston, Trémeau and Texier were evil incarnate. After rigging the primary, they had tried to cover their tracks and silenced anyone who knew anything. One of the Pinguets, or maybe both of them, had come up with the idea. Mukki had agreed to share the information he had to make it possible. And Trémeau had hired lackeys to tie up loose ends, including anyone who tried to uncover her misdeeds. In other words, Winston and me.

He wasn't all wrong, but I couldn't help but feel his explanation was too clear cut to be true to life. Too simple and abrupt. I knew that Texier had had nothing to do with it. He had really believed we were behind the fraud. And Texier's exclusion meant that Trémeau had been forced to go through other people to put everything together. Other people who were less competent and significantly less precise than her right-hand man. They were, in fact, so incompetent that she rigged the election and still lost! Despite the media frenzy surrounding her candidacy during the primary, Trémeau had lost by quite a lot. She was much weaker than everyone thought, and the Boss that much stronger.

And given how badly she managed the fraud from the beginning, I doubt she improved from there. She must have had Mukki—the weakest link—under surveillance, and as soon as his behaviour seemed to indicate he wanted to talk, things had got out of hand. Had she asked her lackeys to kill him or just to keep him from talking? I have a hard time imagining her ordering a murder. Voter fraud, sure, but murder, I still had doubts. I suspect that the redhead got carried away.

Neither Winston nor I could explain, however, why Mukki had chosen Winston to blow the whistle. Remorse over betraying the party? Fear he might meet with the same fate as Pinguet's son, whose car accident must have seemed suspicious? Maybe. My best guess is that he chose the kid because he wanted to work with the only person close to the Boss who had no chance of recognizing him. And maybe he had fond memories of Winston's father. We would probably never know.

Despite all her mistakes, Trémeau's unbelievable turpitude and audacity left me perplexed. With her plans dashed by the failed fraud and her future threatened by Mukki, she had chosen to cast aspersions on us. She had incriminated us with the sincerity of an aggrieved party beyond reproach. It disgusted Winston. Me too, but I couldn't help but feel a sliver of admiration for her survival instincts and unfailing determination.

Deep down, I believe the Boss will win. He was so impressive at the last rally that I can't imagine him being defeated. It's absurd, of course, because he may very well lose, but I just can't make myself believe it. I can *feel* that he's going to win.

But my conviction doesn't warm my heart. I can't find it in me to feel happy. A new life is about to begin for the Boss, a new beginning, but all I can see is the end. The end of a quest that I have been on since I started working for him. The end of a close relationship built on absolute trust but now worn down by doubt. The end of the team we built around the Boss. The end of my job.

I'm an apparatchik. I did my utmost to help my Boss take power. And now he's about to. Now it's time for him to let me go. I know my world too well. Presidents don't need the apparatchiks who got them to where they are. They don't sack them—at least not right away. They find new positions for them, as MPs or ministers, advisors or court jesters. Sometimes they think they need to keep them around, but that just means they haven't come to terms with their new position as president yet.

Exercising power has little to do with the fight to conquer it. Both are difficult, but they're profoundly different. I gave everything I had to help the Boss in his conquest. I'm not sure I have anything left to give. And, when it comes down to it, I can't help but wonder if the Boss still wants anything from me. If I asked him point blank, he'd skirt the issue and assure me I was wrong. His immediate comfort and prudent nature might override his reason. But, in the end, he knows that I know that we both know that a pure apparatchik has no place working for a real president. I'm the shadow of his shadow. Nothing more, nothing less . . .

I'm proud to be an apparatchik. I don't want to become a distant advisor mulling over my past glory in a remote wing of the Elysée Palace, taking advantage of the schemers by dangling before them my so-called proximity to the Boss, which actually no longer exists.

I might as well move on.

Maybe Winston would come and see me occasionally and keep me in the loop. Maybe he'd come for advice, who knows. I could always decide to write a book or two.

How many times have I wondered if the moment has come to leave politics?

But how could I pry myself away from it all: the power, the influence, the campaigns, the people, the machinations, the Boss . . .

That's the problem when you're a shadow. You can't ever leave your master unless it's dark or the light is at its zenith. I had suspected the Boss of the blackest deeds, but he was innocent. I couldn't leave him for that. But maybe the giant spotlight of the presidency would lead him to send me on my way . . .

In a few minutes, I'll have the first forecasts. I'll have to phone him. I've been waiting to make this call for twenty-five years. He's probably had his answer ready for a lifetime.

It will be up to him to decide my fate.

And up to me to make sure everything goes smoothly.

Acknowledgements

Thank you to our wives and children, who encouraged us and supported our efforts without ever suggesting that writing books, on top of everything else, was perhaps not the best idea.

Thank you to our bosses. For everything. There's no point looking for them in this novel, but they've inspired us much more than they'll ever know.

Thank you to our friends Bertrand, François, Frédéric, Gilles, Guillaume, d'Arju, Sarah, and Sophie-Caroline, who once again rose to the challenge of reading and editing our prose. We are very grateful, and any errors that remain are our fault alone.

Thank you to everyone who believed in us and helped us along the way: the team at Lattès, but also Pierre, Koukla, and Christopher.

Thank you to Edouard for suggesting the term "Shadows". Thank you to Gilles for adding "In", and "The".